The
Alder Bed

A novel by
A n n e t t e   M a r t i n

 FriesenPress

Suite 300 - 990 Fort St
Victoria, BC, V8V 3K2
Canada

www.friesenpress.com

Copyright © 2018 by Annette Martin
First Edition — 2018

Excerpted from River of the Brokenhearted by David Adams Richards, published in 2004 by Anchor Canada, with the permission of the author and by arrangement with CookeMcDermid. Copyright © Newmac Amusement Inc. 2003.

Dana Francoeur
Permissions & Contracts Assistant
Penguin Random House Canada Ltd.
320 Front St. West, Suite 1400
Toronto, Ontario, M5V 3B6

ISBN
978-1-5255-2561-2 (Hardcover)
978-1-5255-2562-9 (Paperback)
978-1-5255-2563-6 (eBook)

1. FICTION, FAMILY LIFE

Distributed to the trade by The Ingram Book Company

ACKNOWLEDGEMENTS

Thank you to the community of New Perlican, which afforded me a beautiful setting for the story. In setting it here, where I grew up, I avoided the problem of having to create a new town from scratch. I also thought readers would find the history of that part of Newfoundland, and the names of local sites (e.g. the Sittin' Rock, Peter's Finger) as interesting as I do.

I used the correct names for most parts of the town, but not all (e.g. the Burnt Hills) and I've inserted houses willy-nilly (e.g. Lena's house is where the SUF Hall was situated in my day.) Family names are random English names that you might find anywhere in Newfoundland and are not linked to any real-life person.

Thanks to various editors, especially Katherine Barrett for her encouragement and ongoing interest. Thanks to Bea, Christine and Audrey, who bravely ploughed through the manuscript in its early stages, and to Shirl and Burla, for reading it later and offering support and helpful comments.

And thank you to the people at Friesen, especially Publication Specialists Josh Robinson and Astra Crompton, who patiently brought me through the tech stuff, often rescuing me after I'd stupidly messed up.

DEDICATION

To my mother and my grandmothers.

And to New Perlican. In Captain Ken's words, "a gem, as pretty and compact a place as you'll find anywhere."

Fisher Family Tree

1. Ken Fisher m. Sally (Green) Fisher

Children:
Will (Jean)
John (Molly)
Lew (married late, wife unnamed)
Lexie (Dan)

2. Lexie Fisher m. Dan Connor, 1915

Children:
Iris b. 1915 (m. Ben Simms)
Daisy b. 1920 (m. Steve Gordon)
Rose b. 1922 (m. Calvin Barrett)

3. Iris Connor m. Dr. Ben Simms, 1946

(Iris had a child, Marie, at nineteen
while living at home. Child lived only 6 weeks.)

3. Daisy Connor m. Steve Gordon, 1944

Children:
Lex b. 1943
Barb b.1946
Donna b.1947
David b. 1950

3. Rose Connor m. Calvin Barrett, 1946

Children:
Marie b. 1946 (deceased 1955, polio)
Libby b.1947
Peter b.1951

PART ONE (Lexie)

All the art of living lies in a fine mingling
of letting go and holding on.

(Henry Havelock Ellis)

One

January, 1914. They knelt, one on each side of an old trunk in Carrie's mother's bedroom, frantically searching for something to dress up in. Something that would fool people when they went into the houses, where they'd speak in strange high-pitched voices. Maybe have to do a little dance. A dance they'd yet to make up.

"Can't believe the Missus is finally gonna let you go out jannying," grumbled Carrie. "I mean, you'll be finishing school in June. 'Bout time she loosened the apron strings!"

Lexie rolled her eyes. "Yeah. But you know Mother and her rules. She said I had to wait 'til I was fifteen and that was that!" A delicious word from a history lesson popped into her head. "She's a tyrant, that's what she is." Not that Lexie would ever say that at home. Her mother was the boss and no one, including herself, her three older brothers, not even her father, could sway the woman from her beliefs.

Carrie pulled a long, black dress out of the trunk. "Hm-m." She stood up, turned to the mirror and held it against her body. "Nope, don't want all that stuff clinging around my legs when I'm trudging through the snow." She frowned down at Lexie. "There's nothing good here. Maybe I'll wear Dad's oilskin suit again." Carrie was an old hand, she'd been going out jannying on her own for years.

"I think you're right," Lexie agreed, pushing herself to her feet. "I'll ask Mother for one of her old dresses, stuff it with something to make me look fat."

People always told scary stories about jannying. Lexie was feeling a little nervous about it but she wouldn't admit that to Carrie. "John says to watch out for trolls under the bridges," she said, shaking her head at the idea but half believing it anyway. John was her middle brother, the short, funny one. The one who teased her about everything.

"Huh," grunted Carrie, her face folded in a frown, "that's something John *would* say. He was just trying to get you going. Ignore him."

Later, back at the house, Lexie began her preparations for the big night. She was so excited she felt a little lightheaded. "This piece of curtain should do to cover your face," her mother said, coming downstairs with a piece of white, gauzy material draped over her fingers. "It's easier to see through than a pillow case."

Lew, three years older than herself and the youngest of her three brothers, lurked nearby. He was watching them with a hateful look on his face, probably jealous because he was being ignored. Lexie often thought her mother must have had high hopes for that boy when she'd named him Llewellyn Jones Fisher after Bishop Llewellyn Jones, their Church of England bishop. A less suitable name she couldn't imagine!

Her father, Captain Ken Fisher, sat smoking his pipe and watching them through the blue haze curling around his blonde hair, the Fisher trademark. It pleased Lexie when people said she resembled her father, the straight nose, narrow face and deep-set blue eyes. And the white-blonde hair of all the Fishers, (albinos, some people called them.) But unlike her father's thick mat, Lexie's hair was straight as a whip and tended to fly away in all directions. Her mother kept it cut short; she said it was the only way to control it.

"How do I look?" Lexie asked, twirling in front of her father in her mother's old, blue dress with the red polka dots. "I stuffed it with pillows. Do I look fat enough?" His opinion was the only one that counted.

"I think you might even bounce if you fall down," he replied, a smile creasing his ruddy face, roughened and reddened from the years sailing his fishing schooner to the Labrador.

A knock sounded from the porch, then a squeaky voice. "Any jannies in t'night?" It was Carrie, rigged out in a fisherman's oil skin suit, brown eyes sparkling through two holes cut in a flour sack pillowcase. On her head she sported her favourite winter covering, a peaked cap with fur-lined ear flaps, a familiar marker to everyone who knew her.

"Make sure you stay away from the rowdies," her mother warned. "You never know..."

"Oh, now Sally," her father interjected, "let's not spoil it for her. As you said yourself, they'll only go to the houses they know. There's no call to worry."

Sally nodded briefly. "Well, I s'pose." As the acknowledged head of the household, Sally ran the domestic side of things. But for all her mother's stern façade, Lexie knew it was her father who provided the calm guiding hand. Even so, he had to make everything seem like Sally's idea or she'd ride her high horse about not being appreciated.

**

Free at last, Lexie and Carrie hurried out into the moonlit night, the snow thick on the roads, on the roofs of houses and the tops of fences. They headed up the hill to John's house. A good place to start because John and Molly were an easygoing pair who got full value from events like jannying and enjoyed sharing them with their young children, Kenny and Kate.

"Give us a dance now, before we guess your names," Molly urged, as they entered her kitchen. Awkward and self-conscious, they shuffled around the floor while Molly pretended to think.

"It's Miss Prim and her sidekick, Carrie," said John, with one of his ongoing jokes. He called Lexie "Miss Prim" because, in imitating Will when she was young, she'd started calling her parents "Mother and Father" instead of the normal "Mom and Dad."

"Buzz off, John," Lexie snapped, seeing him grin as she raised her veil. "You know it's too late to change now." After the usual fruit cake, Molly sent them off with a little swig of blueberry wine. "No need to mention it to your mother," she whispered to Lexie.

On the way down the hill they met four jannies hobbling along like old men. They were covered in white sheets tied at the waist with rope, and one of them wielded a sythe. "I'm the grim reaper," he growled, as all four of them surrounded the girls and began to sway back and forth, moaning low in their throats.

Lexie felt her stomach lurch as she grabbed Carrie's arm. Were they corpses who'd escaped from the graveyard?

"Get out of our way, you creeps!" Carrie screeched, pushing between two of the swaying creatures and dragging Lexie behind her. The disguised figures stepped back, offering no resistance as the girls darted out of reach.

"What a queer bunch," Lexie muttered breathlessly, her heart in her mouth as they ran down the hill toward the harbour and Uncle Joe Fisher's house, kicking up snow as they went. "Who are they?"

"They're from across the Barrens, I think, maybe Victoria," Carrie fumed, her voice angry but also a little trembly. "The same ones were around last year. Don't know why they'd come all this way, probably up to no good."

**

The Harbour Road followed the curve of the harbour along its north side and continued toward Bloody Point, at the harbour entrance. The houses along the road looked full face toward the water, garden patches and sheds tucked behind fences at the back. Tonight they were all lit up, beckoning any jannies who might wander by.

Joe Fisher lived on the corner of the Harbour Road, a few yards from his brother's house, with his wife, Julie, and their son, Frank, who was the same age as Lew. Years ago, Joe and Ken had started a fish trading business together but Joe had long ago given up the sea. "I feel a damn sight safer on land," he'd say, to anyone who'd listen.

"Well, we have visitors," smiled Julie, as the girls went in. "Hm-m, that dress looks familiar. Doesn't it, Joe?"

"Right!" Joe's face shone scarlet from sharing his rum with his visitors. "I remember Sally wearing that dress. Must be Lexie and the Hall girl. Okay, show your faces."

Before they left, Julie poured the girls a glass of berryocky, a tart Christmas drink made from boiled partridgeberries. Carrie always swore it burned holes in her stomach.

PART ONE (Lexie)

After a few more houses they stopped in the Five Roads, the central area of town, to take a break. "Jeez, I'm full of berryocky and fruit cake," grumbled Carrie, her breath coming in tart, sugary plumes on the frosty night air.

A sudden movement at the entrance to the Orange Hall startled them. "Hey girls, want a swig? Best shine on the shore!" They looked to see three boys loitering on the steps of the hall, passing a bottle back and forth. "Come on up, we'll keep ya warm," their voices full of false bravado. Cripes, thought Lexie, this night is just one fright after another.

"Frig off," Carrie bawled. "You're nothin' but sleeveens." Satisfied, she huffed off down the road, Lexie behind her. "Let's go, Lexie. One more house and that's it. How 'bout Drover's, there by the Long Bridge?"

The Drover house, the last house on the right before the bridge, fronted the main road through the community. Dark and deserted since old man Drover had died a year ago, it was now said by the children to be haunted.

Down below the house was a river, long ago mistakenly named the "Brook," that ran through a thick grove of alder trees extending about a hundred yards behind the house. The Brook traced a rocky course from the Beaver Pond, three or four miles back in the woods. It entered the village at the back of the Canvastown road, then meandered through the Alder Bed, as it was called, finally hurling itself under the bridge to become one with the water of the harbour.

The Alder Bed loomed black and mysterious behind the Drover house and few young people would brave the dark, dank path, even by day. There was also the occasional rumour of someone being bullied by ruffians here, or frightened by ghosts or coming upon a nasty sight not fit to be described.

As Lexie and Carrie approached the house, they heard shouting and swearing from down through the Alder Bed, down near the Brook in the place where young children swam in summer. "Listen," whispered Carrie, "it's a fight. Let's sneak down and see what's going on. A bit of excitement to end the night."

"I dunno." Lexie stared at the wall of black behind the Drover house. As a young child, she'd been brought here in the summer to paddle about in the water with the other children. 'It'll help with your shyness,' her mother had declared. What it *had* done was give Lexie a fear of drowning. And a fear of dark paths through dense groves of trees.

But Carrie, pillowcase mask pushed up over her cap, was already creeping into the bushes at the edge of the trees. As Lexie hesitated, she heard shouts and shrill laughter from the other side of the Long Bridge; a rowdy bunch of jannies, undoubtedly tipsy. Wary of being caught here alone when they came by, she followed Carrie into the darkness.

As they arrived at the end of the path, the moon reappeared from behind the clouds, lighting up the scene at the water's edge. They saw six people staggering about in the snow, four of them in white sheets, the ones they'd met earlier, and two others. Sythe-man was shouting about someone stealing his liquor.

"Fuck off back where you come from," came the slurred words of one of the other two. There followed a volley of cursing and accusations as they all came together in a full-on fight, the sounds of breaking glass and ripped clothing, and shouts of "bastard" and "bloody thief," echoing through the Alder Bed for several raucous minutes. Then there was silence.

Suddenly, as if by a prearranged signal, the four grim reapers turned and ran off toward the Canvastown road, leaving their victims motionless in the snow. "They're dead," Lexie whispered, stiff with cold and fright. "I think they're dead."

But then, the two losing fighters stirred. There was moaning and talk of a broken rib as, vowing revenge, they got themselves to their feet and stumbled toward the path. Lexie gasped. They were going to pass within inches of where she and Carrie were huddled.

"That's Dan Connor, the one in front," Carrie whispered. "Not the first scrap *he's* ever been in."

Lexie knew of Dan Connor but he wasn't someone she encountered in her daily life. She'd heard the girls at school talk about him, how handsome he was, how funny. And she knew that he played the accordion at dances now and then. She'd seen him there, seen the girls flock around him. Other than that, Lexie had never given him a second thought, nor even a first thought. Carrie, however, always snorted at the mention of his name.

The boys came staggering up the path, the sound of crunching snow indicating how close they were. Carrie touched Lexie's arm in warning as Lexie held her breath. She craned her neck for a better look and as she did, a band of moonlight rolled across Dan's face as if to highlight his features, to favour his face alone.

Mesmerized, Lexie stared at the high forehead above prominent cheekbones, the soft, almost-feminine mouth pulled back in a smile, or was it a grimace of pain? She drew in a breath, felt Carrie poking her. "Quiet, they'll see us."

But suddenly, the two figures loomed above them. "What the hell?" Dan Connor snarled, as he peered down at the two of them crouching in the snow, a fat lady in a dress and a fisherman in oil-skins. "What's going on?"

Carrie pulled Lexie to a standing position, her cramped muscles straining to support her weight as she was hauled out of the bushes. "We're not doin' nothin'." Carrie's voice seemed uncharacteristically meek as she moved to push past the boys.

"Hang on, there!" The boys stayed where they were, giving not an inch of space. "You were watching us, weren't you?" Dan sneered, his voice holding a threat. "Nasty habit for young girls, eh Harold?"

"Jesus," sputtered Harold, "who the hell are they?"

"You know who the hell I am, Harold Perry." Carrie bristled briefly, then caught herself. "It's late, we got t'go home." The moon had disappeared again, everything was dark.

Dan glared at Lexie. "Well, it's young Lexie Fisher from the harbour," he said, insolently, breathing the smell of alcohol into her face. "Almost all grown up, aren't ya'?" He reached down, yanked at the hem of her dress. "What's under all that stuffing?" he snapped, as Lexie darted out of his reach.

What was happening, Lexie wondered, why were these boys being so nasty? And why wasn't Carrie being her normally cantankerous, outraged self, demanding that they get the hell out of her way?

"Listen, can you just let us go?" said Carrie. "We're late getting home."

"Not 'til *we* say so," said Dan, roughly, as Harold grunted his agreement.

Lexie now understood that she and Carrie were at the mercy of these two angry, unpredictable boys. And Carrie was being careful not to challenge them in case they turned ugly.

Just then, a loud laugh and a manic scream sounded from the main road. "Hey, that's Joey and the boys," said Harold. "We said we'd see 'em later, 'member? Help them test their new batch."

"Right," Dan grumbled, "Joey always did have bad timing." He moved close to Lexie, the sour smell on his breath wafting into the air around them. "Lots of drunks on the prowl tonight," he murmured. "Better get home, little girl. Dangerous out here in the Alder Bed after dark." He turned suddenly. "C'mon Harold." And they ran off into the trees.

After a moment of stunned silence, Lexie and Carrie followed them through the alders, hurrying single file on the path, back to the Drover house and the main road. "Damn that Dan Connor," Carrie grumbled, now thoroughly outraged, "I shoulda kicked him in the nuts." But Lexie knew she wouldn't have.

Later, in her bed, Lexie mulled over the events of the evening; the feeling of helplessness as the dark, menacing figures blocked their way, Carrie's unnaturally mild tone of voice as she tried to distract them from –from what? It seemed to Lexie that, where angry, young men were concerned, even Carrie Hall backed down.

Then she thought of the moonlight caressing Dan's face, the way it had affected her, and she felt silly. Probably just overly sensitive from the excitement of her first time jannying, the eerie sight of a bunch of ruffians scuffling in the moonlight. Anyway, her mother must never know about tonight's adventure. Otherwise, her first time jannying would be her last.

**

A month later, in the midst of a frigid February, Lexie and Carrie hurried along to the Five Roads and the lights of the Orange Hall. There was a social tonight and think of it, they were going to join in the dancing for the first time! For Lexie, it seemed the next logical step in the long-awaited process of growing up, because in June she would finish school with her Grade Nine, the highest level available locally. She hoped tonight's experience would be less harrowing than her last.

The Janny Night incident, mixed as it was with so many confused feelings, still played on her mind, the excitement of the night quickly turning to fear as they encountered the dark elements of the Alder Bed. And, though she was embarrassed to admit it to herself, Lexie felt a continuing fascination with Dan Connor.

Full of nervous excitement, they crunched along the snow-packed road, their way lit by a bright moon and four months accumulation of snow. "I thought Mother might have second thoughts about this but she kept her word," said Lexie, her voice muffled by the scarf pulled up over her mouth. "But I'm glad Father will be there to guide me." She shivered in the frosty evening air, her eyes tracking the glistening ice crystals dancing across her vision.

They ran up the steps, weaved their way through the crowd milling around the games and ticket draws and went straight to the room behind the stage where suppers were being served. As a wave of hot, steamy air hit them full on, encasing them like a blanket, Lexie noticed fingers of moisture snaking slowly down the walls. An army of auxiliary women, faces shining with sweat, squeezed between the tables shouting their warning. "Hot tea, hot tea!"

Lexie stopped to look around the room, to take in the moment. The place seemed to crackle with excitement. Delicious smells invaded her senses, her ears rang with the clatter of cutlery and the chatter of diners. "Carrie, there's your mother," she shouted, over the din.

Jenny Hall came rushing over, wiping her face with her apron as she jigged around the tables. "My God, it's hot in here." Then, pointing, "There's a couple empty chairs over there by the wall. I'll be back in a minute with your meat teas. Jiggs Dinner is too heavy with all the excitement." With that, she raised her tray over her head and darted off toward the kitchen.

**

Stomachs full, the girls wandered down to the main floor to try their luck at the penny wheels while they waited. After an hour or so, a buzz began to ripple around the room. A short, stout man, his nose suspiciously red, made his way unsteadily across the stage, flung himself into a chair at the front and heaved a red button-accordion up to his lap. "Awright, people, get yourselves geared up." A well-known local character, Billy Smith was famous along the shore for his ability to keep playing while almost unconscious from drink.

"Father's not here yet," Lexie said, quietly, half hoping now that he'd forget.

Strains of "Mussels in the Corner" drifted down from the stage as four circles of eight began to form on the floor. People stood three deep around the perimeter, some of the older ones sitting on chairs, everyone bobbing and tapping in time to the music.

Mr. Hall appeared, an amused smile on his face. "Well, Carrie, are ya' ready?"

Carrie turned an anxious glance toward the dance floor. "Well, I might mix everybody up," she whined. "Can we wait 'til the next one?"

As the first dance ended, Lexie spied her parents pushing toward her, her mother frowning as, mopping his brow and grinning, Uncle Joe came wandering over to join them. "Hello, Sally. S'pose you won't be dancing, not with those Methodist feet!"

"Never mind *my* feet," snapped Sally, scowling at the source of constant irritation in her life. "Just you try to stay on yours!" Joe was the only one brave enough to tease her. Although, John sometimes came dangerously close!

"Might as well get it over with," shrugged Carrie, as her father reappeared offering his arm. Billy Smith began to stomp the rhythm with scuffed, hobnailed boots and the hall echoed with the familiar tune. *"I'se the b'y that builds the boat..."*

Carrie melded into the circle like a veteran, her face relaxing in a broad smile, chestnut hair bouncing on her shoulders as her father swung her around. She came off the floor looking pleased with herself. "You're next, Lexie. Don't be a chicken."

"Okay, Lexie, let's go," coaxed her father, beckoning her forward. And just as they'd taken their places on the floor, she saw him. Dan Connor, climbing up to the stage, Billy Smith passing him the accordion. "Looks like Billy is taking a break," her father said.

Lexie stared as Dan settled himself on the chair with the instrument. He looked confident and handsome, his eyes searching the room, grinning and nodding to this one and that. He suddenly turned to Lexie, looked straight at her, his eyes melting into hers. She felt her knees go rubbery as, cheeks burning, she tried to turn away but couldn't.

"Okay, let's go," Dan shouted. "The Irish Washer Woman."

Flustered and half dazed, Lexie tried to follow her father in the patterns she'd watched for years but the steps suddenly seemed foreign to her. The tempo gradually increased, the floor bouncing up and down in time. Over the noise, she heard her father shout, "Last swing."

Round and round they went, the colours swirling past Lexie's eyes, making her dizzy. She felt her legs give way and then she was on the floor, struggling to get to her feet, while above her the dancers kept swinging.

The hall had suddenly gone quiet. Her face burning with embarrassment, she took her father's hand and he pulled her to her feet. "It's okay, Duckie," said a woman, patting her on the shoulder. "You're not the first one ever did that."

Lexie hurried off the floor, thinking how stupid she must look, thinking Dan Connor must have had a good laugh. And across the room she saw Lew, watching her with a triumphant grin on his face. "I want to go home," she whispered to her mother.

**

Back at the house, Sally hovered as Lexie continued to brood about her fall from grace. She wished she hadn't been in such a hurry to grow up, because at that moment the challenge of the grown-up world just seemed too much to handle.

In four short months, she'd be finishing school as a young adult. The prospect of leaving the nest didn't seem nearly as exciting as it had yesterday.

Two

Lexie could hear the excited voices of her schoolmates fading down the path into a summer of unknowable and highly anticipated pleasures. Her eyes scanned the familiar objects in Mr. Bickford's classroom. The neat rows of wooden desks, the pot-bellied stove in the middle of the room, the globe on the table at the front, the map of the world on the wall with the British Empire, including Newfoundland, in pink. And the farewell message on the blackboard, *HAVE A GOOD SUMMER*, with optimistic emphasis on the word *GOOD*.

"Jeez, how did it go by so fast?" Carrie muttered.

Lexie grinned. "Are you saying you'll miss it?"

"No, I certainly won't," she huffed. "It's just, I don't know, just feels strange."

The door to the adjoining classroom opened and the principal of the three-room school came in bearing an armload of slates. As usual, he was covered in chalk dust, his vest, his trousers, his hair and the tip of his nose all bearing the telltale traces of his profession. It was easy to see why the boys, and some of the girls, Carrie included, called him "Snowball" behind his back.

"Are you two still here?" Mr. Bickford crossed to his desk and dumped the slates into a drawer. "Figured everyone would be long gone by now, especially you, Carrie."

"Thought we'd say goodbye, sir." Carrie looked sheepish. She'd really only stayed behind because Lexie had promised her mother she'd say thank you to Mr. Bickford before she left. Sally Fisher wasn't one to ignore proper deportment.

"Thank you, sir, for everything," Lexie said, shyly, her eyes on the bare wood floor. "And have a good summer."

"Thank you, Lexie. Yes, capelin time is almost here now. After that, I hope to visit my relations in Bell Island." He reached for his coat on the back of his chair and walked them to the door, hunting through a bunch of keys as he went. "Got to lock up, the other teachers are already gone." He sounded anxious to get away himself. "Off you go now, enjoy your summer."

They poked along the school path and turned down Indian Meal Road. "Y'know," said Carrie, "I thought I'd be happy to leave school but I sorta feel like a boat cut adrift. Other years we knew what was coming in September. Sure, we'd grumble about it but at least we knew." She kicked at a rock, sent it spinning off into the grass verge.

They walked slowly down the Harbour Road, the water on their right a moody grey. Oblivious to the activity around the stages, the boats tied up alongside, men shouting back and forth, they approached the huge, three-storey building looming over the landwash with a long wharf stretching out into the water. Lexie had often seen three or four schooners tied up there at a time, waiting to take on supplies or unload a catch. Over the door was a wide, wooden board, the words painted in black. *Fisher Marine Supplies.*

There was a tap-tap at the big front window and Will Fisher, who managed the store for the family, came out to the steps. "Here's our two scholars," he said, smiling as he handed them each a fifty-cent piece. "There you are, a little something to mark the grand occasion."

"Thanks, Mr. Fisher," Carrie gushed. "I'm pretty sure Mr. Bickford is happy to be rid of me."

Lexie smiled up at Will, took in the blonde hair, the mild expression in his blue eyes. He was the oldest of her bunch of brothers, the tall, serious one, and maybe her favourite. "Thank you, Will," dropping the coin into the pocket of her dress.

She glanced across the road to her own house, a square, two-storey with a mansard roof that looked out over the harbour. "There's Mother in the window waiting for me." She stepped away from the others and motioned with her arms, pointing toward herself and the area known as Bloody Point at the entrance to the harbour. Her mother nodded and gave a little wave. "Carrie and I are going for a walk on the Point," she explained to Will.

"All right then." Will turned to go back into the store. "Be careful on the Flat Rocks."

They left Will and continued along the road to the Point, settling back into the sombre mood that had been dogging them all day. Lexie didn't know why Carrie was moody, it certainly wasn't because she was sad at leaving school. But as for herself, she would miss the daily routine, the pleasure of learning new things. Although bothered by shyness, and the cursed red cheeks that made her reluctant to speak up in class, she was already feeling the loss of something important. Guess we're not children any longer, she thought.

**

Mm-m," murmured Lexie, as they walked out to the point of land at the harbour entrance, "I love that smell." The air was mild and still. And heavy with the wild, sweet scent of the low-growing crow-berry bushes carpeting the wide bank overlooking the water of Trinity Bay. The hard, black pellets that grew here were called blackberries but Lexie thought they looked more like buckshot. It took ages to pick enough to make a pudding.

The girls sat on the rocky outcrop, dangled their legs over the edge and gazed moodily across to the other side of the long, narrow bay. The shoreline opposite was almost hidden behind a low haze hanging over the water, the sky a uniform grey. Below them the red ledge, known locally as the Flat Rocks, sloped gently into the cold water of the bay.

"Do you believe the stories?" Carrie asked, lazily. "You know, how the Flat Rocks turned red from blood, in the fights with the Frenchmen?"

"Could be," Lexie replied, shrugging.

"Not much of a fair fight, was it?" Carrie mumbled, her mind elsewhere. "French soldiers against poor English settlers. Chasing them in the woods, burning down the houses. Buggers!"

Lexie smiled at the comment, so typical of Carrie. "Just think, Carrie, we've been friends since the first day of school. That part of our lives is over now."

Carrie grinned. "I can still see your mother dragging you along to the teacher's desk, you wailing like a stuck pig."

Such an embarrassing memory, Carrie never missed an opportunity to bring it up. "Well," said Lexie, indignant, "I was a year late starting because of pneumonia. I didn't want to go at all."

"Got used to being pampered, did you?"

"I s'pose. Anyway, Mother was having none of that. But what I didn't know was that you were skulking in the corner that day. The teacher motioned to the back of the room and there you were, arms folded, watching the whole performance."

Carrie grimaced. "You can stop now, you don't have to go on."

"Oh, but I do. As I recall, you led me over to a table and informed me, in serious tones, that we should arrange Miss Drew's slates." She pointed at Carrie and laughed. "Such a teacher's pet back then."

"God, Lexie, will you never let me live that down!" Carrie waved listlessly at two men rowing their boat out to the fishing ground. "No wind for the sails today," she murmured.

"No, too calm. Anyway, whether the Flat Rocks are red from spilled blood or not, let's go down and look for snails, like we used to!"

"All right," Carrie mumbled, halfheartedly, standing up and brushing the back of her dress. "S'pose we should, for old time's sake."

They scrambled down over the rocky bank to the flat, red surface dotted with shallow, watery depressions. The creatures that lived in these depressions, with their colourful shells of pink, yellow, and blue, had always been magnets to young hands and eyes.

"*Snail, snail, come out of your hole. Your father and mother is black as the coal, up in the chimney corner.*" They were ten again, chanting the familiar rhyme, all their attention focused on the small snail pinched between thumb and forefinger. Slowly the round, black disc, the snail's eye as the children called it, began to emerge.

Lexie suddenly burst out laughing. "Feels silly at our age, doesn't it?"

"I know." Carrie shook her head. "Did we really believe these dumb creatures come like that because we call 'em? We can't get our dog to do that, for God sake!"

"It's more likely they just don't like being out of the water." Lexie dropped the snails back into their watery hole and turned toward the outline of coast just visible in the haze on the other side of the bay. The water in between was dark and smooth, like a pool of oil.

Carrie started down toward the edge of the rocky platform, where the movement of a weak swell was drawing the water in and out, in and out. "Carrie, get back here!" Lexie shouted.

Carrie stopped in her tracks. "God, you sound like my mother."

"Well, you know what people say." The legend went that if you slipped into the water here, you'd be pulled across the harbour by an underwater tunnel and end up over by Jean's Head, drowned! It wasn't just the snails that drew children to the Flat Rocks. The sense of danger had always made the place more fascinating.

"The water is so peaceful," said Carrie, wistfully. "Hypnotizing, isn't it?" Reluctantly, she turned back. "Oh well, let's go home, Lexie. Our time for callin' the snails is over."

**

They crossed the pitted surface, climbed up the rocks to the headland and started back the path toward home. Preoccupied with her thoughts, Lexie barely noticed the familiar scene before them. The harbour, still as a mirror, reflecting the houses and stages crowding around it, and the hills behind. Small boats moving across the flat surface of the water, trailing their gentle wakes behind them. And across the harbour, the Long Bridge and the hills of the Southside, the houses clinging like barnacles to the steep slopes.

Carrie finally spoke. "Suppose now I'll have to find something to do. Otherwise, I'll be stuck in the house with Mom, cooking and cleaning. And looking after the young ones. God, I can't stand youngsters, never gonna have any." She groaned. "S'pose I could find a housekeeping job somewhere. Not that I'm anxious to work in some big house in Carbonear, cleaning up after a bunch of mucky-mucks. Some old bag treatin' you like a slave, the old man spyin' on you through the crack in the door. Heard that often enough, haven't we?"

The tirade was winding down so Lexie jumped in. "Mother's been saying I should consider teacher training in St. John's. Like she said, I always did like school." Realizing what Carrie had just said, she stopped, turned to the frowning face beside her. "Did you say you might go into service? But you hate housekeeping!" She shook her head. "Now I've heard it all."

"I don't have much choice, Lexie. Unless I hook up with a rich man, and they're not too thick on the ground around here. You're lucky, your crowd has a bit of money so you can take teacher training if you want."

Suddenly struck by the difference in their family means, Lexie felt the hot shame creeping into her cheeks. She was quiet for a moment, wondering how she could make amends for the inconsiderate remark. "Why don't I ask Father to help?" she said suddenly, her voice rising with excitement as an idea took hold. "We could both be teachers."

Carrie threw back her head and raised her hands to the sky, the gesture Lexie always found comical. "Lexie, you've been at school with me for nine years, did I look like I was enjoying it?" She shrugged. "Actually, I wouldn't mind going in service in St. John's. Lorna King went last year, said she'd let me know if she hears of a place." The twinkle was back in her eye. "Yeah. We'd both be in St. John's. Days off we could marl around downtown, look in the shops."

Lexie let the idea sink in. "Our folks would make us wait a year or so before we go, but it's something to look forward to. Over the summer we can make plans."

"Right." Carrie pointed to the wharves at the foot of the harbour, where a man was tying up a white boat with green gunnels. "Look, Dad's in from fishing." She grabbed the hem of her dress and scooted away, waving and calling to her father. Lexie, forgetting her new status as a young lady, picked up her dress and followed Carrie across the grassy bank and down over the flake.

Mr. Hall smiled as they ran out onto the stagehead. "Last day of school, eh girls?"

"Good haul today, Dad?" asked Carrie.

"Yeah." He grinned. "So many fish out there today, they were jumpin' in the boat by theirselves." He gestured with his pitchfork, what the fishermen called a prong. "Stay out of the way, now, don't get your clothes dirty."

Lexie watched Carrie's father at his work, the muscles of his arms straining as he threw the fish up to a tub on the stagehead. "Look at this one," he said, proudly, dangling a huge codfish on the end of the prong. "Must be five feet, I'd say."

"Maybe six," Carrie added, kneeling over the edge of the stagehead, all thoughts of soiling her dress forgotten.

Lexie tapped Carrie's shoulder. "I should go before Mother calls out a search party."

"Okay," replied Carrie. "See ya' tomorrow."

**

Lexie walked along the landwash, her thoughts wandering as she watched the rhythm of the waves, the water swooshing in to tickle the rocks, then dancing away in a gurgling retreat. Over the years, she and Carrie had spent hours here, catching crabs, popping kelp bubbles, searching for smooth pieces of coloured glass. In winter, they hopped pans. Well, Carrie hopped pans. Lexie couldn't see the fun of jumping from one ice pan to another as they sank in the water under her weight.

Not that her mother was always aware of these activities. Sally wasn't happy with Lexie's friendship with Carrie at all. She called Carrie a "wild girl," which was sort of true but Lexie didn't care. She admired Carrie's fearless attitude, the wild girl added some excitement to her life.

Still, for all the aggravation from her mother, Lexie felt lucky to have been born into her family. Not counting Lew, of course. And she was glad she lived in this small outport on Newfoundland's Avalon Peninsula.

She'd been born in the summer of 1898. "At a time of great hope for the turn of the new century," her father had told her. He taught her to respect her time and place in history, and her heritage. "Be proud of your home," he said. "New Perlican is a gem, as compact and pretty a place as you'll find anywhere. And just think, the name may even have started out as *Pelican*, the name of Sir Francis Drake's famous ship."

Lexie dearly loved her father and therefore, she loved her community. And she knew its long history. The long, deep harbour, protected as it was from the open water of Trinity Bay by rocky outcrops on both sides of the narrow entrance, had attracted settlers as far back as the 1600s and European fishing boats long before that. And, to her mind, the ring of dark, spruce-covered hills hovering protectively in the distance just added a sense of coziness to the place.

The thought of going to St. John's was exciting, but at the back of Lexie's mind was the feeling that she might not be up to living in a big city. To live among strangers, people with different ways who didn't know her, who wouldn't be as kind as her own family. Again, not counting Lew. And she'd miss the people of her community, the ones she'd grown up around, who knew her almost as well as her family did.

But Lexie knew that if she wanted to be a teacher, and she could easily see herself standing at the head of a classroom, that was the only way. The alternative for a girl like her was to wait at home till her mother, or one of her brothers, spotted a suitable marriage candidate and brought it to her attention, or maybe helped set things in motion.

But in her heart she didn't feel ready for marriage yet. Maybe, over the summer, she'd get used to the idea of leaving home. Still, she thought, I'll never be happy to leave this place.

Three

Lexie sat at the window and watched the children going by on their way to school, walking in noisy bunches of two's and three's, some bouncing with enthusiasm, others dragging their feet. She almost wished she could go with them.

She'd felt restless all summer, her mind full of racing thoughts about the future. When she did drop off, she had strange dreams. Like running down a dark path toward a flashing light, only to find that no matter how far she ran, the light never got any closer.

Maybe it was normal to feel anxious after just finishing school in June, then turning sixteen in July. Her life was on the edge of change. In another year, she might find herself in St. John's, training to become a teacher. Or, would she become paralyzed by a fear of the unknown and just stay home?

She knew so little about herself, her capabilities. Her world here had always been safe and comfortable. She'd never really been tested, never had to use her inner strength to get through a situation. Assuming I have an inner strength, she thought, glumly.

Since school had ended, her mother had tied her to a stifling routine of lessons; lessons in soap making, lessons in crocheting, knitting, sewing and cooking. "Everything a girl needs in the event an eligible man shows up at the door," her mother had said once, a tight smile creasing her face. Only half joking, Lexie suspected. And as Carrie would probably say, half a joke was as close to a whole joke as the Missus ever came.

To be honest, there *were* times when the idea of marriage and children appealed to Lexie. She admired the cozy family life her older brothers had, sometimes even imagined herself as a wife and mother. Maybe after teaching for a few years she'd find exactly that.

Meanwhile, at least she was living here on the Harbour Road and not on a back road, in among the trees. The harbour was the centre of the community, she was witness to all the important events. In the spring, she watched the boats streaming out the harbour, the men cradling their guns, trembling with the knowledge of seals resting on ice pans.

But best of all, at this time of year, the schooners would be returning from Labrador. Crowds would hurry to the wharves, angling to see a husband or father in the flesh, anxious to know he'd survived another voyage. The homecoming was not always joyful however, because until the ship had arrived in the fall, a family might not know that their man had died during the trip. The body might have been buried back in Labrador, or even preserved in brine and brought home for burial. The people who made their meagre living from the sea were not unacquainted with danger and loss.

"I wish Father would hurry up and get home," Lexie said, to her mother. "It would make life more exciting for a while." His return in the fall was the highlight of Lexie's life. Please God, her father would soon be home for the winter. She couldn't wait.

She pictured his schooner, the *Lexie*, poking its nose around the Point, sailing proudly up the harbour to tie up at Fisher Marine. Captain Ken would come walking up the wharf, tall and handsome in the clothes he wore on the ship; a short, black coat over a heavy roll-neck sweater, the ones they called Gernseys, heavy, wool trousers tucked into rubber boots and a wool cap pulled down over his mat of yellow hair.

"I hope he's healthy," said Sally. "He always looks weary when he arrives. And his beard so thick and untidy, I have to remind him to trim it right away."

"Carrie says I'm like the Queen," Lexie said, proudly, "having my name on a ship."

Sally threw her a quick look. "Remember what the Bible says, Lexie. *Pride goeth before a fall*." Lexie held back from rolling her eyes.

Her mother seemed to rely on these sayings as guides in raising her children, this being one of her favourites.

"Maybe he'll bring me a present," Lexie said, changing the subject, "to put with my other keepsakes." He'd brought her lots of things from his trips, sealskin mittens, pretty beads, smooth rocks. Things that would teach her about another part of the world, as he put it. He was always trying to teach her things.

"Your father spoils you," Sally observed, her lips drawn tight in judgement. "I don't hold with spoiling a child." Lexie longed to point out that Lew kept a wooden boat in his bedroom, a sleek, green schooner under full sail made by an old man Father had met on one of his trips.

As Lexie slouched into the pantry to start the dishes, she glanced through the window and frowned at the dreary, drizzly day ahead. A misky day, Uncle Joe would call it. This time last September, she'd still been in school. How she missed it! "There's the young Mitchell boy," she said, feeling grumpy and mean as she gave in to the urge to tattle, "late for school as usual."

The Mitchells and the Turners were the two other merchant families in New Perlican, both with much larger holdings than the Fishers. Bill Mitchell outfitted five schooners for the Labrador every spring but never went to sea himself. Lexie knew the Mitchells well, they often came to play cards with her parents during the winter.

"Huh," Sally snorted. "Grace told me the boy is going to quit school after this year. He'll go right into the business, of course, likely as crew on the ships. He doesn't have the education nor the character for anything else, far as I can tell." She rubbed blackening onto the stove with wide swipes across the dampers. "Can't see him taking over the Mitchell enterprise, the lad's been nothing but trouble since he's born. Luckily, there's older brothers."

Lexie raised her eyebrows at this pronouncement. The same might be said of Lew, and how she wished she *could* say it. A knock on the door pushed the rebellion out of her mind. "Bit early for visitors." Wiping her hands on her apron, she went out to the porch to see who it was.

Bill Mitchell, the father of the boy her mother had just condemned as worthless, stood on the back steps. He was holding a piece of paper in his hand and looking past her into the porch. "Lexie, is your mother here? I need to see her." The tall, big-boned man with steely blue eyes and coal-black hair looked very serious this morning.

"Yes sir, come in," Lexie replied, standing back from the door.

"Hello, Bill." Sally smiled, as she turned from her task. "I see one of your schooners is already back, must have had a good summer. I expect Ken any day now." Mr. Mitchell came as far as the kitchen doorway and stood there, cap in hand. "Come in, sit down. No need to stand on ceremony." Sally grabbed a rag and began to wipe her hands. "What's Grace up to this morning? Blackening the stove, like me? Awful dirty job!"

He sat down awkwardly on the daybed, long legs splayed to the side. "Grace is, uh, can't say, really. Doing something, I suppose." His voice faded as he spoke.

Something felt wrong. Lexie stopped washing dishes and went out to stand by the table.

"A dreary day out there," her mother continued. "A cup of tea to warm you up?"

Mr. Mitchell shook his head. "No. No Sally, thanks." He looked wretched, his eyes flitting here and there, resting on everything, seeing nothing. "Sally," he said, finally, "I've got bad news." He held out the paper. "The Lexie has run aground off Bonavista. One of our skippers got this telegram when he tied up in Heart's Content."

As Sally fell back in the rocking chair, Mr. Mitchell ran into the pantry, grabbed a glass from the shelf and dipped water from the bucket. "And Sally," he murmured, handing her the glass, "there's more, I'm sad to say." He gave Lexie a look that made her heart stop. "There was a storm, it swamped the ship. Ken and one of the crew were swept overboard. I'm so sorry."

"They're gone?" Her face collapsed. "Ken is gone?" Her voice sounded feeble.

"The men from around there, from Bonavista, managed to save the rest of the crew. But Ken is gone, Sally. I'm sorry." He turned to Lexie. "You're pale, Lexie. Not feeling weak, are you?"

Lexie had a ringing sound in her ears, it took several seconds before she realized he was talking to her. "A little," she murmured, her voice sounding far away.

"This is it, then," Sally said, quietly, "the news I've been dreading all those years, ever since I married him." Her face was ashen but there were no tears.

"I can send the wife over 'til Will gets here from Heart's Content," Mr. Mitchell said.

"No, thank you, Bill, you go on home. There's no need to send Grace over, we'll be fine."

The bearer of bad news looked around, uncertain whether he should stay or go. "Well, if you're sure." He nodded to Lexie. "Send for us anytime." He patted Sally's shoulder and left.

**

Lexie left the house and raced up the hill, her legs so rubbery she thought she'd fall in a faint before she got there. As she opened the door, she collapsed in tears. "C-come. Mother said come," was all she could get out.

Molly took one look at her face. "It's your father, isn't it? C'mon, Kenny, Kate, we're going down to Nan's." They hurried down the hill, the children stumbling along beside Molly while Lexie followed in a daze, trying to catch up. "John won't be back from across the bay 'til tomorrow," Molly said, between breaths.

They arrived just as Will and Jean pulled up in the carriage. The kitchen seemed crowded, everybody sitting around looking stunned as Lexie remembered her mother's words. *Pride goeth before a fall.* She went and sat next to Jean. "Such a shock," said Jean, quietly. "We'll miss him so much."

"All right, everybody." Will came down from upstairs and everyone turned to him, looking relieved that someone was taking charge. "Mother is resting so we'll have to be quiet. As you've heard, Father and Charlie Seymour, the red-headed boy from Heart's Content, were both thrown overboard in the storm. Their bodies were recovered, thank God."

At the mention of the Seymour boy, Lexie's mind flashed to the past fall. Her father just home from Labrador, bringing his crew to the house for a lunch after unloading the schooner. The five men standing awkwardly inside the door, glancing shyly around the kitchen as they rolled their caps in their hands. The smells from their rough, oily clothes, smells of fish and salt water, and the sweat of long hours of work.

They'd settled into the meal, looking awkward in the use of utensils, their gnarled hands stiffened by icy water and marked by the scars of old injuries. Two of them had "water pups" on their wrists, angry raised blisters, infections from dirty, salty wristbands rubbing against their skin as they worked.

"Wonderful spread, Missus." Charlie Seymour, the Heart's Content boy, the youngest of the crew at fifteen. Bright blue eyes, a face full of freckles and a head of orange hair. So mischievous, glancing at Lexie now and then, half a grin on his face.

And her father, smiling and happy as his men rehashed the high point of the trip, the wind suddenly changing direction, leading them to a good patch of cod. Both gone now, two more lives lost to the sea. And Lexie knew her life would never be the same.

"It's gonna be a long night," Molly said, interrupting her thoughts. "Jean, come and help me make sandwiches. And Lew, check on your mother now and then." Lew had been sitting in sullen silence in the rocking chair. He looked surprised that Molly had noticed him.

"Thank you, Molly." Will looked so much like Ken, the mild, blue eyes and gentle mouth, the white-blond hair and beard. "You know," he said, quietly, "Father was only sixty-one and in good health. He might have lived another twenty or thirty years." There was a sudden tremour in his voice. "The bodies will arrive in Whitbourne by train tomorrow. I'll take my horse, Uncle Joe and I'll pick them up in his long cart. By that time, John should be back from across the bay."

It was just daylight when Will and Jean got ready to drive home. "Get your coat, Lexie," said Will. "You'll come with us."

"But Mother needs me," she said, at the same time feeling guilty for wanting to escape her mother's distraught face.

"It's all right," Jean whispered, as they settled in the carriage. "Your mother is fine, John and Molly are there." She leaned over, wrapped the blanket snugly around Lexie's shoulders.

Will's red gelding trotted along the Harbour Road to the Five Roads and turned right toward Heart's Content, his hooves echoing into the cool air of the surrounding hills, hovering dark and eerie in the dim light. As they reached Birchen Hill, the long, steep hill leading down into Heart's Content, Lexie remembered the local legend. The ghost of Birchen Hill, the Woman in White. She pulled the blanket up around her face and closed her eyes tight.

As soon as they were home, Jean sent her off to bed. "Sleep late," she said. "You need the rest." Lexie buried her head in the pillow and cried until she drifted off. She dreamt of a man floating among gently swaying seaweed, colourful fish dancing around him, his white hair and beard shining up to the surface of the water like a beacon.

**

Lexie rose around noon feeling tired and listless. She pretended to eat some toast while Jean moved halfheartedly from one household chore to another, talking quietly to her about her father, saying all the expected things, her father's pride in her, his expectations.

Jean was a tall, sturdy woman with a nest of thick, auburn hair and green eyes that crinkled when she smiled. Her face, with its generous mouth and a nose just a little too long, was frank and open, inviting confidences from others. "Y'know, Jean," Lexie said, quietly, thinking back to when Will had first brought Jean to the house, "I was real nervous to meet you at first."

"Nervous?" Jean replied from the pantry. "Of me? Why on earth?"

"Well, your family had moved here from St. John's and you lived in a big company house." Jean's father had taken a job at the Cable Station and moved his family into one of the grand "company houses" with the mansard roofs that looked out over Heart's Content from a high ridge at the back. "I was expecting some high and mighty lady, full of airs, looking down your nose at outport people. But you weren't like that at all. Thank goodness."

Jean nodded her understanding. "Some of the people in these houses are from as far away as New York and Montreal, even England. I suppose they're needed to run the Cable Station but you *could* say they have little in common with the local people."

"Some people call them high knobs," said Lexie. And, of course, there was Uncle Joe, who said the people in Heart's Content had become "a bit high-minded since the Trans-Atlantic Cable was dragged ashore in 1866."

Jean sat down at the table. "Well, speaking of nervous, I was scared to death of meeting your mother." She smiled. "Will had warned me that I might find her a bit stern. He was right, of course, but we all got through it. We even survived her reaction when we bought this house and moved up here to Heart's Content. A full three miles away!"

"Yes, I remember. Well, you know how it is around here, the sons usually build close to the family when they marry. Mother was worried people might think the Fishers had had a falling-out. She always thinks about the family's reputation."

Jean looked surprised. "Thank you for telling me that. I thought she blamed me for the move!" Her eyes misted up. "But there was never any doubt that your father liked me. I told Mom if Will was anything like his father, he was worth keeping. And he's so much like Ken."

Lexie passed the afternoon in the library at the back of the house, watching the fishing boats sail lazily past the large window overlooking the harbour. She loved the large Victorian with its gables and fancy trim, its solid presence on the harbour side of the main road.

Jean came in later, carrying a tray with a pot of tea and a plate of biscuits. "You know, you can stay with us as long as you like," setting down the tray. "After the funeral, a bit of distance might be good. Now that you've finished school, we could talk about your plans, see what ..."

"No, Jean," Lexie interrupted, "I can't think about the future right now. I'll go home tomorrow, I want to be with Mother for the funeral." A tear ran down her cheek and dropped to her hand. "I always thought Father would be around in the future, a good part of it, anyway." She shook her head. "Why would God allow something like this to happen?"

Jean stiffened as she turned to the window. "God works in mysterious ways, that's what we're led to believe." A wall of fog had crept in from the bay, hiding the lighthouse behind swirls of grey mist. "But sometimes I think all the prayers and rituals do no good at all, except to keep us from going crazy. I used to pray for children when we first got married, I don't anymore." When Jean turned around, her eyes were full. "Sorry, Lexie, I shouldn't have brought all that up now."

"That's okay, Jean. I often wonder, myself, about God and heaven and all that. We keep praying our men will be safe at sea but it still happens. And now it's happened to us."

**

The church was packed full, all eyes focused on the family as they waited for the minister to begin. Lexie could almost feel her mother chafing under the scrutiny.

The past few days had been difficult. The men from the Orange Lodge had come to lay out her father's body in the parlour, two of them staying at night with the coffin. People arrived with plates of food, reaching out to express their sympathy with shy, halting words as her mother, pale and downcast, went through the motions of thanking them.

"I am the resurrection and the life..." Lexie swallowed the lump in her throat and focused her eyes on the altar. She'd attended funerals before but now it was her own father lying inside that plain, wood coffin. Jean touched her arm. "Are you all right?"

On and on it went, the readings, the hymns. Then Will's halting, heartbreaking words of praise for his father, and it was over. *"There is a green hill far away ..."* Ken's favourite hymn faded behind them as they walked down the aisle behind the coffin, Sally holding tight to Will's arm. The Pall Bearers carefully made their way down the steps, John and Lew bearing their share of their father's weight. The congregation followed them outside and stood around waiting for the procession to form so they could fall in behind.

Henry Martin, the hearse driver, looked dignified in his funeral outfit, a threadbare, black suit and a black bowler hat. As he picked up the reins, the horse tossed his head and snorted. A woman flinched. "It's okay Ma'am," came the voice from the driver's seat. "Don't need to worry 'bout ol' Nick."

The Orangemen, in the sashes and aprons of their Lodge regalia, led off and Henry clucked the big, black horse into his slow, steady walk. Behind them came the two carriages, Joe's and Will's, with the younger family members walking behind. At the end came the congregation, men in black armbands, women in black hats with net veils, children running alongside.

The sombre parade snaked slowly along the dusty, dirt road, past houses with black ribbons tied to door knobs and blinds drawn tight. "The Missus seems to be holding up," Carrie whispered, as she walked along with Lexie.

Lexie looked ahead to Uncle Joe's carriage, saw her mother sitting rigidly upright next to Julie. "You know Mother. She'd never do anything that would make her the subject of suppertime gossip."

The cemetery was on the side of a steep bank off the rough road leading inland from the Five Roads. The area was known as Canvastown, the name harkening back to the tilts built by the early settlers, crude shelters covered with sailcloth, or canvas. Almost three hundred years later, the population had grown, the original poor dwellings now replaced by small bungalows and houses with slanted roofs called salt boxes.

The Lodge members started up the steep hill with their burden, heads down over rough, overgrown ground to the place where the Fisher graves waited. Arriving breathless at the top, Sally stopped to look around her. "Here they are," she murmured, "the children we lost, Ken and me. And over there, Joe and Julie's daughters." She shook her head. "Now Ken is gone. After all the care and struggle, this is what it comes to."

Flushed from the climb, Reverend Fairchild waited at the grave as the men of the congregation guided their wives around the brambles and rocks and gooweddy bushes. The children darted among ancient graves and low bushes, competing to be first at the top. They took no notice of the flat rocks peeping up through trampled grass, grave markers of the unfortunate children who'd died in the diphtheria epidemic of the 1880s.

"In the midst of life we are in death..." Lexie felt her throat tighten as she steeled herself to endure the rest of the ceremony. Her father, the quiet presence at the centre of her family, and of her world, was gone. She felt angry at God for taking him so soon.

Finally, arms outstretched, the reverend asked God to accept Ken Fisher, His faithful servant. John and Will bent to the ground. "Earth to earth. Dust to dust..." Lexie saw her mother flinch at the hollow sound of dirt hitting wood.

Sighs of relief rippled through the crowd as everyone let out a breath at the same time. The women turned up collars against the damp and glanced around to see where the children had wandered. Some of the men, caps in hand, shuffled over to shake hands with Will and John, nodding shyly to Sally as they passed. Another funeral had been seen to its end.

Reverend Fairchild hurried to Sally's side and took her hand. Murmured a word to Lexie and the others and turned wheezily to begin his walk down the hill, where Henry Martin was waiting to drive him back to Heart's Content. "Looking forward to his easy chair and a big glass of brandy at the Rectory," Molly muttered.

The family hung back, waiting for the crowd to disperse. "The sky is getting dark," said Joe, "rain coming soon." He turned to the others. "Here Sally, take my arm." He looked around for his son, spotted him wandering off. "Hey, Frank," he bellowed. "Get your ass back here, help your mother down the hill."

Lexie didn't move, didn't want to move. Didn't want to go back to her life without her father. "C'mon, Lexie," said Molly. "Let's get home before the weather turns."

Lexie looked back at the mound of cold earth covering her father's coffin. "It doesn't feel right to leave him here alone." And what would her life be without him?

"C'mon," urged Molly, "the clouds are soon gonna burst."

Lexie glanced toward the hills in the distance where shelves of thick, black clouds churned and gathered. "Yes, s'pose we'd better go." Molly took her arm and led her down the hill, leaving her father behind to face the rain alone.

Four

It had been two weeks since Ken Fisher's death and a pall of gloom had settled over the house. Lexie and her mother moved about in a fog, household chores kept to a minimum. Lew stayed away most of the time, only coming home at night to sleep.

Will and John would come to visit, sit staring at the floor for long minutes. "We have to get back to the business," Will would say, sounding listless and unconvincing. "We'll soon have a load of cod to handle." And John would nod vaguely. But the business remained unmanned, the brothers seemed to lack the energy to carry on without their father.

Lexie had come downstairs after a fitful night, had taken her usual perch at the kitchen table when she noticed the excitement outside. Groups of youngsters were scurrying along the road, laughing and pointing toward the mouth of the harbour.

"Three schooners coming in," she said, carefully, as she glanced at her mother.

Soon, people would come streaming down the Harbour Road to watch the ships unload tubs of dried, salted cod, the result of six months labour on the Labrador. Lexie remembered the delight she'd felt at the sight of her father's ship, her namesake, edging its way around the Point. She thought she'd never be as happy again.

Sally sat in the rocking chair in her black mourning dress, her Bible unopened in her lap. "Yes, I hear the commotion." She sighed. "The end of another fishing season. Happy for some, sad for others."

The door opened and Will came in. "How are you, Mother? Thought I'd check on you before I get busy weighing." He looked a little brighter today, his eyes had gotten back their focus.

"I'm fine Will, don't worry about me. It'll be hectic for you now with the schooners tying up to unload."

"Our own ships are coming in, too, the *CWG* is just outside the Point. She looks pretty low in the water, that's a good sign. I expect the *Huron* won't be far behind." Will stooped to glance out the window. "Some of the early schooners are already setting anchor for the winter. Won't be long, a forest of spars'll span the whole width of the harbour."

New Perlican's sheltered harbour had long been a winter haven for schooners. And a place for daring youngsters to test their courage by jumping from one deck to another without landing in the icy water.

"I think of what your father used to say," Sally said, her eyes filling up. "Winter's the time for tired men and their ships to rest before the next fishing season is upon them."

Will looked at Lexie and raised his eyebrows in question. "Sure you're all right, Mother? Jean and I can spend a few days with you, if you like."

"No, no, we're managing. I have Lexie and Lew with me, I'm fine."

"Well, if you're sure. Actually, Mother," he said, carefully, "John and I had a talk. Gave ourselves a kick in the pants, you could say. We need a family meeting to discuss things, you know, how to proceed without Father."

Sally nodded. "Yes, it has to be done. I'll leave it to you, Will, I'm just not up to it." Ken had left the business to Sally, with Will as manager, but she looked in no state of mind for meetings.

**

The kitchen seemed to shrink in size as the brothers filed in. Lew, who didn't usually bother with meetings, had been ordered by Will to attend this one. "No pisstail girls allowed," Lew muttered, as he passed Lexie's chair. She glared at him, her face hot and spiteful.

"Lexie, let's finish the yarn," said her mother, missing the exchange as she returned to the kitchen after seeing the boys into the parlour. "Hold it taut, now."

Furious about Lew's comment, Lexie stretched the skein of wool tight between her outstretched arms while her mother wound it into a ball. In her mind, she saw herself stretching it around Lew's neck!

Settling gloomily into her monotonous task, Lexie glanced out the window. Dan Connor was strolling along the road, hands in his pockets, a cigarette dangling from his lips. He turned to the window, saw her looking out and grinned as he doffed his cap. The brazen thing! Lexie continued to stare 'til he'd passed out of sight, her cheeks reddening at the memory of her embarrassing moment at the dance last winter.

After an hour or so, the brothers came out of the parlour and stood around. "Well, Mother, here's the situation," Will began, apparently pleased with the meeting. "We've lost the *Lexie,* our best ship, but we still have the *Huron* and the *CWG.* John says he'll take over as skipper on one of them and our old reliable, Skipper Jed, can carry on with the other."

"I'll take the *Huron,*" John said, confidently. "Skipper Jed can have the *Cow Wants Grass.*" Lexie smiled at John's old nickname for the *CWG* but she was pleased for him. For several years he'd looked after provisions, as well as the repair dock across the bay in Deer Harbour, but he'd always wanted to be a skipper.

"And now we come to Lew." Will glanced meaningfully at his mother. "He's nineteen, time to pull his weight. He'll get a list of duties on land, supervised by me." Everyone turned to Lew, who scowled and dipped his head.

John smirked. "Hear that, Lew? No more hidin' behind Mommy's skirts."

Lew flushed a deep, angry red and glared at John, fists clenched. "Keep that shit to yourself. I can do my share, don't you worry."

"Enough, John," Sally warned, frustration clouding her face as she laid a hand on his arm. "And Lew, the language. Use some restraint, both of you, this is family."

Lexie watched the flame spread up John's face as he chafed at being chastised in front of everybody. Her middle brother was funny but he was also quick to anger. She held her breath, waiting for the moment to pass.

John resembled his mother in appearance, being short and thick with the round face and turned-up nose of Sally's people, the Greens from Hant's Harbour. But, in temperament, they were very different, one being the model of restraint, the other impulsive, never having a feeling or thought to which he wouldn't readily give expression. Lexie had more than once heard her mother wonder where in the name of heaven she'd got him.

"All right, John," said Will, quickly stepping in. "Better get home, Molly is holding supper. I'll stay and go over everything with Mother." With a last glare at Lew, John left to walk home.

Lexie was relieved that Will was staying for supper. With Lew still stewing about John's comments, he might try to take out his bad mood on her. "So, Lew," Will said, "you'll be cutting wood with Ron Bailey. You know him well enough, he's been cutting our wood for years. That'll take care of you for the winter months."

"Cripes," Lew sputtered, "that cantankerous, old hangashore! You can't look at him sideways, crabby old bugger." He glanced slyly at his mother through the fringe of white hair that always fell into his eyes. "I heard he's a bootlegger."

"Listen here," Will said, sternly. "Bailey's never given us any trouble and he appreciates the work we give him. So whatever he's like, you'll go with him and not another word!"

Lew headed for the stairs, muttering under his breath. Sally stared briefly at Will but, once again, didn't interfere. Lexie wondered whether her mother had finally decided to stop protecting Lew and let him grow up.

**

Molly had taken it upon herself to get Lexie out in the fresh air, to get her "moving forward," as she put it. Last week it had been picking partridgeberries on the Burnt Hills, this week it was digging potatoes. "Meet me in the garden after breakfast," she'd ordered. Lexie wanted to stay in her room and sleep, but Will had said she must make an effort so she got up.

The late September day was sunny and cool as Lexie wandered up to the Fisher gardens on the hill above Molly's house. She found Molly laughing with seven-year-old Kenny as she dumped the bucket of potatoes on the pile for him to bag. "Is Kate helping?" Lexie asked the white-haired boy, who tossed a look at his four-year-old sister and rolled his eyes.

"They'll soon be getting excited about Bonfire Night," said Lexie, taking a prong and walking into the drills. "I remember my first Guy Fawkes. I was only four. Father lugged me up the hill on his shoulders, my eyes burning from all the smoke in the air. But I was fascinated by the crowd, the flames, the flankers shooting up into the air as the boys poked at the fire." Her eyes teared up at the memory.

"Lexie," said Molly, "there'll be times he'll come to you like that, in a memory. Just remember, they're good memories. Not everyone has that." She looked out over the houses down below. "Yeah, soon be Bonfire Night. John and Kenny'll be busy scrounging wood and stuff for the fire, piling it up here with the potato stalks."

Lexie grinned. "And lots of blassy boughs." She loved the local word for dry spruce boughs, which had probably started out as "blasty." "I like how they flash into flame when you throw a match on them."

Molly grinned. "John gets real nervous when November rolls around. Watches over our wood pile, ladders and the like, like a broody hen over her eggs." She scanned the picket fences around the gardens. "Even the fences aren't safe around Bonfire Night." Adding, as she bent to the drills again, "By the way, you get to do this again tomorrow."

Lexie looked out across her community on this crisp, fall day and remembered how her father had loved this place. She could almost feel him smiling down at her.

They left the garden an hour later feeling tired but happy. As they approached Molly's house, Lew came bolting through the yard holding a hand over his nose. There was blood on his shirt. "Lew!" Molly shouted. "What happened? Where's John?" Lew just pushed past them with a murderous look on his face.

John was in the pantry washing the scratches on his cheek. "Oh, you're back," he said, avoiding Molly's eyes.

"John, what happened to Lew?" Molly demanded.

"He came in here all riled up about the meeting, says we ganged up on him." Then, seeing that Molly was looking riled up herself, "No, the youngsters weren't here, they're down at your mother's. But Lew had it coming, the lazy bastard! And I told him if he tells Mom, I'll tell her he's been stealing stuff from the store and trading it for moonshine. I've been keeping tabs on him for ages."

"And what'll he tell his mother about the blood?"

"He'll say he bumped into a door, like I told him to say. No need to mention it to Will or anyone else. Lew deserved it and he got it, and that's the end of it!"

After listening in disbelief to John's explanation, Lexie turned and hurried home. In her mind she saw the anger in John's face, the blood seeping through Lew's fingers, his eyes full of shame and hate as he glared at her. What was happening to her family? Since her father had died, there seemed to be nothing but strife and anger.

Her mother smiled as she went in the door. "Lexie, I've been waiting for you. Been thinking about partridgeberry jam ever since you left." Lexie suddenly remembered that her mother had asked her to make jam when she got home. "They're lovely berries," sifting them through her fingers. "Are you all right? You seem distracted."

"I'm fine, Mother. Just tired." She had to put the incident with Lew out of her mind and concentrate on the jam. Her mother mustn't find out that her boys had been at each other's throats.

She set the berries on to boil and delicious smells, tart fruity smells, wafted through the house. Then came the bottling, usually her favourite part but today she hurried through it, hardly noticing what she was doing. After the jars cooled, she placed them on shelves in the backhouse with the rest; jars of blue, red, and yellow, each reflecting the colour of the jam inside, all lined up and ready for use over the winter.

Sally nodded her approval. "You did a fine job." Her eyes filled up as she lingered over the jars for several minutes, arranging and rearranging them in a certain way. "Your father loved partridgeberry jam, remember?"

"Yes, he said it tasted like fall." Her father was with them, no matter what they were doing.

**

Lew came in after supper, angling his swollen nose and bruised eye out of his mother's view. "Got a knock in the woods today," he said, giving Lexie a warning glare. "The saw flicked back, hit me in the face."

"Dear Lord, what else can happen?" Sally moaned. "And you missed supper. Sit down, I'll get you something."

"Think I'll go to bed," Lexie said. "I'm tired, all that fresh air." She lay in bed thinking of Lew and John fighting, Lew stealing from the store and drinking at the moonshine shacks. An hour later, she heard her mother coming up to bed. Lew was still downstairs.

Lexie was well aware of Lew's hateful personality but sometimes she felt pity for him. Being short and stout with white hair and a pug nose, he was ridiculed by other young people for his appearance. Lexie had heard him called names like Stump and Piggy, and worse. On top of that, he had two handsome older brothers, neither of whom liked him very much. And neither do I right now, she thought.

She was drifting off to sleep when she heard a sound at her door. Opening her eyes in the semi-darkness, she saw Lew standing over her. "Lew, what are you doing?" He smelled of liquor, must have the stuff hidden somewhere around the house or maybe in the shed outside.

"See?" he whispered. "I can come in here any time I like." He reached down, grabbed her breast and squeezed. Lexie couldn't move. She could only stare up at him, fearful of what was coming next. But thankfully, after another moment of lurking above her, he turned and left.

Lexie lay still for a minute, her thoughts racing as tears flooded her eyes. Her own brother had threatened her! Molested her! She should tell her mother, but would she believe her precious Lew capable of something like this? Besides, her mother was still grieving, Lexie didn't want to add to her burden. And John was out of the question. She'd just have to keep this awful secret from the family, at least till she'd thought it through.

She got up and jammed a chair under the door knob. Carrie was the only one she could trust.

**

They had met, as usual, at their favourite place, Norman's Hill, on this cool, sunny Sunday afternoon. Lexie had just finished telling Carrie about Lew, his stealing and drinking, the fight with John a few days ago and how he'd sneaked into her room.

Carrie frowned. "Lexie, no! You have to tell your mother. Or maybe Molly."

Lexie shook her head. "I can't upset Mother, Carrie, she's had such a hard time lately. And Molly would just tell John and he'd murder Lew on the spot. You know he would." She started to cry softly into her handkerchief.

"Yes, he would," Carrie agreed. "But it's horrible to think of your brother doing that, your *brother*! Don't cry, Lexie, we'll get through this. I can see you don't want to tell anyone but if he does it again, you'll *have* to."

"I felt so small and helpless, Carrie. You'd think I could jump up and push him away but it was like I was paralyzed." She shook her head at the memory. "I suppose he was angry at John and took it out on me."

"That's no excuse!" Carrie was still outraged. "The bastard should be punished but okay, we'll let it go 'til you're ready to tell and when you are, I'll be right there with you. Problem is, you'll have to carry the memory in your head."

"I know. Thank you, Carrie, for listening." They sat together in silence for several minutes.

Carrie finally spoke. "Saw Lew and Dan Connor together the other day, smoking cigarettes on Harry's Bridge. Dan yelled out to me, something stupid of course. Birds of a feather, they are!"

"That's strange," said Lexie, surprised that Dan would bother with Lew. "They never used to pal around together."

Carrie smirked. "Probably met up at the shine shacks. Can you imagine what the Missus would say about that?"

"She wouldn't be pleased, that's for sure," said Lexie, somehow uncomfortable with Carrie's obvious dislike of Dan and weary of thinking about Lew. "And now we have a war to think about." The conflict in Europe was on everyone's mind these days. Britain had declared war on Germany in August, the colonies were being asked to help out.

"Yeah. Don't s'pose a war on the other side of the Atlantic will hurt us, though, will it?"

"Will says most of the men are talking about joining up." Lexie was afraid to give voice to her fear that John might go overseas, leave Molly and the children behind. Lew, on the other hand, could leave today as far as she was concerned.

"Heard about a fight in the Five Roads," Carrie reported. "Two men going at it over whether we should help Britain or not." She sighed. "Cripes, there's so much to worry about."

"Yes. Since Father died, everything seems to be falling apart."

Carrie nodded. "Just think, 1914 will be in the history books. The date of another war, something for the youngsters to memorize in school." She paused. "Maybe Dan and Lew will go overseas together. Maybe they'll stay over there afterwards, we'll be rid of both of them."

They stood up to stretch their legs, looked out from their high vantage point at the top of Norman's Hill and drew their coats and scarves tight around them in the chilly, fall air. "The view from here is lovely," Lexie said, dreamily.

Carrie turned toward Vitter's Cove on the back side of the hill. "Can you imagine the settlers up there on Peter's Finger in the old days, watching for pirate ships?" She pointed toward the long finger of rock stretching seaward from the ridge overlooking the Cove Beach. It was named after Peter Easton, the infamous pirate of the 1600s. "Now there's a war, we might have to go up there ourselves and keep watch for German ships."

"John goes up every summer, gets ice to make ice cream for Kate and Kenny."

"John would, wouldn't he? He's just fearless enough to crawl down that cave. Mom won't let Dad go down there. She's afraid he'll get stuck."

They turned back toward the harbour and the Southside. And the narrow road winding northward along the shore toward Turk's Cove and Winterton, the former Scilly Cove, recently renamed in honor of some politician.

Below them, the white houses huddled together, chimney smoke rising lazily to the sky as painted schooners rode anchor side by side in the harbour. Small boats, hauled up now for the winter, lounged around the landwash, their white bottoms round and sleek. "Like seals sunning themselves on the rocks," Lexie whispered, unwilling to disturb the stillness.

"Please God, we won't lose any more sealers this year," Carrie said, quietly. The past spring, there'd been two sealing disasters. Two hundred fifty men had been lost, some abandoned by their ship to freeze on the ice. Several of them had been from Trinity Bay.

"Father used to say the sea can be kind but it can also be cruel," Lexie replied, a lump creeping into her throat. "It's true, isn't it?"

They sat in silence looking out over their community, every crook and corner as familiar to them as their own hands. When Carrie spoke again, she sounded unnaturally serious. "A lot of bad things have happened lately. Let's hope there won't be any more."

Five

The day was still, the harbour calm, the early October air sharp and deeply quiet; Lexie could hear the women talking from way down on the Point. She meandered down the Harbour Road with the parcel of dried tomcods Carrie's father had given her, stopping every so often to dab at the frozen potholes with her toe, just to hear the crinkling sound of the shattering ice.

This was her favourite time of year. A time of sweet regret for the passing of summer, the community holding its breath for fear of bringing on the first snow that would signal the arrival of winter. This year, she was more in tune with the season than ever. Her father's death had left her with a sense of drifting.

Lexie's days were long now, her life was on hold. The plans she and Carrie had talked about seemed far away. There'd probably be no teacher training in St. John's. Not while her mother struggled to keep going and the boys had to concentrate on the business.

She passed the Fisher Marine building, her thoughts leaping ahead to the warm kitchen stove. As she turned left into her lane, she noticed Lew and another boy walking toward her from further down the road. Carrie had been right, Lew *had* taken up with Dan Connor.

The boys turned into the lane behind her and she heard Dan say, "Look Lew, there's your baby sister. Let's stop and say hello." Lexie looked back in time to catch the scowl on Lew's face. "Hey baby sister, what's the hurry?"

Not sure what to do, Lexie stopped at the gate and waited. Dan came right up to her, grinning as he ran a hand through dark hair combed back from a high forehead. His dark eyes looked straight into hers and he gave her a saucy wink. "Hello, baby sister."

"I have to get this parcel in to Mother. Mr. Hall, um, he gave it to me for Mother." She glanced nervously at Lew as a stream of black liquid squirted from his mouth and pooled on the ground near his boot. When had he taken up chewing tobacco? Mother would be furious.

"Jesus Lew, watch where you're spittin' that stuff," Dan scowled. "Can't you smoke cigarettes like everybody else, for Christ sake?"

Dan's voice was soft, like velvet. And he spoke with a drawl, every word slowly dragged out of his mouth. Unlike most people who, her mother often grumbled, spoke at such a clip that the words fell over themselves in a gibberish. Her mother didn't have a lot of education but she held the belief that everyone should speak "slowly and clearly."

Lexie hovered shyly at the gate while the boys got into some horse-play, Dan poking Lew in the ribs and ducking as Lew flailed his arms about, swearing furiously. Dan was like a spin top, vibrating with energy, his wiry body in constant motion. Howls of laughter transformed his face as he poked Lew and darted out of the way.

Flustered and tongue-tied, Lexie turned and hurried into the house. Dan's laughter, and the image of his handsome face, followed her inside.

Sally smiled as she unwrapped the brown paper from around the salted tomcods. "I hope you'll thank Mr. Hall for me." She cut the small cod into pieces and dropped them into a bowl of water. "There, they'll soak overnight. Tomorrow we'll boil them for supper, with some potatoes and drawn butter. Nothing like something salty to bring the stomach round."

She glanced at Lexie. "Did you run down the road, Lexie? You're all flushed. You children are such a high-coloured lot. The fair complexion and light hair, of course, you get that from both sides." She smiled. "And the red cheeks like apples. Yes, I know, you hate your red cheeks but it comes from good Anglo-Saxon stock, you know."

Yes, the Fisher high colour, and Lexie hated it. It was especially aggravating when she was around boys because she blushed easily and often, much to their amusement. If only she had Carrie's easy way with the frustrating creatures. But she was too shy to flirt and her scarlet cheeks gave her away, so she mostly avoided them.

They were just about to sit down to supper when Lew came in. "How was work today, Lew?" Sally asked, as she ladled up hot vegetable soup.

"Worked 'til dinner time, then Ron broke his saw and we quit." A lie, thought Lexie, as Lew glared at her. "Jeez, you were really blushing when Dan spoke to you." He glanced at his mother, waiting for her to ask the question. "Dan makes all the girls blush."

"Dan who?" Sally obliged.

"Dan Connor. His mother is Lena Parsons, you know, over on the Southside, this end of the Long Bridge." He gave Lexie a sly glance. "I think Lexie likes him, looked like it when we met her in the lane, anyway."

"That must have been when you came in with the tomcods, Lexie," her mother said, eyebrows high. "Yes, I know who you mean. Lena was a Shipp, married Al Connor over the objections of her family, him being a Catholic. Al drowned out on Garlop maybe fifteen years ago. September it was, a gale blowing that day. Afterwards, Lena married Jake Parsons. Dan was a small boy, she had three older children besides.

"Lena's two girls went off to the States a few years ago." Sally was caught up in her story now. "And her son, Max, married a girl from Carbonear and moved over there so there's only Dan left. He could be a help, now that Jake has left the Labrador schooners for the inshore, but I hear he's a bit of an unsavoury character and not reliable."

Lexie held her breath as she listened, afraid to move for fear of interrupting the flow. Lew's mouth hung open, his eyes flicking back and forth between Lexie and his mother. When had they ever heard their mother speak about a local family in such detail before?

Sally got up to pour the tea. "Lena did what many women have to do in such circumstances," she continued, her voice quiet. "But I believe the marriage went well, which is not always the case. Jake Parsons was known to be slow-moving but he was steady and not overbearing."

She sighed as she sat back down. "It could have been me, if your father hadn't built up a business we could rely on." Obviously embarrassed at his mother's rare show of personal feelings, Lew flushed and dipped his head, began to fidget with his utensils.

Lexie was amazed, not only at the momentary glimpse of emotion, but at her mother's knowledge of the Parsons family. Unlike her father, she'd never been one to mingle easily with people and besides, she'd always expressed a low opinion of gossip. This was a side of her that Lexie hadn't seen before. Not only did her mother have deep, personal feelings, but she knew more about the community than she let on.

**

After their chance meeting at the gate, Dan Connor seemed to pop up everywhere. Or maybe, Lexie thought, I've only now started to notice. He'd pass her on the road as she was going to Parker's Store. Or just happen to meet her and Carrie as they were on their way to church on a Sunday. He'd say hello, not much else, but the intensity of his eyes was unsettling.

"I don't know what he's up to," Carrie grumbled, "but it's something to do with you. Better be careful, he's the type can charm a girl into anything. He got my cousin, Minnie, drinking one night. Aunt Beulah gave her the tongue-banging of a lifetime. She's not allowed out anymore 'til she's nineteen."

Lexie didn't remember Dan from school because he'd quit early, as did many who were needed to help in the house or on the fishing boat. But the girls at school talked about him all the time. "He's a rascal," they'd say, with a sly smile that hinted at naughty things. But rascal or not, it didn't dampen their interest.

So, though it was against her better judgement, Lexie couldn't help herself. Certainly, she'd felt dazzled by Dan's good looks since that night in the Alder Bed, his face awash in moonlight as he'd walked toward her. But, more than that, she'd been drawn to him since the night of the dance, when she'd glanced toward the stage and met his eyes. Those eyes had made her feel warm, like he'd singled her out especially.

And now, since seeing him that day by the fence, she felt off-kilter, out of focus, distracted. She tried to recall the night at the Alder Bed, the fear rushing through her as she realized that she and Carrie were at the mercy of the two boys. But now it was different, he was just a boy who made her laugh. Maybe, she thought, when it comes to boys, a girl could feel good and bad at the same time.

But Carrie wasn't drawn to Dan at all. "I don't understand what the girls see in him," she grumped. "Even grown women. Sure, in public they tut-tut and call him a devilskin, but in private it's another matter. I've seen it with Mom's friends. 'My dear, that young Irishman can charm the birds out of the trees,' she trilled, mocking them. Put him outa your mind, Lexie, he's not your type."

It wasn't that Lexie disagreed, exactly, but he was constantly on her mind, the days and weeks of missing her father replaced by new thoughts and sensations. However, she knew her mother would disapprove. "Mother called Dan an unsavoury character," she told Carrie.

"What would she say if she knew the unsavoury character was giving her daughter the rush?"

"But Carrie, there's no harm in it. Dan is just so funny. Well, he's always joking when we meet up with him, right? Mother needn't worry."

Shortly afterwards, on a Sunday night after church, Dan appeared at her side as she and Carrie were chatting on Harry's Bridge. Carrie headed over the Tory Road for home, a disgusted look on her face. Dan grinned at Lexie, gave her a sideways nod toward the harbour and she followed him like someone in a trance.

They started down Indian Meal Road, Dan chatting away about this and that, seemingly unaware that she'd suddenly gone mute. "I told Ma I talked to you, the day I was with Lew," he said, in a half-shy manner. "She told me to leave you alone, you've been through enough without getting tangled up with me. That's Ma for ya, speaks her mind no matter what."

At the corner where Joe Fisher lived, he stopped and turned to her with a comical expression. "I'm not goin' any further. Don't want your old lady to kill me," and he headed back the way they'd come. Lexie walked the last hundred yards in a daze. Luckily it was dark so no one could see the silly grin on her face.

**

The October weather had turned cold, the smell of snow was in the air. They'd begun to meet more often, though not openly. Sometimes after church, Dan met Lexie on the Green, a grassy bank dotted with boulders at the south corner of the harbour. Sheltered by stages and flakes, the Green was a popular gathering place for young people on warm summer evenings. But at this time of year, it was dark and deserted.

"Your dear brother wasn't keen on being a go-between for us," Dan told her. "Bastard had the nerve to ask me what I saw in his skinny sister. Jesus, some brother!" He grinned. "I told him he'd help or he could stay away from me. He'll do it, I'm the only friend he's got."

Lexie smiled shyly in response. It felt wonderful to hear this. She had someone on her side again, someone to keep Lew in line. And Dan didn't seem to mind her shyness at all, he just filled the silence with jokes and funny imitations of the locals. Including "the queen", as he called her mother.

Sometimes when they met, Dan smelled of liquor but it never showed. He was always the same, talkative and restless, bursting with energy. When they parted, he'd kiss her on the cheek and leave running in the opposite direction, toward the Long Bridge where he lived.

Carrie continued to be doubtful. "I know he's good-lookin' and funny," she said. "But there's something about him that puts me off, Lexie, I can't help it."

"You sound like Mother." Lexie grinned. "Isn't that something, you and Mother in agreement over something?"

"Well," bristling at the criticism, "the Missus is not always wrong!"

Disapproving or not, Carrie still helped out. On Sunday evenings after church, she waited with Lexie behind the Orange Hall 'til Dan came. But tonight, she seemed crankier than usual. "He'd better come soon," she grumbled, "my feet are cold."

"I know." Lexie felt bad that her friend wasn't happy. "He won't be long."

Dan soon showed up, breathing hard like he'd been running. "Here's my two women!"

"Don't include me in that group," Carrie snapped. "I'm going home. See you, Lexie."

"Wait, Carrie," Dan said, as she began to walk away. "I've been thinking. Your old man's stable, there behind your house, d'ya think we could meet there? It's too damn cold outside."

"Well, I dunno. This time of year the animals are looked after by suppertime and Dad is in for the night. But what about you, Lexie? You don't have to."

Lexie shrugged. "I-I don't know." Dan's suggestion had come as a surprise.

"Aw c'mon, Lexie," he coaxed. "It's no different than anywhere else, just warmer."

"I s'pose." It was so easy to just go along with him.

"If I get in trouble over this I'll kill somebody," Carrie warned, pointing her finger at Dan.

"Guess I can give Lexie the old key hanging in the backhouse, the one Dad never uses. Shouldn't, but I will." She turned to go. "Better get home soon, Lexie. The Missus is a clock watcher."

**

Three days later, under the pretext of visiting Carrie, Lexie met Dan at the stable. "Come on, follow me," he urged, as he led her up the ladder to the loft. He was holding a small lamp that cast just enough light to make out the summer's hay crop piled loosely to the rafters along one wall. He hung the lamp on a beam and they were enveloped in a soft, yellow light.

Enchanted by the quiet, the lamplight, Lexie felt a sense of unreality, like she was in a fairy tale. "It's so cozy here." She breathed in the

smells of hay and animal, smiled at the notion of the two sheep and
a black pony in their pens below, twitching their ears at the sounds
above them.

Dan guided her down on the hay and put his arm around her.
They hugged and kissed and she giggled at his gentle teasing. She felt
warm and safe here with Dan looking after her, showing her how he
felt. The hollow feeling she'd had in her stomach since her father had
died was slowly fading away.

Suddenly, without warning, Dan stood up, took her hand and
pulled her to her feet. "We'd better get you home before yer old lady
sends for Constable Shepherd."

The next time they met, Dan seemed different. There was none
of the usual teasing that always made her laugh. His kisses quickly
became more urgent. She felt his tongue flicking inside her mouth
and she pulled back.

"It's okay, Lexie," he whispered, hoarsely. "I'm just excited 'cause
I like you. You feel the same, don't you?" His smoky breath was hot
on her face as his hand found her breast. "Relax." His lips found hers
again. He eased her back on the prickly hay and pushed against her,
his hand suddenly underneath her skirt and inside the elastic of her
underpants. "Oh, Jesus."

Before she knew what was happening, he'd unbuttoned his trousers and closed her hand around the hard, smooth shaft. She froze.
In all her fantasies, she'd never imagined this!

"Lexie, can you take off your pants?" he murmured. Without
waiting for an answer, he fumbled her underwear down over her legs
and moved between her thighs. She gasped. "You okay?" pushing
himself up to look at her.

Before she could answer, he began to move in a frantic rhythm.
Then he rolled away and lay back to catch his breath. "Christ, I'd kill
for a cigarette right now," he said, as he buttoned his trousers and
brushed the hay from his hair.

Her face burning with shame, Lexie sat up and began to rear-
range her clothes. She felt disappointed and confused at the way Dan
was acting. Was this how it is with boys, she wondered, does it mean

nothing to them? She lay back in the hay feeling alone and hurt, the cold wetness on her leg a reminder of her misdeed.

"I know it hurts the first time with girls," he said, putting his arm around her. "After that, it won't hurt no more, I promise."

He kissed her gently and even though her mind was still trying to catch up to what had happened, she felt herself responding. They lay back in the hay for a few more minutes, her head tucked into his neck. She felt warm and safe again. Then he pulled her to her feet. They walked to the corner and he kissed her goodnight.

Six

Christmas had always been a happy occasion in Lexie's comfortable life, but this year it was just an unwelcome interruption. The Fishers had planned a flurry of gatherings, all aimed at boosting Sally's spirits on her first Christmas without Ken. Lexie felt obligated to attend, all the while wishing the holidays were over so she could see Dan again.

She couldn't believe she felt this way over someone she'd hardly known a few months ago.

They'd been meeting two or three times a week since early October, Lexie offering various excuses for leaving the house but amazingly, arousing no suspicions. Since Father had died, her mother was not as watchful as she used to be. Lexie had more freedom than she'd ever had.

Certain now that what she felt for Dan must be love, Lexie pushed aside the guilt of deceiving her mother, the niggling at the back of her mind that made her uncomfortable with what they were doing. She looked forward to her time in the loft with Dan and hated every minute she was away from him.

It was almost the end of December, the New Year right around the corner. Lexie was half asleep in her bedroom, resting after a family dinner at Molly's house, when she fell into a lazy replay of their last meeting. The scene rolled through her mind as she lingered over every detail. The loft, warm from the heat of the animals below, is bathed in a dim, yellow light. She leans toward him, passes him the little package tied with red yarn. One of her father's tie clips, she'd taken it from a fancy dish on her mother's dresser that morning. "Jeez, uh, thanks a lot." For once, Dan is speechless.

The memory continued into the familiar daydream. She and Dan are getting married, her family watching proudly as they turn from the altar, man and wife. They smile at each other, a happy couple at ease in themselves. Best friends like John and Molly, or Will and Jean.

A sound from outside roused her. As she rose to look out the window, she caught sight of the calendar on the wall, the one from Parker's Store with the picture of a snowy winter scene. It struck her in a flash and her heart sank. She'd been feeling listless for a couple of weeks, now she knew why.

The panic raced through her body and propelled her out of the house, up the hill to the Tory Road, straight to Carrie's house. Carrie took one look at her face. "C'mon up to my bedroom before Mom butts her nose in."

Safe upstairs, Carrie started in. "God, Lexie, you missed *two*?" She looked crestfallen, then came the anger. "Well, I'm not surprised. Figured you two were at it hot and heavy, what else would Dan Connor want? Well, now you're up the stump and I bet he's not too concerned." She shook her head, tried to calm herself. "God, I feel like killin' you. Damn it, why didn't you listen to me?"

Stung by Carrie's words, Lexie lay back on the bed and closed her eyes. She wanted Carrie to know that Dan did care about her but she felt too sick and upset to try and explain. "I know," she murmured. "I never thought."

"You can say that again! And the Missus didn't notice you weren't gettin' the curse? Cripes, Mom's eyeballs are always stuck into me. Anyway, you'll have to tell the brave *Danno* sometime and there's no time like the present," sneering at the mention of his name.

"I don't know how he'll take it," Lexie said, cautiously.

"You don't know how *he'll* take it?!" Carrie blurted. "Far as I'm concerned, he can take it and shove it ...!" She stopped, glanced quickly at the bedroom door. "Oops, forgot Mom is downstairs."

Carrie thought for a moment. "Tomorrow is New Year's Eve, too much goin' on then. Tell Lew to tell Dan you'll meet him the day after, New Year's Day." Lexie started to shake her head but Carrie was firm. "I know it won't be easy but my dear, you got no choice."

**

The next morning, Lexie helped her mother tidy up the parlour. "As you know, Lexie," said Sally, chatting idly as she dusted, "I am a Temperance sympathizer, as was the family I grew up in. But I've lived with a family of men for most of my married life, and in the interest of family harmony I *have* allowed moderate drinking in my house. Moderate, mind you. And thank God, they had no trouble abiding by my wishes." She paused, a shadow of irritation crossing her brow. "Except for John of course, who occasionally gets led astray by his Uncle Joe."

Sally reached into the cupboard and pulled out a bottle of rum. "After the terrible fall we've had, I think I'll offer everyone a little drink before they go to the Time tonight, no harm in that." She glanced at Lexie. "Don't look shocked, I haven't taken leave of my senses!"

"Mother, I've had a headache all day. I'll stay home with you tonight, you shouldn't be alone on New Year's Eve."

"But, it's the highlight of the year!" Sally looked surprised that Lexie would willingly miss the end-of-year event but she seemed pleased enough to have company while the others were off celebrating. "Well, if you're sure."

After a quiet night with her mother, Lexie went to bed to another sleepless night. She thought of a certain girl at school who'd been the target of gossip, frowned upon for her low morals. Now she knew the truth. She was one of these girls.

What was going to happen to her? Would she be sent away? There was no road back to the way things were, and she didn't know what she'd do if she *could* go back. Would she be able to resist her feelings for Dan, avoid putting her family through the upheaval that was coming? One thing was sure, she'd never be a teacher now.

The next morning, Lexie went downstairs feeling miserable, her head pounding. She'd rather spend all day in bed but it was New Year's Day, she had to try and act normal. As she sat at the table playing with her breakfast, the outside door banged shut.

"It can only be John," said her mother, frowning. "Lord, that boy is noisy!"

"Look alive, Lexie!" John bawled, his voice a knife in her skull. "It's 1915, we can turn over a new leaf." He gently squeezed his mother's shoulder. "Got to be better than last year, eh Mom?"

"Hello, there." Molly came in behind him. "We dropped by to say Happy New Year and tell you about the Time." She looked tired but her face was flushed with excitement.

"Shoulda seen her last night," said John, grinning. "She danced the men off their feet. When young Connor took over the accordion, she jumps up and hollers, 'Keep it comin', kiddo!' and everybody clapped."

At the mention of Dan, Lexie felt the heat rise to her cheeks.

"At the stroke of midnight," Molly continued, "we heard the gunshots goin' off and we all belted out "Auld Lang Syne." By the time we left the hall it had stopped snowing, the sky was peppered with stars. A good sign for the New Year, everybody said."

Molly's pretty face was beaming, her amber eyes glinting with mischief. Lexie wanted to cry. She was keeping a secret from her family. Barring a miracle she was going to spoil their happy New Year.

**

As Lexie approached the Green, she saw Dan pacing back and forth, impatient as usual, the smoke from his cigarette trailing behind him. He looked tiny beside the huge, grey boulder guarding the entrance to their meeting place.

Her father came to mind. Explaining about glaciers, how they'd melted and left rocks all over the Avalon. "You see them in streams, at the top of cliffs, even in the woods among gnarly, old, spruce trees," he'd said. "And sometimes in the middle of a field, like they suddenly dropped from the sky one day." Her father had taught her so many things. And now she'd let him down.

Dan grinned as he came to meet her. "What, no New Year's smile?" He looked tired and a bit scruffy. "You shoulda been at the Time last night, that Molly is some dancer." He laughed, put his hands on her shoulders. "Did you miss me, Miss Lexie?"

She stepped back, dropped her eyes. "There's something I have to tell you."

He shrugged his shoulders and wagged his head side to side, the familiar gesture that usually made her laugh, but not today. "Well, maid, let's hear it, we're not getting any younger. Plus, I'm near dead of a hangover. Me an' Harold went over to Benny King's after the Time. Got into the shine, rolled home around daylight. Wicked head on me today!"

She took a breath and blurted it out. "Dan, I ... I think I'm in the family way."

He froze. "Jesus. Jesus, Lexie, are you joking? I mean ..." He looked stunned as he stared at her, his eyes like black holes in his pale face.

Unwilling to meet his gaze, she turned toward the harbour and Jean's Head, where the lighthouse kept its lonely watch over the bay. Tiny snowflakes spiralled to earth as darkness settled over the Point.

"Jesus Christ!" Dan muttered, angrily snatching off his cap and running his fingers through greasy hair. "That's all I need now! Isn't there anything you can do?" He began to pace furiously, fists clenched, breath puffing into the cold air like smoke.

Her eyes filled up. What did he mean, do something? She'd heard of girls who tried to lose their babies by falling downstairs. And Carrie had told her about a girl who'd died of infection from a piece of wire. He couldn't mean that! The wind gusted up, driving the flurries sideways. Suddenly, she was chilled to the bone.

"Damn it all!" Dan said, angrily. "Me and some fellers were talkin' about joining up. The Brits need men bad. I could get in if I said I was nineteen, they wouldn't care." He pushed his hands deep into his coat pockets and scowled at the masts outlined against the sky. "Jesus, they'll make us get married. Old lady Fisher won't have no bastard baby in the precious Fisher family."

Lexie leaned back against the boulder, her head heavy with exhaustion and disappointment. The snow had turned her brown coat a winter white. Now and then, a cold, wet flake found its way inside her collar.

"You look miserable," Dan said, finally, his tone a little softer as he came near. "S'pose you should tell your old lady right away, she'll need time to get used to the idea. Probably have a heart attack but it's got to be done." He shrugged. "And I'll tell Ma soon as I can, okay? I don't know what else to say, Lexie. I'm in shock."

He still sounded a little angry but Lexie took heart from this small show of concern. His face was in shadows. She tried to imagine the crooked grin, the dark eyes she loved. "You can't stand me now, can you?"

His shoulders sagged. "No, maid, I don't hate you." His voice was almost gentle. "I was there too, remember?" He leaned in, hugged her briefly. "Better get home, storm comin'." He turned up his collar and took off running toward the Long Bridge.

Lexie bowed her head against the wind and pushed down the Harbour Road, her thoughts racing. Dan had been thinking about joining up, that was a complete surprise. He could be killed and she'd be left alone. Would he give up that idea, now that he knew she was carrying his child, or would he go anyway and leave her to face her situation alone? And if he decided not to go, would he forever blame her for ruining his life?

He'd seemed kind at the end. Had he mentioned marriage? Maybe not in those exact words but she was sure that's what he'd meant, anyway.

The powder swirled around her as she remembered a childish pleasure from a lifetime ago. Herself and Carrie making zigzags in newly fallen snow.

"Lexie, that you?" The voice from the squalls startled her. "It's Uncle Joe, Lexie. Didn't frighten you, did I? I'm on my way over the Southside, walk Julie home from one of her sick calls. Better get on home yourself."

"Yes, Uncle Joe," she hollered back, "I'm on the way home now." She turned the corner, saw the lights of home further down the road. Her spirits fell. How would she ever tell her mother that she was carrying Dan Connor's baby?

Seven

Lexie had gone to bed exhausted and got up feeling exactly the same. Full of anxiety for what she had to do, she'd been biding her time all day, waiting for Lew to go out. Finally, after supper, he got ready and left. She and her mother were alone in the pantry, washing dishes.

Lexie chose her moment and turned to her mother. "Mother, I'm in the family way." The words seemed to float in the air between them. Bubbles waiting to burst.

Sally stood frozen to the spot, one hand holding a plate, the other dangling in the dishwater. Lexie wound the dishcloth around and around her hands as the blood, the symbol of her shame, came rushing into her cheeks. Please God, if she could only fall through the floor boards and disappear.

"Lexie, my dear, I must be mistaken," said her mother, hopefully. "What did you say?"

"I'm carrying Dan Connor's baby." Almost a whisper.

Sally's hands flew to her face. Then, as expected, she lashed out. "Lexie Fisher, you went behind my back with that ne'er-do-well and thought you could come away without a mark? What about your good name, your father's hopes ..." Her face a flaming red, Sally fell into the rocking chair, one hand pressed to her chest.

"Mother," Lexie said, quietly, aware of the arrow she'd sent into her mother's heart, "I know this isn't what you wanted for me. I went behind your back, I made a bad mistake." A huge lump of regret threatened to choke her and the tears came. "It just all h-happened so fast!"

Sally looked at her. "Lexie, you're sixteen, he's only a year older. I don't know what to do, m'dear!" Lexie started to speak but her mother interrupted. "We'll say no more about it now, I'm tired. You go on to bed, you're looking peaked." She shook her head. "Why didn't I see it?"

Lexie ran upstairs crying, the sting of her mother's disappointment heavy in her chest. She lay in bed, listening to the creaking of the rocking chair downstairs as her mother picked over the events of the last few months, wondering how she could have missed the signs. And letting go of her dreams for her daughter.

She cried herself to sleep, a deep dreamless sleep, and was awakened by a sharp knock on her door. Lew, with his usual rude signal as he clumped down the hall on his way to bed, his reminder of the power he held over her. She dreaded the time when Lew would find out about her predicament. How he would crow! Meanwhile, downstairs, the rocking chair went on creaking.

**

Waking to the sound of sleigh bells, Lexie dragged herself out of bed and peered through the leafy frost patterns on the window. The sky was a brilliant blue, the world sparkling and bright in its new white coat.

Squinting into the brightness, she saw John pulling back on the reins. "Ho there, Fog. Ho, ya bugger!" his voice loud in the morning stillness. Beside him in the sleigh was Molly, her legs wrapped in a heavy, grey blanket. Worried of what her mother might tell John, Lexie hurried downstairs.

After the usual commotion of stomping the snow from his boots, John came in. "Hello to all," he beamed, obviously recovered from his New Year's imbibing. "We're goin' across to Carbonear for supplies, Mom. Anything you want over there?"

"Well, no, I don't need anything. But if you'd stop by Will's, ask him to come by today. I daresay he and Jean had planned to anyway, but just in case they had something else in mind."

It was early afternoon when Will and Jean burst through the door, rosy-cheeked and laughing after the bracing sleigh ride. Jean looked happy and alive in her grey, hooded coat, the matching fur muff hanging from her neck by a fancy cord. Lexie's heart sank at what was to come.

"And today, mind you," Jean was saying, "Blaze wasn't his cranky self, he actually let me drive. Maybe he's turning over a new leaf for the New Year."

Lexie watched them going on in their usual way. "Of course, Blaze thinks she's the cranky one," Will piped up. "Still, I must say she did him proud. Sitting stiff as a board holding the reins just right, a big smile on her face." He gave his impression of his wife's driving technique. Jean gave him a poke in the ribs.

"Well, I was a bit nervous," Jean conceded, "especially as he began to labour up Birchen Hill. What would I ever do if he stopped in his tracks? But then he settled into an easy trot on the Levels and I knew I'd won him over." She laughed. "As we drove by Howley's Pond, the children skating there all started to wave and cheer. Boy, was I proud!"

Will turned to his mother, his smile fading as he became aware of her distraction. "Mother, are you all right? You look tired. Too much celebrating?" His attempt at a joke fell flat as Sally's face gave her away. "Jean," Will said, quickly, "put on some tea, will you?"

"Yes, Boss," Jean mocked, unaware of the change in tone. She headed into the pantry for water, making a funny face at Lexie as she passed. Lexie tried to smile in reply but her lips felt frozen.

"Will, we have a problem," her mother said, quietly. "I sent Lew off somewhere so he wouldn't be around to hear." She glanced at Lexie. "I'll say it right out. Lexie got herself in trouble, she told me last night. She's been seeing that Connor boy. I had no idea."

Jean stopped in her tracks on the way to the stove. Will's mouth dropped open. Together they looked toward the table where Lexie was sitting. "Dear God," Will mumbled.

"We're going to get married." The words had come out before Lexie knew she was even thinking them. There was no way to take them back without looking like a silly girl. And, for some reason, she didn't really feel like taking them back.

Will took a moment to gather himself. "Lexie," he said, calmly, "I can't pretend I'm not shocked. You know how much we think of you, how we've planned for your future." He looked solemnly at Jean. "Maybe we can help. What if Jean and I raised the baby? You can carry on with your life. Get married someday, have a family. What do you say?" Jean brightened as she nodded her agreement.

Sally gave Will a grateful look. "Well, it makes the best of a bad situation. Lexie?"

Lexie wasn't surprised at Will's suggestion. Responsible Will, always looking to the family's best interests. Besides, he and Jean had always wanted children. To them, it must seem like the perfect solution.

But to Lexie, it felt like they were ganging up on her, dismissing her feelings. "I'm going to marry him," she repeated. "We talked about it and that's what he wants, too."

Even as she said it, she wasn't convinced it was true. Dan had been really angry that day on the Green but hadn't he begun to soften at the end? Or was it her imagination? Like the times she'd envisioned their marriage as she sat in her room writing, "Mrs. Dan Connor," and "Mr. and Mrs. Dan Connor," over and over in her journal.

Jean turned and strode angrily into the hall. Just as quickly she was back, green eyes flashing. "Lexie, you can't marry into that crowd, they're poor as church mice! Dan Connor is a drinker and a layabout, everyone knows that. He'll never make a living, not even in a fishing boat. And in this man's world, we won't be able to help because he won't allow it." She stalked into the parlour and sat alone.

Will continued to try and change her mind but Lexie quietly stood her ground. When Dan really thought about it, he wouldn't turn his back on his own child. And the family would come around when they saw the baby, a grandchild for her mother, a niece or nephew for her brothers. Besides, she couldn't see Dan allowing his child to be raised by a Fisher.

Will looked at her for a moment, his brow wrinkled in puzzlement. He was probably thinking it wasn't like her to go against the family's wishes and that was true. Until now. "Give it some thought, Lexie," he said, "and let us know in a few days."

He was being so kind, so reasonable, that she almost broke down and gave in. Will's suggestion would solve the problem for everyone. But what of her and Dan?

"Poor things," her mother murmured, as Will followed an upset Jean out the door. "Not as cheerful now as when they arrived, are they?" Her face was haggard. "You're making a mistake, Lexie. You need to give some realistic thought to your situation. Hear me? *Realistic* thought. And so must I." She pulled her shawl around her shoulders. "I'm going upstairs to lie down."

**

A week later, Will and Jean had given up trying to change Lexie's mind. Like her mother, they were probably feeling they'd failed her and Lexie was sorry for that, but she couldn't give in yet. She needed to know what Dan was thinking.

"I suppose there's no other choice," her mother said. "I'll have to tell the rest of the family. I'll start with Lew. You go upstairs 'til I'm done."

Later, as Lew passed her in the hall, the curl of his lip told her how much he relished the news of her humiliation. Lexie hurried past him, her cheeks burning. How would the others react, she wondered? Would they shun her?

When John and Molly arrived, Lexie tried to make herself invisible in the corner. How she wished she could spare them this! Molly had been so kind after her father's death, looking after her, prodding her to keep going. And though John teased her, she knew he was proud of her.

John didn't tarry long after his mother had explained the situation. Red to the roots of his hair, he banged out the door in a rage. "I'll kill the son of a bitch!"

"John, don't you do anything foolish!" Sally called after him.

Lexie's spirits rose a little as Molly came to sit beside her. Molly wouldn't be against Dan, she came from a poor, hardworking family just like he did. The slightest hint of snobbery from any of the Fishers always caused her hackles to rise.

Molly reached for her hand, the gesture bringing a tear to Lexie's eyes. "It's been a hard couple days, hasn't it? All them self-righteous people lookin' at you like you let 'em down, brought shame to the family." Lexie held tight to Molly's hand and nodded. "Thing is, my girl, we've got to make a decision. Now, you say you want to get married?" Lexie nodded again. "Well, as you know, I got nothing against the boy for who he is, but he's not someone I'd pick for you myself. Young Dan's got some growing up to do. What about Will's offer?"

"Dan is young yet, Molly," Lexie pleaded. "He'll settle down after we're married. Lots of men are wild 'til they have a family, aren't they? Isn't that true? People always say that."

"Mm-m, yes, people do say that, and sometimes it's true." Molly's voice lacked the conviction Lexie wanted to hear. "Whether Dan will, we don't know, and I somehow doubt it. Do you want to take that chance?" Hearing no reply, Molly shook her head. "You wanted to be a teacher, remember?" her own eyes filling up.

"A fallen woman would never get a teaching job, Molly," Lexie said, quietly, looking away.

**

Now that Lexie's situation was out in the open, Lew took great pleasure in reporting Dan's activities. "Shoulda seen the girls around Dan at the dance last night," he'd say, as Lexie realized that Dan was following his usual routine. His life hadn't changed at all while she'd replaced Lew as the family disappointment.

It was early afternoon, her mother had just left to visit Mrs. Mitchell. Lexie was sitting at the kitchen table when Lew came in from the woods. He was home early, had probably feigned sickness so Ron Bailey would let him go.

Lew went into the pantry to wash his hands and it occurred to Lexie that she was alone in the house with him. She was just getting up to make her escape when he came out, a sly smirk on his face. "Y'know, I've been wonderin'. What is it Dan Connor sees in you? Let's face it, you're not really his type. He likes the wild ones." He moved so quickly she didn't see it coming. "Let's see if I can find out," and his hand was under her skirt.

"Lew, stop!" She stumbled backwards, the chair went flying across the kitchen.

"Precious little Lexie." Lew grabbed her arm, pulled her toward him. "Dan probably gets a kick outa having the Fisher princess chasin' him."

"What's going on?" came the voice of doom from the kitchen door. "What're y'doin', Lew? Where's Mom?"

"She's over at Mitchell's," Lexie gasped, as she rearranged her clothes.

"Good, there's something I started that needs finishing." John grabbed Lew by the collar. "You little Christer! All those years treatin' her like shit, for no other reason but jealousy." He slapped Lew's face hard. "I've had enough! Now this can go on, me beatin' the shit outa you every week, or you can grow up and stop torturing her. Hear me?" Lew nodded. "You know I'll do it, don't you?" More nodding. "From now on, buddy, I'll be watching, got it?"

"Yes, yes," said Lew. "Let me go."

"Get out. Try to be a normal human being and not a bloody outcast. I can be your best friend or I can be a bastard, you decide!" He gave Lew a push, sent him flying into the porch.

John slumped down on a chair. He was breathing hard, sweat running down his face. "Damn that Lew, I'll end up killing him yet!" He looked at Lexie. "Did he hurt you?"

"No, I'm all right," trying to catch her breath. "But I'm glad you came when you did. What's wrong with him? He's always so mean to me."

"I don't know. Surely, at his age, he should be over this childhood jealousy. Lew's always been a problem, but since Dad died he doesn't seem to care about anything." He was pensive for a moment. "I'll have a word with Will, there's got to be something we can do."

John looked at her sheepishly. "I really came to talk to you about, you know, how I acted when I heard about the baby, all that. Molly said to come and be civil and not act like a savage, her words. I wish you'd take Will's offer, Lexie. That Connor boy is no good for you."

She hung her head. "I know I've disappointed everyone and I'm sorry. But I want to see what Dan says about it. Maybe we *can* make a go of it."

John jumped to his feet, his face hot with anger. "You know, you've got a real stubborn streak that we didn't know about." He gave a resigned shrug. "Okay, do what you want. You know where we stand, me and Molly."

**

Sally Fisher wasn't one to let a problem fester. "There's no benefit in putting things off," she declared. "Your condition will soon be common knowledge and I can't see discussing the matter with Reverend Fairchild. Get ready, we're going to see Julie Fisher. She knows about babies, she's helped born enough of them. Besides, she's family."

They found Joe dozing on the daybed, Julie at the table mending a shirt. "Hello, Julie," said Sally. "I see you're busy."

"Sally, Lexie, come in." Julie's smile was warm and welcoming. "I'm not busy, just passing the time with some mending. Joe is not the best company when he's half asleep."

Joe sat up at the sound of their voices, his thinning blonde hair sticking up in patches. "Look who's here. Sit down, sit down."

"Hello, Joe." Sally tried a smile. "Sleeping away the day, are you?"

Joe grinned. "Actually, I was just having a naughty dream about you. Want to hear it?"

"No, I don't! I came to see Julie about something."

"Say no more. Women's talk, I suppose." Joe got up and went to the porch for his coat. "Take your time, I'll be over to Hedley's havin' a yarn."

Julie laid aside her mending. "I'll put on the kettle, a cup of tea always concentrates the mind."

Lexie hung her head as her mother went through the painful details; the pregnancy, Will's offer, her stubborn insistence on marriage. Julie listened carefully without interrupting.

"All right, now we know the situation," said Julie. "Come sit at the table with us, Lexie. It's your life we're discussing." Julie was a God-fearing woman. Lexie expected she'd be judged harshly.

"I want Lexie to take Will's suggestion," Sally said, "but she insists on waiting to see how the boy feels. Of course, I can force the issue, force her to accept Will's offer." At this, Lexie's head shot up. "But what might come of that, a sister turned against a brother? And what of her state of mind afterwards? There could be any number of ill effects and I've thought of all of them."

Julie nodded solemnly as Sally went on. "I'd hoped by now I could sit back, let the boys run the business and turn my attention to Lexie as she enters womanhood." Her voice broke. "It's all gone now, all …" She reached into the bosom of her dress for her handkerchief.

"Lexie, I *am* sorry to hear this today," said Julie, taking Lexie's hand. "You've strayed from the path the good Lord wants you to follow and I'll certainly pray for you. Still, I tend to be practical in most matters. Of all the babies I've borned, I'm betting none of them cared about the circumstances of their birth.

"Sally, you need to know where the boy stands. It's one thing what Lexie wants, might be different for the boy, especially from what you say about him. I suggest you send a message to Lena Parsons and ask her to come with the lad. Hash everything out and see where it leads."

She turned her gaze on Lexie. "In the end, my girl, you might have to take Will's offer, no matter what you want. And if that happens, we would hope the Lord will give you the strength and courage to accept it and move on.

"Otherwise, Sally, you never know. Some marriages start amid doubts but work out fine in the end. As I recall, your own mother, Sarah Jane Green, wasn't too keen on your marriage to Ken Fisher. She had her reasons, Ken was just getting started in business, him and Joe, and they had no money, no family backing. But your father, he thought different, didn't he?"

"Yes." Sally nodded her head, remembering. "I was surprised at the time, Father being a pious Methodist and all. But, you know, I think he believed in leaving important matters to a higher power." She nodded to Julie. "I'll send a note to Mrs. Parsons. Thank you, Julie, for hearing us out."

Eight

It was a bitter afternoon in late January, the winter sky hovering dark and angry over the village. All the houses had lit their lamps early. Lexie watched nervously from her bedroom window as Dan and his mother rounded the corner by Joe Fisher's house, pushing hard against the icy wind blowing off the water. Her mother's message to Mrs. Parsons was about to bring things to a head.

The harbour looked cold and forboding, a frozen mosaic floating in yellowish slush. Huge ice pans had pushed up into the landwash with the tides and were stacked up level with the road. Lexie's eyes fell on the schooners, tugging and creaking with the shifting of the frozen soup. Abandoned at anchor and left to the mercy of the storms, just as she was.

Lexie crept into the kitchen as the visitors came in. Her mother looked the picture of dignity, her greying hair pulled back in a tight bun, a cameo brooch at the high collar of her black dress. She directed them into the parlour, the coldest room in the house.

"Mrs. Parsons, thank you for coming with your son," said Sally, pulling her purple shawl tight around her shoulders. "I think you know the situation. My daughter is expecting a child, your son is the father." Her words were measured and respectful. "I don't know the whole story but it seems they've already discussed marriage. At least, that's what Lexie tells me, and that's what we need to clarify."

Lena Parsons sat quietly on the settee, hands folded in her lap. Dan had perched on the hard chair by the window, the oil lamp on the wall casting one side of his face in full light. At the word "marriage," his head jerked around and he looked at Lexie. In spite of the coolness of the room, there were beads of sweat on his upper lip.

"Lexie has said she wants to marry your boy," Sally continued. "I doubt she's being realistic when she talks about marriage, young girls often have their heads in the clouds. What are your thoughts, Mrs. Parsons?"

Lexie sat hunched over in the green, brocade armchair, a large, blue shawl draped over her shoulders and covering her stomach. As Mrs. Parsons turned to her, she felt overcome with embarrassment, had to look away.

"My dear girl," Lena said, her voice kind, "is it really in your mind to get married? Make no mistake, Dan will do his duty if that's your decision, I've made that clear to him. But even though he's my own, I wouldn't advise you, nor any girl, to take up with him at this point. He's not set up for fishing, not even close." At this, Dan had the grace to drop his head. "Did you think hard about your brother's kind offer?"

Lexie glanced shyly at Dan, then went back to staring at the hooked rug on the floor, the one with the big, blue roses, her mother's pride. "Yes, I did think about it." Her voice was no more than a whisper. "But I want the baby to have a home with his parents. And we're his mother and father."

All eyes turned to Dan, who seemed to shrink further into the collar of his coat. He shrugged. "I, uh, I suppose there's nothin' else to say," he said weakly. "If she wants to get married, we'll have to get married." He shrugged again. "I'm not fussy about giving the baby to Will Fisher, anyway."

Lexie felt a wave of relief go over her. Lots of young men went to the altar through no decision of their own. She hoped Dan was doing it willingly, but if not she was sure it would work out in the end. He'd settle down once he had responsibilities. She gave him a quick smile that was only half-heartedly returned.

"Lexie," Sally said, her voice rising in frustration, "it's not a trivial thing, marriage, and certainly not in these circumstances. You have to be sure it's what you want."

"Yes, Mother," she replied, "I'm sure." Lexie felt more confident now that Dan had more or less agreed to marriage. She could foresee a future with him, herself presiding over their home as a wife and mother. This was what she used to dream of. Yes, it had come earlier than planned but she would chin up and carry on, as her mother always said. Or was it Queen Victoria? Lexie smiled to herself. Sometimes it was hard to tell the difference.

"Well, we'll see," said her mother. "Dan, I think it'd be proper if you came to see Lexie every few days, there's a lot you two need to talk about." She turned to Lena. "If it does go ahead, and we'll see about that as the days go on, I expect the best time for the wedding will be spring or early summer, when the weather gets warmer. Maybe May. Certainly not a church wedding, of course, just a few family." She showed no joy at the pronouncement.

Lena looked at Lexie for several seconds, her eyes troubled. Then she turned to Sally and gave a brief nod.

**

The weeks dragged by. Then it was March, the month of hope for better times. Lexie felt miserable and it didn't help that she was housebound with her mother, who went around sighing and looking sad. Every time Lexie heard that sigh, she felt a pang of guilt. Of course, the guilt was probably going both ways, her mother feeling that if she'd been more vigilant none of this would have happened in the first place.

"I'm living in The House of Guilt on the Harbour Road," she whispered to Carrie, who had to stifle a laugh. If Carrie didn't come by now and then, Lexie thought she might run screaming down the wharf and jump into the harbour. "Thank God, spring is almost here."

She'd spent the winter perched in the kitchen window, watching clusters of children wading through the snow with coasters and horn cats, snow-encrusted mitts molded to their hands or hanging out of sleeves by a string. She was the family shut-in, everyone tip-toeing around her.

"Is Dan still coming by, like he was *ordered*?" Carrie asked, a wicked grin on her face.

"Yes. The first few times were awkward. He was sullen, not much to say." Lexie leaned closer, whispered, "Mother keeps pushing me to talk to him about the future, how he'll support us, that sort of thing. But I think it's too early for that, he's only just getting used to coming here. Well, you can imagine how he feels, Mother looking at him like he ruined her life!"

"Yes, I know that look very well," Carrie said, with a laugh. "And, of course, Dan is not much for taking orders, probably resents being bossed around by a bunch of women."

"I'm nervous of saying the wrong thing, the slightest comment can set him off. He and Frank got into a fight last week because Dan had girls hanging around him at the dance." Her cousin, Frank, Uncle Joe's son, could be counted on to defend her honour. "I hate hearing things like that but I don't say anything." Lexie hesitated. "I hope I'm doing the right thing, Carrie."

"Frank and Dan are numbskulls," Carrie replied, offhandedly. "Hot-headed, stubborn numbskulls."

Lexie felt a need to say more, to discuss her situation further, but Carrie didn't seem interested. She'd been going easier on Dan lately, probably thought it was too late to change things anyway. Which it is, Lexie reminded herself.

"Still, it's upsetting," Lexie persisted, "the girls, the fights. It bothers me."

"By the way, how are things with Lew?" Carrie asked, changing the subject. "Jeez, that was awful what he did. Good thing John stepped in." She seemed determined to avoid any serious talk about Dan.

Lexie had to let the moment go. "Lew is a little better, I suppose, except for the odd rude remark when there's no one around. But he knows John is watching him."

Carrie glanced out the window. "The ice is breaking up. Dad saw seals sunning themselves on ice pans outside the harbour yesterday. And the schooners are signing on summer crews."

"Yes, all signs of warmer weather. Last week, Dan appeared at the back door with a brace of turrs slung over his shoulder. Wanted to know if Mother would like to have them."

Carrie's eyebrows shot skyward. "No! *Dan* being nice to the Missus?"

"Well, he does have a good side, you know."

Carrie was not to be convinced. "Mm-m, too bad he keeps it so well hidden!"

"Anyway, Mother *was* pleased with the turrs. She went bustling away to boil the water, telling Dan they should pick them right away. Ugh, the sickly-sweet smell of hot feathers wafting through the house! I had to fight my stomach just to stay and watch.

"But I couldn't miss the chance of seeing them leaning over the steaming tub together, Mother sloshing the big, black and white birds in the water, Dan going to work on the feathers. I was afraid to speak for fear of breaking the spell."

**

Sally poked her head around Lexie's bedroom door. "It's a nice, early spring day, a rare thing in this part of the world. I opened some windows, blow off the winter stink as Joe Fisher would say. Get up now, m'dear, and see how you feel. Maybe sit out on the back platform for an hour, get some fresh air." And she hurried off downstairs, her tuneless humming filtering back up to Lexie's room.

Lexie frowned as she hauled herself out of bed. Her mother's chipper manner was getting on her nerves; the last thing she wanted to do was sit outside. Feeling huge and useless, she huffed downstairs and slouched into the kitchen, pulling her robe around her. "I'm not hungry," she yawned, lowering herself into a chair by the window.

As she idly traced her fingertips over the familiar red roses of the oilcloth, she glanced out to see Lew going in the door of Fisher Marine. He must be working with Will today. So far, he was more or less following Will's schedule. Some days with more less than more.

"It's mild out," Sally said, setting a pot of water on the boil. "John dropped in earlier. He read in the Carbonear paper that the war isn't going well, England is calling for more men from the colonies. Has Dan said anything?"

Lexie looked up, startled. "Well, he mentions it now and then." She shrugged. "But he's too young to go, he's not eighteen yet. You have to be nineteen."

Sally placed the bowl of porridge in front of Lexie and poured tea for them both. "I already had breakfast, too nice a day to lie around," she declared, proceeding to puff herself up like a pigeon as it dawned on Lexie that something was up.

"Now, Lexie, I want you to listen. You and Dan have got to talk about the wedding, how he'll support you, things like that. You can both stay here 'til the boys can get a place ready, but you'll have to be the one to tell him."

Lexie sat back in her chair. With her mother's words, the weight of coming events became real. She was about to be pushed out of the nest. She felt homesick and she wasn't gone yet.

"If you're still set on marrying him," her mother went on, briskly, "you'll have to take the lead in discussing these things, because I doubt Dan will." Her voice softened. "Will's offer still stands, you know. And the baby would have a fine home."

"Mother, for the last time, I won't change my mind!" Why wouldn't they take her seriously? "All right, when Dan comes by, I'll talk to him!" She stomped back upstairs. Stopped on the landing as she realized what she'd done. Her mother would probably excuse her rudeness on the grounds that her condition was delicate, but she probably shouldn't make it a habit.

**

Lexie and Dan sat together on the back platform, out of sight of the main road. Privacy was necessary now as her condition was noticeable and the subject of much interest in the community. Lexie knew her mother must be devastated that the family was the subject of gossip, people pointing and tittering as they passed the house.

"The weather is finally turning," said Dan, taking off his cap and leaning back to catch the sun on his face. "Soon be warm enough to go troutin'."

Over the winter, Lexie had gotten to know Dan better. He'd talked about some of the things that occupied his time, everyday things like hauling wood with Jake, walking to Carbonear with Harold to get flour. Now and then, he talked about his father, Al Connor, who'd come from Turk's Cove, the small Catholic community between New Perlican and Winterton.

"Old Bridget, my grandmother, never forgave Ma for luring him away from the RC Church," he'd told her. "'Course, the way Ma tells it, the old man was happy to give up his soul for the woman he loved. That's Ma, always with the jokes."

Lexie was glad Dan was in a good mood today because she was getting ready to bring up the matter her mother had mentioned earlier. How would he react to the news that they were expected to live here, with her mother, after the wedding? It would certainly be a delicate operation. Like holding a butterfly in your hand. Press too hard and you might kill it, not hard enough and it might wiggle free.

"Got into it with Frank again the other night," Dan went on, grinning sheepishly as he looked away. "Jesus, can I help it if the girls come around me at the dances?"

Lexie hated to hear him talk like that, but she figured most young men liked to brag. She could imagine Uncle Joe at Dan's age, even her father. The girls must have loved her father when he was young. After they were married, and as Dan matured, this kind of talk would likely end.

"Oh, Frank is just being Frank," she replied absently. "Best to ignore him."

Dan leaned into his hand to light a cigarette and Lexie made her move. "I, uh, I suppose we should talk about where we'll live afterwards," she said, cautiously, wishing she could sound more confident, less timid, around him.

"Yeah? Well, Ma says we can live with her and Jake for a while." He looked uncomfortable. Had he made that up to put an end to the subject? To wiggle free?

"Mother said we can live here 'til the boys can put something up." There, she'd done it!

His head shot around, the black eyebrows pulled downward in a scowl. "You got t'be kidding! Me, live with your old lady? Jesus, is that what she told you to say? Forget it." He headed into the porch. "C'mon, might as well put the kibosh on that right now!"

Sally turned from the stove where she'd been wiping off the kettle with a cloth. "Isn't it lovely, the fresh air?" Then, noticing their faces, "What's wrong, Lexie?"

"Somethin' you should know," Dan declared, "Lexie'll be living over with us after we're married so don't worry, we'll be fine." He lifted the damper, threw his butt into the stove. "It's just 'til I'm set up, anyway, she'll have her own house before long." He turned to go, a crooked smile on his lips. "She'll drop over to see you now and then."

Lexie saw the vein pop in her mother's temple. "Listen here, you young pup!" her voice low and threatening. "Grin all you like, but where my daughter lives is my concern and I'll be the one who decides. Don't forget that!" She made a move toward the poker hanging from the back of the stove. Dan jumped back and headed for the porch.

"Christ," he breathed, when they were back outside. "You can't be serious, live with that old bitch?" He started to roll a cigarette but his shaking hands betrayed him. "Make up your mind," he sputtered, flinging the fixings over the rail. "It's Ma's or nowhere." He jumped the steps and disappeared up the lane toward the Tory Road and the Cove, where his friend Harold lived.

**

The next morning, Lexie and her mother sat glumly over their toast, the tension between them heavy and silent, when a knock at the back door startled them. Sighing heavily, Sally pushed herself up from the table and went to answer it. "Come in, Mrs. Parsons," Lexie heard her say. "We're just finishing breakfast, Lexie is slow to get around those days. Have some tea?"

"No, thank you, Miz Fisher." Lexie could only stare as Lena took a chair at the table. "I won't take much of your time, then I'll be on my way. As I said to Jake, God must have sent me Dan to balance things out 'cause he's more trouble than my other three youngsters put together."

Lexie was instantly alert. Had Dan run off somewhere, run away from her and the baby?

"I hope you don't think bad of us because of him," Lena continued. "It's true, he's different from the rest of my crowd. My girls, Mary and Belle, are on their own, living in Boston." She smiled. "Then there's Max, the oldest. He's a ship's carpenter, married to Ruth Healey, her father is Captain Healey. They live in Carbonear."

Lena sighed deeply. "And then there's Dan! Yes, so far he's a disappointment, but it's not that I raised him any different. Maybe he's what they call a late bloomer, I don't know, but he can't seem to settle into a normal life.

"When he was young, he was so wild I used to call him the "young Turk." That's the old word for pirates, they used to shelter down there in Turk's Cove in the old days. I heard some of the Connors went off with the pirates back then. Maybe the wild streak came through to Dan. 'Course, Jake says who could blame them, piratin' was a damn sight easier than fishin'. I don't know, maybe if his father was around to give him some guidance ..."

She looked at Lexie. "I heard about the snit he got in yesterday, about where you'll live. I wanted to come over and set things right because I'm sure he didn't handle it very well."

"Mrs. Parsons," Sally interrupted, "no one can fault you as a mother. But Dan is still very much a child, as you yourself have said. I thought I was doing them a favour when I suggested they live here."

"Yes, I know," Lena replied, nodding agreement. "But Miz Fisher, I can see no way Dan can live under your roof without you killin' him, and Jake agrees." She smiled at Lexie. "I wish you'd consider our offer, my dear. 'Tis not a palace, but 'til Dan gets on his feet, you'll be welcome. You're not the first one Jake Parsons ever took in. Easy man to live with, Jake is, you won't have no worries with him."

Sally sat pondering. "I don't know. Certainly, the boy and I are a bad combination. Maybe Lexie would be all right with you, it's not that far away after all. And, we have to remember it wouldn't be for long. My boys would soon be seeing about a house. Anyway, I'll give it some more thought." She sighed. "Before you go, Mrs. Parsons, what are you hearing about the war? Do you worry that your boys will go overseas?"

"Well, yes, I do worry. My Max will probably think it's his duty to go, he's the high-minded one. And Dan, well, he mentions it but I daresay he's too young."

**

A few more days, and a few more talks with her mother, and the issue of where they'd live seemed to be settled. Lexie had just propped herself up on the chesterfield in the parlour, trying to find some relief for her aching back, when she heard someone come into the kitchen.

"She's inside," she heard her mother say, in that resigned tone. "Go on in, I suppose."

Dan strolled in and sat down beside her. He looked different today, his handsome face beaming. "How is Miss Lexie?" he smiled. Suddenly serious, he leaned forward. "Got something to tell you. I joined up, me and Harold and a couple other boys. We leave in six weeks." The words hit her like a punch to the stomach. Dan was waiting for her reply but she couldn't speak. "We'll get married before I go," he went on. "You'll be all right over with Ma and Jake."

Lexie covered her face with her hands. "But you're not old enough. And how will I manage without you?"

He knelt down beside her, pulled her hands away from her face. "Right now, the Brits are not exactly fussy about a man's age," he said. "They'll take most of us for the Navy, naturally, what with our reputation for the sea. But, y'know what? This is the best thing for me right now. Help out the poor Brits, see a bit of the world at the same time. Before I settle down, like, right?"

Lexie gave him a weak smile and wiped her eyes. He seemed so different. He was making plans, taking charge. A surge of love shot through her. Maybe Dan was right, he'd have a chance to grow up before coming back to her and the baby. Please God, he'd be safe.

"But listen, you being my wife, I expect you to live with my crowd 'cause you'll be a Connor then." He nuzzled her cheek. "Let's tell the old lady, get that over with." He took her hand and led her out to the kitchen.

Sally turned as they came out of the parlour, an expectant look on her face. "I'm joining up, Missus," Dan said, boldly. "Leaving in a few weeks, we'll get married before I go. Probably only be gone for a couple months, anyway, they say the war could be over by next Christmas."

Nine

Tired after another sleepless, uncomfortable night, Lexie forced herself out of bed by sheer will and peered out the window. "My wedding day," she thought, with a wry smile, as she looked down at her enormous belly. "And don't I look the innocent young bride!"

She'd been miserable for days and was anxious to get the ceremony over with. She'd even begun to resent Dan's good spirits, his excitement about going overseas. In fact, there were moments when she dearly wished he could feel all her discomfort, all the aches and pains, all the fatigue. "Having a baby is certainly not shared equally," she'd complained to Molly.

"I'm sure women everywhere would agree," Molly had replied.

Yesterday, the weather had been mauzy, overcast and drizzly with a thick fog hanging over the bay. But, as Uncle Joe had promised, today looked to be perfect, quite mild for May with definite hints of summer. Joe had even offered his horse and carriage to the Connors. A nice gesture but Lexie knew Joe had no more liking for Dan than did the rest of the Fishers. He probably just wanted to stay involved so he could keep an eye on her.

Lexie glanced around her bedroom. Remembered coming home after school on warm spring days, lying on her bed and listening to the familiar sounds outside; a wheelbarrow rumbling along a flake, men laughing on the wharves, a neighbour chastising her boy. The warmth of the room from the afternoon sun, the buzzing of fat houseflies bumping against the window, usually sent her off to sleep 'til her mother called her to help with supper.

Things had been simpler then. Here she was at sixteen, six months along with a baby out of wedlock, about to get married to the father and say goodbye to him. Her birthday was in a couple of months. It was certainly one she'd not soon forget.

She carefully maneuvered herself downstairs, keeping a tight grip on the rail so as not to jolt her swollen stomach, and was soon caught up in wedding preparations. Her mother, as evidence to her state of mind, was ignoring the odd swear word and letting Molly take charge.

"There, you look like a princess," Molly declared, tying her straight, blonde hair with a blue ribbon that matched her dress.

"A very fat princess," said Lexie, looking at herself in the mirror. Her dress was light blue with a dark blue overblouse. Molly had bought it at Pike's Ladies' Wear in Carbonear and Jean had lent her a navy hat that she said went well with everything.

The door flew open and Lew stomped in. "Mom, is it true what Will said? That I've got to look after the store while you all go to the wedding?"

"That's right," replied Sally, standing in front of the small mirror in the pantry, fixing her hair.

"But Mom, I got things to do. Can't we shut down for the day?" Lew shifted from one foot to the other, nervously licking his lips as his eyes bounced around the kitchen.

Lexie watched with interest. Did Lew really have the nerve to argue with their mother on a day like this, when she was already frazzled? "Lew," came the stern voice from the pantry," did you hear what I said?"

"Yeah, okay," said Lew, his tone as grumpy as he dared. Wisely, he turned tail and left.

**

The Rectory loomed above them as the grey gelding moseyed up the steep lane. John's thick, yellow hair was damp from the effort of coaxing the horse forward, the horse he called Fog. "Because look at his colour," he'd say, "the damn thing disappears in a fog bank."

The large, two-storey building with its white clapboard and red-tiled roof was a match to the church on the right. Two red doors in front denoted separate entrances, one for Reverend Fairchild's quarters and one for the official side of the building. The young reverend, a paunchy, little man with soft, pink cheeks and a high-toned accent, was thirty-two years old and out of England only ten years. He'd only recently been transferred here to serve the three communities of the Heart's Content parish.

Molly began to fuss with her hat. "I hear the jury's still out on the Englishman," she grumbled. "Rumour has it he's got his eye on the big prize, the Church of England Cathedral in St. John's. Ministers, nothing but politicians in long gowns!"

Sally held Molly's eyes in a stare. "Molly, I know you don't like Reverend Fairchild but have some respect, he *is* our minister."

"Sorry, Miz Fisher, nerves talking." Molly glanced at the people waiting outside the Rectory. "They must be tired waiting for us. It's a miracle old Lazy Ass got us here at all." Molly had her own name for the grey horse.

Lexie saw that Molly was in a mood, she'd exhausted her patience trying to get them all organized. And it was a wonder they'd ever got out of the house. Just as they were about to leave, her mother had brought everything to a halt by announcing that they'd wait another half hour, just to be sure they didn't follow too close behind the Connors. "No need to give the locals a parade," she'd sniffed.

John pulled back on the reins and Lexie stiffened. "Oh my! Look at everyone."

Carrie squeezed her arm. "Don't worry, kiddo, it'll soon be over." She made a funny face. "You can't back out now, I even wore a hat for the grand event."

Lexie had to smile at Carrie's attempt to distract her. How would the marriage affect their friendship, she wondered? Would she always have Carrie to look out for her, as she'd done all those years? "Thank God you're here," she whispered, "if only to hold up my stomach!"

At this, they took a fit of nervous giggling. Lexie noticed her mother's quick glance, heard the wistful sigh. Felt the regret like a sudden pin prick.

Dan and his friend, Harold, stood fidgeting as the carriage came to a stop. Threw their butts to the ground, took their time scrubbing them out with their boots. "This is it, man," said Harold, shaking his head. "You're done for!" Dan answered him with an elbow to the ribs.

Harold Perry towered over Dan like a protective tree as he hovered in his collarless shirt and frayed jacket, his trousers too short for his long legs. A mop of brown hair flopped over his eyes as he swatted at the nippers swarming around his head. "Christ, I'm fidgety," he muttered. "Thank God I'm not the one getting married."

"Go on, what woman would want you!" Dan retorted, as Lexie smiled at their banter.

Dan's hair was neatly combed back, a clean white handkerchief peeping out of his upper pocket. Max's wife, Ruth, had begged the suit from one of her relatives in Carbonear and Lena had cut it over to fit. Seeing how the double-breasted style flattered Dan's slim build, Lexie self-consciously rubbed a hand over her stomach. He looked like a shiny new penny, she was a puncheon tub.

"You look nice," Dan said, helping her down and throwing an arm around her shoulder.

"Well, not as nice as you," Lexie murmured, shyly. "How was the drive up?"

"Max was a bit nervous but he did pretty good keeping old Maude on the road."

As John came around to help Sally down from the carriage, Dan jumped forward. "There y'go, Missus," taking her arm. "Easy now, that step is a bit high."

Sally gave him a look, a "you don't fool me" look, but resisted the comment that Lexie knew was on the tip of her tongue. Instead, she took a moment to give Dan a head-to-toe examination. "Well, it's an improvement," she murmured, adding as she regained control of the situation, "Let's go in. Lift your dress, Lexie, you don't want to soil the hem."

"The queen has arrived, the ceremony can begin," Molly whispered.

Sally turned sharply, caught the wicked grin on Molly's face. "Come here, Molly," she said. "I'll take your arm, keep you out of mischief."

**

As they approached the Rectory, Will and Jean came out to meet them. Lexie admired the handsome couple, Jean in a pale green dress, Will in his suit and bowler hat, shoes shining beneath white spats. "Hello," said Will. "We've been waiting for you in the meeting room." There was no hint of celebration in his voice.

Behind them came Lena. At fifty-nine, Lena showed no sign of the hard life she'd lived, her figure trim and elegant in the long, mauve dress she'd borrowed from Molly. Perched atop her greying hair was a plain, black hat with a narrow brim. "Jake said to wish you the best," she said to Lexie, a restrained smile on her face as she looked out over the calm water of the harbour. "He's out in the boat today, where he's most comfortable. I know you understand." She took Sally's arm and together with Max and Molly, they walked into the Rectory.

"Before we go in, Dan," said Will, "I want to wish you both the best of luck. Lexie is very special to us. Jean and I are always here if you need us."

Dan looked up at the much taller Will, his eyes lingering on the suit, the bowler hat covering thinning, blonde hair. "You look like a real posh gent in that get-up, Will," he drawled, his grin impudent. "Thanks a lot but I won't need your help to look after my own wife. From now on, she's a Connor, not a Fisher."

"Hey, back off!" barked John, charging over to stand between the two, poking his finger into Dan's chest. "You don't have to show your ignorance to everybody, they already know."

"Well said, John," muttered Will, looking ruffled and unhappy as he straightened his hat and pulled on his lapels. "C'mon, Jean, let's get this over with."

Dan shrugged and walked over to where Lexie and Carrie were standing. "What's wrong with the Fisher men today? Little sensitive, aren't they?"

Carrie was furious. "Had to go out of your way to spoil her day, didn't you?"

"Oh, don't *you* start. C'mon, Lexie, let's go in. The royal family is waiting."

Lexie flushed with embarrassment as she took Dan's arm. She felt heartsick at the way he'd treated Will. Why did he have to diminish her brother, her lovely Will of all people, at a time like this? Dan disappointed her at times, acting like a spoiled brat like he wanted people to dislike him. He did have a kinder side, she'd seen glimpses of it, but why did he hide it from other people? Maybe, in the future, she could help him understand himself better, but this wasn't the time to dwell on it.

Dan steered Lexie over to the green settee near one of two large windows in the front wall. Carrie sat on a chair beside them, throwing murderous glances at Dan while Harold stood awkwardly nearby, looking uncomfortable as he tried to remain neutral.

Will and Jean sat with Sally near the other window. Lexie watched as her mother leaned over and whispered something to Will, but he was unresponsive, his face downcast. Lexie wanted to run over, beg his forgiveness for Dan's behavior. She longed to see that gentle smile return to his lips.

Max sat with Lena on the other side of the room. He had Dan's dark hair and slim build but his eyes were grey instead of brown and he was taller. Lexie liked Max, his gentle smile, the kind way he treated his mother, who obviously had a soft spot for him. Dan had told her that Max was going overseas, too, and that Lena was having a hard time accepting it.

John stomped in, his clothes rumpled, his face still hot with anger. "Your hair is like a birch broom in the fits," said Molly, grinning. But John didn't reply. He perched on the edge of his chair like a tiger ready to spring and glowered across the floor at Dan.

In the midst of all this, Reverend Fairchild came in and took his place at the front. "Come forward," he announced, solemnly.

"Here we go," said Dan, as he helped Lexie to her feet. He seemed oblivious to the tension in the room, all of it directed at him.

Carrie and Jean stood on Lexie's left, Harold and Max on Dan's right. Harold was sweating badly, every freckle standing out on his pale face as he shuffled his feet and rubbed his big hand around his neck and through his hair. "Harold may not make it," Dan whispered.

"Deahly beloved, we have gathered here..." Lexie's heart did a flip as the minister began. When it came to her part, she stammered through it, her voice weak and unsure. When Dan's turn came, he answered smoothly, "I, Dan, take thee Lexie ..."

The minister looked them over before giving the final word. "I now pronounce you man and wife." Then he stood aside, a satisfied smile on his flushed face as Sally, her lips stretched into a faint smile, hurried over to kiss Lexie on the cheek. Molly and Carrie grabbed her in a hug.

"Reverend," said Will, without enthusiasm, "you're welcome to join us at the house for a bite of supper. I've arranged for them to stay over tonight, it's been a tiring day for Lexie."

Lexie took Will's arm and pulled him aside. "I'm sorry about what Dan said, I don't know why he acts like that sometimes. Please don't tell Mother."

"Never mind it now, Lexie," said Will, as he guided her toward the door, "it's not your fault. Let's get you to bed, you look exhausted."

**

It was early June, two weeks after the wedding, when Dan and the other men received word that they had to leave in a couple of days. The Orange Hall was quickly spruced up with red, white, and blue ribbons, Union Jacks decorating the front of the stage in honour of the new recruits. There was a dinner and some lively speeches about the Kaizer. "He'll soon know how the Newfoundlanders can fight, by Jesus!"

Amid cries of "hip, hip, hurray," the band played them out into a soft summer evening. Lexie waited with Lena and Jake while Dan did the rounds, grinning broadly as he and the other new military men shook hands with everyone and received hearty pats on the back. Lexie was struck by their youth, their desperate determination to leave their home, either out of a sense of duty or a desire to see a different part of the world. Or to escape a mundane life of hardship and responsibility, whether they'd admit it or not.

"We'll hope for the best," Lena said, sighing as she swiped a handkerchief across her eyes.

"I know one thing," murmured Jake, as he patted Lena's shoulder, "Dan's been nothing but trouble all his life but I'll miss the young bugger. Let's hope he comes back a new man."

Lena nodded. "Yes, Jake. *If* he comes back!"

A light land breeze, reminiscent of dwarf spruce, wet bogs and shallow ponds teeming with fat, brown trout, wafted through the crowd. "Ah," someone murmured, "smell the woods?" A couple of the young recruits already looked homesick.

Shortly afterwards, Dan and Max Connor, Harold Perry and five other men left to walk to Carbonear, where they caught a schooner to St. John's. After a period of training, they boarded a ship that carried them across to England.

And just like that, Lexie Fisher Connor had joined the ranks of the women who feared they'd never see their men again.

Ten

The baby had arrived on July twenty-eighth, two months after Dan had left for the war. "What do you think, Miz Fisher?" asked Lena, as she gently rubbed the baby's arm. "Your third grandchild and my first, a healthy baby girl."

Sally smiled down into the crib. "I must say, Lexie did very well."

"I wish Dan was here," said Lexie, as she looked around at her family. "I can't wait to see the look on his face when he sees her. And that might be soon, according to what people are saying."

"She's adorable," sighed Molly, cooing over the crib as she handed Lexie a bag. "Here's some baby clothes of my Kate's. Please God, I'm finished with babies!"

Will and Jake, a matched pair, tall and thin with light hair and beards, stood by the window discussing the war. Lexie had watched Will earlier, the pity in his eyes as he'd looked around at the sagging ceiling, the patched window, the homemade furniture. Jake's old salt box didn't quite measure up to Will's big house in Heart's Content.

It was nothing like the house Lexie had grown up in, either. When she'd first moved here with Lena and Jake, the narrow, dirt road running past the front door often tempted her to go back to her comfortable home on the Harbour Road.

"Here, Jean, sit in the rocking chair and hold the baby," said Lena, carefully placing the baby in Jean's arms and pulling over another chair. "Miz Fisher can sit here beside you."

"She looks like the Fishers, don't you think, Jean?" chirped Sally, as she perched on the chair. "All that light hair."

Jean sat rocking the baby, her eyes bright with unshed tears. Life isn't fair, thought Lexie. Jean and Will would make such fine parents but it would probably never happen.

"She's a little dear, Lexie," said Will, "you must be proud."

Lexie smiled as the baby closed her tiny hand around Will's finger. In spite of all the upset she'd caused him and Jean, they still wished her well. Even after Dan's rude remark at the wedding, which they hadn't mentioned since. She hoped they'd eventually forgive Dan's behavior, which he'd laughed off as "just a joke," but Lexie knew Will wouldn't forget it.

**

A few days later, on a warm, sunny day in August, Joe and Julie Fisher came by. Julie could hardly take her eyes off the baby. "Let's sit out in the yard," Joe boomed, in his loud, hearty manner, "enjoy the sun while we've got it."

"Joe," Julie shushed him, "you'll frighten the baby!"

"Sorry, Lexie," he whispered, a sheepish grin on his face. "Not used to babies anymore."

"You must miss bein' on the water, do you Joe?" Lena asked, after they'd settled outside.

"Well, I used to like the water once, when Ken and I first started the fish trade. Had to give it up though, it was getting to me. I'd think of the great, dark ocean waitin' to take another fisherman down to the bottom, and I couldn't shake it no matter how I tried. Still, I'm glad Ken carried on, he's built up a good business with his two boys. But no, I don't miss it a bit." He grinned. "Still like to watch the commotion around the harbour, though."

"Any news from overseas?" Julie asked Lena.

"Nothing yet. Like everyone else, I have to rely on the postings at the post office, there in Parker's Store."

"Yes, I check it myself," said Julie. "It's not easy to read, mind you, the big words. But sometimes Miss Mabel reads it out to us." Rachel and Mabel Parker were spinsters, sisters to the two Parker brothers who owned the store. They'd been the postmistresses for years.

"Rachel and Mabel don't need a man," grumped Joe. "They got rich brothers. Pinch a copper 'til it bleeds, the Parkers!"

"Maybe they don't want a man," said Julie, with a shrug. "Ever think of it that way?"

"See what I've got to put up with, Lexie?" Joe shook his head. "She's a hard case, I tell ya'."

They relaxed in the warm sunshine. Watched the women on the flakes, hurriedly turning over slabs of salted cod to catch another few hours of sun. And the fishermen on the stageheads, shouting back and forth as they made ready to go out for their second trip of the day. Hovering above were flocks of ravenous gulls, wheeling and dipping, bleating and bawling, and making a great din as they fought over floating fish guts.

Joe chuckled. "See the youngsters over there in the punt? They're leaning over the gunnel, lookin' down at the old Tommy." All the children were fascinated by the remains of the schooner that had sunk there in the harbour years ago. "Keep watching, they'll soon go ass–over-kettle in the water."

Aunt Julie had been quiet for a while. "I was wondering, Lexie," she finally said, in her soft voice. "Do you have a name for the baby yet?"

"No, I don't. Dan said I could choose, as long as the second name is for one of his sisters. He did want that."

"Well, I don't know what you'll think of this but I'll say it anyway. As you know, I've always loved flowers. That geranium I just brought over is a cutting from the big plant in our parlour, the one Joe grumbles about." Joe was taking out his pipe and watching her carefully.

"Our first three babies were girls. They all died of diphtheria, it was real bad in the 1880s." Julie's voice faltered for a moment. "I named them Iris, Daisy, and Rose, for the flowers, but the poor little things never lived no time."

"Yes, Mother told me about your girls. So many children died in those years!"

"T'was a terrible time. My sister lost six, buried three of them within a month." Julie leaned toward her, one woman to another. "Thought I'd ask, would you consider calling her Iris?" She paused. "If you got nothing else in mind, that is."

Lexie was surprised and touched, and a little flustered, that Julie would share such a private matter with her. "Oh, Aunt Julie! I-I'll certainly think about it."

Julie smiled and patted her hand. "Good. Take your time, there's no hurry. But enough of that, too nice a day to dwell on sad times. Besides, Joe is giving me that look."

After they'd left, Lexie picked up the geranium Aunt Julie had given her. "Iris Mary," she said, softly, trying out the name, savouring the words on her tongue.

"What's that, Lexie?" asked Lena.

"The baby's name," she said, feeling excited. "Iris Mary. What do you think?"

Lena came and picked up the baby. "Iris Mary." She smiled. "Won't Mary be proud! And so will Julie." She danced the baby around the kitchen, making up a song on the fly just as Dan liked to do. "*Tis a proper dandy name, yes sir, yes sir, a proper dandy name it is.*"

Lexie smiled as she watched them. Lena had come to mean a lot to her, Jake too. They were generous, hard-working people who'd welcomed her into their humble home. And how different Lena was from her mother! Lena thought nothing of cleaving splits, sawing wood, she'd tackle anything. Sally Fisher sawing wood? Lexie couldn't imagine it.

**

The war went into its second year. Recruitment had been relentless, several other young men had shipped out since Dan and his group left. Everybody was preoccupied with the overseas news, who would get the telegram saying someone had been killed or wounded.

Lena had just left for her daily walk to Parker's Store when Carrie came in. "Jeez, this place seems empty," she grumbled. "Bloody war!"

"I know. Lena goes to Parker's every day to get the latest news. She hardly sleeps anymore, keeps expecting to hear something bad."

"Things are not good for the fishermen, either. Dad says there's no markets and besides that, they can't get salt. I'm gonna have to help out."

Lexie knew what Carrie meant. "You've heard of a job."

"Yeah, Lorna finally wrote me about a place in St. John's. I'm leaving in a couple days, Dad is taking me to Harbour Grace to catch a boat. You'll have to save the gossip for when I get time off." She reached into her pocket. "Oh, before I go. Iris, come over here, you little doll."

Iris had grown into a healthy toddler with the Fisher looks and Dan's sense of fun. At the sound of her name, she came waddling over, eyes glued to the tiny pair of blue socks in Carrie's hand. "Made them for you, myself," said Carrie, as Iris grabbed the socks, pulled them on over her hands and toddled off. "Hm-m, guess I shoulda made mitts instead," Carrie muttered.

The next day, Lena's trip to the post office brought results. "Finally," she said, coming in with a smile on her face, "a letter from Dan."

Lexie scanned the envelope. "It's from their training base in England, postmarked over a year ago. But he'd be on a ship by now."

Good trip over, Dan wrote. *Lots to see over here, not much like home. The training is tough, they don't put up with no foolishness.* And a word of comfort. *Don't worry, the Brit Navy is looking after us.* The surprise came at the end. *Max met up with some fellows from the Newfoundland Regiment, thinks he might join up with them instead of the Navy.*

"That's funny," Lena said. "How did Max get interested in the Regiment?" She tut-tutted. "Dan could have explained!"

Not long afterwards, Mona Wells came by with a picture postcard from her son, Alec. Dan was in the picture with him. "They look good, don't they?" said Mrs. Wells, her smile proud but anxious. "See on the back, Alec said I should show it to you."

Lexie studied the picture. "They're in British Navy uniforms." Across the front of the round, white hat was the name *HMS Endurance.*

"Two little boys dressed up in sailor suits," Lena murmured.

Six foot two Alec was sitting, Dan standing beside him, a hand resting lightly on Alec's shoulder. "Dan probably made Alec sit down so he wouldn't look so short," Lexie said, smiling at a memory. "He's touchy about that."

She thought of the dream she'd been having, she'd kept it to herself for fear of making it come true. Dan is on the deck of a ship, looking out over a rough sea. Turning to her with that crooked grin, he leaps over the side and the water takes him under. She always wakes with a terrible feeling of dread.

Lexie looked into the handsome face, the dark eyes staring defiantly at the camera. She noted the arch of his eyebrows, the way he held his shoulders. Funny, she'd almost forgotten these things. If he never came back, would his features fade completely from her memory?

Afterwards, she and Lena sat for a long time without speaking. "The war seems more real now, doesn't it?" Lexie said, quietly.

PART TWO (Dan)

Life's under no obligation to give us what we expect.

(Margaret Mitchell)

Eleven

April, 1919. Dan Connor stood on the dock in Portsmouth, England, waiting to board the ship for his second trip across the Atlantic. A return trip this time. He was going home.

He'd spent the last four months of the war at a Royal Naval Hospital in Southend. His ship had been blasted to hell, he'd been left clinging to a barrel 'til he was rescued. Spent his days at the hospital sobbing his guts out, his nights screaming bloody murder. And he had a roar in his head that made him want to crawl into a hole and die. "Shell-shock," said the doctor, "common thing in war."

He'd been so excited to come over here, to get away from Lexie and Ma, find some room to breathe after the fuss over the baby and getting married. He wasn't like Max, the man of honour, who'd seen it as his duty to help the Brits. Dan had just wanted to escape.

But the war had quickly put an end to any expectations of fun and adventure. The cold, the blood, the noise, the smells, the damned, uppity Brit officers had exploded all his senses into a new reality. Then came the attack on his ship and lying in a hospital like a battered old schooner in dry dock, waiting for the doctors to make him seaworthy again. Sometimes, he had the gall to feel cheated but that was bullshit. No one had forced him to join up.

The noise in his head hadn't gone away completely but had gradually subsided to a dull roar. The hospital had given him day passes into the town of Southend, and eventually, full release into a hostel in London, thirty miles away. He was a bloody wreck, deaf in one ear, panic-stricken at loud noises and full of anger. But still, they'd turned him loose on the town.

Through his time in London, Dan had suffered sudden, debilitating flashbacks of the explosion. Of flying through the air and plunging into the heaving ocean, gasping for breath, sure he was going to die. He'd fought emotions that shook him to his core; one minute raging at the rescue party who'd dragged him back to this lousy world, the next, bursting into tears of gratitude that they had.

He'd visited the London bars and the whorehouses, tried to be the old Dan Connor, but it felt like he was pretending, playing a part. And he missed his friend, Harold Perry. The so-called confirmed bachelor was overboard in love with Dotty Bradford, daughter of one of their training officers. He was living with the Bradford's in Bristol now, looking for work. There was a wedding on the way. And a baby, for Christ sake!

Try as he might, Dan couldn't find it in his heart to feel happy for his old friend. Harold could look forward to a new start in England, Dan was going home to his old life in Newfoundland. And he was tired. He didn't feel up to the challenge, the energy it would take to fit back in, make a life back there. He wondered if he could run away, get lost in Europe and never be heard of again.

**

A few weeks later, he got off the train in Heart's Content and walked the three miles to New Perlican. Before going into the house, he stopped to look around Jake's property hugging the harbour at the Southside end of the Long Bridge.

The place looked like Dan felt, too tired to keep going. The rickety fence leaned in over the yard like a spent sentry at the end of duty. At the back, the flimsy, old flake pushed off from the bank and wobbled across the landwash to meet the lopsided stage, itself long overdue to collapse into the water. Nothing's changed, he thought. Jake was never much for upkeep.

Dan took a breath in the porch as he realized he was about to see his daughter for the first time. He knew he looked pretty bad, a bag of bones with hollow cheeks and sunken eyes. Bad enough to frighten a four-year-old child.

The women came rushing toward him as he went in. "Ma, how goes it?" he said, dropping his clothes bag on the floor.

Lena grabbed on to him like she was afraid he'd disappear. "I can't believe you're here," talking into his neck, her voice breaking.

He turned to Lexie, who was quietly waiting her turn. "It's okay," he said, feeling her tremble against him as she tried to say something through the tears. "Take it easy. I'm here now."

He turned to the rocking chair, where a fluff of curly hair and two big saucer eyes peeped through the rungs. "Who is this, I wonder?" he said, kneeling down beside the chair, scratching his head, pretending to be puzzled. "Is it a little maid from the Cove?"

"No, I'm Iris," came the tiny voice.

"Iris. That's a pretty name. Can you come out here for a minute? I might have a present for a little girl with yellow hair and big blue eyes."

She crept out from her hiding place, head down, hands clasped in front, cheeks glowing red. "Christ," he muttered, under his breath, "she's a pure Fisher!" She had on her best dress for the occasion, the blue picking up the colour of her eyes.

Iris glanced at her mother for courage and stood eyeing Dan as he held out the rag doll with red yarn hair and a green, polka dot dress. "This is for you," he said. "I brought it all the way from Halifax. You can take it to bed every night for company."

She reached for the doll and squeezed it to her chest. A sweet smile lit her face. "Say thank you," Lexie coaxed. "T'ank you," Iris whispered, hiding her face behind the doll.

He leaned over and kissed her forehead. "You are welcome, young Missy. Now, why don't you go and think up a name for her, poor thing's got no name yet!"

Iris ran to the daybed, clutching the doll in both hands. A few minutes later, she crept over to the table where they were sitting and touched his arm, the touch so light he hardly felt it. "Her name is Redhead," she whispered.

Dan would never understand why, but at the touch of the child's hand he felt a rush of emotion pass through him. "Good for you," he said, weakly, holding back tears. "That was quick. You must be a smart cookie!"

After Iris and Redhead had been persuaded to go to bed, Dan sat at the table and tried to relax while Lena brought him up to date on the local gossip. "Jesus, it's good to have plain food again," he said, savouring the tastes he'd been craving, salt cod and potatoes with drawn butter and onions, and Lena's fresh bread drenched in Crosby's molasses. And a cup of strong tea. "That Brit tea is like dishwater."

Lexie and his mother were thin, their faces drawn. The war years had obviously been hard on them. "Any more tea, Ma? And tell me about Max. He's been home a couple years now, how's he doing?"

"Well, he's makin' the best of it." Lena got up for the teapot. "He was in the hospital over there for over a year after that July. His leg was all splintered. They fixed it up best they could but he's walking with a bad limp. His job as a ship's carpenter is over, he's finished with the boats for good." She poured the tea, the feelings raw on her face. "Damn war!"

"Yeah, that was a shock, when he left us and joined the Regiment." Dan shrugged. "We tried to talk him out of it but that's what he wanted so what could we do?"

Lena nodded. "What Max said was, he met up with some of the men from that first bunch that went over, the Blue Puttees, and he was drawn to them, to the spirit among them." She shrugged. "It may have been that simple, who knows? At any rate, he ended up in Scotland, training with the Regiment."

Dan felt the anger rising. "Jesus, then he ends up at Beaumont Hamel. Lucky he survived, I s'pose, most of the Regiment was killed." His fist hit the table. "Beaumont Hamel was nothin' but a slaughter, everyone knows that. Just another exercise to the Brass, lots more cannon fodder comin' in from the colonies. Bastards!"

"Even in this little place," Lena said, "we had four killed that day, the Gordon brothers and two Strickland cousins. And four wounded, five if you count Max." Wiping her eyes with her apron, she got up to clear the table. "We'll never get over it, never," she murmured.

"So what's Max gonna do now?"

"You know Max, he'll tell us when he's good and ready. He's only now getting around a bit, some days he can't get out of bed. But he wants no pity so you don't dare help him."

She looked thoughtful for a moment. "I saw him last week. Joe Fisher had to pick up freight in Carbonear, he took me along. That's when I caught something Max said to Ruth. I could be wrong, but I think Ruth's father, Captain Healey, is looking to help them set up a little business, general store, something like that. But don't repeat it, for God sake, and get me in trouble."

"See what I mean?" Dan snapped. "Luck! This damn life is all about luck. Max had the good luck to marry Ruth Healey. Her old man'll see they don't fall into poverty like most of the vets."

"I'm sure my brothers would help us, Dan," said Lexie, quietly. "We only have to ask."

"Well," Dan replied, surprised that she'd spoken up like that, "we'll see. Thing about that is, you always feel beholden." He knew he was being contradictory but he had no desire to examine his statement. Besides, he doubted the Fishers were in any mood to help him.

Lexie left it at that and thank God his mother didn't comment. Not that she wouldn't at any other time, but she probably saw how close to the edge he was.

Dan sat back wearily and looked around the house, took in the sagging floor, the stained wallpaper, the poverty he'd left behind four years ago. Only now he had a wife and a baby. He let the women's voices fade into the background and he was back in England. A weekend leave with Harold, the bright lights of London, beer flowing, women laughing.

Three thumps and a clatter sounded from the ceiling, disturbing his daydream. "That's Jake, he's awake," Lena said. "Dropped his cane when he knocked on the floor. He's in bed all the time now, the pain pills put him to sleep. He said to send you up when you got here."

**

The old stairs creaked under his weight. Bloody place about to fall down, Dan thought. He remembered when they'd moved here, Ma and four youngsters, the raggle-taggle-gypsies-o. Jake didn't bat an eye, he just moved aside and let Ma take over. T'was a rare man who'd do that.

Nervous of what he'd find, he crept into the small bedroom. Jake opened his eyes. "Well, look here," his voice ragged and weak. "I was expectin' the young pup we sent away but here's a Navy man." The tired eyes managed a twinkle.

Dan pulled a chair over to the bed. "How ya doin', Jake? Jesus, man, you still in bed this hour?" He cringed at the false note of cheerfulness in his own voice.

"Nah boy, it's not by choice," Jake murmured. "My insides is goin' against me. I'm even turning yaller, ya notice?"

Dan felt his breath catch. At seventy-two, Jake wasn't a young man but Christ, he looked a hundred, a shrunken shell of himself. The skin of his face had melted away to a thin film that barely covered his skull. "Jaunders, Jake, that's what the yellow is." He stopped trying to sound cheerful, no need to insult the man. "I'll see Dr. Bursey tomorrow, see what he can do."

"No, never mind that, don't get Lene's hopes up." Jake's voice was fading. "We talked it over, she knows it won't be long now. What I want to know is, can I count on you to keep an eye on her after I'm gone?"

Dan felt the blood drain out of his face. His throat felt paralyzed, he could hardly get the words out. "Jake, you know I'll look out for Ma. I'm usually in her bad books but I'd never see her hard done by."

"Good. Go on down now." The yellow eyes closed. "Get to bed. You look dog-tired, all that travellin'. Tell Lene I'll have some tea when she's ready."

Dan reached over and touched Jake's shoulder, was shocked to find it was all bone, no muscle at all. He backed slowly out of the room, the anger like bile in his throat. Here's the luck again, he thought, and Jake had the bloody, bad luck to get cancer. This shitty dog-eat-dog world just kept hammering away, there was nothing you could do but scratch and claw and try to stay alive. You might as well get what you could while you're here.

He went downstairs slowly, had to hold tight to the rail so he wouldn't sink down on the steps and bawl his guts out. Lena looked at him as he went into the kitchen. She could see how he felt, always could. "He wants some tea," Dan muttered, as he collapsed on the daybed.

Lexie sat motionless at the table, the lamp on the wall behind casting her face in shadow. Now and then, Dan noticed her glancing his way. He closed his eyes, felt himself getting irritated at her stillness. Her expectations.

He'd felt no joy at the prospect of coming home. And from somewhere in his mind came the realization that he felt no tenderness toward Lexie. Is that what he was now, after what he'd been through? A hollowed-out man? And was Lexie aware of the change in him? Was Ma? Christ, how he wished he had a cabin in the woods where he could be completely alone. No one to expect things of him that he couldn't give.

"You two get off to bed," said Lena. "I'm sleeping down here. Keep the fire in for Jake's tea, give him his medicine when the pain gets bad. Go on."

**

They crept upstairs so as not to wake Iris in her little cubbyhole down the hall. Lexie stood aside in the small bedroom, made room for Dan while he undressed quickly, threw his clothes over the chair in the corner and jumped into bed.

He watched as she fumbled with the buttons on her sweater, her face hot with embarrassment. She turned to the wall, squirmed out of her dress and petticoat and pulled on the long flannel nightdress. Then, seemingly relieved to escape his silent scrutiny, she gave him a look of shy uncertainty, got into bed and turned out the lamp.

Right away, he turned her around and lifted her nightdress. Took her quickly, without a word, got a quick release from the feelings building up inside him. Afterwards, he rolled over and fell into a deep sleep. Neither of them had spoken.

Twelve

Dan had been home for over a month and he'd yet to feel comfortable in his own skin, let alone his old life. Aimless and disconnected, he wandered around the community, often walked over to the harbour to sit on one stagehead or another as the men went about their work.

He watched the fishermen, the skill bred in them over centuries, and thought about the men in his own line, the Connors from Ireland. Who was the stupid bastard who'd decided to jump ship and stay here in this brutal land? Likely some poor urchin picked up in the slums of Dublin, hired to work for pittance on a rich Englishman's fishing schooner.

He smoked cigarettes and watched the creatures in the water below. The bottom feeders, conners, cussers, flatfish, crabs, sculpins, and nipsy-tansies, darting about, nibbling on sound bones and fish guts that fell through the trunk hole as the fishermen split their fish.

The fishermen never bothered him. "My son, you're not the old Dan Connor, that's for sure," they told him. But allowances were made. "Who can tell what these boys went through over there?" he heard them mutter to each other.

Dan had spent hours on the wharves when he was a boy, lying face down, dangling a hook in the water. After they'd moved in with Jake, he was pretty much left to himself all day, his mother and the others always working at whatever they could do to survive, fishing, the garden, berrypicking. His sisters, Mary and Belle, had scrubbed floors for old ladies.

Back then, he'd get up in the morning and head for the wharves, hang around and chat with the fishermen as they worked. The old fellows would grin and tease him, laugh when he came back with a saucy remark. And here he was, twenty-one years old, still hanging around the wharves.

Toward the end of June, the fog and drizzle set in for two weeks of Capelin Weather. As they'd done since time began, the small, silvery fish rolled in on the waves to spawn and everybody headed to the Cove Beach to scoop them up in buckets and castnets.

As usual, Lena joined in the excitement. "It's Capelin Weather," she crowed, "the end of school and the beginning of summer. No wonder the youngsters love this time of year." She clamoured through the yard with her wheelbarrow, two buckets crashing side to side as she rolled over the humpy grass. "See ya', Lovey," she called out to Iris, who watched her from the step. "I'll bring back some capelin for supper, okay?"

Iris clapped her hands in reply. "Okay, Nanny."

Dan watched his mother hurrying across the Long Bridge, head down over the barrow handles. Why couldn't he have inherited her disposition? Lena had a joyful heart, she could get excited about anything. He, on the other hand, had "the Irish melancholy," as old Bridget, his Connor grandmother, always said.

**

When the capelin left, they took the mauzy weather with them but the warm days that followed did nothing to take the chill out of his bones. Dan could almost feel the cold, North Atlantic water coursing through his bloodstream.

He wandered all day and spent his nights drinking with his service buddies. One of them had a still in the woods near the Beaver Pond. There were five of them, "Old Sweats," they called themselves, yet none of them was over twenty-two.

They sat around on rocks and tree stumps with their jars of shine, thinking about the war but talking about anything else. The Newfoundland government had put a ban on alcohol just before they'd got home from overseas. "Suspicious timing," said Ralph

Strickland, a Navy vet like Dan. "Nothin' like sticking it to the vets. Got to smuggle the good stuff over from St. Pierre now."

"I give it five years." Dan smirked into his drink. "I mean, they almost had a riot down the shore a few weeks ago. That ban'll sink like the Titanic, people won't stand for it."

He'd been fourteen when the Titanic went down. He and Harold had walked to Heart's Content to see if there was any work around the wharves and someone told them about it. They'd run all the way home without stopping. His mother had fainted at the news.

The Titanic event had stayed with Dan. It changed the way he saw things. What sense did it make to work hard for the future when you may not live to see a future?

"Not like the old days, is it?" came the eerie voice of Gene Brown, a young man of nineteen who'd lived through Beaumont Hamel and would never be young again. "Remember when everybody went to the Times, danced all night?" As usual, he sat by himself in the darkness at the edge of the lantern glow, quietly drinking himself into a stupor. And, as usual, they'd drag him home at daylight, throw him into his porch before his mother could start in on them.

"No, not like the old days," said Dan. "Won't be again, either. Back then, you could get a drink just by showing up somewhere. Now, there's nowhere to go." A couple of the old moonshiners had died while they'd been overseas. Everyone else seemed to be settling into marriages and babies.

"Zackly right." Larry Banks, another lost soul, lay spread-eagled under a spruce tree. Wouldn't be long, he'd be passed out cold.

As the alcohol hit his bloodstream, Dan began to feel calmer, almost happy. The July night was clear and warm, the woodsy scent almost overpowering. The ripples on the surface of the pond glinted like diamonds in the moonlight. "Sometimes, I wish I was a boy again," he said, wistfully. "I was freer then than I'm ever gonna be again."

It was hard to believe what he'd been like as a boy of five and six years old. Left on his own all day, he'd wandered everywhere, conversed with the high and the low, merchants or poor fishermen, made no difference. He was everybody's kid back then, he got attention from the whole community. Not to mention that he'd learned a lot about human nature.

"Know what you mean," said Ralph. "Too bad we had to go to school."

Dan grinned. "School never slowed me down because I hardly ever went. Couldn't stand being cooped up, rather be in the woods or down around the wharves."

He remembered sneaking into sheds and houses, sometimes taking things, sometimes seeing things and understanding things other boys his age had yet to learn. "Saw something once I never forgot. I was hanging around this house, thought it was empty. Stood on a rock to look in the window and saw a man and a young girl on a bed. She was struggling, he was holding her down."

"No kiddin', who was it?"

"Never told anyone at the time, too scared I suppose. It was Bob Turner, one of the merchant clan. That young girl left town soon after, probably raised Turner's bastard back in her home community."

"The prick," said Blackie Walters, his cigarette glowing red as he sucked in the smoke.

"'Course he got away with it," said Ralph, a sneer in his voice. "That kind always do."

"Yeah," said Dan, "far as I remember there was nothing else about it. The upstanding churchman went on about his business, his money and reputation intact." Dan hated people like Turner, their power over poor people like him. He'd never admit it to anyone but sometimes, in the dark of night, he resented the circumstances of his own life that kept him from being one of them.

**

Dan was having a bad day, he needed the relief that came with alcohol. He walked down to the Flat Rocks and stared across to the other side of the bay. Imagined the people over there, laboring on the wharves and in the gardens. "We're all slaves!" he screamed at the churning water as white horses, liberated from the depths by gusty winds, skimmed the tops of the waves.

He thought of Harold, the fun they'd had kicking around. As much as Harold had preached the single life, he'd lost his freedom, too. He was working on the docks in Liverpool now, working to support a wife and kid. Nothing turned out the way you thought it would.

As he stood on the headland, his body racked with craving, he stared across the harbour to the road leading down the shore and it hit him. Uncle Leo, his Dad's brother in Turk's Cove, always had a batch of something going in the hayloft.

A half hour later, he was in Leo's yard. Leo came out of the house smiling. "Good to see you, Dan. C'mon up to the loft, let's have a yarn." He slapped Dan on the back. "It's Sunday, Mary's gone visiting. No one to bother us."

Dan felt pleased at the welcome he was getting. "Lead on, Uncle, I'm right behind you."

"Still some hay left up here," said Leo. "Last year's crop lasted us pretty good, got old Sid through the winter, anyway." He grinned. "Sid is on his summer holidays now, grazin' the lanes and rocky clearings from here to Winterton. But just watch, this fall I'll have to chase the bugger all over hell to get him back in the stall! Got a lot of gypsy in him, Sid."

Dan laughed. "Go on, Leo, you think the world of that little, black pony."

Leo reached for two tin cups hanging from a beam. "Always good to have a drink with my brother's son," he said, pouring the homemade spruce beer. "You look more like Al every day, y'know that?"

Dan didn't remember his father. But when he was young, he'd walk down to Turk's Cove, listen to stories about how Leo and Al grew up. How they'd walk to the dances in Winterton, or make spruce beer in a shack in the woods.

A light breeze wafted up from the beach, bringing the salty smell of dried kelp. The beer, the warm, muggy loft, the comforting smells of horse and hay were like drugs. Dan felt his body grow heavy as the tension ebbed out of him.

PART TWO (Dan)

They talked and drank through the afternoon and at five o'clock, Leo roused himself. "Better get straight before Mary comes home. C'mon in the house, get a lunch before you walk back."

They got unsteadily to their feet, yawning and stretching and grunting with the effort. "Right," said Dan, his tongue thick and lazy in his mouth. "For sure, Lexie and Ma are gonna check me out the minute I get in the house. Women! Always there to put the kibosh on a good time."

"Well, yeah," Leo replied, carefully, "sometimes it seems that way. Then again, that might be the reason we feel free to enjoy ourselves, right? 'Cause we know they won't let us go too far." He rolled his eyes. "That's what Mary says anyway, but don't tell her I repeated it."

**

An hour later, Dan was on the road for home. It had been good to see Leo but now he had to suffer the scrutiny of the women back at the house. He didn't do well with pushy women, they made him feel moody and irritated. Like Ma, definitely a pushy woman! That was something Lexie had in her favour, she wasn't pushy. But as he recalled from the marriage fiasco, she did have a strange stubborn streak that had taken them all by surprise.

But whatever their type, all the women went for him. When he was young, he'd been a particular favourite of the older ones. They had a soft spot for polite, little boys, and he could act the part to perfection. "Here comes the little Irishman," they'd beam, as he went smiling into the kitchen, following the smell of fresh baking.

He'd sit on the daybed and munch his cookie while Missus This or That told him boring stories of her young days. One of the old bags used to touch him through his trousers, feel around his crotch with her old, veined hands. Almost made him gag but he got a penny out of it every time so it was worth it.

Later, he'd discovered he had a knack for music. Practiced on his father's old accordion 'til he could play well enough to help out at the dances. The girls went crazy for him.

Then came the shine shacks, the old boozers giving him free drinks as long as he played music and sang a few songs. He'd only been fourteen or so. Some of the women hanging around there had taken a fancy to him, taught him a lot of things.

His mother had figured out what was going on, given him a good old-fashioned reaming out. "From now on," she'd said, "you'll earn your keep. You can help Jake with his fishing."

"Wine, women, and song, Ma," he'd said to her. "Only things worth living for." That's when she'd slapped him hard across the face.

Almost home now, he looked down over New Perlican from the top of Smut Hill and felt like running in the opposite direction. His black mood had returned, it always did.

Maybe he should have told Leo about the quandary he was in. About being home, about his feelings, or lack of, for Lexie, about Jake so close to death, about everything. He'd come close once but the words had stuck in his throat. And anyway, what would Leo have said? Give it time, it'll work out, or some such blather.

No one had the answer to how he was feeling and Dan couldn't explain because he didn't have the words. Neither did he have the words for how he'd feel when Jake's time came. It wouldn't be long now. Jake no longer ate or spoke to them, he just slept all the time. But Lena was prepared, he could see that.

**

On a warm summer night two weeks later, Dan woke at the sound of a knock on the bedroom door. He opened his eyes in the dark, saw the outline of his mother standing silently in the doorway. His heart lurched in his chest. "Oh, Jesus, he's gone."

Dan followed her back to the room where Jake had spent the past year suffering in silence. Stood quietly in the doorway, his eyes full in the soft light of the lamp.

"C'mon in," said Lena. "He won't hurt you. Never did before, he certainly won't now. He's out of his misery, that's the important thing."

PART TWO (Dan)

Dan pulled a chair over to the bed, tried to say a prayer but the words wouldn't come. He heard a sniffling sound, turned to see Lexie standing behind him, crying softly into a handkerchief.

Lena had got up in the night to check on Jake and found that he'd died in his sleep. "Just like him, isn't it?" she said, her eyes shining. "Slipped away while I was downstairs. Never one to make a fuss." She gently pulled the sheet up over the yellowed, wizened face. "Go over and tell Uncle Gil. He's an Orangeman, he'll set everything in motion. I daresay they've been expecting it so it's just to let them know."

Dan nodded. They'd all been expecting it but that didn't make it any easier.

Thirteen

Jake was gone. Dan had known it was coming but he wasn't prepared for the feelings that followed. He sought the company of his buddies and the comfort of their moonshine, passed the nights in oblivion, caring for nothing and nobody. He crawled home one day at noon to find Lena waiting for him with that look on her face. She was ready for a fight.

"I got somethin' to say." He opened his mouth to argue but she raised a hand to stop him. "You're killing Lexie with your drinking and your moods. She was a happy girl while you were away. Now she's timid, like she's afraid to speak for fear you'll growl at her. You don't talk to her, you never notice the baby, it's not right."

Lena pointed to the chair and he sat down. "Maybe old Bridget was right. 'Watch for signs in the youngsters,' she said, in that Irish brogue, 'signs of the black dog, the melancholy. It's in the family.' And that's what's happening with you now."

He snorted. "First time you ever gave credit to old Bridget for anything. Christ sake, Ma, I just got home from overseas. Gimme some time."

"Don't get your hump up, I'm saying what needs saying because no one else will. You got a family, you need work to support 'em and a house to live in. Jake would say the same if he was here, 'course he wouldn't say it to you, just to me. But mind my words, if you keep wandering around, drinking with that crowd, you'll get in the habit of it. And then you'll be no good to nobody."

"Jesus, Ma, there don't seem no point to nothin'. Jake worked like a dog, now he's gone. And Max, a young man, he's a cripple. There's no hope here, you work like a slave and die poor, and that's it!" Exhausted from the anger, he leaned his head on the table and the tears came. "Know what, Ma? I d-dunno if I can look after myself, let alone anyone else. Not only that, I got no mind to try."

Lena sat quietly while he cried it out. When the worst was over, and he was blowing his nose and feeling sheepish, she spoke up again. "Yes, Dan, I know life is hard," softer now, but careful not to sound like she was giving in. "Always was for us here but we keep going, you hear me? That's what we do, we keep going."

She gave a jerk of her head toward the window. "Caleb Drover's old house there across the bridge from us, I heard his son is thinking of selling. I want you to go and see him, see what he can do in the way of price. And proud or not, if the Fishers offer any help you'll take it and be grateful!" Old Caleb Drover had died years earlier. He'd been a widower for years, a mean, stingy sort and a favourite target of idle youngsters out for a bit of mischief.

Dan knew he was outflanked but he didn't want to let Lena win too easily. "Huh, sounds like you've given this some thought."

She ignored his childishness. "The son is Heber Drover. He's been living in Harbour Grace for years, there's no way he'll ever come back here. He and the old man never got on, anyway, I figure he'll be damned glad to be rid of the place. Besides, the house needs work, there's not many would take it on."

**

On a warm, July day a week later, Dan was on his way across the Barrens with Joe Fisher. His mother had reamed him out pretty good and truthfully, he still didn't feel that much different but he had a plan, that would do for now. He'd go as far as Carbonear with Joe, then catch a ride to Harbour Grace, where Heber Drover lived.

The ten-mile stretch of road across the Heart's Content Barrens was a narrow, rutted trail that meandered across a bald expanse of peat bog, rocky outcrops, and shallow ponds. "Trying to get across here by horse and cart is enough to loosen your goddamned eyeballs,"

Joe growled, cursing in frustration as he tried to keep the horse moving, "or any of yer balls, for that matter!" Joe made regular trips to Carbonear to pick up freight at the train station, so he knew every rut and sunken rock that might break an axle.

"Jesus, easier to walk, isn't it!?" Dan hung on to the side of the seat so he wouldn't be pitched out onto the road. If his Irish melancholy hadn't already been shaken out of him by Ma's haranguing, this trip should certainly do it.

"This road was built in 1836," Joe shouted, above the noise of the cart wheels rumbling over the bumpy track. "It replaced the old foot-path the Red Indians used to walk on, back before our people came here. Been neglected ever since."

Joe snapped the reins. The horse responded with a brief burst of energy as they passed a white bungalow at the side of a pond. The Halfway House. "There was nowhere to take shelter here in winter 'til the government overlords finally gave in and built this place. And y'know, even after that, our schoolmaster, Mr. Fenley, perished here in a snowstorm."

Dan knew all about the merciless wind that roared across this empty terrain, snow drifts as high as a horse's head. He'd been caught in storms before, had to wait it out at the Halfway House with other stranded travellers. "Yes, I know about Mr. Fenley. Ma used to tell the story to me and Max when we were young." History is like today in these small places, thought Dan, time standing still while the rest of the world moves on.

Joe chuckled. "Silas Ryall was the first caretaker, a good host, too. I had to put in for the night more than once. Usually left the next day with a big head, slept it off in the sled while old Maude followed her nose and took me home. Got a built-in compass, Maude."

**

Dan left Joe and his stories at the Carbonear train station. "Good luck, m'son," Joe said. "Lot of people depending on what you and Heber Drover decide today."

Dan spotted a lumber cart and begged a ride the last few miles to Harbour Grace, a large town with a long history of shipping and trade. And piracy. Peter Easton had ruled these waters in the 1600s, raiding ships travelling between Europe and the States. He'd had his headquarters on a little island just offshore that was easily defended from the British Navy.

As Dan pondered the pirate life, he decided it sounded pretty good. Take from the rich and keep it, he thought, nobody telling you what to do.

After some searching, he found his way to Heber Drover's row house on the harbourfront. The man who opened the door was short and barrel-chested with a bald head and a face set in a scowl, a younger version of old man Drover. But that was where the resemblance ended.

"Come in, Dan," Heber said, pleasantly, after Dan had explained who he was. "Yes, I know Lena, fine woman. If she told you to come here, I'd be interested in what you have to say."

Heber listened carefully as Dan talked. "I'm married now, got a young daughter, born while I was overseas. They lived with Ma and Jake while I was gone." He looked away for a moment to hide his eyes. "Poor Jake just died, cancer."

"Sorry to hear that. Jake was one of the good ones."

"Anyway, Ma says I've been lying around long enough, now I have to take charge of my family. She's probably right, usually is. So that's why I'm here, to see if you'll sell me the old house."

"Must be hard to settle back into normal life after being in a war," said Heber, his voice kind. "Your poor brain is still dealing with it all."

The comment was unexpected. Dan tried to speak, say something casual, but his throat had closed shut. He was horrified to think he might cry in front of this man.

Heber suddenly got up from his chair. "Never mind," passing Dan a glass. "We'll have a drink of St. Pierre rum, just smuggled over in a friend's schooner." Dan watched as Heber poured a stiff one, maybe he could see how much he needed it. "And you must be hungry."

"So, about the house," Heber continued, after they'd had their drink and a lunch. "The old man let everything go after Mom died so it's in bad shape." He paused. "But hell, if you want 'er, take 'er. Ten dollars and she's yours!" He grinned. "It's a bit low but there's some satisfaction in it for me too, you know. The old man was a god-damned miser. He'll roll in his grave at the price I'm asking."

**

Dan arrived home from Harbour Grace in a fine mood. He watched their faces as he talked about his trip, Lexie and his mother smiling with pride. He was proud, too. "I never thought he'd agree so fast," he said, laughing.

"And thanks to Will for giving us the money," Lena chimed in. "That's what happens when families work together."

"Yes, all right, Will did us a favour. You don't have to rub it in. Anyway, now we need help with the house so the wonderful Fishers can do us another favour. I'll ask Lew myself, he probably wouldn't come for anyone else. Lexie can ask the rest of 'em."

The Fishers turned up to help, as they were asked. They might not like me, Dan thought, as he watched Molly and Jean going in and out with buckets, but they'll do anything for family. Anything to improve the lot of their sister, the one who went and married a ne'er-do-well!

And who'd have believed it? He and John Fisher were on the roof, working side by side. After the wedding, he'd thought John might catch him some night and beat the shit out of him. Going overseas had probably saved his life.

Lew had shown up to lime the fence. As usual, he and Lexie hadn't said a word to each other. There was always something wrong between those two, even though they were grown up now and Lexie was out of the house. Dan had heard Lew was seeing a woman from Chapel Arm. What woman would want to look at that face for the rest of her life, he wondered?

By early August, the house was almost in order and Lexie seemed excited. "Lena and I can wave to each other from across the bridge," she said.

"You women are like birds, aren't ya?" teased Dan. "You have to have a nest."

They were tidying up around the yard when a cloud of dust blew up and a horse and cart pulled in at the gate, Max pulling hard on the reins. "Ho there. Cripes, how do you steer this thing?"

Max' wife, Ruth, sat smiling beside him in the seat. "Meet Flossie, my cousin's stubborn mare," she chuckled. "Got a mind of her own." Dan gave Ruth the once-over, found himself admiring her slim figure and lively brown eyes.

Max lifted his bad leg, placed it over the edge of the seat and somehow got himself down from the cart. "Ruth charmed some bits of furniture out of our friends at church," he said, limping around to the back and lifting the sailcloth. "There you go, couple chairs, daybed, a few other things."

"Oh Ruth, thank you." Lexie smiled as she looked over the things they'd brought. "You, too, Max. Come in and see the house."

"It's just a common Newfoundland house," said Dan, feigning modesty as he showed them around. "A plain two-storey with an almost-flat roof." There was the usual backhouse, an extension of the porch for storing bulk food and preserves, a kitchen with a small pantry off to one side, and a parlour. "Old man Drover used the parlour as a bedroom," he said. "Probably too shaky to climb the stairs." Upstairs there were two small bedrooms and a tiny storage room.

"Yoo-hoo," came a call from below, as Dan tried to hide his frown. They went downstairs to find Sally Fisher, who'd certainly qualify as a pushy woman, standing in the doorway. This was her second visit since they'd moved in. I'll have to discourage this, thought Dan, or she'll soon be running my life.

"Hello, Mother," said Lexie. "Max and Ruth brought us some things for the house. We've just been showing them around."

"Mrs. Fisher," said Max, "nice to see you." Ruth smiled and nodded hello.

Sally smiled in return. "Such a nice day. Thought I'd take a walk, drop in to see how everything is going. They've done a nice job, don't you think?" She turned to the door. "Well, you've got company, I won't stay. Maybe I'll drop in on Molly before I go home." She nodded to Ruth and Max. "See you again, I hope."

"Let's go out back," said Dan, after Sally had left. "Too nice a day to be indoors."

They stood on the back platform and looked down over the alders to the Brook, the river that snaked through the Alder Bed. "It becomes wider and deeper at a certain spot," Lexie told Ruth. "The young children swim there all summer, they call it the swimmin' hole."

"Just think," said Ruth, "in a few years, you'll come out here and watch Iris splashing about with her friends."

"Yes, she talks about it all the time. She and Lena are off berrypicking today, I needed her out of my way so I could get some work done."

Dan watched Max nodding and smiling as he puffed on his pipe. Thought he was a big businessman now, with the General Store Ruth's father had set up for him. Lucky bastard! Some people always seemed to do well, no matter what.

**

The weather turned to the cool of fall and Lexie seemed to be settling into married life. She was still quiet, never much to say that caught Dan's attention, but she was getting to know Dora Miller, the old biddy up the lane, so he figured she must talk sometimes.

Otherwise, young Iris took up most of her time. She liked to take the girl down to Lena's garden on Bloody Point. It was on the side of a hill overlooking the harbour, had been in the Shipp family for two hundred years or more. "The view is lovely," she'd say, in that dreamy, breathless tone. Lexie was strange like that, she noticed things like the view, the way the clouds moved, the mood of the water. She and Lena had grown attached to each other while he'd been overseas. What did old Sally think of that, Dan wondered?

As far as the bedroom was concerned, Lexie was his wife and she was there when he wanted her. She'd even got used to his nightmares, his sudden jumping awake as his ship exploded yet again. Dan liked that she was quiet. He saw no need of bedroom talk, it got on his nerves. And Lexie must feel the same way because there was never anything out of her in bed.

But, for Dan, home life wasn't the answer to his restlessness. By November, he was at loose ends. The winter had set in way too early, blizzard after blizzard blocking the roads so the doctor couldn't get through. And to make matters worse, there was a sickness on the go. They were calling it the Spanish Flu.

Dan and his Navy buddy, Ralph Strickland, were sawing wood in Ralph's shed. Dan stored his wood there because he hadn't gotten around to building a shed of his own yet. "Jesus," he said, "we'll either freeze to death this winter or die from that flu. I might even die of being cooped up with the women!" Lexie was expecting again. That was how things usually worked out, a baby every two years, not much you could do about it. Lena had moved in with them to help out.

"Yeah," said Ralph, grunting as he pushed on the saw. "Gonna be a long haul 'til spring."

Dan didn't say so, but sometimes he thought he might not make it to spring. He was stuck in poverty with no way out, and he was feeling hopeless. The community itself seemed hopeless. The families who'd lost their men were destitute and most of the ones who had come back were disabled in one way or another, either in body or mind. "There are days when I think I might lose my grip," he said, laughing as if he were joking, "like some o'them poor vets we see around." But he wasn't joking.

This was as close as Dan came to talking about his feelings, but he was on the edge and he had to do something. "Y'know what?" he said, as they took a break from sawing. "I'm thinkin' of going to the lumberwoods. Get away from here, make a bit of money at the same time." The Grand Falls paper mill, with its relentless appetite for new wood, drew men from across the island when fishing stopped and winter supplies were low.

"Slave work for slave wages," said Ralph.

Dan knew all about the rough, filthy camp conditions, the endless days of backbreaking work. But he had to get away. "I know, but man

I'm desperate. I'll tell the women any day now, get that over with. Then I'll take off from this damn place for a few months."

It was a stormy, early December day when he left, the wind off the harbour driving snow into the alders behind the house. He had to walk to Heart's Content, take the train to Whitbourne, then catch the one for the Western run. "Great day for a walk," he joked, going out the door with his clothes bag on his back, trying to hide the relief on his face.

Fourteen

"Daisy Belle, I like it." The baby had been born on April second, 1920, while Dan was away in the woods. He leaned over the crib, took the tiny hand in his. "And look Ma, the dark hair, the square chin. It's a Connor this time. Bet her eyes'll be brown, too, like her Daddy's." He grinned at Lena. "Thank God. I was worried she might look like the Shipps."

"Devil!" Lena cracked him on the arm. "You'd be lucky to get a Shipp, my son. We're a good-lookin' bunch, the Shipps are."

"Christ, I'm exhausted." He slumped down at the table and rubbed his hands over his face. He'd lost weight, the old bib overalls and flannel shirt hung off his frame. "Almost six months in that hell-hole! I planned to stay 'til June but I couldn't hold out. Between the bedbugs and the lice, and the stink in the bunkhouse, I figured if I didn't go home, I'd go mad." He shrugged. "Well, a little bit of money is better than none."

Dan watched Lexie as she picked up the baby and went to the rocking chair to nurse her. "You look pretty good, Lexie. Feeling okay now, are ya?" He rubbed a finger over the baby's cheek, couldn't believe how soft it felt.

"Yes, I'm fine," she said, quietly, glancing at Lena.

It struck Dan for a moment that something had passed between the two of them, a recognition, an understanding, something. He thought Lexie seemed distracted, lost in her thoughts. Probably still not over the baby, it had only been six weeks or so since the birth.

Iris had been waiting quietly but her patience wore thin. "Will you be here for my birthday, Daddy?" She grabbed his hand and looked up at him, the big, blue eyes sending waves of desperate love his way.

"That's right, my big girl turns five in July." He scooped her up in his arms. "*I got two young girls, one big, one small, E I E I O, The big one's getting pretty tall, E I E I O,*" dancing her around the kitchen as Iris giggled and joined in to the tune of "Old MacDonald."

After Iris went to bed, they sat around the table with a cup of tea and a plate of Lena's fat-pork buns. And some dried capelin. "That's the last of 'em from last summer," she said. "They saw us right through the winter. Soon be Capelin Weather again, we'll get fresh ones."

"They're perfect, Ma, nice and salty." Dan sat back to roll a cigarette. "Suppose I'll have to look around, see what's on the go for work." He aimed a wicked grin at Lena. "I'll start with Uncle Gil. He's kin, surely he'll take pity on me."

"Well, you know Gil," Lena shot back. "He thinks you're fickle as hell but he'll likely give you a berth. Too good-natured, like all the Shipps!" She paused. "I'll be going back to my old shack tomorrow, or what's left of it after that awful winter we had. Fix up the hen-house, get some new chicks somewhere to replace the poor things that froze to death."

Lena's face fell. "I shouldn't complain, compared to some I got off lucky. I can't stop thinking about the two little babies we lost. No, there's no one sorry to see the end of this bloody winter."

Dan was anxious to tell them about his new idea. "While I was away in the lumber woods, I met up with William Coaker. Have you heard of him?"

Lena nodded. "Something to do with a fishermen's union, I think."

"That's right." Dan had come to believe in Coaker's plan. It had given him something he hadn't had before, a reason to get up in the morning. "Think about it. A union will change the old way of doing things. The common man will be in control. He'll set the price of his catch, not the merchant. And I'm gonna do what I can to help the cause."

"You seem serious about this," said Lena, looking doubtful but not saying so.

"Well, I went to some of Coaker's meetings. He explained how it's been all along, with everything favouring the merchants. Haven't I been saying the same thing all this time? He says it's time to change the system and he's right! He'll change it through politics."

"What will you do?" Lexie asked, in a vague, offhand way. That was how she seemed, vague. Like her mind was elsewhere.

"I'll drop in at the lodge meetings around here, talk to the men about the benefits of a union. Shouldn't be hard to convince them once they realize what it could mean. When the government sees that we have support, they'll have to agree to Coaker's bill."

Dan planned to spend the summer and fall working toward a union. He knew his reputation might be a stumbling block but he felt strongly that the information was crucial to the men in the area. He'd promised Mr. Coaker he'd spread the word and he meant to keep his promise.

It wasn't just the hope of better prospects that had attracted Dan. It was William Coaker himself, his single-minded belief in the cause, the fury in his words as he rallied the men in the halls. "Coaker could almost raise the dead with his speeches," he told Lena.

Dan appreciated that Coaker had spent time with him. He'd treated him with respect, listened to his gripes against the high knobs, the merchants who grew rich at the expense of poor men. Dan saw in William Coaker something of himself, not as he was but as he'd like to be.

**

When Dan went to the Orange Hall for his first talk, the men seemed surprised that he was taking an interest in a matter of public concern. And Dan really couldn't blame them, his record in community affairs was rather dim. "But think what it would mean," he told them, "to stand together for fair treatment, fair prices."

"What if the merchant won't buy from us?" asked one man. "We'll be left with rotting fish."

Dan nodded. "Yes, but the merchant makes his living from buying and selling our fish. He'll have no choice but to buy, unless he wants to go out of business."

Another man stood up. "What if some of the fishermen decide to stay with the old truck system, how will the union work then?"

"Well, it won't," said Dan, seriously. "Everyone has to buy in or it can't work. And if Coaker wants to get a bill passed in the government, he needs our support." Afterwards he left so the men could talk among themselves. He hoped they'd see the sense of the issue.

Through the summer and fall, he continued to follow through with his plan. He went fishing most days, Lena kept an eye on him about that. But after supper he'd head out walking, talk himself into lodge meetings up and down the shore. Get home in the wee hours, exhausted but wound up from arguing with the men, hoping to say the one thing that would convince the stupid bastards to try something new. Some nights he'd have to walk down through the Alder Bed to the Brook, let the sound of the water wash over him, calm him down, before he could go to bed.

"Christ, I'm too nervy to sleep," he said one night, as he got into bed. He'd walked down to the Brook but he was still restless. "That meeting in Hant's Harbour was a struggle." There was no response from Lexie as he reached for her in the dark. She murmured sleepily, then turned slowly toward him. The act was over before she was fully awake.

Dan was puzzled. Lexie seemed numb to the workings of her own house. He wondered if she noticed him at all, as he came and went at all hours. And she seemed tired all the time. Sometimes, he'd come home from the wharf to find her asleep on the daybed, the baby crying in the crib and young Iris wandering about the Alder Bed by herself.

"What's wrong?" he'd ask her. "Are you feeling sick?" Maybe she was overwhelmed with the youngsters, they were a handful now. If so, she'd have to get over it, other women did.

As the weeks went by, he grew more and more impatient. The housework was falling behind, dirty clothes piling up, the youngsters looking scruffy. "So, Lexie, should we hire a servant to help out?" he said, sarcastically, trying to point out her failure as a wife and mother. "There's lots of young women out there wanting to go into service."

He didn't care if the remark affected her or not, he was too pissed off to worry about that. If his wife couldn't cope with the housework, it was a mark against his manhood. Other men would say he had no control in his own home. Besides, if he was making an effort for the family, the least she could do was pull her weight.

"C'mere, Iris," he said one morning, before he left for fishing, "would you like to help Daddy?" Iris nodded her head eagerly. "When I get home, I want you to tell me what Mommy's been up to all day. Can you do that?" He pulled playfully at a blonde curl.

"All right, Daddy," Iris whispered, giving her mother a wary look.

Lexie looked at him but there was no surprise, no anger, no expression of any kind on her face. He left without a word, Iris waving to him from the window as he headed across the Green on his way to the harbour.

**

Another lean and hungry Christmas had come and gone, the long winter of '21 stretched ahead. One evening, before heading for a meeting down the shore, Dan dropped in on his mother. He wanted to know if she knew anything about Lexie's condition. "Any switchell left in the pot, Ma?" he asked.

Lena was washing dishes. "Sure. Sit down, it's still hot." She poured the strong, black tea into his cup. "I was wondering," she said, carefully, "is Lexie all right? Not sick or anything, is she?"

Dan shook his head. The woman must be a bloody mind reader. "That's just it, I don't know. Lexie never did say much but now she's like a clam. She's always tired, I do know that. Don't know what she'll do when young Daisy starts walking, then she'll have two to chase after."

"Lexie is not a strong girl," said Lena. "I've come to see that over the past few years. Maybe she *is* overwhelmed. I hope you're not getting after her about the housework. The young ones are enough of a handful, the housework can get done when it gets done."

"Poor little Lexie, got to treat her with kid gloves."

"Never mind your mockery, it may be more serious than we think. I hadn't planned to tell you this, but a few days ago I went over with some leftover soup for their dinner. I heard the wails as I neared the doorstep. Little Daisy was crying to break her heart, and Iris doing everything to make her stop. Besides that, the fire was out, it was cold in there. And Lexie was sitting on the floor with a pile of dirty clothes scattered around her."

"I don't know what her problem is. Her mind's just not right since I came home, she can't seem to handle the normal stuff. But she's got no more to do than other married women!"

"Anyway," Lena went on, "I got the fire going, made porridge for the children. Then I got Lexie underway to make the beds while I started the wash. But Dan, the way she looked. The girl is still only twenty-two years old but she looked so much older, so care worn. I asked Dora Miller up the lane to keep an eye on her the rest of the day."

Lena thought for a moment. "I wondered if I should talk to Miz Fisher, see if she's noticed anything, but I haven't done it yet. After all, it might be a passing thing. And there's something else you should know."

"Just full of news today, aren't you?"

"Never mind the smart remarks. That's part of the problem, you never take anything serious. Do you remember me saying how, after Daisy was born, Lexie got low-minded? Some women are affected like that after childbirth. She kept saying it was like a fog settled over her.

"People came to see her. They'd comment on the baby and wish her well, but she could hardly work up the energy to acknowledge them. I even had to prod her into breastfeeding. I did my best to help her but I wonder, is she still in that fog, do you think? If so, you'll have to give her time to come around. I know you're not a patient man by nature but it's time you learned."

Dan snorted. "I'm thinkin' she's just not up to marriage and children. Some days I get home, the house is in slings, the youngsters scruffy. I'm getting fed up, I can tell you that."

"Dan, you've got to be gentle with Lexie, let her rest as much as she needs. Never mind bawlin' and hollerin' about the housework. She's your wife, not your slave."

Lena paused, looked him in the eye. "Remember the day we went to Miz Fisher's together? Lexie was all for marrying you, and against my better judgement as you know. She had no thought to letting Will take the baby, she was willing to put her future in your hands. Now ask yourself, Dan, are you the sort of husband she envisioned at the time?"

He jumped up from the table and banged out the door. His own mother was taking sides against him! Well, so what? The women all stick together in a crunch. Besides, Ma couldn't begin to understand his feelings, the effort it took to keep going in this world. To not give up and crawl into a hole.

The main thing now was the union, his way out from under the thumb of the high knobs. He'd set himself up with a boat of his own. All the fishermen would stand together, they'd make a decent living for once.

Dan could finally see a future in front of him. But he was exhausted. He never slept anymore for the thoughts and ideas running in a loop around his brain. The union was a real possibility. He hadn't cared about anything as much in a long time.

Fifteen

In the spring, Dan's plans for his future came to a halt. He made a decision, he was getting out of this Godforsaken hole! But first he had to tell Ma. He had no idea what her reaction would be.

"Where did you come from?" Lena looked him over as he walked into the kitchen and threw himself into a chair. "Another meeting about the union, I s'pose."

"Damn the union and all who sail in her!" Dan said, bitterly. "I'm finished with it. Prime Minister Squires, the bastard, he killed Coaker's Union Bill." With a sigh of resignation, he got up from his chair, went over to the window and looked toward the harbour. "You can't win against the merchants, they got all their buddies in the government. What I *really* can't understand is why the Catholic bishop came out against it. You'd think the Irish crowd would need a union as much as we do. But that's that, so to hell with it!"

"Mm-m, thought something was up," Lena said, quietly. "Your misfortunes are usually of your own making but I can see it's different this time. The union was something you believed in. I'm sorry it didn't work out, but don't crawl back into that sour way of thinking, life is all about luck, you may as well not bother to try, all that stuff. I don't want to hear it."

"Why not? It's the truth. I'm sick of being poor, Ma. Living hand to mouth, wearing raggedy, stinking clothes. There's no luck coming *my* way, I can see that."

"It's true, poor people carry the taint of poverty like a perfume. Still, we can't give up." She reached for the kettle. "Why don't you make me a few shavings for my fire in the morning and I'll cut us some raisin bread. Been face an' eyes in the dough all day, we may as well sample it."

"A man should go somewhere he can get ahead," Dan grumbled, preparing her for his news as he stomped out into the backhouse.

He took out his pocket knife and began the job of shaving thin curls on the side of the kindling splits. Making shavings, Lena's remedy for a battered spirit when he and Max were boys. Dan smiled to himself. Splits, shavings. Would anyone understand his language in the new place?

As usual, the half hour's solitude calmed him down. He sat and attacked the bread, devouring six slices drowned in molasses before he stopped. "Good cup of switchell, Ma," he said, as Lena started to pick up the dirty dishes.

He plucked a splinter from the shavings, started to clean his fingernails. "Had this idea the other day. Maybe had a feeling the Union Bill wouldn't pass, I don't know." He sat back, took out his cigarette papers. "I'm thinking of heading to the States. Another winter here, scratching for a living, and I'll be fit for the Mental. Christ, anything is better than lookin' at Lexie mopin' around the house!"

Lena jerked her head around. "What in the name of God will you do down there? And you'd leave Lexie with the youngsters, the way she is?"

"I'll be able to send money home," he protested. "This feller from Winterton is going in the fall, staying with his sister in Boston. Thought I'd write Mary, see if I can stay with her and Pat. They got their own house now." He shrugged. "Worth a try. Maybe she'll take pity on baby brother." He gave her a big grin, hoping to soften her up.

Lena sighed. "Well, maybe it'll be okay, you wouldn't be the first one had to go away to work. And it'll give you a chance to reflect on the important things, your family, raising your children." She gave him a hard stare. "Long as you stay away from the drink. I've noticed you're getting back into it a bit lately."

He scowled. How was it that Ma knew so much? Maybe she was a witch. "For God sake, don't go on about that now."

"What does Lexie say about you leaving?"

"Haven't told her yet, but I'm pretty sure she won't object. Probably won't even know I'm gone." He stood up to leave.

"Wait a minute, Dummy," she said, turning to go upstairs. "You can walk with me to the wharf, stand guard while I dump the slop pail." She hollered back over her shoulder. "Too bad the women don't get paid for dumpin' the slop pail every night. Be no lack of money then, by God!"

"Never mind, Ma," he called up after her. "When I get rich in the USA, I'll build you an outhouse like the high knobs got. You and old lady Fisher can have tea in the yard and admire your two-holer!" From the top of the stairs came a hoot of laughter. Dan smiled. No matter what came, Ma never lost her sense of humour.

**

In May, Dan got a letter from Mary. *These are hard times, Dan. People from all over Newfoundland and the Maritimes are coming to the Boston States to look for work. You can stay with us 'til you get on your feet. Pat agrees.*

He waited till the children were in bed, then he broached the subject. "Lexie, I'm leaving for the US in the fall, after fishing season," he said. "Already got it set up to stay with Mary 'til I can find a job."

She nodded. "Yes, Lena told me."

"Is that all you got to say? Will you be all right with the children?"

"Yes, Iris can help me, I'll be fine."

He shook his head. Iris was only six years old, how could she help? "Okay, if you say so."

Dan was on top of the world all summer, waiting to finish up the fishing season and make his escape. He even spent time playing with the children, laughing with fourteen-month-old Daisy as the sturdy little girl bounced around to his accordion music. She looked more like him every day.

But Iris understood that he was going away for a long time. "I don't want you to go, Daddy," she'd say, tears running down her cheeks. She followed him around, watched his every move as if memorizing his features. A man had to be made of stone not to feel bad.

The time of leaving finally arrived. "Lexie, you'll have to ask John for a load of wood for the winter. I stored some up in Ralph's shed but you'll need more. Y'hear what I'm saying?"

Lexie looked at him blankly. "Yes."

"And try to keep up the housework, don't let everything go to the dogs." A slovenly household reflected on him. "Ask Dora for help if you need it."

Dora Miller, the woman up the lane, had taken an interest in Lexie and the children since they'd moved here. Maybe too much interest, he wasn't keen on her sour face when he came home with a few drinks in.

He'd tell the old bat to mind her own business, but he needed her to help Lexie out while he was away. She'd told him yesterday that she was three months along.

**

In September, Dan and Sam Moore, from Winterton, left for the States aboard an American freighter; Captain Healey, Max' father-in-law, had arranged a working trip for them. "There's no sense having kin if they can't do you a favour now and then," Dan said, grinning as he watched the Carbonear waterfront fade in the distance.

The trip was like food to a starving Dan. He settled comfortably into the freedom of language and behaviour that comes with all-male company, gladly accepting liquor in return for a few songs and jigs on someone's accordion, a custom that had followed him most of his life.

They docked in Portland, Maine, unloaded barrels and crates under the eyes of the burly skipper they called Bumpy. "Hey," shouted Leroy, one of the crew, a big fellow from Tennessee. Dan could hardly understand a word he said. "Y'all wanna come with me an' Billy Joe after we're done, get some grub somewhere downtown?"

Dan and Sam followed the Americans to a restaurant called Olsen's Steak Joint. "Now," said Leroy, after they'd finished, "it's time for dessert. Me an' Billy Joe know just the place."

"The place" was a two-storey, brick building with a red light over the door. "Is this what I think it is?" asked Sam, hanging back from the steps. "Good Lord, I'm not going in there."

The Americans guffawed but Dan wasn't surprised. Sam was a serious member of the Sally Ann's. "All right, you go on back," he said. "I'll be right behind you, just want to have a look inside." Besides, he didn't want to look bad in front of the Yanks.

He followed the two men into the building. Found himself in a fancy parlour, where several women in various states of dress and undress lounged around on settees and couches, sending sultry glances their way.

"Pick one, Danny boy," said Leroy, rubbing his crotch in anticipation. He pointed to a young blonde sitting in the corner. "I'll take Blondie there."

The woman came over and put an arm around Leroy's broad shoulders. "Long time, no see, Darlin'." Obviously not Leroy's first time here, thought Dan, as Leroy winked and disappeared up the stairs with the girl.

Dan hesitated as Lena popped into his head, that old disapproving look on her face. But then a young girl with long, dark hair walked over to him. "You go wiss me?" Obviously from some other part of the world, just like he was.

"Sure." He'd pay with the money Max had given him for emergencies.

Sixteen

Mary lived in the blue-collar suburb of Lynn, Mass. "So good to see you," Mary gushed, pulling him into a bone-crushing hug. She looked good, young and slim like Dan remembered. "Come on in, Pat is waiting to meet you."

Dan dropped his suitcase in the hall and followed Mary into the kitchen. A well-built fellow with auburn hair and Irish blue eyes got up from the table. "Pat Shea," he said, shaking Dan's hand, "great to meet you." He nodded toward a young girl sitting at the table. She was staring at Dan with big, blue eyes. "This is our daughter, Mary Ann. She's four."

"Hello, Mary Ann," said Dan. "You look like your Grandmother Lena, did you know that?"

The girl blushed as her mother ruffled her reddish-brown hair. "He's right, you do. I wish you could meet your Gran."

"My daughter, Iris, is your cousin," said Dan. "She just turned six. Maybe you'll meet her someday." Mary Ann beamed from all the attention she was getting.

"You look tired, Dan," Mary said. "Pat, show him to his bedroom, or what we'll call his bedroom, and I'll make a lunch."

As Pat led him downstairs to the basement, Dan remembered Mary saying in her letters that Pat was an easy-going guy who stayed away from the taverns. That would be right up Mary's alley, she was like an old Temperance biddy about drinking.

"We got married in 1917, before I went overseas," said Pat. "Took an accounting course after the war, lucked into a job with the city. We just moved here, I've been working on the basement in my spare time. We set up a bed in the unfinished bedroom. It's not the Ritz but you should be comfortable."

Dan settled in with the family, spent a week or so riding around on the buses, getting to know the city. Before long, Mary was nudging him toward a job. "Lynn is known as the city of shoe factories. Bet you didn't know that, did you?"

"Is that a fact?" Dan grinned. "My, the things you learn in the US of A!"

"There's lots of jobs at the shoe factories. But they're being snapped up pretty fast so you should check on it soon." Another pushy woman, thought Dan. Not long before they're telling you what to do.

"Yeah, I will. But you said we'd go see Belle. After that I'll start looking."

**

Belle lived in downtown Lynn with her husband, Tony Marino, and their three children. Their apartment was above the fruit store Tony's father had started when he arrived from Italy years ago. "Dan," Belle cried, hugging him tight, "it's been so long! Gosh, you were only twelve when we left, and now look at you." There were tears in her eyes as she looked him up and down.

Belle was Dan's favourite sister. She was easy-going, not intense and picky about everything like Mary. "Well, here I am, all grown up," he said. "Let's have a cup of tea and catch up, you can ask any questions you want."

"Christ, Mary, what happened to Belle?" Dan said later, as he and Mary walked down the street after leaving Belle's flat. "She looks dragged through a knothole. Good thing Ma can't see her, she'd put the run to that Wop she married."

Mary cringed. "Don't say Wop!" muttering out of the corner of her mouth. "There's foreigners here, Italians, Poles, all kinds. Wanna get your face punched in? Belle's just tired. She works two jobs, part time at the dress factory with me and she cleans offices some nights.

But Tony's a good guy, a hard worker. He'll take over the store when the old man retires."

Dan couldn't help laughing. "Yeah, he *wohks hahd*," mocking her Boston talk.

She punched his arm. "You buggah!" There it is, thought Dan, an old Newfoundland word in a Boston accent.

Swirls of red, orange, and yellow leaves danced around their feet as the trees flailed their bare limbs about, waving goodbye to another family they'd nurtured over the summer. Dan and Mary pulled up their collars against the wind and ran for the streetcar.

Once in their seats, Mary continued her update on Belle. "Belle called her little one Lena, Ma was so pleased. Hard to believe she's a year old now."

"Well, let's hope Belle is finished with babies. I mean, three is enough, the way she looks!" He grinned. "Jesus, that young Sal is a real W... Marino!"

Mary turned to watch out the window for their stop and Dan studied her profile. So much like Ma now, the Shipp pointed chin and grey eyes. Her dark hair was cut in the modern way, a bob Mary called it. What would Sally Fisher make of it all, the short hair on the women, the way they smoked and drank in the Speakeasies? He tried to imagine Lexie here in Boston. Christ, in his mind Lexie seemed as old as her mother!

"Hey, Sis," he said, "it's only three o'clock. Let's get some o'that Yankee ice-cream before we go home."

"All right. Just don't gawk at the women, you never know who's got a husband in tow."

They got off the streetcar and ducked into an ice-cream parlour near Mary's house. Dan scanned the stream of young women coming in the door. Pretty women, brash and confident in short dresses, lip-sticked mouths puckered around the ends of cigarettes. One girl had a long cigarette holder like he'd seen on movie posters. These Yankee women were something!

He noticed Mary's frown. "Never mind the girls, Mr. Connor," a sharp edge to her tone. "That should be the least of your worries, you've got another kid on the way."

He almost told her to get off his back but he bit his tongue. "Yes, Ma," he laughed. "You're just like her, y'know that? Anyway, a cat can look at the Queen long as he don't bite."

"Be serious, Dan," Mary said. "Think of poor Lexie, three kids to look after all by herself. I know Belle has three kids but at least she's got Tony to help her. You need a job so you can send money home. Then, at least, she'll be able to feed them properly."

He ignored her. "I can't get used to the short hair on the girls," he said, "but I sorta like it. Hope Belle don't cut hers though, all that red hair she got from old Bridget. The rest of us, you, me and Max, we're black Irish. Remember Bridget telling us that?"

They walked home through the busy streets, Dan looking around and pointing at the buildings, the parks. "I must say," said Mary, the edge back in her voice, "you seem to take to city life."

**

Another week of no job and Mary was ready to lay down the law. Dan came home from the tavern one supper time to face the two of them standing inside the door, waiting. Okay, he'd pushed it as far as he could. Now he'd have to take Mary's marching orders.

"Dan," she said, as Pat nodded his support, "we've decided it's time you got a job. I'm disappointed in you. You've got a family waiting at home, they need money."

Pat stepped in. "Take a couple weeks to get a job and find a place to live." He almost looked regretful for giving Dan the heave-ho. Unlike Mary, who'd come to the place of no return.

Dan held up his hands. "Don't have to say anything else, I'll get on it tomorrow."

He got a job at a shoe factory, cutting big pieces of leather into small pieces of leather. Said goodbye to the Shea's and moved into a rented room downtown. By Christmas, he knew all the watering holes within a ten-block radius. Makeshift taverns selling Maritime moonshine and St. Pierre rum were popping up everywhere. "Prohibition'll never work," he told some men at the tavern. "Wait and see if I'm not right."

He went to the movies, became a big fan of Mary Pickford. "She's from Canada, did ya know that?" one of the women at the factory told him. She thought Dan was from Canada. He didn't bother explaining the difference between Newfoundland and Canada, the Yanks didn't know there was another world outside the States.

There were lots of women at the factory who caught his eye and they were interested in the "good-lookin' Canadian," as he'd heard himself described.

"How 'bout we go to a movie?" he asked one of them, a buxom redhead with long legs.

"Maybe," she replied, coyly, "long as my husband don't find out." Dan took a pass. He was in no hurry to get a pounding from Mr. Redhead.

He was making twenty dollars a week, eighty a month. He sent home twenty, held back thirty for his rent and kept the rest for his entertainment. It was just too easy to dart into a tavern on his way home at night. The life was much to his liking. If he could dodge the Immigration bulldogs, he thought he might stay on a while. Maybe forever.

The following March, 1922, he got a letter from Lena. The baby had arrived. Another girl, her name was Carrie Rose.

PART THREE (Rose)

I shall never cease to marvel at the way we beg for love and tyranny.

(Francine du Plessix Gray) *Lovers and Tyrants*

Seventeen

Spring, 1932. Nine-year-old Rose Connor, the youngest of Lexie's three daughters, sat with her mother at the breakfast table, urging her to eat her toast. Lexie was always slow to come around in the morning.

"Hurry up and finish," snapped Iris. "I want to get the dishes cleared up." And Iris was always grumpy in the morning.

"C'mon, Mother, finish this piece." Rose didn't want to send big sister into a spin this early in the day.

**

Rose had been born in 1922, while her father was in Boston. He'd arrived home in the summer of '28, a strange man suddenly appearing in the doorway with a clothes bag over his back. Rose had been six at the time. If Dora Miller hadn't been there, she'd have run away in fright.

Her sister, Iris, a tall, pretty girl, almost thirteen and already looking grown up, had gone rushing over to the man, squealing with delight as he lifted her up in a big hug. Iris had left school by then, had been running the house with an iron hand since Rose could remember.

Rose's other sister, Daisy, had been eight. "It's your father, Pet," Dora had said, frowning severely toward the man as Daisy ran behind her skirt, "he's home from Boston." Daisy had only been about a year old when he'd left so she had no clear memory of him, either, but Rose could definitely see Daisy in the stranger's dark looks.

"All right, you two," he'd said, his tone overly jolly, "come and see what I've got. Look, here's *Anne of Green Gables* for Daisy, and *The Alphabet* for Rose," passing the book to Rose, patting her blonde head. "Rose, you look just like your mother, y'know that? Another Fisher through and through." He glanced at Dora. "Can't get away from the Fishers, can we?

"Anyway, it's Daisy who looks like her old man, eh Daisy?" No response from Daisy. "And here's something for Iris and her mother." Iris had grabbed the hairbrush and headed for the old mirror in the hall, the one that made everything look wavy. And that's when Lexie had come downstairs. She'd stopped in her tracks and stared at her long-lost husband as if she were seeing a ghost.

That had been almost four years ago. Rose, now almost ten, still remembered the little kernel of joy that had inched its way into her chest that day. Everything would be better now, she'd thought. They'd have a father like other children, someone to depend on. And best of all, Iris would no longer be the boss.

But things hadn't worked out that way. Almost four years on, just like while her father was in Boston, the family still relied on other people for food and firewood. People like Rose's grandmothers, Sally Fisher and Lena Parsons, as well as Aunt Molly and Uncle John Fisher. And, of course, their guardian angel, Dora Miller, who lived close by with her husband and two girls, Blanche and Lucy. Dora was always bustling in and out, bringing loaves of bread, checking on Lexie. Looking after them.

And Iris, sixteen now, still ruled the roost. She'd gotten used to being in charge while Dan was away and nothing had changed since his return. She continued to growl at her mother for any little thing, for not eating, not getting up on time, for anything, depending on her mood. And Rose had become her mother's caretaker and guardian because Daisy no longer lived at home.

Shortly after his return, Dan had decided that Daisy should quit school and go to live with Gran Parsons. "Better you help your grandmother than waste time in school," he'd said, as Daisy stared at him in horror and disbelief. "Besides, lots of girls your age leave school to help out." Surprisingly, Gran had gone along with the decision. Rose still resented her for it.

Rose had begged her father to change his mind. "But Daisy loves school," she'd pleaded. "She's real smart, the principal said so." In the back of Rose's mind, she'd remembered something Daisy had said. 'School is the best thing in my life. If I didn't have that, I'd run away.'

Thank God, Daisy hadn't run away but Rose missed having her at home. Still, there was nothing they could have done to change things. They were just kids, their father was the boss.

Sometimes, Rose felt like an orphan. Daisy lived somewhere else, her father wasn't around much, and her mother was slowly withdrawing into her own world. According to Gran, Lexie hadn't been herself since Daisy was born. "Some women are just delicate," she'd said. "Seems like they feel too much. They get overwhelmed by everything, by hardship, children, the expectations of other people. Overwhelmed by life, I guess you could say. But she's your mother, Rose. Be kind to her, treat her as well as you can." Gran obviously hadn't seen Iris in action.

**

Rose was taking her mother's dishes into the pantry when her father and Marcus Crane came rushing in. "Get us a lunch, Iris," Dan ordered. "We're goin' down the wharf. There's a coal boat in, might get a couple days work unloading her." Rose led her mother over to the rocking chair, away from the loud, masculine voices, while the men made themselves comfortable at the table. Iris got busy frying eggs.

Marcus was a big man with a bushy, black mustache, an incomer to the community. Her father had met him a year ago when he'd come in on a fishing schooner. The two of them must have clicked because Dan had brought him to the house and introduced him. "Marcus is finished with fishing. He's gonna stay here, build a cabin in the woods. Live the simple life, eh Marcus?" At this, the two men had shared a grin. "He wants me to help him build it."

This cabin had become the subject of many a squabble between Dan and Gran Parsons. He'd begun to spend most of his time there, neglecting his fishing berth with Gil Shipp, Lena's brother. "Gil is soon gonna dump you. How will you feed your family then?" Lena would grumble. "And don't think I don't know you and Marcus Crane are making moonshine back there in the woods." Shortly afterwards, as Gran had predicted, Dan was let go from the boat. The Connors were again living hand-to-mouth.

Rose watched the men gobbling their food, hurrying to finish and get away from the house. She'd noticed that about her father, he was always anxious to get away. Throwing on his coat and going out the door, cigarette smoke trailing after him. Rose thought maybe he was more suited to living in a cabin in the woods, like Marcus, than living with a family.

"Everything is goin' tits-up, Dan," Marcus grumbled. "Businesses laying off everywhere." As usual, they were talking about the Depression. Her father called it a bank crash and Rose couldn't figure out how a bank could crash. A sled might crash into a fence, a boat could crash on the rocks, but a bank?

This crash had happened about three years ago, around the same time as the Burin Peninsula had been hit by a Tidal Wave. You wouldn't have thought it could be felt here in Trinity Bay but the house had started shaking in the night. And the water had rushed out of the harbour, leaving the boats stranded on the mud bottom. Later, they'd heard about houses being dragged out to sea on the wave, with people still in their beds. Rose often had nightmares about it.

But unlike the Tidal Wave, the Depression was still going on. Rose had heard her father and Marcus talking about the drought on the prairies, men jumping on trains and crossing the country looking for work, lining up at soup kitchens in the cities. It all sounded so frightening and strange that Rose sometimes wondered if they were making it up.

Rose didn't understand much about the Depression but she saw how her family, and the families around her, were affected. The fishermen couldn't get supplies because they couldn't sell their catch. Of course, there was lots of food if you liked cod, but they ate it every day and Rose was plain sick of it.

"You're lucky to have it," Gran Parsons chastised her. "We're sending salt cod up to the Canadian prairies to keep them people from starving and you're complaining because we have lots of it!"

A lot of people were getting sick, especially children. Most of them had quit school so when Rose stopped going, no one got mad. She'd only just started Grade Two but she didn't care. She never wanted to go to school anyway. She wanted to be home with her mother.

"The Cable Station in Heart's Content is letting go most of their workers," said Dan, heaving back from the table with his rollup. "Some of the upper crust might have to go on the dole. Can't say I pity 'em much."

He had no pity, either, for the Fishers, whose business was failing. A few months ago, Lew and his wife had left for Grand Falls where he hoped to get work at the paper mill. Rose had gone to see them leave. She'd stayed with her Grandmother Fisher all day, watched the old lady's eyes fill up every time Lew was mentioned. "I'm very much afraid, Rose," she'd said, "that Will and Jean might be next to leave." But Rose didn't believe that would happen, not Will and Jean!

**

Later that morning, Iris grabbed her coat. "Going over to Gran's for eggs, Rose. I've started the wash, you and Mom carry on with it. Try to have it done by the time I get back."

An hour later, the door burst open and Carrie Hall blew in, red-faced and puffing as she untied the bandana from around her head. "Woo, breezy out there. March winds, as they say."

Rose was delighted to see her mother's friend. And Lexie was all smiles. "So good to see you, Carrie. You haven't been out here for ages." Carrie was a servant in the house of some big shot in St. John's.

"I know," said Carrie, grabbing the bucket of clothes. "Need help hanging it out, Rose? Here, I'll carry the bucket, you bring the pins."

Back in the house, Carrie shrugged off her coat. "So, how's our Carrie Rose? All right, let's play the game." Rose giggled as Carrie held out two closed fists. Rose touched the left one, picked the nickel out of Carrie's hand and turned to show her mother. "See, I *am* your fairy godmother. And didn't you just have a birthday?"

"Yes, March the third." Rose was pleased that Carrie had remembered. "I'm ten."

"Ooh, you're a big girl now." Carrie reached into her pocket and took out a red, rubber ball. "There y'go," bouncing it on the floor. "Found this in the attic where I work, the youngsters in there are too old for it anyway. Happy Birthday, Rosebud!"

Rose scooted over and caught the ball. "Thank you, Carrie." It was her first store-bought toy.

"But Carrie," Lexie persisted, "what are you doing out this way in the middle of the week?"

"Yeah, it's a surprise. Mom almost had a heart attack when I walked in." Carrie looked uncomfortable. "God, I might as well say it. Richard and I are going to the States, Lexie. We're getting married before we go. 'Bout time, I s'pose, we've been keeping company for years."

Lexie's face fell. "Seems what everybody is doing those days."

"Things aren't good here, Lexie. Richard lost his job on the paper last month. We're heading to Detroit, he figures there might be some opportunity there. If he can't get on with a newspaper, he'll try the car plants." Carrie's eyes misted over. "Will you be okay, Lexie? You had it hard while Dan was away. How is everything now?"

Rose sat cross-legged on the wood box, rolling her nickel around in her hands and thinking about the peppermint knobs at Parker's Store. But her ears were open to what they were saying. Rose was always alert to what was going on around her.

"Well," said Lexie, "he gets the odd few hours once a month, unloading coal boats. Otherwise, there's not much." Rose remembered a few weeks ago, Gran telling her father to go to Heart's Content and get a dole slip. He'd caused a great uproar. Said he wasn't going up there, cap in hand, to no government man. He'd left the house in a rage, came back later so drunk he could hardly stand.

"I see," said Carrie, putting on her coat. "I worry about you, Lexie. What if something happens and I'm not here to help?"

"Don't worry, I've got Rosie here with me." Rose felt a sudden pride at her mother's comment but at the same time there was a twinge of unease in her stomach.

"Rose is just a child, Lexie, she can only do so much." Carrie looked worried as she hugged them goodbye. "I'll write," she said, her voice thick.

Rose watched through the window until Carrie was out of sight. Afterwards, her mother sat for a long time without speaking. "Will we ever see Carrie again?" Rose asked. Her mother didn't reply. She'd gone into one of her fogs, as she called them. Sat in her rocking chair all afternoon, rocking slowly back and forth while Rose watched over her.

When Iris came home, the wash was still only half done. "Christ, do I have to do everything myself?" she bawled, as Rose scurried around, throwing dirty clothes into the lukewarm water.

Dan came dragging home from Parker's Wharf at suppertime, his face black from coal dust. "What's the problem?" he asked, seeing Lexie slumped over in the rocking chair.

"Carrie and Richard are getting married and going to the States," Rose told him.

"Finally gonna marry her, is he?" That was his only comment, but Rose could see by his scowl that he was affected by the news. She knew he'd like to be back in Boston if he could, because when he talked about his time there it was the only time his face ever lit up.

**

May brought warmer weather and everyone settled in for a long summer. Dan was preoccupied with the news of Amelia Earhart's upcoming flight across the Atlantic. "Gonna do it by herself this time," he said, amazed at the courage of the American woman. He was fascinated by the idea of air travel, kept track of all the daredevils who came here to make their names by flying across to Europe.

Rose noticed the big smile on Iris' face. "We're gonna meet up with some people and walk over to Harbour Grace to see her take off," she said, smugly.

"You come, too, Rose," Dan offered. "Do you good to get some fresh air."

"No," replied Rose, dismissing the suggestion as Dan shrugged. "I'll stay with Mother." She'd noticed that even Lexie seemed more alert lately. "Mother," she said, "it's a lovely day. Do you want to go in the woods, like we used to?" It had been a while since they'd gathered firewood together, it used to be their favourite thing.

"Oh, yes," Lexie replied, smiling at the prospect.

"Not 'til you help me wash the windows!" said Iris, still looking smug as she poured Dan's tea.

They left the house in late afternoon, the air still warm after the mild spring day. Strolling along the New Road, the path leading into the woods at the back of town, they came to Frank Sutton's Field at the side of Big Pond. This was where the older children liked to swim, probably because the water was deeper and more dangerous here than at the Brook. Even better, Big Pond was back in the woods, out of sight of nosy parents.

After a few more minutes, they came to their spot. "Here it is," said Lexie, smiling, "the Indian village." The men stacked their wood here to dry, standing the sticks up on end so they looked like teepees scattered around the clearing.

Rose breathed in the heavy scent of spruce trees as she helped her mother lay out pieces of rope and sailcloth. Then they tramped through the woods, over ferns and blueberry bushes and lime green mosses, searching for sticks, blassy boughs, log ends, anything that would burn in the old Waterloo stove at home. Lexie hummed her favourite hymn, "Abide with Me," and Rose smiled to see her happy.

After an hour or so, they tied up the sticks and started back, dragging their load behind them. Rose ran ahead to the huge boulder crouching at the side of the path; the "sittin' rock," so called because it was shaped like a chair. Her mother caught up and they sat for a while, feeling the warmth on their faces, listening to the birds twittering around them. Then they walked home together in the early evening calm.

The house was empty, there was no sign of Dan or Iris. "I'll boil some eggs for supper," said Rose, thankful that they always had eggs from

Gran's hens. She was pleased that the walk had gone well. There'd been no sign of the dark mood that was so much a part of her mother.

But after supper, as often happened after a good day, Lexie's mood began to change. By nine o'clock, she was agitated. She rocked and cried and rubbed her hands together while Rose hovered nearby and wondered what had upset her.

It was late when Iris came strutting into the house. "I was over at Gran's," she said, her face broody and defiant. "Daisy needed help with the cleaning."

Rose said nothing but she knew different. Iris and a boy had just come across the bridge arm-in-arm, she'd been sneaking around with boys for a while now. At sixteen, it wasn't unusual for a girl to have a boyfriend but it was different for Iris. Dan often warned her about 'whorin' around.' He wasn't raisin' no bastard, he'd said, and don't forget it.

Iris tossed a glance at her mother. "Not another crying jag." She yawned and headed upstairs.

An hour later Dan came staggering into the kitchen, squinting his eyes in the lamplight as he scowled to see them still up. "Jaysus, what now?" he drawled.

"Mother isn't well," said Rose. "I've been trying to get her to bed."

"Not well, eh?" Dan muttered. "Big surprise there!" Maybe Daisy was right, thought Rose. The only thing he cared about was drinking at Marcus Crane's. And it must be true because he spent most of his time there.

Rose was helping her mother into the downstairs bedroom when Iris came flitting down the stairs in her nightdress. "I'll get you a lunch, Daddy," she chirped, in that goody-goody voice she used when speaking to her father.

"Okay, Iris. That'd be a bit of all right," he muttered, as he flopped on the daybed. Most nights that was as far as he got.

Eighteen

The winter of '33 brought more cold weather and more poverty. Iris had run out of yeast again, had sent Rose over to get some from Gran Parsons. "I can't feel my feet," Rose whined, as she limped back into the house. "I think they're frozen." She looked around. "Where's Mother? She was in the rocking chair when I left."

Iris shrugged. "I dunno."

Rose was about to check upstairs when the door banged open and Lexie rushed in. She stomped over to the rocking chair, her face an angry glare.

Behind her came Daisy. "I found Mom sitting in a snow bank, crying," she fumed, as she roughly helped Lexie off with her coat. "Took a tantrum when I tried to bring her home."

"Mother," asked Rose, "why were you crying?"

"Want to play with the girls."

Daisy rolled her eyes. "Two little girls were pulling a sled along the road and Mom tried to jump on. They got scared and ran away. Well, they're five-year-olds, they didn't know what she was doing!" She turned and faced Rose, hands on hips. "She's getting worse, Rose. People are talking about her, the boys laugh at her. Can't you make her stay home?"

"Don't you think I try?" Rose's voice rose in anger as she felt her eyes well up. "I had to go over to Gran's for yeast. I can't be everywhere, can I?" It was Iris who'd let her mother slip away but Rose wasn't going to point that out. "She sneaks out when I'm not looking. If I try to talk to her about it, she gets upset."

Daisy quickly backed down. "I know, Rose. I know you do your best." She glared at Iris, calmly kneading dough at the table and ignoring the whole situation. "Well, anyway, she's home now. I'd better go, Gran wants some wood brought in."

"Yeah." Rose could hardly speak for the lump in her throat. Daisy's words had cut her.

As Daisy turned to leave, she went over to the rocking chair where Lexie was calmly rocking and humming to herself. "I'm going now, Mom. Try to stay home, okay? It's cold out." Lexie smiled and nodded, and continued humming.

Lexie's behavior was increasingly worrisome. Sometimes she was childlike, she'd have little tantrums if she didn't get her way. And sometimes she was embarrassing in public, which bothered Daisy the most because Daisy was someone who chafed at humiliation.

Rose still blushed at a particular memory. She was following her mother on one of her sudden wanderings, trying to steer her toward home, when Lexie started flapping her arms and cawing like a crow. "Caw, caw, I'm a crow, a big, black crow."

People on the road had begun to stop and stare when, out of nowhere, Dora Miller appeared. "Hello, Lexie. Can I walk home with you?" Dora had linked arms with her and they walked home together, chatting like old friends. That night, when Rose went to bed, she'd done a rare thing. She'd said a prayer of thanks for Dora Miller and all she did for the family.

**

Rose's chaotic family life was fast becoming more than she could handle. As her mother's condition deteriorated, her father's drinking got worse. At Christmas, he stayed out on a drunk from Christmas Eve 'til well after New Year's. Marcus Crane brought him home barely alive. "Better stay out of his way today," Marcus muttered. "Got in a brawl with some bootleggers last night. He's sick and cantankerous, you don't want to cross him."

Marcus lugged him into the downstairs bedroom, Dan's bedroom now since he'd banished Lexie upstairs. This meant that Rose had to share a room with Iris. Some nights Iris would come out of a sleep and sit bolt upright in the bed, gasping for breath and sweating. Rose never asked what was wrong, she knew Iris wouldn't tell her.

Marcus hung around the house with her father all winter. "Call me Marcus," he'd say, stroking that bushy mustache, "you know me well enough by now." But Rose kept her distance, she was intimidated by his size and his forceful way of talking.

Iris wasn't intimidated at all. She'd settle on Marcus' knee and sip his moonshine, throw back her head and laugh, the way she did when she was around men. "You're funny," she'd giggle, and he'd hug her close. Rose sometimes thought Iris was like two different people. One Iris craved attention, the other Iris hated the world.

When Marcus was around, Rose stayed upstairs with her mother. Sometimes she'd lie with her 'til dawn, listen to the loud laughter and the dirty language down below as her father banged on about his favourite subject, politicians.

"Squires is carrying on with a woman here in New Perlican," she heard him say. "Sneaks in town after dark in that fancy car, the one the taxpayers paid for." As far as Dan was concerned, all politicians were crooks. He especially hated Richard Squires, the former Newfoundland Prime Minister, who'd been run out of office last year during a riot in St. John's.

Dan and Marcus talked about Lexie, mocking her for the way she was, how she talked to herself or sat staring for hours. "She's a millstone around my neck," Dan would say, his voice thick with alcohol. "Got dragged back here, now I'm saddled with a nut case."

"Whad'ya mean, dragged back here?"

"I was workin' in the US but I never had proper papers. Bloody Fishers informed on me!" Rose, lying half asleep beside her mother in the upstairs bedroom, had no idea what he meant by papers. But she wondered if this might explain his hatred of the Fishers.

Then, one night, she heard Marcus say something that shocked her to attention. "You know, Dan, there's a place in St. John's for people like her. You should look into it." Were they just talking nonsense or did it mean something more?

**

Rose turned eleven in March but the family didn't notice. She didn't say anything, it wouldn't mean much if she had to remind them, so she wandered down the Harbour Road and up the hill to Molly's house. Molly always remembered.

"Here's your present, Rose. Happy Birthday." Rose smiled as she pressed the soft, wool socks against her cheek. Molly and her knitting! "Wait, there's more," added Molly, passing her a brown paper bag. "Raisin cookies, a rare treat those days with everything so scarce. By the way, your Grandmother Fisher wants to see you."

As Rose entered the kitchen, a smile touched Sally Fisher's lips. "Happy Birthday, Rose. I made a cake, thought you might turn up today. You didn't bring Lexie with you?"

"No. I asked her to come but she paid no attention." Rose wondered if she should tell her grandmother what Marcus had said, about sending her mother away to a hospital. But it might have been drunk talk and she didn't want to worry the old lady for nothing. She'd be eighty soon and besides, Molly had said she was having some heart trouble.

"I'd go over to see Lexie more often but Dan is always so hostile." Rose had heard this from her grandmother many times before. "She's not doing well, is she, Rose?"

"No. And it's getting harder to get her to eat."

"I thought we might take your cake over and let her enjoy your birthday with us. It can be my reason for visiting." She sighed. "Never thought I'd need a reason to see my own daughter." She gave Rose a cautious glance. "I don't know if I should tell you this, Rose, but you know the situation. You're living it every day." She paused before going on.

"When your father was in Boston, Lexie had a hard time. You were just a baby so you won't remember. But Lexie wasn't keeping on top of things very well and besides, Dan had stopped sending money home. So I told John to go over and bring you all home here. And, you know, she absolutely refused to come. John came back breathing fire he was so mad. But that's Lexie, none of us can understand the way she is, we just have to live with it."

Rose didn't have anything to say to this. She felt sorry for her grandmother, for herself, for everybody involved, but no one could change the way things were.

"Something else, Rose. I'm sorry to say Will and Jean are leaving, they're going to Montreal. The Depression, my dear, there's no business. We have to close the store."

"What? They can't leave." Rose started to cry. The two people who'd been hovering in the background like guardian angels all her life were leaving. What would happen to her, now?

"Yes, you'll miss them. We all will." Sally dabbed at her eyes. "They have to make a living, Rose. Jean has an uncle there, he's going to help Will find a job. "

Rose was struck with a frightening thought. "Are Uncle John and Molly leaving, too?"

"Thank God, no. John and his boy, Kenny, are going to stay with the *Huron*, the one schooner we have left, and try to ride it out. It's a good thing Lew got away when he did, though I have to say I was against it at the time."

**

They left the Harbour Road and took the shortcut across the Green, Sally puffing as she pushed through the heavy, late-winter snow. "I hope Dan isn't home," she fretted.

"He didn't come home last night, so probably not." Rose was used to his nights away.

"Well, no matter. Unpleasant as Dan may be, Lexie is my daughter and I'll check on her."

As they went in, Lexie turned in her rocking chair. She was wrapped in the black shawl Dora had given her, the ghost of a smile on her thin face. Sally brushed her hand over the straggly, blonde hair. "Lexie, Love, are you alone?"

"Iris was supposed to wait 'til I got back," said Rose, angrily. "Where did she go, Mother?"

Lexie nodded and smiled. "Yes, gone. Back soon."

Rose dropped the cake on the table. "Damn it. You can't trust Iris for anything." It was the first time she'd ever used bad language in front of Grandmother Fisher.

"Now, now, Rose, calm down. She can't have been gone long, there's still some wood in the stove." Sally turned to Lexie. "I made a birthday cake for Rose, would you like some?"

Lexie nodded. "Cake for Rose." She looked at Rose and smiled and Rose smiled back, her eyes full. It had been a few years since her mother had marked her birthday. It wasn't her fault but Rose felt the loss all the same.

As she cut into the little fruit cake, Rose wondered if her mother would ever be well again, would she ever come back from wherever she'd gone. That was how Rose thought of her mother, like she'd gone away and left them all.

The door opened and Iris came in. "Iris," Rose grumbled. "You left Mother alone!"

Iris threw a glance at her grandmother before she replied. "I went to see someone, Rose, and none of your business. Cripes, I was only gone fifteen minutes." She spotted the cake. "I'll have some, too."

They were just finishing their cake and tea when Dan walked in. The first thing Rose saw was the gun he was cradling across his chest. He looked like he'd been in a war. His eyes were bloodshot, his face covered in stubble and he was filthy. Rose could smell him from across the kitchen.

"Dad," cried Rose, "you've got a gun!"

"Yeah, Marcus gave it to me, he had two. Well, it's March, soon be spring hunting." He glared across the kitchen at Sally. "Having a party, are we?"

"No, I came to see Lexie. I'm worried about her." Sally looked aghast at Dan's appearance, her eyes flicking from his face to the gun. "I brought her some of Rose's birthday cake."

"Rose's birthday, is it? Hey, Happy Birthday, Rosie." Dan sank down on a chair, settled the gun across his knees. "Get me that old can of gun oil in the backhouse, Iris. Got to get this thing ready, ice'll be breakin' up soon." He turned back to Sally. "Checking up on me, I s'pose."

"Listen here, Dan, Lexie is my daughter. I have the right to see her when I want, and what's wrong with that? Can't you be more welcoming?"

Dan stood up and slowly, deliberately, heaved the gun to his shoulder. "Get out, old woman. Now I got a gun, you never know what might happen. Especially when I'm hung over." He cocked one eye, sighted along the barrel. "Go on, get the hell back to Fisherland. I'm the head of this house and what I say goes!"

Sally looked horrified. In her haste to get up from her chair, she stumbled and Rose ran to her. "It's all right, Rose," she said, breathlessly, "I'm leaving." As she opened the door, she paused to look back. "You're evil, Dan Connor. I wish I'd stopped Lexie from marrying you when I had the chance, because you'll be the death of her."

"Get out," he repeated. "Any news of Lexie from now on, you can get from Rose." He glanced at Rose. "Walk her home, Rose. If she falls, we'll have another Fisher uproar."

Nineteen

The Depression dragged on. Rose saw the strain in the haggard faces of her neighbours, heard the despair in their voices. Everywhere in the colony there was poverty, illness and unrest as people marched in protest, demanding help from the government.

Alone with her worries, Rose felt worn down and barely able to carry on. After another night of listening to her father and Marcus in their drunken rambles, she heard Marcus say it again. "A hospital for people like her." Now it was time to tell someone.

The next morning after breakfast, she took her mother back up to bed. Hopefully, she'd sleep away the afternoon. If not, Rose would have to trust that Iris would be responsible, for once. She left the house and headed across the bridge to Lena's.

As soon as Gran smiled at her, Rose started to cry. "Rose, what's wrong? You must be overtired. Here, lie down on the daybed. Maybe you should stay the night, I'll go over and tell Iris not to leave your mother alone."

Rose spent the afternoon resting while Gran hovered with a cup of her dogberry tonic. After supper, Gran pulled a hot beach rock out of the oven and dropped it into an old, wool vamp. "There, this'll keep your feet nice and warm. Go to bed now, Daisy should be up soon." Rose hugged the warm rock to her chest and headed upstairs. Some of her panic had started to melt away under Gran's attention. It felt good to be looked after.

Daisy came up not long afterwards. "God, I'm tired," she said, her eyes drooping with fatigue as she undressed. "Didn't sleep well last night. Had a nightmare, something about a man trying to lock me up in a tiny room. Must have screamed because Gran came running. Never got back to sleep after that."

Daisy got into bed and started searching around, under her pillow, under the sheet, under Rose's pillow. "Got to leave the lamp lit for a few minutes," she muttered. "Little buggers have been gaining on me lately, sometimes I'm too tired to bother." Years ago, Jake would bring bedbugs home from Labrador in his clothes bag, Gran was still trying to get rid of them.

"I'll help," said Rose, as they set about picking the tiny, brown insects from the feather mattress and dropping them into a jar.

"We hung the mattress on the fence in February," Daisy grumbled," figured the frost would do the job. It did for a while but we'll have to keep workin' on it." She flopped down in the bed. "That's enough. I'm beat."

"Dais," Rose whispered, as they settled down in the darkness, "Gran thinks I'm sick but that's not it. There's something I have to tell you."

"Hurry up," Daisy mumbled, "before she hollers at us to get to sleep."

Rose took a deep breath. "Dad and Marcus are talking about sending Mother away. They say there's a place in St. John's that take *people like her*. That's how they said it. I think he might really do it." She started to sob, pulled the blankets up over her mouth to drown the sound.

Daisy sat up. "The bastard!" she whispered. "John and Molly should know about this. I'll go and see them tomorrow." She sighed. "Wish Will and Jean was here, they'd know what to do."

Rose nodded her head in the dark. Will and Jean had left for Montreal at the end of March. They'd left a hole in the Fisher family, an empty spot where there used to be comfort and support. Rose still had nights when she'd cry herself to sleep for missing them.

"Mom is getting worse, though, isn't she?" Daisy said, her voice breaking. "I think she may need more help than we can give."

"Girls!" came the shout from downstairs. "Tis way past time you two was asleep!"

**

Daisy was true to her word. The next day, John barged into the house looking murderous. "Dan, I hear you're making plans for my sister."

"Nothin' to do with you," Dan drawled. "I saw Dr. Bennett. He said Lexie needs to be looked at in St. John's. A quick appointment in May, we'll be back the next day." He shook his head in disgust. "Jesus, even the Fishers should be able to see the woman is not well."

Rose saw John's shoulders sag as the truth of the statement hit home. He was quiet for a moment, fighting inside himself. His sister needed help but he had no say in her care. "Yes, I know she needs to see someone. Why don't Molly and I go along with you? It might be easier for her if we're there."

"Listen here, Fisher," said Dan, impatient now, "this is my wife we're talking about, understand?" He reached behind the stove. "Maybe I should be clearer," bringing the gun to his shoulder. Since he'd got the gun, he seemed to use it as an extra threat when something got under his skin. At any rate, it was always close to hand in case he needed it.

John flinched and jumped back. He stared at Dan, his face ashen.

"Clear enough now?" Dan lowered the gun, a satisfied look on his face. "I'll take charge of my family and if you crowd come snooping around, I'll take action. Keep this in mind, John. I'm the head of the house. The law is on my side."

John turned to go, his fists clenched, a look of pure hatred on his face. If her father hadn't been holding the gun, Rose was sure John would have killed him.

**

May had arrived too soon. Rose woke early to the sun's rays dancing on the wall across the room but she took no pleasure in it. This was the day she'd been dreading and she felt anything but sunny.

She went downstairs to find her father going about the house whistling. He'd been up early, had washed and shaved and put on a clean shirt and trousers. "Get your mother ready, Rose, Vic'll be here soon." Vic Tucker, from Heart's Content, ran a taxi service. He was going to take them to St. John's.

Rose went back upstairs, her heart like a stone in her chest. "Get up, Mother. You're going in the car today, remember?" The night before, Rose had told her they were going for a car ride. She'd used her mother's fascination with cars to trick her into getting up and around, and she wasn't proud of it. "There's the car, now," she said, as she watched Vic pull up at the gate.

Lexie jumped out of bed and allowed Rose to comb her hair and pull on her old, cotton dress, the only one she had that wasn't worn thin. It hung on her bony frame like a brin bag. Her eyes full of tears, Rose gathered up her mother's few belongings, put them into a wicker basket and they went downstairs.

Lexie refused to eat breakfast, she'd almost given up eating altogether by then. Rose stared at her face, the dark circles under her eyes, her mouth full of bad teeth. At only thirty-four years old, her mother looked like an old woman.

"Better get ready," said Iris, taking away the bowl of porridge. "Daddy is anxious to go."

Just then Lena and Daisy came rushing in, their faces full of concern. "Lexie, I had to come and see you before you go," said Lena, taking Lexie's hand. "Take care, my dear, we'll see you when you get back."

Lexie paid no attention. "Car ride," she murmured.

"Okay, time to go," Dan announced. "We'll pick up Marcus on the way. Got to, he's payin' for the taxi. Or should I say, he's *bartering* to pay for the taxi." Probably bartering moonshine, thought Rose, bitterly.

Lexie got up from the table and picked up her basket. Pranced out the door and down the steps with a big smile on her face, like a child going on a picnic. "The poor girl," whispered Lena, her eyes filling up.

Everyone came outside to watch them leave, Daisy hovering near her mother, her face contorted from holding back the tears. Rose wasn't surprised, Daisy liked people to believe she didn't have feelings.

"Wait, wait!" Everyone turned as Sally Fisher came hurrying across the road from the Green, waving her arms. She looked Dan in the eye. "Yes, Dan, I know what you said about staying away. Shoot me if you like, but I'll say goodbye to my daughter."

"What do you mean, stay away?" Lena's eyes bored into Dan. "What's going on? Of course you can speak to your daughter, Sally. Go ahead." Dan fell back, moving quickly away from his mother's angry eyes.

Sally went over and took Lexie's hand. "You're just going to talk to a doctor, Lexie. I'll see you tomorrow or the next day, when you get home." Lexie's eyes never left the car.

"Christ sake," grumbled Dan, "let's get on the road." He guided Lexie into the back seat and hopped into the front with Vic.

As the car pulled away from the fence, Rose glanced up the lane toward the Miller house. Dora was watching from her bedroom window.

**

Dan arrived back the next day but Lexie wasn't with him. "Where's Mother?" Rose asked, as he walked into the house.

"Oh, the doc said she needs some tests. We'll have to go back in a few days, pick her up." Rose caught a glance between him and Iris that made her wonder. Was he telling the truth?

For the next week, Rose worried. "I'm wondering about what Dad said," she told Dora. "Do you think he left Mother there for good and isn't telling us?"

"I don't know, Pet. But if he did, there'd have to be papers wouldn't there? He'd have had to sign something."

Rose thought about the dresser in her father's bedroom. "If I can find a time when he and Iris are out, I'll sneak into his room and check his dresser."

Dora frowned. "I don't know, Rose. Think it through before you do anything rash."

"He doesn't care about Mother," Rose went on, her anger growing. "Last year he walked to Harbour Grace to watch an American woman taking off in a plane. Now he can't even make the effort to see Mother in the hospital."

"I know Rose, I know."

"I'm gonna check the dresser. I have to see if there's something there."

Her chance came the next morning, when Dan and Iris left to walk to Carbonear to see Max. "We're going, Rose," called Dan, as they hurried out the door. "I'll tell Uncle Max you said hello."

Rose watched them through the gate. As soon as they were out of sight, she crept into his bedroom. In the top drawer of the dresser, she found a package of letters and papers tied up in a piece of white yarn. She sat down on the bed, had just begun to pick at the yarn when a shadow spread across the floor.

"What the hell?" Her father stood in the doorway, dark eyes flashing. "Good thing I forgot my jacket, isn't it? What are you doing in here?"

Rose dropped the papers and jumped to her feet. "I-I."

"Tell me, Rose, I'm in no mood to wait around."

"All right, I will," she shouted, anger and tears driving her on. "I-I think you left Mother in St. John's for good, I was looking for something that told me I was right."

"Oh, you were," he drawled, a sarcastic smirk on his face. "Well, since you're so keen to know, I'll tell you. We went to the Blackwood Hotel. A doctor came to see her and said she should be admitted to the hospital. I signed the papers and that was that. That what you wanted to hear?"

Rose stared at him wide-eyed as she realized she'd been right. He and Marcus had left her mother behind without a word and headed on home. "How long will she be there?"

"How do I know? 'Til she's normal, I s'pose." He folded his arms. "So now you know. T'was only a matter of time 'til I told you anyway, so you can pass it on to the rest o' the clan." He proceeded to look her up and down, his eyes resting on her arms, her chest. "You got more nerve than I gave you credit for, little Rose. Growing up fast, aren't you?" The anger spiked again and he went to the door. "Now get out. If you come in my room again, we'll see just how much nerve you *do* have!"

**

Rose hated her father for abandoning her mother like that. "I can't think of Mother in that place," she said to Daisy.

"I know, Rose, but Mom couldn't go on like she was. Maybe they'll make her better and she'll come home and be fine."

"Maybe." Rose understood that her mother needed help, but she was so far away. "Our doctor should have helped her here at home. She didn't need to go to St. John's."

"Well, Gran says we should get some news soon."

Rose snorted. "We won't get any news because he'll never go to the hospital to see her. Other men would, they'd hitch a ride on a freight schooner, maybe, even walk. But not him."

Without her mother to care for, Rose was at loose ends. She felt invisible in her own house now, as her father and Iris hardly spoke to her. She stayed away as much as she could, couldn't bear to be around them, to see the back-and-forth between them.

They'd get along fine for a while, then he'd stay away for a few nights. He'd come home sick and hung over, and Iris would go about banging pots and muttering under her breath about being a slave. Finally, he'd come around and pay attention to her. Iris would go back to catering to him and everything would be smooth again.

Rose moped through the days and weeks, hoping for news that never came. She found some comfort at her grandmother's where Sally Fisher had taken on the job of writing letters to the hospital, asking for news of Lexie.

"We've got to stay on top of it," Sally muttered, head bent low over the paper, her face flushed and determined, "else the news will go to Dan and we'll never find out how poor Lexie is doing." Rose admired the tough old woman. Grandmother Fisher refused to give up on her daughter.

The first reply, when it came months later, was brief and disappointing. *There is no change in her condition.* The next letter was much the same, adding the painful note that *Mrs. Connor seems contented and doesn't ask about home.* That was the part that hurt the most.

Twenty

It had been almost a year since they took Lexie away and Rose missed her more than ever. John had gone to see her in the fall, when he'd delivered a boat load of freight to St. John's, but Lexie had sat looking at him as if he were a stranger. It had hit John hard. "He cried when he told me about it," Molly told Rose.

Rose had cried, too. "Mother's left us forever, hasn't she?"

"Don't say that, Rose," consoled Molly. "In a few months, John might get another freight job. I'll go with him if it's a time of year when the sea is calm. But we have to be patient, jobs and money being what they are right now."

Rose had felt hopeless that day, as she'd sniffed back tears in Molly's kitchen, but Gran was there to pick her up. "The best you can do for your mother is keep your hopes alive," she'd said. "You have to get out more. Do things with Daisy, be around people."

So today, at Gran's insistence, Rose and Daisy mingled with the crowd in the Five Roads to watch the New Year's Day football match. Rose wasn't much interested. It looked more like chaos to her, a crowd of red-faced men and boys galloping around in the snow, kicking an inflated pig's bladder. And all for the glory of winning a tin cup for their side of town.

"Dad is watching Iris like a hawk these days," she confided to Daisy, keeping her voice low. "Warned her to stay away from the young bucks. Actually, he told me the same thing last week, said now that I'm almost twelve he'd better know where I'm at all the time. Can you believe it? Finally noticed I'm around. Anyway, I think there's a blow-up coming."

"Good," muttered Daisy, her eyebrows clenched in anger. "Maybe they'll kill each other!" Daisy had never forgotten the terrible day he'd yanked her out of school. She carried around her bitterness like a well-worn purse, so she could reach in for a savage remark whenever it was required.

At that moment, a heavy, bald man landed in the snow at Rose's feet. "He was tripped," cried Rose, pointing indignantly at the culprit as the bald man's language turned the air blue.

"It's every man for himself," said Daisy, her dark eyes tracking the play of a sandy-haired, young man on the Harbour team. "Steve Gordon is pretty good, isn't he?"

**

A week or so later, Dan came home earlier than usual complaining of a sore throat. "Where's Iris?" he asked, as he rooted around in the pantry for the Vick's VapoRub. "Why the hell is she out on a cold night like this?"

"She's over at Gran's, I think. Said she wouldn't be long." Rose had to lie because Iris was likely with one boy or another, thinking her father would be out late.

"She'd *better* be over at Gran's," he muttered, swallowing a heaping spoonful of the greasy mixture, then slathering some all over his throat. "Hey, Rose, get your ass out there on the steps. The Northern Lights are jumpin' all over the sky. It's really something!"

Rose hurried outside and looked up. There it was, the rare sight she'd heard about but thought she'd never see. She held her breath and watched as the colours danced and weaved across the cold, clear sky, like green and yellow phantoms visiting from out beyond the stars. "Dad was right, for once," she whispered to herself. "I *am* glad I got my ass out here."

Suddenly, she caught a movement from across the road as two people, clearly visible against the fresh snow and the bright night sky, came strolling along the path from the Green. It was Iris, arm-in-arm with Bert Parker, one of the Parker's Store crowd, a tall, skinny fellow with sandy hair, big ears, and hollow cheeks. He always reminded Rose of a fox.

Rose frantically waved her arms, hoping to warn them off, but then the familiar scent of Vick's VapoRub hit the night air. As soon as her father saw Iris and Bert standing in the middle of the road, he lost his interest in the Northern Lights.

The roar that came out of him bounced from one side of the harbour to the other. "Get the hell inside!" Iris darted for the steps. The heir to the Parker business empire bolted back across the Green, heading for the safety of home.

Rose scuttled in and curled up on the daybed to wait out the storm. Helpless to prevent it but unwilling to leave, she felt the familiar sense of dread settle in her stomach. Iris stood motionless in the kitchen, teeth clenched, fists tight at her side. As Rose saw her sister steeling herself for the onslaught, she felt her eyes well up in pity.

"You whore!" Dan bawled, his lip curled in disgust. "Get upstairs and clean yourself up!"

Looking relieved to have escaped so easily, Iris tried to move past him. But as she did, Dan grabbed a junk of wood from the woodbox. He caught the hem of her old, grey coat and swung at whatever he could reach, legs, hips, back, shoulders, as Iris struggled to get free. White with rage, he kept swinging and cursing 'til his breath came in gasps and he collapsed against the wall. The wood fell from his hand.

Iris made for the stairs, howling like a wounded animal. Rose darted up behind her, ran into her freezing bedroom and crawled under the quilts. Would he follow them upstairs? She held her breath, tried to listen above the thrumming in her chest. Above the sound of Iris' sniffling and cursing across the hall.

After a few minutes, Rose heard the outside door bang shut; he was heading for Marcus Crane's. "Dear God," she whispered, into the cold, dark room, "where will it all end?"

After this incident, the tension in the house ramped up. Iris would take more beatings, not only when Dan had caught her with a boy but even if he *thought* she'd been with one. Iris took it all without a word of protest. It was like she'd found his weakness. She kept turning the screw, even if it meant she'd be punished for it.

The strange thing was, in between the beatings everything was calm. Rose would come home and find them sharing his home brew like old drinking buddies. Until the next upheaval. Iris was truly the woman of the house now.

**

Rose turned twelve in March. By day, she did the jobs Iris told her to do and left the house, spending time at Grandmother Fisher's or Molly's or Gran's. At night, she lay awake missing her mother.

She woke up one cold morning feeling logy. She was tired and headachy and her limbs felt like lead, but she knew she'd better get up. It was wash day, Iris was sure to be in a bad mood. She hadn't been feeling well lately and it took less aggravation than usual to rile her up.

"Where's Dad?" Rose asked, as she went into the kitchen.

"Left to walk to Carbonear, see if Max can give him some flour and stuff. Max's shop is still hanging on, least he can do is help us out."

"Maybe he'll send over some boots," Rose said, hopefully. "The sole is coming apart on my old ones, my feet are always wet." Max had brought them winter boots before, when they were younger. Before the Depression.

"I wouldn't expect new boots if I were you," Iris scowled. "We're just hoping he can give us some food. Anyway, I'm waiting for the water here."

Rose pulled on her leaky boots, grabbed two buckets and a hoop to support their weight, and trudged down to the Brook. Returning half frozen, she set the buckets down and hung her stockings near the stove to dry.

As Iris began filling pans and placing them on the stove to boil, Rose noticed the straining waistband of her cotton dress. Suddenly, everything made sense, Iris' pasty look, her recent habit of lying down in the middle of the day. Another storm was coming.

Rose knew it wouldn't be long before her father caught on. "So, Iris," he drawled, sitting back one night after supper, "explain this. We're half-starved but you're getting fat." Sarcasm was his favourite way to start a racket. "How come?"

Iris backed up against the door frame and peeped at him through the curls hanging over her face. The look gave her away. "Wouldn't listen, would you?" he bawled, dark eyes flashing. "Fucked around 'til you got knocked up, probably been with every young Christer from here to Carbonear! Was it the Parker brat? By God, if it was, there'll be hell to pay."

Rose heard the slap as Iris stumbled forward into the hall. Dan opened his mouth to say something, changed his mind and stormed out of the house. The dam had burst. The tension of the past few weeks had been released in a violent five minutes.

**

By summer, Iris' condition was common knowledge but she took no pains to hide. She went out when she felt like it, looked everyone straight in the eye and dared them to comment. But at home, things were different. The baby wasn't mentioned. Iris was expected to go about her housework as before.

Iris never talked to Rose about what she might name the baby, whether she wanted a boy or a girl. And certainly nothing about her feelings, that wasn't Iris' way. But now and then, Rose would catch her sitting with her hand on her swollen stomach, her face full of despair.

Daisy was disgusted with Iris' situation. "Wonder who the father is," she mused one day, a smirk on her lips. "Could be Bert Parker, I s'pose, but I can't see the Parkers taking Iris into the family. Chalk and cheese there. However, if Bert *is* the father, I can see Dad trying to finagle money out of them."

Rose thought of her mother and how she might feel about Iris and a baby, but she pushed away these thoughts. "Well, Iris went with all the boys," she said, uncomfortable with talking about it, "so it's hard to know."

"True. And we're not likely to find out who it is from the sweet, little mother, are we?" Besides looking like the old man, Daisy could be just as sarcastic at times.

On the morning of September seventeenth, Iris suddenly grabbed her belly. "Jesus," she barked, "go get Aunt Julie. Quick!" When Rose came back with Julie, Iris was rolling around in the bed, cursing like a sailor.

"Iris," Julie said, sternly, "if I was you, I'd get on the Lord's good side because you're gonna need His help from now on. And right now, you need *my* help, so watch the language!"

Rose watched Iris fall back in the bed, a stunned look on her face. You never took the Lord's name in vain around Julie Fisher without being chastised.

"Rose, you'll have to be my nurse. Get the kettle boiling," ordered Julie, "then bring me something I can tear into strips for cloths." Rose looked around frantically, wondering what to do first. It wasn't enough that she was about to see her first birth. She also had to help out!

After an hour of Iris' grunting and screaming, Julie smiled. "Hot water, Rose." As Rose came back with the kettle, a slimy head appeared beneath Iris' nightgown. Iris howled and the baby slid into the blanket Julie held ready. "It's a little girl," said Julie, her voice soft. "Dip the knife in the water, Rose, and hand it to me. Quick, now!" As Julie moved to cut the cord, Rose felt the old weakness pass over her. "Sit down 'til it passes, m'dear," Julie chuckled. "Can't have our head nurse fainting on us."

After a tense few seconds, a piercing squeal filled the room. "Welcome aboard, little one." Julie washed the tiny baby, wrapped her in a flannel sheet and placed her in the bed beside an exhausted Iris.

Julie had just left when Dan came home from the garden carrying a brin bag half full of vegetables. "The baby came," Rose said carefully, meeting him at the door.

He grunted and followed her upstairs. As they went in the bedroom door, Rose saw the look Iris gave him and it almost broke her heart. She was begging his forgiveness.

"Now then," he drawled, looking down on Iris and the little bundle lying on her chest, "you got it over with. But don't think the house is gonna turn into a nursery. Keep the young one upstairs outa my way. Whatever's got to be done, do it up here." His lip curled. "As they say, you made your bed!" And with that, he went downstairs to get his dinner.

"Never mind him," Rose ventured, hoping to make Iris feel better. "I'll help you look after the baby." Iris stared at her, the blue eyes questioning.

"What are you gonna call her, Iris?" Rose asked, daring to hope.

"I don't know, maybe Marie."

"What about a middle name? What about Marie Rose?"

"No, just Marie."

"Well, I was wondering ..." But Iris had already turned away. "Never mind."

Twenty-One

A month later, Iris still hadn't gotten her energy back. She was pale, her eyes ringed with dark circles. And she was under pressure from Dan; everything to do with the child, nursing, changing, everything, had to be done upstairs, away from him.

So it was Rose who took over the care of Marie. She loved the gurgles, the drooly grins, the way the baby clung to her when she picked her up. She spent hours upstairs holding the baby, murmuring words of comfort as she dreamt of having her own child someday. The baby gave her a purpose, added some joy to her life.

The days had gone by quickly, it was already the end of October. Rose had got up, as usual, to change the baby before going down to breakfast. But something was different this time, the frail, little body felt limp as Rose tried to shift her to her shoulder. Alarmed, she looked into the baby's face, saw that her eyes were closed.

Rose gently placed the baby back in the crib and ran to the landing. "Iris," she hollered, "come up quick! The baby's not movin'."

Iris came upstairs grumbling. "What's the racket?" She picked up the baby, held her out at arm's length. The baby's head fell forward. "My God," Iris murmured, "go get Daddy."

Rose left the house running. She crossed the Green and made for the Point, where her father was working in the garden. The cold wind off the harbour slashed through her thin dress as she raced through the potholes, breaking the skin of ice that had formed overnight, splashing water up over her stockings.

She ran past two old men leaning against a boat in the landwash. Felt their eyes follow her along the Harbour Road, imagined what they were thinking. *Look at the scrawny youngster with no coat on in this bitter wind. Got t'be one o'Dan Connor's crowd, poor little mite!*

She was almost there, might just make it before her breath gave out. She saw her father picking up old potato stalks, throwing them on the pile for Guy Fawkes next month. Rose raced across the damp earth, touched him lightly on the shoulder.

"Jesus, maid," he said, jerking his head around at the touch of Rose's hand. "What the hell are you doin', sneaking up behind me like that?"

Flinching at the anger in his sweaty, dirt-stained face, Rose tried to speak but she was shivering so hard the words got stuck. "Iris said, uh, Iris said—." Finally, crying and sniffing back the tears and snot running down her face, she stammered, "I-I think the baby's dead. When I picked her up, she was limp. Iris said to come home. C'mon, we got to go!"

Her task completed, she collapsed to the ground on her knees, felt the water soaking into her wool stockings as she sobbed into her frozen hands.

"Okay," said Dan, pulling her to her feet, "let's go see what's goin' on." He grabbed his old Navy coat off the fence post and dropped it over her shoulders. "There, you need it more than I do."

She pulled the heavy coat around her and followed him up the road, running awkwardly beside him as he scuffed along in his rubber boots, scattering loose stones as he went. They passed Sally Fisher's house, then Joe's. A little further on, as they turned left to take the shortcut over the Green, Rose began to hang back.

Iris was standing by the stove, wide-eyed and staring, arms folded across her waist. "She's not moving, I think she's dead," her voice flat, without emotion.

Rose ran upstairs and stood shivering over the crib, waiting for them to follow. She was chilled to the bone, wet stockings bagging around her ankles, the muddy hem of her thin dress hanging low in front.

The baby lay still, the veins under her skin giving the tiny face a blue cast. She was wearing the pink bonnet Molly had knitted her. Iris had covered her with an old patch quilt and tucked it under her chin, as if a little warmth would bring her around. Rose touched the tiny turned-up nose, the same nose as Iris and Uncle John. The Green nose, from Grandmother Fisher's side.

Dan came into the room and threw back the quilt. Put a finger on the baby's neck and lifted a delicate eyelid. Then, shaking his head, "Well, whatever happened, she's gone. I'll have to send word to Dr. Bennett." Iris turned pale and sank back on the bed.

"Here we go, another faint," Dan grumped. "The Fisher blood strikes again!" He passed Iris the glass of water from the dresser. "Listen, Iris, the baby's gone, you have to get used to it." As Iris began to sob, he put a hand on her shoulder. "Might be better anyway. You'll have less to do, right? You'll get your health back, we'll go on like before. Stop crying now, it'll be okay."

Rose's mouth dropped as she realized he was *relieved* the baby was gone. He had his housekeeper back without anything to interfere with his routine. Anxious to remove herself from his presence, she willed her legs forward to her bedroom.

Shivering from cold and shock, Rose stripped off her wet clothes and put on her other dress, the one that didn't have holes. Then her spare pair of wool stockings and on top of that, two old sweaters, one left behind by her mother. Her stomach clenched and she remembered that she hadn't eaten since a slice of bread the day before.

"Go and make some tea, Rose," came the voice from across the hall. She went downstairs, trying not to think about the cold, little body in the other room.

**

"Now then, girls," said Dan, as he finished his tea, "I have to walk to Heart's Content and get the doctor. He'll have to sign some papers. Probably say it was one o'them infant deaths you hear about. These things happen, nothing we could've done. Iris, you're still pale. Get some rest, you'll have to answer the doctor's questions later. Rose, you go get Ma." He put on his rubber boots and scuffed out through the gate, blowing smoke as he went.

Lena was in her rocking chair, knitting. Like most women, she knitted year round, kept a supply of mitts and vamps on hand to barter. "Sit down, Rose, Daisy'll be back the once. She's gone down to Parker's with some eggs, my cluckers are layin' real good those days."

"Dad said to come over."

Lena took a look at Rose's face and nodded. "Let's go," throwing aside her knitting and grabbing her coat.

Iris, wrapped up in a quilt on the daybed, watched without a word as they came in and went straight upstairs. The baby lay as if asleep. Lena touched the cold cheek, curved her hand around the pink bonnet for a moment and bowed her head. "Yes, my dear, she's gone."

Turning at the sound of the stifled sob, she put a hand on Rose's shoulder. "Oh Rose, it wasn't your fault. God wanted Marie with Him for reasons only He can know. Wipe your face now. Bring me some warm water, then you can go downstairs. I'll wash the dear, little soul and wait 'til the doctor comes.

A miserable hour later, Rose saw Dr. Bennett's car, one of the few on the shore, pull in at the gate. Dan was asleep in the front seat, head thrown back, his old, tweed cap covering his face. As the doctor hurried upstairs, he flopped down at the table. "Sit up, Iris. Try to look half alive when he comes down, he'll want to talk to you." He scrubbed his hands over his face, the way he did when he was tired. "Jesus, I'm bushed."

When Dr. Bennett came back downstairs, Rose noticed that everyone sat up straighter, just like when the minister or the school principal came in. The doctor checked his pocket watch, pushed it back into his tiny, waistcoat pocket and threw his bag on the woodbox beside Rose. He looked grumpy and anxious to be on his way.

Rose glared at the short, stocky man with the light hair and mustache who stood peering at them through wire-rimmed glasses. Dr. Roy Bennett had taken over for old Dr. Bursey a few years ago. Rose blamed him for sending her mother away, something she felt Dr. Bursey would never have done.

The doctor placed a chair near the daybed where Iris had propped herself into a sitting position, the quilt covering her legs. He leaned toward her, elbows on his knees. "Iris, your grandmother told me the events of the morning," looking intently into the blue eyes, "the baby found lifeless in her crib, and so on."

He spoke slowly and carefully, as if to a slow child. "I see no overt signs on the child. The only plausible explanation I have is Crib Death. Another way of saying I really have no idea, as no one does in such cases, of course. Do you have any sense, yourself, of what may have happened?"

Iris shook her head. "No doctor," she whispered, shy in the great man's presence. "Rose hollered and I went up and she was just limp." She lowered her eyes, tucked the quilt tighter around her legs.

Dr. Bennett reached for Iris' arm, held her wrist while he looked at his watch, then laid the arm gently back on her lap. "You're a bit the worse for wear, my girl. Better take it easy for a few days. Been a shock, no doubt." He slewed his chair back to look at Dan. "I did notice the baby seemed underweight, Dan. Was she not thriving?" he asked bluntly.

"Well, Doc, Iris was always saying the baby was sickly and not feeding good. But then, Iris is young, she wouldn't know much about it." He shrugged. "I dunno."

Lena turned from the stove where she'd been warming herself. "Julie Fisher borned the child, Doctor. She told me the baby was underweight and would need an awful lot of care." She reached into her sleeve for her handkerchief. "The poor, little thing just wasn't strong enough to go on."

"Yes ma'am, maybe you're right." He turned to look at Dan. "Maybe Mother Nature does what's best in certain circumstances. Anyway, Constable Shepherd will have to be notified, unexplained death and such. I'll call him myself, soon as I get home."

He shrugged into his overcoat, put on his hat and went to pick up his bag. "Huh," he grunted, peering at Rose over his glasses like she was an interesting bug. "Here's another one with very little meat on her bones." He went out the door, leaving Rose red-faced and grumpy.

Dan scowled as the door closed. "Shepherd won't be any trouble," he muttered. "Me n' him are old drinkin' buddies."

**

When Reverend Fairchild came by the next day, Rose suddenly remembered what Molly had told her. About the scene in the Rectory all those years ago, when Dan Connor and Lexie Fisher had stood in front of the young Reverend. "Lexie was pregnant with Iris," Molly had said, her voice breaking. "Looking ahead to a happy life with her new husband."

Lexie was locked away in a hospital now and Reverend Fairchild was about to bury her granddaughter, little Marie. Rose felt heavy with the sadness of it all.

The minister readied himself to go upstairs. "The two of us and Iris will be sufficient, Mrs. Pahsons," he said quietly, in the clipped English accent. In a few minutes alone with the dead baby, with only Lena and Iris looking on, Reverend Fairchild baptized the child. Marie Connor, deceased daughter of Iris Connor, father unknown. A fact so recorded.

They buried the baby in a corner of the cemetery, in a small, wooden box Dan had cobbled together the day before. Rose watched from outside the fence as the Reverend said a few words. Watched her father place the box into the hole and scrape some frozen soil and moss on top, while Iris stood like a statue between Julie and Lena, her face empty and hard. As they bowed their heads for the Lord's Prayer, Rose walked away, her throat tight with tears.

Over the next few weeks, Rose grieved the little girl she'd grown to love. And she pondered the many things she didn't understand. The baby had been fine during the night, when she'd got up to give her the bottle. What had happened between then and the morning?

The weeks passed. Rose looked on as her father and Iris went back to their normal routine. All signs of the baby had been removed, the crib, the tiny shirts, the pink, knitted cap. Little Marie might never have happened.

The child had lived six weeks. She'd spent her entire life in a crib in an upstairs bedroom, her only comfort the thin arms of a twelve-year-old girl. The snow came and settled in drifts over the grave, and Rose mourned in silence.

Twenty-Two

By the spring of '36, Lexie had been away for three years. Any plans to visit her had been put aside as two years earlier the hospital had sent word that they were quarantined for TB, the disease being rampant all over. Sally's persistent efforts had resulted in a single letter from the hospital at the end of last year. It contained a disheartening note. *The patient shows sporadic signs of lucidity but overall, she is nonresponsive.*

Rose was tormented by questions. What was her mother going through? Did she ever think about her family? "I worry about Mother," she said to Lena. "The other night I dreamt the nurses found her dead in her bed. I can't get it out of my mind."

"Well, maybe you need something to occupy your time," said Lena. "Ask Molly, she might be glad of some help. Your Grandmother Fisher just moved in with her and John." She tut-tutted. "About time Sally made the move, I mean she *is* over eighty!" Rose caught the grin on Daisy's face. Lena was closing in on eighty herself.

Molly seemed happy with Rose's offer. "And your grandmother will get to see more of you, she'd like that." Flushed with success from her first attempt at independence, Rose decided to ask her father if she could help with the garden on the Point.

"Go ahead," he said. "But if you find the treasure, it's mine." There was supposed to be pirate treasure buried somewhere on Bloody Point. He always said he knew where it was but, of course, he never got around to searching for it.

"Well," said Rose, "if it hasn't been found in three hundred years, it's doubtful I'll find it now."

Dan gave her a long, appraising look. "What's this? Is little Rose getting a sense of humour? Maybe you can help our Daisy, she's a real sour ass." And you're an asshole, thought Rose, indignant at the comment about her sister!

Rose's days were full now. She especially enjoyed the solitude of working in the garden, watching the boys rowing lazily around the harbour in borrowed punts, their shouts and loud, raucous laughter echoing around her head as they called out to her.

But now and then, she felt restless and impatient. "Gran, I think I'm going crazy," she said. "Sometimes, I feel nervy, like I can't stand to have people around me, and I don't just mean Iris." She paused. "Do you think I might get sick like Mother?"

Lena smiled. "Oh, Rose, don't be so hard on yourself. You've just become a woman. You're growing up, that's all. We all feel like that at your age." She grinned. "You'll feel it again when the change of life comes."

Later that day, as Rose came in from the garden, Iris tossed something at her. "This telegram came," she said, her face a blank. "It's from the hospital. Go ahead, read it."

Rose started to read. *Mrs. Connor is very ill with TB. We will keep you— keep you—.*

"Informed, Rose, informed!" shaking her head at her sister's lack of education. "Anyway, there's TB all over the island, you must have expected it." It had been said that the St. John's Sanitorium was over-flowing. Three people from New Perlican had been taken there over the past few months.

Rose had to sit down as a wave of weakness passed over her. It was happening, the thing she'd been carrying in her mind for weeks. "But she's in a hospital," she said, still hoping. "They'll make her better, won't they?"

Two weeks later, another telegram arrived. *May 15, 1936. Dear Mr. Connor, I am sorry to inform you that Mrs. Connor passed away early this morning. Please make arrangements for the body to be picked up at the train station in Carbonear tomorrow. Dr. L. Jones.*

On hearing the words read aloud, Rose fainted. She came around to the smell of liniment, Iris holding the bottle under her nose and poking her in the shoulder. Her father was sitting at the table, the telegram dangling from his hand.

"Okay, Rose, you back with us? All right, I got things to do. Got to see Joe Fisher about taking his horse across the Barrens tomorrow." Rose closed her eyes, listened to him making plans. He might have been going on a holiday. "On the way I'll run over, tell Ma and Daisy."

Rose glared at him. "You could have gone to see her. John would have taken you along when he went that time."

His face hardened. "Is that what you think, that I'd go to John Fisher with my hand out? Don't *ever* mention it again!" He grabbed his coat and left, banging the door behind him.

Iris had been doing the wash before the telegram came. She was back at the tub now, her face dripping from the steam. "Iris, don't you feel even a little bit bad about Mother?" The words had escaped from Rose's mouth before she could stop them.

Iris spun on her knees. "You know what?" she hissed. "Her bein' dead won't make a damn bit of difference to me. Not a goddamned bit!" She turned back to the washboard, scrubbing furiously, splashing water up her arms and over her chest.

As Rose fell back on the daybed, chastened by Iris' outburst, the door opened and Daisy came in. "Mom is gone." She sat down heavily at the table. "Never had much of a life. Did she, Iris?"

The silence festered for several seconds, then Iris jumped to her feet. "Maybe she was better off in there, ever think o'that?"

Daisy exploded from the chair. "You'd like to think so, wouldn't you? And sad as it sounds, maybe she *was* better off because all you ever did was bawl at the poor soul. Probably caused half her problem." At sixteen, Daisy was almost a woman herself now. She was no longer afraid of Iris.

"You bitch!" Iris flung the scrub brush into the tub. "Makin' snide remarks, like you know what you're talking about! Think I've had it soft all those years?" She yanked the door open. "Get out!"

Daisy darted to the door, her face rigid with anger. "See ya at the funeral," she sneered, slamming the door so hard the dishes rattled in the pantry shelves.

Rose knew what was coming. "I'm not your slave," Iris growled, looking more upset than angry as she headed for the stairs. "Get off your ass and finish this wash."

**

The next morning Rose paced the floor, waiting for her mother's coffin to arrive. Dora Miller had come to wait with her. "I didn't say goodbye to my dear friend when she left," Dora said, her eyes full. "But I'll make sure to welcome her back home now."

Finally, they heard the sound of hooves outside as Joe Fisher guided his horse to a stop at the gate. Beside him in the driver's seat was John, his face pale and twisted with emotion.

Rose stared at the plain box on the back of the cart, her breath catching in her throat. "This is hard for you, Pet," said Dora, putting her arm around her shoulder. "Stay near me now, 'til they bring her in."

Rose had hoped the coffin could stay at John's until the burial, but her father had other plans. "Set it up between two chairs in my bedroom," he told the men, as they glared at him with disgust. Even in death, thought Rose, Mother isn't free of him.

"Rose," said Dora, "why don't you come up with me and Jonah tonight?"

"No, thanks anyway, Miz Miller. I looked after Mother for a long time. It wouldn't be right to leave her now."

"Yes, I understand," sniffling into her apron. "Give me a shout if you need anything."

That night, Rose lay awake thinking about her mother's body lying in a box in the downstairs bedroom. She longed to look at the familiar face again, tell her mother how much she'd missed her. But the coffin was closed and she didn't know why. Did her mother look so different that Rose wouldn't recognize her? The only thing Rose was sure of was that this was the end of the hope that her mother might someday get well and come home, the hope that had been keeping her going these past few years.

She got up the next morning with a dull ache across her forehead. Her father was finishing his breakfast like it was any other day. "When will Mother be buried?" she asked.

"Day after tomorrow. Reverend Fairchild was notified, everything is ready."

"I heard Carrie Hall is here, came all the way from Detroit," said Iris, from the pantry.

Rose saw her father scowl. "Came all this way for a funeral? She's crazy as she always was!"

Later that morning, there was a knock at the door and Carrie came in, handing Iris something wrapped in a cloth. "Raisin bread from Mom, just baked," she said. Her eyes were red, like she'd been crying. "I'm sorry to hear about your mother, she was ..." She sat down at the table and rooted in her pocket for a handkerchief.

"I'll make some tea," said Iris, nodding at Rose to go sit at the table with Carrie.

"Gosh Rose, you're fourteen," said Carrie. "When I left you were only ten, just a kid." Rose remembered the day Carrie had come to tell them she was leaving. For days after that, her mother had hardly spoken a word.

"Did you get the birthday cards I sent?" Rose nodded shyly. "I was so proud when your mother named you Carrie Rose and asked me to be your Godmother. You look like her, y'know." Rose nodded again, afraid to speak for fear of crying.

"And how's Daisy? Still the strong, silent type, I guess." Carrie grinned. "You always knew Daisy's state of mind by those dark eyebrows. She could really pull 'em down when she was in a bad mood."

"Did you come for the funeral?" Iris poured tea and sat down herself.

"No, I'd been planning the trip for a couple years, saved every bit of extra money I could between layoffs at the factory. It's been tough with the Depression but things are looking up lately." She sighed.

"Mom writes me all the time so I knew Lexie was in the hospital." She brought out her handkerchief again. "I was just too late to see her."

Iris glanced toward the downstairs bedroom. "Go on in if you like, but the coffin is closed."

Carrie nodded. "Yeah, it was TB, maybe that's why. To keep it from spreading." She ran her fingers through short, brown hair styled in soft waves. "I'll spend a few minutes with her before I go. Right now I need a smoke." Iris and Rose stared, wide-eyed, as Carrie brought a cigarette package out of her pocket. "Mom gives me hell if I smoke in front of her. She says I've been corrupted in the States, maybe it's true, I don't know."

Dan came in with a yaffle of wood, dumped it in the woodbox. "Well, Carrie," he drawled, "long time, no see. Comin' home for a funeral, eh? Must be doing well down there."

"I didn't come for the funeral, just happened that way." She eyed Dan closely. "I was really surprised when Mom wrote me that Lexie went in the hospital. What drove her to that, I wonder?"

Dan shrugged. "Can't say. Life is hard, isn't it?"

"Harder for some than others," Carrie replied, holding his gaze again before rising. "Thank you, Iris, for the tea. I'll spend a moment with her now, before I go."

"Don't be too long," snapped Dan. "Max and Ruth are comin' to pay their respects."

Carrie turned quickly, stared at Dan. "Mm-m, respect. Better late than never, I guess." Ignoring his dark look, she took Rose's hand. "Come with me, Rose, I need moral support."

They stood in front of the coffin, Carrie's hand on Rose's shoulder. "Wish I could take you back to Detroit with me, Rosie, for her sake," Carrie said, quietly. "Maybe in a few years you can come down and live with us, me and Richard. He works at a newspaper office. We could help you get a job."

"Do you have any children?" Rose asked.

"No, I don't." Carrie dipped her head, a tiny smile on her lips. "Funny, I remember Lexie and me talking about that once, a long time ago." She reached for her handkerchief and sat back on the bed. "She should have listened to me, Rose. About a lot of things."

Rose sat quietly beside Carrie until the crying was over. "Mother would be glad you came."

"You always called her Mother, didn't you? You were the only one who did, I thought it was so cute when you were little." Carrie smiled. "Come to think of it, Lexie did the same thing. Guess you copied her, didn't you, Honey?" Rose nodded back at Carrie, happy to hear her mother spoken of in a kindly manner.

They went back into the kitchen, Carrie still dabbing at her eyes. "I gotta go now, Carrie Rose. Mom is waiting for me." She hugged Rose hard. "I'll see you tomorrow at the church." She turned at the door. "There's something I regret, Dan. A small thing, I suppose, but it may have made all the difference to how things turned out. I wish I'd never agreed to let you use the loft, back at the beginning."

As Carrie hurried out the door, Rose watched her father's features twist into an ugly scowl. Whatever Carrie had meant by the comment, it certainly had an effect.

**

A month after Lexie had been buried, Sally Fisher passed away quietly in her sleep. "Everyone says she died of a broken heart," said Molly, after the funeral, "and they're probably right. It's not natural to outlive your children."

Rose walked along with Molly and John, keeping an eye ahead to where Daisy was strolling with Steve Gordon, the boy she had a crush on.

"Mom hung on all those years," said John, "waiting for Lexie to come home. After Lexie died, I think she just gave up."

Rose thought back to the many times she'd arrived at Grandmother's house to find the old lady struggling over a letter to the hospital, her poor eyes inches from the paper as she whispered words aloud to herself. Words that might explain to these people how much she missed her daughter. And how much it would mean to receive news of her.

"I spent a lot of time at Grandmother Fisher's after Mother was taken away," said Rose. "I'll miss her."

Molly smiled. "I will, too. Isn't it funny? Years ago, when John and I were courtin', I used to think Miz Fisher figured I wasn't good enough for him. But, y'know, while she was living with us, I came to see her in a different light. She confided in me about a lot of things. Especially her regrets about the early days after Ken died, what she might have done differently."

John put his arm around Molly. "Guess we all have those regrets," he said, quietly, his eyes full.

Twenty-Three

With the loss of her mother and now Grandmother Fisher, Rose was thrown adrift once again. Memories of her mother were never far away, as now and then something would catch her unawares. A woman with blonde hair tied back with a ribbon, the smell of spruce trees, and especially, someone idly humming, "Abide with Me." Her mother would spring vividly to mind and Rose would feel the memory like a physical pain.

Her father had passed her the job of drying his catch, such as it was, on the flake behind Gran's house. The local fishermen had washed their hands of him, but sometimes he'd walk down to Turk's Cove and go out in the bay with his old Uncle Leo, his father's brother. "You're lucky Leo is willing to put up with you," Lena would mutter, her tone lacking the usual spirit. Has Gran finally given up on her son, Rose wondered?

But Rose didn't mind the work. On sunny days, she went over to the flake every few hours to turn over the stiff, yellow triangles so they could dry properly. At the end of the day, she stacked them in round pooks and covered them with boughs for the night.

It was a late afternoon in July. Finished for the day, Rose was busily covering the fish when everything went dark. Looking up, she saw a huge object floating over the top of Norman's Hill. It was shaped like a big, fat cigar.

Frightened, she took off in a mad dash across the bridge and into the yard, where her father was sawing up wood. "There's s-something in the sky, floating over Norman's Hill." She had trouble catching her breath. "I'm afraid it's gonna fall on us."

He laughed. "Yeah, I saw it. It's an air balloon, Rose, something the Germans invented. It's called the Hindenburg, actually carries people back and forth across the Atlantic. It floated over St. John's a while back. There was a picture in the paper, you could see people waving from the windows."

Rose shook her head. "What? But ..." She couldn't believe what she was hearing.

He chuckled at her confusion. "Never mind, it won't last. It'll be planes that take people across to Europe. They can't do it yet but there are people workin' on it all the time, tryin' out different engines." He shook his head. "Balloons won't stand up to passenger travel. They're filled with gas, that's what keeps 'em up there. Jesus, anything can happen with gas."

Rose stared at him, her heart full of grudging admiration. He was always surprising her with the things he knew. And now and then, when he was in the mood, he took the time to explain something she didn't understand.

She thought how rare it was to catch a glimpse of his softer side. Like the day she went to tell him the baby had died, and he'd wrapped his coat around her shoulders. Was this why her mother had loved him, back at the beginning? And what had changed him into the hard drinking, pitiless man they knew?

The sighting of the balloon had been a big event and a topic of conversation for weeks, but Rose quickly put it behind her. What could it possibly mean to someone like her, a fourteen-year-old girl without a mother who didn't know what the next day would bring? Passenger balloons or passenger planes, none of these things caused even a ripple in her life.

**

A few days later, Rose was on her way home to supper, hot and tired after a busy day. She was thinking about the fish and brewis Iris had said she was going to make when she saw a brown car at the gate. What had her father done now, she wondered? Was he in trouble with the law?

Nervous of what she'd find, she went around to the back door and crept into the hall. "I figure the thing'll blow up," her father was saying. "Bound to happen, it's filled with gas, for Christ sake!" He was still talking about the Hindenburg, hadn't really stopped since the silvery tube had floated over Norman's Hill a month ago.

"Yes," said a man's voice, "might be a bad experiment in the end."

Rose stepped timidly into the kitchen, saw a tall man with dark hair sitting at the table with her father, and a woman perched on the daybed. "Ah, here's Rose now." Dan got up and steered her toward the table. "Rose, this is Mr. and Mrs. Butler. They're from Whitbourne."

As the strangers looked her over, Rose could only imagine what they saw. A skinny girl with short, blonde hair cut straight across, sweaty bangs sticking to a high forehead, scrawny arms peeling from sunburn and tired, blue eyes looking back in confusion. To add to the picture, the hem of her old cotton dress hung down on one side where it had caught on the longer of the flake. Quite the sight, all right.

The strange man stood to meet her. "Hello, Rose. You look like you've been working hard." He was so tall his head almost touched the ceiling.

She squinted up at him and twisted her mouth into what she hoped was a smile. The woman on the daybed stirred and nodded, murmured something that might have been hello. Rose waited for this strange puzzle to be solved. She had a feeling she wouldn't like the answer.

"Rose," Dan drawled, in his best company voice, "the Butlers are here to take you back to Whitbourne to help out in the house. I told 'em you're a good worker. Get cleaned up now, and pack your stuff." He gave a quick nod toward the stairs. "Go ahead."

Still confused and feeling slightly dazed, she looked around for Iris, who was nowhere in sight. "Rose, wake up," her father said, the hint of impatience creeping into his voice. "Listen, you're big enough now to do housework and earn your keep. So go ..."

Mr. Butler broke in. "You'll be all right with us, Rose. Whitbourne is not all that far away." He sounded kind.

Mrs. Butler wiggled off the saggy daybed and yanked her dress back into place over wide hips. "We've got a big house, Rose," her thin smile at odds with her matter-of-fact tone. "And four youngsters, three, six, eight, and twelve. Mr. Butler works with the railway and I run our little General Store, so we could really use some help." Rose was trying her best to follow what the woman was saying. "We'll give you a dollar a week and you can live in."

They were all waiting for her to say something. Mr. Butler smiled as if to encourage her. Still, she couldn't find her voice.

"This'll give you a bit of money and some training for later on, Rose," Dan spoke up. "Go on now and get ready, the Butlers want to get back before dark."

Rose held back the tears 'til she was upstairs in her bedroom. Bone weary from working in the hot sun all day, she had no energy to protest. Anyway, it wouldn't change her father's mind. He'd come up with the plan and it would go his way, like always. Shocked into submission, she washed herself, tied up her few bits of clothes into an old flannelette sheet and floated downstairs like a sleepwalker.

As she went into the kitchen, Mr. Butler turned to Dan. "Thanks now, Dan. She'll be fine, don't worry." He put on his grey, felt hat and went out the door. Mrs. Butler picked up her purse, nodded to Dan and followed her husband. Rose fell in at the end of the line, moving forward like someone in a dream. Or a nightmare.

"There you go, Rose." Mr. Butler opened the car door for her. "We'll soon be on our way." As she crawled into the back seat with her bundle, Rose was immediately seized with a rush of excitement and fear. It was the first time she'd ever been in a car!

The huge machine bounced through the potholes, kicking up dust and scattering rocks as it sped along. Rose stared out the car window, wide-eyed and slightly dizzy as the houses and trees flew by. When they rounded a corner, she grabbed the seat for fear of tipping over into the ditch.

They were soon leaving New Perlican and driving along by the Burnt Hills. Rose looked out over the dusty, stunted trees on the side of the road, saw people scattered about the hills, leaning over patches of berries. Was Daisy out there, picking blueberries for Gran?

They drove through Heart's Content, past the house Will and Jean used to live in. Rose felt the tears fill her eyes. Would she ever see them again? Would she ever see home again? Maybe she'd been sold to these people for good!

On they drove, through the small communities along the Trinity Bay shore; Heart's Desire, Heart's Delight, Cavendish, Whiteway, Green's Harbour, on and on, the names melting together in her head. She was amazed to find there were so many places up this way. She'd heard of some of them, of course, but had never been to any of them. And she knew nothing about Whitbourne, except that it had a railway station.

"The drive'll take a couple hours," Mr. Butler had told Rose, when they'd started out. After that, neither he nor Mrs. Butler made any further attempt at conversation, neither with her nor with each other. Weary of watching out the window, Rose leaned back and stared at the backs of their heads, his thick, black hair, her small, green hat with a feather on the side. She took deep breaths to keep from crying. What was going to happen next, what would be expected of her?

Finally, they pulled up in front of a large, three-storey house with a veranda running along the front. Still holding her bundle, Rose followed the Butlers into the house. "Praise the Lord, we're home," Mrs. Butler exclaimed, as her children came to meet them.

"Shirley, Evelyn, this is Rose," she said, as the two little girls gave Rose a shy smile. "She's the new maid." So that's what I am, thought Rose, nice to know. "And this is Jacob." The eight-year-old stood looking at her, a sullen smirk on his face. This one was likely *not* going to be her favourite!

"And here's Allan, the oldest. He's twelve." The tall, lanky boy smiled as he nodded hello. He looked like his father, the same black hair falling over his forehead, big brown eyes with long lashes. Although two years younger than she was, his gaze caused Rose's cheeks to burn, which irritated her and made her blush even more.

Sitting with the family at a supper of baloney sandwiches, Rose felt awkward and shy, and still stunned at being carried miles away from home without warning. "You must be hungry, Rose," said Mr. Butler. "Don't be shy, make a long arm." Even so, Rose had to force herself to eat.

"We'll look at your room now," Mrs. Butler announced, after supper. They walked up two long flights of stairs to a hot, stuffy room in the attic. "You're overlooking the back garden," she explained, pointing to a small dormer window. "We plant vegetables down there. Had to cut down some trees last year, it was getting too shady."

Rose looked down from the window, saw several big trees that were different from any she knew. "The trees around here are bigger than at home," she said, to fill the space left by Mrs. Butler's comment. It only served to make her more homesick. She wanted to cry, to fall on her knees and beg the woman to take her back home.

"Yes, things grow well around here. The Commission set up a farm nearby, it's called Markland." The colony had faced bankruptcy around '34, was now governed by a British Commission. "Trying to make farmers out of fishermen," Mrs. Butler snorted. "Bloody Englishmen and their ideas! Except for the cottage hospitals, of course, that *was* a good idea."

Rose thought of the new hospital in Old Perlican that everyone at home was so grateful for. "Yes, we have one down the shore from us."

"So, here's your room," said Mrs. Butler, as Rose's gaze swept across a single bed with a feather mattress, a washstand with a mirror and a large white basin and jug, and a small dresser that would easily hold her few rags. A slop pail stood in the corner.

"This can serve as a night table." Mrs. Butler pointed to an orange crate covered with a flowered, cotton skirt. A small oil lamp sat on top. "There's a Bible there in the top shelf."

The Butlers must be Bible people, Rose thought, remembering the small cross hanging from the mirror in the car. Were they Holy Rollers, the ones who got up in church and started talking crazy? Daisy had told her it was called "speaking in tongues." Sounded a lot livelier than the long, mournful services at her own church, not that Rose had been there lately.

Against the faded green and white roses of the wallpaper hung the only picture, a sampler with red, white, and blue stitching. *There'll Always be an England*, with the Union Jack in the corner. "My father was in the Great War," Mrs. Butler commented. "Died at Beaumont Hamel, I was just a young girl."

"Yes," said Rose, "my father was in the war, too." Maybe that was the reason her father drank so much. It was hard to know because he never talked about it.

"Now that we have a new king, maybe there'll be no more wars. Although there's all that talk about Edward and that Wallis Simpson woman. Divorced twice already, she is." Mrs. Butler shook her head and tut-tutted. "The brother would have been a better choice, don't you think?"

Rose had no opinion on that. She did remember, however, that when her father had heard the news about Edward, he'd gone all out with the celebrations. Any excuse!

"So, any questions?" asked Mrs. Butler, as Rose shook her head. "All right, then. Before you go to bed, I want you to get Shirley and Evelyn washed and into their bed clothes." Adding as she turned to go, "Tomorrow, we'll go over your duties."

Dispirited and lonely, and still confused, Rose dragged herself down to the first floor, hauled a bucket of hot water up to the second floor and went through the motions of washing the girls and helping them into their nightgowns. The little ones giggled as Rose tucked them into bed but she was too tired to respond.

After hearing bedtime prayers, Rose crawled back up to her room in the attic. Relieved to finally fall into bed, she turned out the lamp and let the darkness settle over her. She fell asleep instantly.

**

The next morning, Mrs. Butler went over the household routine while Rose stumbled from one task to the next, trying her best to follow instructions. It wasn't long before she knew what her worst duty would be. Every morning, she had to empty the chamber pots and slop pails in the outhouse out back. What a way to start the day, she thought! But the work routine was well-established so she'd have to try her best to fit in. She had no choice but to resign herself to her predicament.

"I get breakfast ready myself every morning," Mrs. Butler explained. "At ten, a local woman comes in to cook dinner for noon. She'll serve it, clean up afterwards and prepare supper before she leaves at four. Flo Gosse has worked for us since her husband died in a woods accident some years ago. A quiet woman, you'll like her." Rose's spirits lifted. There was another person working here, someone to talk to who wasn't a Butler.

Mrs. Gosse arrived promptly at ten. "Hello," she said quietly, offering her hand. "Flo Gosse, nice to meet you. I should mention, I like to work without chit-chat. No offense meant, dear, just my nature."

A little put out by the curt remark, Rose gave a quick nod and shook the woman's hand. "Rose Connor. Just arrived yesterday. Didn't know I was coming 'til I got here." Kidnapped, really, she thought, bitterly.

She soon found out how quiet the woman really was. There was no small talk, even when they ate dinner together in the kitchen. Other than frequent updates on the weather, the woman had nothing to say except, "T'was foggy last night," or "Goodness, so hot out there." Mrs. Gosse worked quietly all day in her hairnet and flowered apron and left just as quietly at four, leaving Rose to serve supper. She had to grab her own on the fly while she was washing the dishes.

Washing for such a crowd took all day Monday. The rest of the week was filled with chores; making beds, dusting, cleaning lamps, bringing in coal, washing floors, there was no end to it. Rose struggled to stay one step ahead of Clara Butler's sharp tongue.

Only at night, in her bed, did Rose have time to ponder the mystery of how and why she'd been sent into slavery in Whitbourne. Did her father owe money to Mr. Butler? Was she part of the repayment? Nothing would surprise her.

She thought of the two of them, her father and Iris, alone in the house now. Maybe it was as simple as getting rid of her. They'd gotten rid of Daisy, then her mother, and now herself. He was the big boss, Iris was his slave. No one else to aggravate them.

Twenty-Four

Rose struggled on. Beside the housework, there were the children to look after. The two little girls were easy but young Jacob was under-foot all the time, teasing them, making them cry. And Rose had to be careful of how she treated him because he was obviously Mommy's pet. She longed for school to open so she could be rid of the little pest.

Allan was seldom around the house, but sometimes he'd tell her about some of the things he liked to do. "Me and my friends meet the trains and sell candy and ice-cream from Mom's shop to the pas-sengers," he said one day, as he counted out change at the table. "Had a good day today, usually do when the weather's warm." Then, he surprised her with a question. "What's it like in New Perlican, Rose? Who's in your family, how many brothers and sisters?"

Rose gave an inward shake of her head. How could this boy, a pampered child in a loving home, ever fathom the Connor crowd? What would he think if she told him some of the things she'd seen? Like the bitterly cold night her mother had been locked out of the house. The memory was still raw.

Rose had woke to a sound from downstairs, found her mother in the kitchen shivering in her nightdress and slippers after wander-ing outside in the night. Her father had come staggering out of his bedroom in a belligerent fog of liquor fumes and cigarette smoke. "Christ, can't I get a break from this crazy woman?" He'd pushed her mother outside and locked the door behind her. "If she wants to go outdoors, let her go outdoors."

For the rest of the night, Rose had lain awake listening to her mother whimpering on the steps below. At daylight the next morning, her father had hollered up the stairs. "Go get her, Rose. Don't want that bitch, Dora Miller, to see her. I'm in no mood for her lip this morning!" And he'd gone back to bed. Rose had helped her mother upstairs. Then she'd brought her some hot tea and climbed into bed beside her, warming her with her own body.

What would the handsome, young Allan Butler say to a story like that, Rose wondered, as she pretended to have something to do and hurried upstairs?

**

By October, Rose was in a bad way. She couldn't keep up the work load and she was exhausted all the time. Impossible as it seemed, because she could hardly get any thinner, she'd even lost weight. Life was funny. She was finally in a place where the food was plentiful and she was too tired to eat it.

As hard as she tried, she was still getting reprimanded by Mrs. Butler for this or that shortcoming. She dreaded the end of the day, when the mistress would come through the door with that grumpy look on her face. How did Mr. Butler put up with the old sourpuss!?

Strangely enough, in her silent presence, Mrs. Gosse, the day worker and part-time weather forecaster, had become the calm centre of Rose's hectic day. They were working quietly together in the kitchen, Rose stoking the stove, Mrs. Gosse cleaning trout for the Butlers' dinner, when the older woman glanced at the table. "Is that the Mister's lunch over there? He must have forgotten it. Put on your coat, Rose, and get on down to the station. No need to hurry."

Rose strolled along in the crisp, fall air, alert to the screeching of blue jays overhead, the squadron of starlings bombarding a flaming dogberry tree in the next garden. It crossed her mind that she could run away right now, ask someone the way out of Whitbourne and start walking, back down the shore toward home. But she'd have to sleep in the woods at night, was she brave enough for that? And what if she met some ruffians out looking for trouble?

The pros and cons of making an escape occupied her mind until she suddenly found herself at the station. Mr. Butler came over to the counter with a worried look on his face. "Rose, what happened? Is anything wrong at the house?"

"No sir, you forgot your lunch. Miz Gosse said I should bring it down to you."

"Oh, my Lord." A relieved grin sparked the dark, good looks. "Clara keeps telling me I'm losing my memory, maybe she's right. Thanks, Rose."

Rose left the station wishing she didn't have to go back to that big house where she felt alone in her misery. Maybe she'd get another letter from Daisy today. That always helped a bit, even if it made her homesick to see Daisy's slanty writing on the envelope.

She was crossing the station yard when, from somewhere among the carriages and carts, she heard her name. She stopped and looked around, thinking she'd misheard. Then she saw him step out of a car. But it couldn't be Uncle Max. It was a ghost! As she wavered between staying and running away, the image started toward her. When he touched her arm, she almost fainted.

"Rose, what are you doing here?" He looked like he'd seen a ghost himself. "You don't look well. Are you all right?" He craned his neck, scanning the area. "Are you with someone from home?" Right away, her eyes filled up. "My dear maiden," he said, "tell me what's going on."

It was Uncle Max all right, he always called her and Daisy maidens. "I-I thought I was seeing your token," she sniffed. "I thought you were going to die."

"What? My token?" Max chuckled. "Well, for one thing, if I was going to die I'd have to see my token, not you. Calm down now, I'm here in the flesh."

He led her to a bench and between sobs, she told him the whole story. As he listened, his face darkened. "Get in the car, Rose, you're goin' home!" At that moment, she loved Uncle Max more than anyone in the whole world.

They drove right to the Butler house, Rose sniffling all the way. She raced upstairs, tied her belongings back in the sheet and lugged it down to the kitchen where Mrs. Gosse was waiting. The woman who'd hardly said two words to her in all this time walked her to the door and surprised her with some kind last words.

"The job was too much for you, child. You go on home with your uncle. I'll mind the lasses 'til the Butlers get home." Then, with one raised eyebrow, "Herself will send you what's owed, I'm sure." So, the quiet lady had her own opinions after all! As a last surprise, Mrs. Gosse pulled her into a brief hug. "Cheerio, Rose. Good luck."

**

Max hardly spoke as they drove through the small communities, each one similar to the last, the houses clustered around a harbour, dark, spruce trees on the hills behind. They all look to the sea for their survival, thought Rose, just like my own place. They drove along by the Burnt Hills and it struck her. It was almost November. Blueberry season was long over, even partridgeberry time had come and gone.

"I'll go in first," said Max, as they pulled up at the door, and Rose fell in step behind him. Her father was sitting at the table with a cup of tea, a cigarette burning in his fingers. When he saw Max' face, he turned pale under his normally dark complexion. "Calm down, Max. I thought she was old enough to handle it, if she's not, she's not. Sit down, have a drop of tea."

"You are one lowlife bastard, Dan. That maiden was nowhere near ready to go into service and you know it. It was too much, she was doing the work of two people. Well, now she's back and the next time she goes away, it'd better be her own choice. Hear what I'm sayin'?"

Dan nodded his head several times. "Sure Max. Look, I didn't mean no harm. Maybe you're right, she was too young." He gestured toward the hall. "Go on upstairs, Rose, put your stuff away. Go over to Ma's, see what Daisy is doing. She'll be real happy to see you."

He sounded caring but Rose knew better. He'd backed down from Max like the coward he was and he was never going to be any different.

Meanwhile Iris, obviously shaken by the actions of their mild-mannered uncle, was standing open-mouthed in the pantry door.

"Okay, Rose, I'm going home," said Max. "I'll be around to see how you're doing, don't worry." And he was gone. Rose stood for a moment, the bundle of clothes at her feet, and looked at the people who could make her life really miserable from now on. But that was nothing new. Besides, she had Uncle Max on her side now.

And the sour face on Iris made it clear what her dear sister thought of her return, but that was nothing new, either. The main thing was, she was home and looking forward to seeing everyone, Daisy and Gran Parsons, Dora and the Miller girls, and Molly and John. And the harbour! She couldn't wait to see the harbour, the way the water changed colour, sometimes an angry dark blue, sometimes oily black and smooth as glass. Or a pretty baby blue, her favourite.

Funny, the things you miss when you're away from your own spot, Rose thought. Whitbourne didn't even have a harbour. Lots of nice, big trees but it was built in the woods, for God sake, there was no fresh, sea air to breathe. Iris could sulk all she wanted, Rose was too happy to be home to worry about big sister's moods.

The next day, she took the money she'd earned in Whitbourne and proceeded to Parker's Store. She bought tea, flour, sugar, raisins, and some bacon and proudly presented the parcel to a tight-lipped Iris. She also bought a length of blue cotton for Molly to scun up into a dress for her, and some red, patterned material for Gran to do the same for Daisy. It was the first time she'd ever bought anything with her own money and it felt wonderful!

Twenty-Five

Rose would always say that May of 1937 was notable for three events. First, on May sixth, the Hindenburg had crashed and burned somewhere in the States, thereby confirming her father's opinion of a gas-powered balloon. Second, on May twelfth, Mrs. Butler's recommendation having somehow reached the ears of the British government, the crown had passed to Edward's brother. George VI was the new king of England.

And third, Rose and Lucy Miller were going into service in Old Perlican, an old community further north along the shore, the first-settled of the two towns with similar names.

"The notice at the Post Office said the Rogers outfit needs two servants," Rose had told a dubious Lucy. "Whatd'ya think?"

"I dunno," Lucy's eyes wide with fear and possibilities. "Old Perlican is fifteen miles away! I'll have to see what Mom thinks."

Dora Miller had quibbled a bit but in the end she gave Lucy permission to go. And, as expected, Rose's father was only too happy to send her off, to Old Perlican or anywhere else for that matter. It had only been seven months since she'd left Whitbourne, but the hated ordeal had done something for Rose after all. It had given her the confidence to leave home and this time it was her own choice!

Uncle Max drove the excited fifteen-year-olds as far as New Chelsea, where a young man by the name of Calvin Barrett, a Rogers employee, picked them up. "Things are looking up already," Lucy whispered, and they giggled as the car got underway.

Young Mr. Barrett had a pleasant face and a head full of brown curls and when he spoke, which was seldom, his voice was so soft they could hardly hear it from the back seat. "You're a good driver, Calvin," said Lucy, in a suddenly-breathless voice as the shy, young man glanced at them in the rearview mirror.

"Uh, thanks," came the halting reply, a band of colour creeping up the back of his neck.

The Rogers family ran a big operation, fish plant, marine supplies outlet, several schooners and a general store, among other things. In fact, they seemed to own most of the town, one of the few businesses to have survived the Depression.

The girls were given responsibilities upstairs and down in the "big house," everything from cleaning and laundry to helping the cooks. "Still, it's not as hard as Whitbourne," Rose commented. "That Butler woman was a slave driver." The pay was five dollars a month, a fortune to her and Lucy.

The summer was hot and dry. On their day off, the Rogers servants strolled around town in light summer dresses and straw hats and felt privileged to be associated with such a well-known family. In August, Mrs. Rogers sent them out on the surrounding barrens to pick bakeapples for the kitchen. This was Rose's favourite job.

For once in her life, Rose Connor found herself free of worry. She thought she might even be happy but how could she know for sure when there was nothing in her previous life to go by.

**

Two years later, war broke out in Europe. Britain was again looking to the colonies for help.

March 3, 1941. Happy Birthday, Rose, you're nineteen and still going strong! Guess what, Dad is going to St. John's to work on the new American base, he's actually going to get a real job. Probably just wants in on the prosperity coming our way. There's lots of jobs around, none as hard as fishing. (You'd better sit down for the next bit.) With Dad gone, Iris has to go into service. She's talking about going to Bay-de-Verde.

At this point, Rose stopped reading Daisy's letter. She read the first part again. Yes, Iris was going to be in Bay-de-Verde, only ten miles away. Way too close for comfort!

The rail line to Heart's Content is closed down, the letter went on. *They're taking up the tracks. Everyone around here is mad about it. It was too good to be true, wasn't it? Nobody cares about the small places. And guess what? Steve Gordon and I have been keeping company, as Gran puts it, for a while now. Just thought you should know, ha, ha. Love, Daisy.*

Rose smiled, remembering Daisy's interest in Steve when she was fourteen or so. Watching him play in the New Year's football game, confiding to her that Steve had walked her home one day and "don't tell Gran."

Most of the young men in Old Perlican had joined up, Calvin Barrett among them. He and Rose had become good friends by then. Calvin was quiet and steady, not a loud, obnoxious braggart like some of the fellows she met. "Calvin would make good husband material," Lucy commented, with a wink.

Rose wrote long letters to Calvin, telling him about the people they knew, who was doing what and, in Lucy Miller's case, who she was doing it with. She kept company with Calvin's mother, knitted socks and mitts for her to send him, to keep him warm in the cold, damp French winter. And then, something she'd never foreseen in her early life, she went back to school.

May 12, 1943. Dear Daisy, I know you won't believe it but I been going to night school, Miz Rogers said I shuld go cause I was smart and I did. Maybe my spelling will get better now. The teacher said to reed the newspaper in between classes, and I try but it's hard to find time to reed a paper what with the extra work since a cuple of the girls went to St. John's for jobs. Different jobs, like in restrants, movie houses and offices on the militry bases. I hear St. John's is louzy with servicemen, Yanks and Canadians everywhere. and no truble to get one to take you to a movie sometimes. I'm temped to go there myself.

The men from here are finding jobs in construkshun, and for cash money which is better than the old truck sistem in the fishery. They talk about the music on the bases, swing music, so called, and the people they meet from all over Canada and the States. God, everything is in flux since the war started, isn't it? Nfld will never be the same again. Write soon, love Rose

**

The war ended in 1945. The town of Old Perlican held a supper at the hall for returning servicemen. "Hurry up and get ready," Lucy Miller simpered, looking pleased with herself in her best dress. "You don't want to be late. Corporal Calvin Barrett will be there in his uniform. It's our duty to go and welcome him home, you know."

As they hurried into the hall, Lucy was barely able to contain herself. "Ooh, look, there's Calvin. My, he's certainly filled out since we saw him last!"

"Probably just the uniform," Rose replied, suddenly aware of her racing heart as she looked him over, "but he does looks more manly, doesn't he? Wonder if he's still shy."

"Only one way to find out," Lucy declared, skipping across the floor to where Calvin was lining up for his supper. "Hey there, soldier," just like she'd heard in a movie the last time the travelling showman came to town, "not speaking to your old buddies?"

Calvin blushed red as he turned and saw them. "Oh, hello. How's it goin'?"

"We're here to welcome you boys back home," breathed Lucy, posing prettily, one hand on her hip, the other primping her short, brown hair, newly curled.

Rose rolled her eyes. "Don't mind Lucy, she's being Ginger Rogers today." She gave Calvin a nervous smile. "Welcome back, buddy." For some reason, she felt a little short of breath.

It wasn't long before Calvin and Rose were going for strolls around town. There soon developed an understanding between them and eventually, a more serious consideration on Rose's part. "He's different, somehow," she said to Lucy. "I mean, he's the same, but still different. More grown up, I suppose."

Lucy grinned. "You're a goner, Rose Connor!"

Rose and Calvin were married in the winter of '46. They were just getting used to their new status when a letter came from Daisy. *Aunt Julie died last month, less than a year after Uncle Joe. Frank said he'd sell you her house on the Harbour Road if you want. It needs work but if you and Calvin are willing, he'll give you a good deal. (Can't wait to meet Calvin. And for you to meet Steve. I know, you knew*

Steve Gordon long before this but he's a lot older now. We're married women, did you ever think you'd see the day?)

As Rose read the letter, she pictured New Perlican as it looked from the top of Smut Hill. The pretty, little town nestled beneath surrounding spruce hills, the houses all painted white, boats coming and going in the harbour. It was the place she loved.

Best of all, she'd be close to Daisy. No one knew her as Daisy did. They'd been through their own war, they'd survived Dan Connor together. Daisy had a daughter now. She'd named her Lexie, after their mother, and Rose was happy about that. Soon, Rose hoped, she'd have children, too. She and Daisy would share the joys and frustrations of motherhood together.

Calvin needed no convincing once Rose had told him there was a house waiting for them. "And I've got my own boat," he said. "I'll be my own boss for a change."

Rose thought of Iris who, as far as she knew, was still in Bay-de-Verde. Her worry that Iris might seek her out in Old Perlican and try to bully money out of her hadn't happened. By now, her big sister might have put down roots. She might be married, might even have children. Would they ever see her again, Rose wondered.

PART FOUR (Daisy)

Hope has two daughters: Anger for the way things are and
Courage to change them.

(Paraphrased from St. Augustine)

Twenty-Six

September, 1960. Daisy Gordon watched Lex pacing the yard, impatiently waiting for Jerry Downey's taxi to pick her up. Daisy could hardly believe it, her oldest was going off to university. "Are you sure the boarding mistress knows you're arriving today?"

"Mom, you've asked me that five times! Yes, she knows." Wound tight as a drum. Daisy couldn't blame her, any seventeen-year-old would be nervous to leave a three-room school in a small place to attend university in St. John's. And Lex had only just turned seventeen two weeks ago, on September first. Way too young to leave the nest.

It had been Kate Fisher, Molly's daughter and Daisy's cousin, who'd first mentioned university to Lex. "Premier Smallwood wants more teachers for the province," she'd said. "He's offering free tuition at Memorial to anyone going into Education."

Kate was a teacher herself, here in New Perlican. One of those spinster teachers commonly seen in many outports, happily unwed and totally dedicated to her work. She'd watched Lex coming up through the grades, had seen how she liked school, how she worked to get good marks. Like her mother in that regard, thought Daisy, allowing herself a small, prideful smile.

Kate had filled out some kind of form for Lex and she got a bursary, so she had enough to cover her board. But hopefully, Kate had something in mind for the three years after this. Otherwise, Lex' first year at Memorial could be her last.

Money was tight, Steve didn't make enough to pay for any of it. Last month, Steve had even come close to wondering why a *girl* would need so much education. Daisy had thrown him a look that warned him not to venture further with that line of thought. Sometimes Steve disappointed her.

The porch door banged open and the other three tumbled out of the house. "Taxi's comin'," shouted Barb, Daisy's second oldest, a sturdy fourteen-year-old with her mother's dark colouring. Thick braids bouncing around her shoulders, she skipped over to join her big sister. "Are ya' nervous?" bouncing restlessly from one foot to the other.

"'Course not," Lex snapped, as Daisy grinned at the two of them, the back and forth that never stopped. Lex knew enough not to show Barb a hint of weakness or she'd be needled to death over it.

Behind Barb came Donna, thirteen, followed by David, a skinny, ten-year-old with the Connor red hair. Donna, slim and blonde, stood near Daisy, arms folded across her chest. She was the quiet one. And what choice did she have, coming behind two gabbers like Lex and Barb?

As the taxi rolled to a stop at the gate, Daisy saw the scowl cross Lex' face. She'd spotted the three passengers in the car, one in the front and two in the back. Lex could hardly stand being crammed into their old Chev with her siblings, let alone share with strangers.

"David," ordered Lex, her mouth tight with annoyance, "put my suitcases in the trunk."

David nodded in obedience to "the bossy one," as Lex was sometimes known around the house, and ran over to the taxi. As he bent to his task, Daisy's eyes fell on the battered cardboard suitcases. Why hadn't she borrowed some nicer ones from Molly or Kate?

Lex came over and gave Daisy a hurried, awkward hug. She wiggled her fingers at the younger ones and crawled into the back seat beside a large woman eating potato chips and a teenage boy with pimples. She looked so miserable, Daisy almost felt like dragging her out of the car and telling her to stay home.

"Big day," said Jerry, grinning as he closed the trunk, "lots o' nerves."

Daisy nodded. "You won't forget what I asked you to do, will you, Jerry?"

"Don't worry, I won't forget." Jerry was a Winterton boy, Daisy had known him for years. She'd asked him to leave Lex 'til last when he dropped everybody off, make sure she seemed all right as she got out of the car.

Lex gave them a wobbly smile as the car started to back out the lane. Daisy and her three remaining children stood and watched as it crossed the bridge and drove out of sight.

**

An hour later, the youngsters straggled out the door for school, Barb, as usual, leaving just enough time to make the nine o'clock bell. Daisy made herself a cup of tea and sat down in Gran's old rocking chair to ponder this new development in the family's fortunes.

She thought back to thirty-something years ago, when her father had dragged her out of school and sent her over here to live with Gran Parsons. She'd been overcome with grief at giving up the one thing that got her away from the turmoil, her father's drinking and roaring, her mother's gradual retreat from reality. Daisy would never forget the look on little Rose's face when she realized she'd be left to cope on her own. But the old man didn't care. Dan Connor was never one to bother with anyone else's feelings.

Somehow, thought Daisy, they'd both survived their early years. Rose had gone into service in Old Perlican and married Calvin Barrett, they were living back here now. And Steve Gordon had come along to change things for Daisy. Pregnancy being the change, with Lex arriving in '43! They'd got married in '44, Steve on leave from the Merchant Marines before leaving again to join his ship.

Gran had looked after Daisy and the baby while Steve was away. The dear soul had died suddenly just after the war, and as she'd promised, had left Daisy the house. Daisy still missed her. Sometimes, she imagined she could hear Gran's voice giving advice on this or that, as she liked to do.

Daisy started as she suddenly realized someone was standing in the kitchen. She'd been so deep in the past that she hadn't heard the door open. "Thinking sad thoughts, eh Daisy?" said Molly. "Missing Lex already. Did she get away OK?"

"Yeah, think so. You know Lex, not one to admit being scared. Barring homesickness, we'll see her at Thanksgiving so we'll hear it all then."

Molly sat down at the table. "Pour me a cup o'tea now, I see you just brewed a pot," loosening her coat. "That Lex! She bugged me all summer to tell her about her Grandmother Connor. Me and my big mouth, I let it slip one day that Lexie wanted to be a teacher herself once, so now she's probably more determined."

"I'm not surprised. Lex has been wondering about Mom ever since her teen years. She was a kid who had to know things, and she'd never let up 'til she was satisfied."

Molly grinned. "Like the time she wondered when you and Steve got married."

"Yeah. She and her friend, Betty, were tittering about pregnancy, or people getting pregnant before marriage. Young girls, you know how they are. I knew she was wondering about me and Steve so I finally just gave in. Not only was she conceived before the wedding, I told her, she was already *born* before the wedding. Shoulda seen her face! Thought it might teach her a lesson about digging for information, but it didn't."

"No, it didn't. She's still going on about her grandmother."

Daisy nodded. "Maybe she feels a connection because of having the same name as Mom, I don't know. Anyway, I've always tried to put her off, telling her Mom died in a hospital in St. John's. That's enough for her to know. The rest of it isn't meant for young ears, at least that's what I think."

**

Lex arrived on the Friday for Thanksgiving weekend. The first thing she said was, "You'll never believe who I saw in St. John's!" shrugging off her coat, the new, beige raglan Daisy had ordered from Eaton's catalogue. Daisy looked at the girl standing in front of her, flushed with indignation and outrage, and she knew who it was right away.

"Theresa, that's my roommate, and I were walking along Merrymeeting Road this day," Lex went on, "and I see a familiar shape coming toward us. Another clue, he was taking both sides of the sidewalk. I was just praying he'd go by but, damn it, he recognized me. So then I had to introduce him to Theresa. Embarrassing or what!

"Anyway, he said hello to Theresa, then he says, 'Come up for supper sometime, Lex.' As if I'd go anywhere near him! Meanwhile, Theresa is standing there speechless so I had no choice but to explain my weird, alcoholic grandfather to her. I tell ya, that old man is a nuisance!"

"Well," said Daisy, "you might see him in there now and then, but try not to let it bother you. Take your things upstairs now, get ready for supper." And Lex huffed off, grumbling to herself.

Daisy knew Lex would always be bothered by her grandfather. Lex liked predictability and he was anything but. He was usually drunk when she saw him, as likely to grab her in a hug as forget who she was. Or stagger and fall down at her feet. The other children felt the same, of course. But Lex had gone a step further, declaring she'd never call him "grandfather" or anything like, and had settled on "old Dan" or "the old man."

Dan had been living in St. John's since the war. He'd come back home for a few months after '45, when his job on the base finished up, but he wasn't content. Daisy knew he'd never go back to fishing. "Going back to the city," he said. "Too quiet around here."

He'd met a widow at his tavern around that time. She'd taken him back to her house for the night and he never left. He was only about fifty at the time. Still a nice-looking man, and charming when he wanted to be, so Daisy could see how it could happen. Besides, from what she'd seen of Mamie Doolen, they were a good match. Mamie was as much an alkie as he was. And with lots of money from her dead husband, she was just what Dan needed.

The late forties had been a chaotic time in the colony, with some people agitating against Britain, some talking of joining Canada and some looking to the US. Dan had supported Joey Smallwood, of course, with his talk of the benefits of joining Canada, the free money flowing down from Ottawa. Daisy, herself, had thought it was all a set-up between Britain and Canada. Britain would be free of Newfoundland, Canada would get hold of certain resources.

Anyway, Dan had settled in with the widow Doolen. "Living in sin," he'd say, grinning unashamedly. They'd come out to New Perlican once every summer for a visit. Sometimes, they'd motor down to Bay-de-Verde to see Iris, Dan driving Mamie's Buick like he owned it. Actually, now he *did* own it because Mamie had died last year and left him her car, her house and her money. Old Dan had really struck gold the day he met Mamie Doolen in that tavern!

With Dan living in St. John's and Iris in Bay-de-Verde, married to Dr. Simms as Dan had told them, Daisy had been enjoying peace for some years. She just hoped Lex wouldn't be bothered by her "weird grandfather," now they were both in the same town.

**

Rose arrived the next morning. "Where's Lex? How was her first month at university?"

"Seemed to go okay. Likes her roommate, getting used to the big classes." Daisy raised her eyebrows at Rose. "She just left to go up to Molly's, probably wants to bug her some more about Mom. S'pose she's been after you, too."

Rose nodded. "All the time, and not only about Mother. One day she wondered how I came up with Marie's name, was it for someone in Calvin's family. The girl is relentless." A quick grin, "Stubborn like her mother. Anyway, I told her there was nothing to Marie's name except I liked it."

As usual at the mention of Marie, Rose teared up. Her eight-year-old daughter, her firstborn, had died of polio in the early fifties. Daisy remembered the old magazine pictures, children lying inside big, steel drums with just their heads sticking out. Iron lungs, they were called, a horrible name in itself. The vaccine had come in '55, too late.

"If Marie had lived, she'd be Barb's age now," said Rose, wiping her eyes. Her two other children, Libby and Peter, were close in age to Daisy's two, Donna and David. Rose loved them dearly but, as Daisy knew, they'd never take the place of the child she'd lost.

The outside door banged shut and Lex came in, cheeks red from the October chill. "Hey, it's Aunt Rosie," she said, all smiles. "I went by your house, Libby told me you were here."

"I brought you some partridgeberry jam I made last month, a treat to take back with you. Don't say I never gave you anything."

Lex picked up a jar. "Partridgeberry, my favourite, Thanks, Aunt Rose."

"So, you got on good in your first month?"

"Coping, I guess. Some of the classes are huge, not much like here. By the way, next year the university is moving to the new campus on Elizabeth Avenue. I heard it's gonna have underground tunnels connecting all the buildings. Can you believe it?"

"Well," said Rose, "you'll have lots to tell your father when he gets home."

Lex smiled. She was Steve's sandy-haired clone, a real Daddy's girl. "Yeah, can't wait."

Steve worked on the coastal boats, carrying freight and passengers around the island. For the first few years, he'd only got home for a month in January, during freeze-up, and two weeks in the summer. But now, thanks to his union, he had more time off in the winter, when Daisy needed him home the most. Depending on ice, of course, but he was usually home from mid- December 'til mid-February.

Steve was home for Christmas now, it made life a lot easier. Better for the kids, too, especially David. And luckily, he was an outdoors man, loved hunting and fishing, cutting wood. Wasn't under Daisy's feet all the time like some men.

"Mom," said Lex, heading for the fresh buns in the pantry, "Grandmother died at a hospital in St. John's, right? Which hospital was it?"

Daisy looked at Rose, rolled her eyes. "Why, is it important?"

"Just wondered." Lex shrugged. "You never did tell me."

"It was the Mental Hospital, all right?" Rose snapped, shaking her head in frustration. "What difference does it make?"

Lex shrugged again. "None, I guess. Good buns, Mom," heading upstairs as Daisy and Rose stared after her, shaking their heads in unison.

**

Lex finished her year in May. After lying around for two weeks with nothing to do, she was wondering how she could get money for next year. "I don't know, Lex," said Daisy. "There aren't many student jobs around here. Did Kate help you apply for another bursary?"

"Yeah, but there's no guarantee I'll get one. I was thinking, Mom, your sister lives in Bay-de-Verde, right? There's a fish plant down there, they'd probably pay well for a summer job."

Daisy almost fell over. "Lex, where do you get the ideas? I haven't seen Iris in twenty years, and she certainly doesn't know you. How in the name of God did you think of that?"

Lex grinned sheepishly. "I sorta listened in one day when you and Rose were talking about the old man, how he goes down to Bay-de-Verde most summers to see Iris. I could hitch a ride with him. If Aunt Iris likes me, maybe she'll help me out."

"But I thought you couldn't stand your grandfather. You always go upstairs whenever he comes, grumbling that he's drunk, he's gross, this and that."

"Yeah, I know. But maybe it's time Dan Connor did something constructive for a change."

Daisy stared at her for a moment. "What do you mean?"

"Well, we've put up with him and his drinking all our lives so I figure it's pay-back time. Whad'ya think?"

"I'll let you know after I talk to your father. Which means don't get your hopes up!"

The next day, Daisy went over the road to the pay phone to call Steve. According to the shipping news on the radio last night, his ship was in Lewisporte.

But Steve wasn't shocked at all. "Lex should be a lawyer," he laughed. "She's got that connivin' lawyer mind. Let her go, Dais, she needs the money. And, as you yourself always say, a girl should get an education."

In the end, Daisy's ambition for her girl overcame her objections. Besides, it was Lex who would have to be around Iris, not herself. And money was money, as Steve had said.

**

Not long afterwards, Dan arrived early for his summer jaunt to Trinity Bay. He came shambling in the door, jacket hanging off one shoulder, grey hair sticking up in tufts. He smelled of a mixture of sweat, liquor, tobacco and gasoline, his life in a malodorous soup.

Daisy went about her work, watching out of the corner of her eye as Lex started in softening him up, as she called it. "Would you like a cup of tea?" a big, false smile pasted on her mug.

He squinted at her with narrowed, bloodshot eyes, realized who she was and drawled, "Well, 'tis young Lex. Almost growed up, aren't ya'. Yes, Darlin', I'm dry as a bone."

He drank his tea, rambling on about his car, his pub and the friends he had there, his heart problem and the medication he had to take, all barely understandable between the slurping and the slurring. Butter wouldn't melt, thought Daisy, as she watched Lex listening politely, murmuring "yes" or "no" at appropriate times. Finally, Dan sat back with a satisfied sigh and took out his cigarette papers.

"What's the news from Aunt Iris down in Bay-de-Verde?" Lex piped up. "Are you going down to see her soon?" At this point, Daisy had to sit down to watch the performance.

Dan licked the edge of his roll-up and struck a match. "Iris is doin' okay, I guess. Livin' in that big house by herself now, since Dr. Ben died a couple years ago." As a cloud of smoke obscured his face, he took a coughing fit. "I try to stay in touch," he said, gasping for breath. "Never know when she'll loosen the purse strings, right?"

"I was wondering," said Lex, acting all innocent as if the thought had just occurred to her. "I got nothin' to do right now, no summer job. Maybe I'll go along when you go, kill some time."

"Sure, Lex. Up to Daisy, of course, but I wouldn't mind the company."

Daisy gave him the eyebrows. "As long as there's no drinking. Can you promise me that?"

"Certainly," he muttered, getting up from the table. "Whad'ya think I am, an alkie?" And, as evidence to the obvious, he stumbled over the doorstep and fell into the porch.

Daisy frowned at Lex. "I don't know about this," shaking her head as she went out to help the old drunk to his feet. "He'd better keep his promise or there's no Bay-de-Verde for you, summer job or not."

"Mom," Lex said, afterwards. "You don't believe he'll keep that promise any more than I do. But that road down the shore is too potholey to drive fast, you couldn't go more than forty if you wanted to. And if I do get the job, next time I'll take the bus down." She held out her hands, palms up. "See, problem solved."

What do I say to that, Daisy wondered, as she thought how nice it must be to be young and full of optimism?

The following week, she watched from the gate as Lex ran across the bridge and climbed into the car with the old man. "She's got guts," muttered Daisy, feeling unsettled as she turned back into the house.

Twenty-Seven

Daisy sat at the kitchen table and looked out at the broody, late-October sky. A lot can happen in a year, she thought. Lex was in her second year at MUN, now. Iris had come through for her last May, arranged a job at the fish plant so she could make enough money to go back. Lex had worked in Bay-de-Verde all summer, she'd even stayed at Iris' house.

When Lex arrived home in August, Daisy had been waiting to give her the third degree. What was Iris like, what did she talk about? Lex had commented that Iris only asked about a few people in New Perlican that she remembered, who was married, who was dead, that sort of thing. There was nothing of significance that Daisy could get mad about.

Daisy had doubted that Lex would stick it out at the fish plant but she'd been proved wrong. And the job had been good for her. She'd left for St. John's with confidence, looking forward to her year at the new university campus. She'd told them all about it at Thanksgiving, the buildings, the trees, the tunnels. The opening ceremony in the auditorium, Prime Minister Diefenbaker's jowls wobbling with pride as he welcomed special guest, Eleanor Roosevelt.

But Lex hadn't seemed herself at Thanksgiving. She'd seemed tired, even a bit low. And no wonder, the girl was probably run ragged from trying to take everything in. Still, Daisy had got after her about her health, getting more rest.

Not for the first time, Daisy wondered how her own life might have been different if she hadn't been hauled out of school as a young girl. Kate Fisher had been her teacher, a young thing just starting out. Daisy had admired Kate, she'd even dreamt of being a teacher just like her but it wasn't to be. She'd never told a soul about this, not even Lex. The feelings were still nish, too raw to be exposed.

She looked across the bridge and shook her head. The old house looked better than ever with fresh paint and new windows. The old man had hired two boys for the summer, to get the house ready for Iris.

This was the shock of the century! Iris was coming back here to live, going to rent the house from the old man. Maybe having Lex around all last summer had triggered something in her, made her want to move back. Though God alone knew why she'd want to.

Daisy sighed and glanced around, wondering what little task she could do to keep busy. The house was just too quiet. Steve wouldn't be home for six weeks so it was just herself and eleven-year-old David here, which he rarely was.

Donna and Libby, never one without the other, were going to school in Carbonear. They were enrolled in a new program doing high school and secretarial courses at the same time, a great opportunity. But they were boarding over there with Steve's Aunt Marge so they only got home weekends. And then there was Barb, Daisy's problem child. Barb had flown the coop. She was off to the big city, Toronto.

Daisy wasn't hungry, but it was noon so she got up and fixed a sandwich for "lunch," as Lex had started calling the mid-day meal. Apparently, it was the modern way. What used to be called dinner was lunch, what was supper was dinner. No one seemed to know where supper had disappeared to. Daisy couldn't see it, changing the names of things just to change them.

But everything was changing those days. The television telling women how to dress, how to act, what to buy. News reaching them the minute it happened, like that Bay of Pigs thing in Cuba, black people in the States demanding their rights. And the Women's Lib stuff, which somehow struck Daisy the wrong way because wasn't she "just a housewife?" Yes, change was in the air all right. Daisy wondered again where it would all lead.

PART FOUR (Daisy)

After lunch, she'd never get used to calling it that, she threw on a jacket and walked over to Rose's. It was calm out, maybe they'd go for a walk.

"Good day in the bay?" she asked Calvin, as she went in. Calvin was a man of few words, you had to start the conversation or he'd just sit there. He and Steve couldn't be more different, Steve never *stopped* talking. But they got on well, spent a lot of time together when Steve was home, fishing, rabbit slipping, even moose hunting a few times.

"Yes, good day on the water," Calvin replied, quietly. "Nice and calm." He nodded a couple of times. "Nice and calm." And he went back to his bowl of soup.

"S'pose the old house is almost ready for her highness," said Rose. She was taking bread from the oven, her face scarlet from the heat.

"Yes, she'll probably be here any day." Daisy shook her head. "God, I dread to see Iris coming back. When she lands, it's probably best for us to stay away 'til we see what's what."

"Yeah, though it'll be hard to avoid her in a place this small. I don't know about you, but the thought of Iris moving back to her old stomping grounds makes me nervous. I mean, it's been twenty years."

"I dreamt about her the other night. Dreamt she was knocking on my door, crying out something about a baby. God knows how I dredged that up."

"It's long past the time Iris should be crying about the baby," grumbled Rose, as she set the loaves on a rack in the pantry. "Anyway, enough of that, what have you heard from Barb? Is she surviving up there in Toronto?" She looked wistful for a moment, her eyes misty. "If Marie was alive, she'd probably be up in Toronto, too. And wouldn't they be havin' a ball!" Barb's name never came up but Rose thought of Marie.

"Barb is doing okay, I think. Had a letter yesterday. Said she heard of a job in a store and she's going for an interview." After Barb failed Grade Ten last year, Daisy had given in to her nagging and let her go to Toronto to find a job. She and a friend from here were staying with the friend's Aunt Velma 'til they got on their feet. Daisy felt okay with it to a certain extent, but she worried too.

Rose caught her frown. "Now, Dais, I know you worry but Barb is tough, she'll be fine. Donna and Libby now, couldn't see the two of them up there in that place. Can hardly see them going to Carbonear, let alone Toronto."

Daisy nodded her agreement. "I know. But, as Steve says, so far, so good. Three kids more-or-less out of the house, and one to go."

"Just think. Wasn't so long ago you were refereeing fights between Barb and Lex. Now Barb is in Toronto and Lex is at university. Lots of changes." Rose sent her a look, almost like she was going to tell her something, but the moment passed and she reached for her coat. "Calvin, we're going for a walk, maybe down to the Point. You can put your own dishes away." She grinned. "Now, don't you get rowdy while I'm gone and tear up the house."

Calvin smiled calmly in reply. He was used to her teasing.

**

Later, as Daisy was getting supper ready, she glanced out the window to see David running across the bridge full tilt, his book bag slapping against his legs. The fog had come in with a heavy drizzle during the afternoon, he was probably soaked from playing ball after school.

At the same time, she caught sight of a taxi pulling up at the gate of the old house. The fog was so thick she could hardly make out the figure darting in out of the rain. Iris, coming back under a cloud, the same way she'd left.

When the knock came at the door later that evening, Daisy almost jumped out of her skin. Surely, Iris wouldn't have the gall to come over here, would she?

"Mom, it's Andy Lewis," David called, from the porch. "His mother says to come quick." Daisy knew right away what it was. Dora Miller had been unwell for weeks.

Dora was lying unconscious on the floor in her bedroom. Bea Lewis, who lived nearby, was on her knees watching over her. "I was afraid to move her 'til you got here," Bea whispered.

"She just fell to the floor," whimpered the terrified young girl who'd been staying nights with Dora. "I didn't know what to do so I ran to Miz Lewis."

"You did fine." Daisy patted the girl's shoulder. "Go on home now, I'll drive Miz Miller to the Old Perlican Hospital." She knelt down beside Dora. "Here, Bea, help me get her up to the bed. Then you can send Andy over to get Rose, if you would."

Daisy and Rose stayed at the hospital all night, watching over Dora. Early the next morning, as pink streamers drifted lazily across the eastern sky, Daisy watched Dora take a deep breath. Her muscles relaxed, the grimace of pain left her face. The heart machine stopped beeping.

She went over to where Rose had fallen asleep in a chair. "Wake up, Rose," poking her in the shoulder. "Dora's gone. I'll get the nurse."

They drove home together later that morning. "Everything happened so fast," said Daisy, her voice thick with emotion. She remembered the early days, Dora coming into the house smiling, a loaf of bread wrapped in a dish cloth. Or sitting with her mother, talking quietly to her about the weather, her vegetable garden, Jonah's goats.

Rose was sobbing around a huge wad of tissues. "It's like losing Mother all over again! And what about Blanche and Lucy? You'll have to contact them, tell them their mother is gone."

"Yes, I'll call them. I'll call Lex, too. The funeral will likely be Saturday, she can take the bus Friday evening." The new bus service to St. John's and back every day made it a lot easier for Lex to get home when she wanted to. Not that she wanted to very often, too much going on in her life at the university. "Dora used to knit Lex a new pair of mitts every September for her birthday, remember? I think she had a soft spot for her because of her name."

Dora's daughter, Blanche, arrived by taxi from the St. John's airport the next afternoon. She lived in Saskatchewan now, Daisy hadn't seen her since '45 or so. Like thousands of other Newfoundland women, she'd met her serviceman husband during the war and moved to his part of the world afterwards.

"How ya been, Daisy?" Blanche seemed her old, feisty self but she looked older than her years, her face lined and leathery. Farming must be a hard way to live, thought Daisy, as Blanche glanced around the yard where she'd played as a child. "Ivan and I talked about coming out east someday, let Mom meet the youngsters, show them where I'm from." Her voice was wistful. "But we never had the money. Farming is like fishing, up one year, down the next."

The other daughter, Lucy, arrived later that day from Old Perlican, where she'd lived since '37, when she and Rose went into service with the Rogers operation. "Good to see you, Lucy," said Rose, to her old friend. "Not such a happy occasion, though. Won't be the same without your mother." Lucy nodded, unable to speak for crying.

"You girls get some rest now," said Daisy. "We'll see you tomorrow at the church. Don't worry about food for the reception, Rose and I'll make sandwiches."

**

After the funeral, Dora's house began to fill up with the many people who loved her. Daisy thought if Dora was looking down from heaven she'd be pleased, because if there *was* a heaven Dora would certainly be there by now. "Looks like the whole town is here to pay their respects."

Rose grinned impishly. "And to see how the years have treated the Miller girls."

"Lex said she'd be a bit late to the reception, had something to do first." Lex had arrived by bus the night before. Daisy was glad she'd made the effort, it showed she had a good heart.

It was almost an hour later when Daisy saw Lex come in. There was someone with her, a woman with a bandana tied around her head. They made their way through the crowd, over to the chesterfield in the front room where Blanche and Lucy were holding court. Blanche glanced around casually, then she did a double take. "Sweet Jesus, 'tis Iris Connor!"

PART FOUR (Daisy)

The mourners in the crowded room stood frozen in place as they stared at the newcomer. Daisy could imagine what they were thinking; Iris Connor, the hard case, was back after twenty years away. She sidled out to the kitchen to find Rose.

"Did you...?" Rose's face was a landscape of emotions; surprise, nervousness, anger.

"Yes, I saw her." Daisy was miffed that Lex had gone behind her back. "And I know what happened. Lex went in to Iris' after the funeral and persuaded her to come up here."

"Lord, she looks like a million dollars. Older, of course, her blonde hair mixed with white, now. But she's aged pretty well."

"Mm-m, the madam is well turned out, all right. New raglan, matching beige shoes." Daisy heard the peevish note in her own voice, felt the ball of resentment settling in her throat. Iris had the nerve to intrude here, at Dora's final goodbye, knowing it would take everyone's attention away from the purpose of the gathering.

Iris' pretty features and smooth complexion were unchanged. And the lovely, thick hair, not as curly now but wavy, the blonde and white mixing well together. She'd put on a little weight over the years but she was forty-six now, only to be expected. Rose was the only one who'd stayed slim; Rose's secret vanity, her girlish figure.

"There's something different about her," said Rose, but Daisy wasn't paying attention. Her mind was racing. Lex was about to steer Iris out to the kitchen where she and Rose were hiding.

The thought had just entered her head when Lex appeared at her side. "Mom, Aunt Rose, I made Aunt Iris come up and see everybody while they're all in one place. Maybe head off some of the gossip, right?" She turned as Iris walked over. "Here she is. I'll leave you here now, Aunt Iris. I'm starved, where's the grub?" And she headed back to the front room and the food table.

There was a hush as all eyes turned expectantly toward the three women standing awkwardly near the kitchen window, not a smile among them. After a tense few seconds, Rose jumped in. "How ya settling in? Guess you've got everything put away by now."

"Almost," replied Iris. She might have been speaking to strangers. "Still a few things but there's all summer for that." She looked to Daisy, who was standing with arms folded.

"Hello, Iris," said Daisy, quickly, not wanting to seem hostile now that Rose had broken the ice. Though why she shouldn't be hostile was another question. "If you need some heavy lifting, I can send Steve over when he gets home. Just let me know."

"Thanks a lot, I might do that." Iris looked toward the front room. "I must go and speak to a few people. Then I'll leave so they can talk about me," a trace of the old mischief in her quick grin. "I'll see you later, then." With a nod, she walked away.

"My God, that was something, wasn't it?" Daisy whispered, letting out a breath. "And everyone watching her, suppose they took in every word."

Rose nodded. "Nothing like a bit of gossip to lighten up a funeral reception." A puzzled look crossed her face. "I dunno, Dais, like I said, she seems different somehow. Once, funeral or not, Iris would've come in here, get all the attention going her way in seconds." She sighed. "Early days yet, of course. I'm sure she'll be back to herself before long!"

Twenty-Eight

Daisy got up on Monday morning feeling exhausted. Lex had gone back to St. John's and thank God for that. All weekend, it had been nag, nag, nag. "You and Aunt Rose should go over to see Aunt Iris." The girl was a real pain when she set her mind to something.

Lex had gone down to Iris' after the funeral reception, never got home 'til after midnight. "What in God's name were you doing over there with Iris?" Daisy had grumbled, the next morning. "Can't be that much to talk about." It seemed the two of them had become close since last summer and it bothered Daisy.

She didn't want Lex to fall under Iris' influence. Last fall, she used to wish Lex would come home more often. Now that Iris was on the scene, Daisy would rather Lex got even more involved at university, kept herself busier than she already was. What about a boyfriend, maybe that fellow she mentioned now and then, the one she said was in her class? Mel something, had a different last name. Petley? Petrie?

Of course, Lex never gave a simple answer to a question. "I'm tellin' ya, Mom, I'm gonna be first in line when Aunt Iris makes her will. I mean, I did spend a whole summer with her, I think she likes me. And really, you and Aunt Rose should go over and say hello. She won't bite."

Out of the mouths of babes, Daisy had thought at the time, but maybe Lex had a point. The longer she put it off, the harder it would be to get along with Iris in a civil manner. So, a week later, before she could change her mind, Daisy headed across the bridge. Knocked on Iris' door and stood nervously on the step, shifting from one foot to the other.

Iris appeared holding a cigarette high in one hand. There was a split second while she stifled her surprise, then, "Come on in, coffee's still hot from supper." She motioned Daisy toward the table and went into the pantry to pour the coffee.

Daisy glanced around the old house. Her last memory of the place was the day her mother had left for the hospital, jumping into Vic Tucker's taxi with her few belongings in a wicker basket. A chill rippled across her back. *Someone is walking over your grave.*

"You've made some improvements," Daisy said, casually, determined to keep it light. This was *not* going to be one of those gushy reunions like you saw on TV. "The new gyproc in the hall looks good. You'll need some wallpaper, now, there's some nice stuff at Benson's in Winterton," holding back from offering to help, at the same time feeling uncharitable.

Iris arranged the cups, the milk and sugar, on the table. "Daddy phoned yesterday, he's coming out tomorrow for a few days," blowing smoke toward the ceiling as she sat down. "He says I can rent the house for a while. I'd buy it if he'd sell it to me but he won't give me a straight answer." She took a last drag, stubbed out the butt in the ashtray. "Did he used to stay here much?"

"Him and Mamie, for a week or two in the summer. Same time as he'd go down to see you in Bay-de-Verde." Daisy dropped her eyes. "Maybe he'll come more often now."

Iris paused to light another cigarette. "Yeah, you could be right," eyeing Daisy through a cloud of smoke.

On her way back across the bridge, Daisy wondered again why Iris would come back here, subject herself to the scrutiny of the people who remembered her. Anyway, she was relieved it was over, that first visit. Better to get it over with before Steve came home.

She couldn't wait to tell Rose because Lex had been bugging her about Iris, too. Rose might as well do it or there'd be no peace. "No matter how we feel about Iris," she'd tell Rose, "we don't want to look mean spirited or we'll be the ones they gossip about instead of her."

**

Not long afterwards, Steve arrived for his winter break. "The snow is late this year," he said, the next day, as he hauled on his old woods clothes. "Let's hope it holds off for a while."

Daisy smiled. As if snow would keep Steve Gordon out of the woods. "Bring me back some frankum," she called after him, remembering how Dora's husband, Jonah, used to gather spruce gum for them when he went in the woods.

Later that day, Rose popped in. "Well, Lex should be pleased. I went to see Iris. Saw the old man's car outside so I darted in." She was flushed and a little breathless. "He was tellin' Iris to get him some lunch, he was gut-foundered, something like that. Drunk, of course." She winced. "Got a knot in my stomach like I was ten again, just from being back with him in the old house."

"How was Iris? Was she friendly?"

"Like we were on the best of terms," said Rose, looking slightly puzzled. "She offered coffee. I sat down, listened to Dad going on with his foolishness. How glad he was to rent Iris the house, he had the best daughters in the world, all that old shit. I didn't stay long. Never really got the chance to talk to Iris, the old bastard wouldn't shut up."

"And how did Iris act with him?" Daisy wondered.

"Well, it wasn't like the old days. 'Course she's older now, lot of water under that bridge! But the old man, he seemed right at home there with Iris catering to him." Rose looked her in the eye. "You don't suppose it'll be the same as before, do you?"

"Let's hope not. Can you see Iris and the old man livin' back here? Him staggering around town all day, Iris chasin' the married men. We'd be the talk of the town again. May as well move if that happens."

"Who's moving?" asked Steve, coming in from the woods. He looked from one to the other, his rosy face a question mark. "Something I should know, Dais?"

Daisy grinned at his expression. "Nothing to worry about, Steve. I'll keep you informed."

"What're you two cooking up now, I wonder?" he muttered, as he headed back outdoors.

**

Now that the old man's visits were done 'til spring, Daisy went over to see Iris the odd time. She made the excuse of helping with suggestions for the house but it was really curiosity. Was Iris the same girl she remembered?

"You and Iris are thick as thieves now, are you?" said Rose, a trace of resentment in her tone.

"Not really. I'm here by myself a lot so I drop over now and then. Suppose I'm wondering how long it'll take for the old Iris to show up." Daisy paused, started again. "Rose, you said Iris seemed different. Well, I find that, too, but there's nothing I can put my finger on."

"Yeah," Rose agreed. "I know what you mean but I can't explain it, either."

"Probably all in my head but she seems like someone finally at peace, like she's made a decision or something." Daisy waved away the idea. "Oh, I'm just talking nonsense."

"Y'never know with Iris," said Rose. "Maybe when Ben died, she got the urge to get back to her roots, as they say. You hear of people doing that after they've lived away. Can't imagine it in Iris' case but you never know. Does she ever mention Dad or his visits?"

"No, not much. Apparently, he still likes his walks down through the Alder Bed late at night."

Rose nodded. "Yeah. Used to say the water relaxed him, 'member? Fell in one night, came home drenched. Pretty drunk at the time, of course."

Daisy was becoming frustrated with the whole issue of Iris' return. "Y'know, now that she's back, I remember how it was and I get mad all over again. Sometimes I blame him, other times I blame her. Either way, I end up with all the old stuff going through my head." She dropped her eyes. "It was worse for you, you were alone with them after I went over to Gran's."

"Yes, Daisy, but that wasn't your doing. Sure, sometimes I felt hard-done-by but then I'd think, there's no need for both of us to suffer. Because you being there wouldn't have made any difference to how things were." Rose managed one of her crooked smiles. "Besides, you were only across the bridge if I wanted to see you."

"We were like checkers on a board, being moved around at the whim of the old man."

Rose sent her a long look. "Dais," she said, carefully, "did Lex tell you anything about Mother lately, about when she was in the hospital?"

"No. But Lex knows Mom was in the hospital. What do you mean?"

"Well, I'll tell you what she done, you won't believe it! When Lex went back to St. John's this fall, she went to the hospital. The Riverview it is, now. She saw the head man there and got permission to see Mother's records. Not only that, she forged the old man's name on a letter to say he supported it. She told me about it at Thanksgiving. "

"She did *what*?"

"She's got copies of the whole thing. Gave it to me to read." Rose's voice faltered. "Christ, Dais, Mother had that breakdown because of what she put up with at home, you know that. And when she went in there, they labelled her a lunatic. Lex said that was the common word back then, it was 1933, after all. But Mother, a lunatic ..." She tried to stop the tears but they came anyway. "Tha- that's what they called her, Dais. I can't bear it."

"Hush now, Rose, calm down." Daisy awkwardly patted Rose's back, the old, brown Mary Maxim she never seemed to take off.

"Daisy," Rose sniffed, "Lex knew I'd tell you so don't be mad at her. She'll be home for Christmas soon, you can talk to her then."

**

After Rose had gone home, Daisy sat and stared out the window. She was dumbfounded at what Rose had told her, at what Lex had done. Then she remembered Lex' low mood at Thanksgiving. She'd put it down to fatigue after a busy start to her year.

But that wasn't it at all. Lex had gone back in September fully intending to go to the hospital and she'd done just that. That's what was on her mind at Thanksgiving. But to forge her grandfather's name on a letter!? Christ, she could end up in jail!

Daisy has always been proud that Lex and Rose got along so well. It was understandable, they shared the same sense of humour, the teasing manner. But now, Daisy felt a tinge of jealousy that Lex had gone to Rose and not come to her own mother. And yes, Lex knew Rose would tell her about it eventually, but still...

Daisy wasn't like them. She was more comfortable keeping things to herself, things about how she felt or what her memories were. She'd always been like that, didn't see the good it did to talk about the bad old days. The times she'd cried herself to sleep, or had her feelings hurt.

Maybe this is how it works, she thought, people who keep secrets have secrets kept from them. She was certain Lex could give her chapter and verse on *that* theory, something from another psychology book most likely.

For the rest of the day, Daisy brooded about the house. She picked up her knitting. Donna wanted a pair of blue mitts to match her winter jacket. The child rarely asked for anything so Daisy wanted to get them done for Christmas. But after a few minutes she threw the knitting aside. She couldn't concentrate, her mind was bouncing all over the place.

Now she had to wait for Christmas to have a talk with Lex. A serious talk, not an easy thing for Daisy to do. The hard part would be hiding her mood from the family 'til then.

Twenty-Nine

Lex arrived on Friday, December twenty-second, a few days later than she'd planned. Daisy watched her get off the bus at the end of the bridge. Watched her struggle through the snow drifts in the lane, dragging her suitcase, shopping bags hanging off her arms.

"God, the bus was packed," Lex grumbled, as she came puffing through the door. "I know, I'm late getting here. Stayed a few extra days. Theresa and I went to see that movie everyone is talking about, *Breakfast at Tiffany's*." She threw the bags on the table. "David, Donna, don't touch anything while I hang up my coat. I'm warning you!"

David and Donna gave each other a bug-eyed smile. "Ooh," they murmured together.

Daisy saw the packages sticking out of the bags. In the midst of exams, Lex had made time to go shopping with the fifteen dollars Daisy had given her to buy presents for the family. She'd have to put off their talk till after Christmas Day, it'd be cruel to spoil the girl's fun.

"Okay," called Steve from the front room. "Let's get this tree decorated." And immediately there was chaos in the house. Daisy had always let the youngsters decorate the tree, back when Steve didn't get home for Christmas. But since he'd been on the new schedule, he liked to take charge of the job. Caused more confusion than if he'd just let the kids do it themselves.

"Okay, Donna, you can put on the special decorations," said Steve, taking a sip of his rum and coke, "the fancy birds and bubble lights and whatnot. David, check the bulbs, make sure they're all working. And Lex, as usual, will do the icicles."

And, as usual, Lex started to complain. "I always get the worst job." But she took the box over to the table and began to pull thin strands of tin foil free from the clump. "Why do we always take them down and throw them in the box any old how?" Same complaints every year.

After the tree was done, Lex grabbed her coat. "Mom, I'm going visiting. First, it'll be Aunt Molly. After that," she continued, pulling her wool hat down over her ears, "I'll drop in on my buddy, Betty Cole, then Aunt Iris. A full afternoon, be drunk as a lord by the time I get home."

Lex was back to her old self, the teasing and foolishness. Unburdening herself to Rose at Thanksgiving had obviously helped her state of mind. Daisy thought ahead to Boxing Day, when she and Lex would have to talk. She'd wait no longer than that to clear the air.

Finally it was Christmas Day. Daisy dragged herself through the long hours, guiding the family through the regular routine, pretending she was enjoying it. After supper, she and Steve went over to the pay phone in the Five Roads to call Barb.

"Guess what?" Barb crowed, as Daisy took the phone. "I'm working in a bank now. Told them in the interview my school records got lost in a fire." And through the line came the big ha-ha's.

Daisy shook her head. But it made sense in a way, Barb had never had any trouble with numbers in school, just everything else. "Barb, what if they check?"

"Mom, they'll never check. These people up here think we don't have any telephones in Newfoundland." Again, the laughs. "Well, gotta go. Maybe I'll get home next Christmas, if I can save up the money. But I was thinking, Donna and Libby should come up to Toronto after they finish their courses. They can stay with me and Helen, we'll help them get settled."

Daisy frowned as she hung up the phone. She couldn't see it, Donna and Libby living in Toronto.

**

On Christmas night, the weather turned bad. The next morning, they woke to high winds and blowing snow, huge drifts piling up in the lane and against the side of the house. Everyone would be house-bound on Boxing Day.

After a late breakfast, Steve and David, looking spiffy in their new Christmas sweaters, headed for the chesterfield and the sports on TV. Donna wasted no time hurrying to her bedroom to play the new Brenda Lee album Lex had given her for Christmas.

Young girls are so lucky nowadays, thought Daisy. Back in her day, all they had was work, every day the same, nothing to brighten up their drab existence. And certainly no record players. Daisy was glad for them, sure, but she was also a bit envious of what she'd missed out on.

Lex helped her with the dishes. Afterwards, Daisy waited a few minutes, then she followed her upstairs to her bedroom. Lex was already sprawled on the bed with the book she'd got for Christmas. *To Kill a Mockingbird*, a strange title in Daisy's opinion. Of course, there being no bookstores in New Perlican, Lex had been forced to pick it up herself in St. John's.

Daisy stood motionless in the doorway, a pulse jumping in her throat, sweat running down her back. "Aunt Rose said you had something to tell me."

Lex turned quickly, cheeks in full flush. "God, you made me jump! You must have your Hush Puppies on." That was Lex, trying to be funny in a tough situation. The grin faded, however, when she saw the look on Daisy's face. "Right," she sighed. "No time like the present."

Lex went over to the makeshift desk Steve had cobbled together for her when she was in Grade Six, explaining as she hunted through her briefcase, "I did it in September. My roommate's sister works at the Riverview, that's what the hospital is called now. She set it up with Dr. Brent. I told him I was doing family research."

Lex pulled out a file, turned to face Daisy. "I guess Aunt Rose told you I signed the old man's name on a letter. Dr. Brent seemed to need some reassurance that I was serious," trying to sound tough but her eyes were misting. "By that time, I didn't care if I was a criminal or not. I couldn't stop 'til I knew everything. A bit obsessive, I guess you could say.

"Anyway, I was pretty low when I came home at Thanksgiving. I was trying to decide how to tell you or if I *should* tell you. I didn't know if you'd want to hear it or not."

"Yes, I remember you weren't yourself. I thought you were just tired."

"Anyway," Lex went on, "I left the house one day that weekend feeling lousy, I was sad and mad at the same time. I ended up at Rose's, she was there by herself. I told her everything. Didn't mean to go behind your back but I had to get it out. I figured Aunt Rose would tell you." She handed over the file. "I'll leave you to read it now. It's hard, Mom, it's really sad."

Daisy hesitated, tried a grin that didn't quite come off. "Well, after all the trouble you went to, I suppose I should read it." She reached for the file, felt her eyes filling up. "My poor mother. Seems so long ago, she left one day and that was that, almost like she disappeared. Rose had just turned eleven, I was thirteen. We just carried on like she was never there at all." She wiped her eyes with her apron. "I always felt bad about that."

"You were just a kid, Mom, there's no need to feel bad." Lex took her arm and guided her over to the bed. "Take all the time you need. I'll keep the menfolk outa your hair." She turned and left, closing the door softly behind her.

**

As Daisy read, she knew she'd carry the words to her grave. The matron's cold remarks, the pitiful letters from Grandmother Fisher, a sad, old woman trying not to offend as she begged for news of her daughter. The old lady had had no formal education but she'd done the best she could.

July 6, 1933... Dear Matron, would you kindly rite me a few lines and let me no how my daughter is feeling, my daughter Mrs Dan Connor or Lexie as I call her. Poor dear child, I am nerly tore up about her. I rote to doctor Jones dident get any answer yet. I was talking to a lady today, she was a visitor to the hospital for ten years her daughter died there. She said the hospital always reply every letter. Please kindly let me no how Lexie is. Mrs k Fisher

In another letter, *Remember me to her and if she is well enough let her look this letter over.* And lest these important people should be offended by this difficult request, *if not I am satisfied.*

Daisy could only shake her head. The old, reliable class system had been in full flower at the time, it had come over from England with the settlers. Of course, there were more than a few vestiges of the system still around, you didn't have to look very far to find them.

A letter had finally come back from the hospital matron, and here Daisy met the arrogance and disrespect typical of the upper classes. There was also some pertinent information concerning her mother.

December 15th, 1933, Mrs K. Fisher, New Perlican. Dear Madam: In answer to your letter of last summer, complaining you got no answer to the letter you wrote. It is quite possible if you did not stamp the letter it would not reach this Hospital. The law is, as I understand it, that every letter must be stamped, and it is probably just a chance that your letter to me passed unstamped. Your daughter is somewhat improved, but unless someone is there to be responsible for her, she is not fit yet to look after her own household. Her outlook is more favourable now but mentally, she has a long way to go before we can pronounce her cured. This letter will serve for the whole family. Yours very truly, Lady Field, Matron.

One after another, the memories toppled through Daisy's mind. She saw her mother sitting in the rocking chair, staring at nothing. Or wandering the roads, sometimes crying, sometimes singing a shaky version of "Abide with Me." She saw people grinning at her, pointing at the crazy woman.

How broken her mother had been! And to Daisy's own shame, once she'd moved over with Gran Parsons she'd more or less distanced herself from her mother's life. She hadn't been brave enough to stand by her side, as Rose had done.

A note from the doctor read: *On one occasion, when Mrs Connor was having a lucid moment, she hinted at some kind of trouble with her husband at home. And that she was worried about her daughter, Iris. Would not state in what way, only burst out crying when subject was mentioned.* Puzzled, Daisy decided she'd have to ask Rose about that.

Another note shocked Daisy to her core. *Today, another lucid few minutes. Mrs Connor appeared full of rage. Blurted something about her brother finding her home alone and forcing her, as she called it. It was early fall, her husband had just left for the States. She muttered something about her daughter Rose. "The girl is cursed," something like that.*

I tried to reassure her that she'd already have been pregnant about three months before the incident with her brother so her daughter is fine. But she became agitated and I had to cancel the session. This lady has had a very bad time of it!

Daisy fell back on the bed. The tears came unabated.

Thirty

Over the last few days of the holidays, Daisy kept to herself as best she could. She was with the family in body but her mind and her feelings were galloping off in all directions. How could it be that words on a page could affect a person so deeply?

She thought of telling Steve the whole story, letting him share her burden, but something held her back. For him to see her like this, troubled and weak, how would she get back to where she'd been, where she felt halfway in charge of herself? She couldn't do it, couldn't let herself look pitiful in his eyes. Couldn't let a man get the upper hand over her. Daisy had vowed that would never happen again, not after growing up under Dan Connor.

Lex had left on the twenty-ninth, she and Theresa had made plans to go back early. Donna and Libby had waited 'til today, January first, Daisy had just waved them off for Carbonear on the bus. It's 1962, she thought, as she threw on her coat, whatever will it bring?

She hurried across the bridge, straight for the Harbour Road and Rose's, the cold, north wind slashing at her face like sharp knives. It was starting to snow.

"Sit down, Dais." Rose's face was grim as she pulled out a chair at the kitchen table. "I can see from your face that you read Lex' papers."

Rose dumped boiling water into the teapot with more energy than was required. Stray drops hissed and bubbled across the hot stove. "I know how bad you feel. After I read it, I was mad enough to spit tacks. The way that matron answered Grandmother's letters. Probably thought, them are just poor people, lower class people. No need to be polite to them." The kettle banged against the damper as Rose plopped it back on the stove. "Snotty English bitch!"

"It had to be Uncle Lew who raped her, Rose. The bastard raped her." A fog of hopelessness threatened to swamp her as she looked out the window to the Point. To the flakes and stages that had belonged to the Williams clan for as long as she could remember. The harbour was empty now, all the boats hauled up for the winter. There was a loneliness to it.

"Yes," said Rose, quietly. "Maybe that's what pushed her over the edge. Not only that her brother had done that to her, but thinking her pregnancy was from him and the baby she was carrying, me, that I'd be affected somehow. Poor thing." She shook her head. "I always thought Lew was creepy but it was more than that, wasn't it? He was deranged."

"Yes, I think you're right," replied Daisy. "But there was something else in the file. The doctor said Mom mentioned some trouble at home. That she was concerned about Iris but would get upset if he asked her about it. What did he mean, why would she be concerned about Iris?"

Rose's expression changed and a phrase came to Daisy from something she'd read. Deep sorrow. That's what she saw on Rose's face. "Rose, what is it? What's wrong?"

"There's something I never told you, Dais. Dad and Iris were doing bad things. We caught them in bed one day, Mother and me both, so she knew about it too. I was maybe eleven, it wasn't long after you went over to Gran's." Rose began to rock back and forth on her chair, unknowingly mimicking their mother.

"What!?" Daisy felt a heaviness in her chest, she craved a deep breath but couldn't draw in enough air. "You knew this all along and didn't tell me?"

"What would have been the point, Dais, wouldn't have changed anything. You were living at Gran's, away from the craziness. The least I could do was leave you that way. Besides, I didn't know how you'd take it. You might have come over and raised hell. And if you did, what would it be like for Mother and me at the house afterwards? I had to protect her."

Daisy walked into the hall. Tried to calm her heart, get her breathing back to normal. Would anything in her life, the life she'd built for herself, ever feel normal again?

"Tell me how you came to see them," she said, coming back into the kitchen. She wanted to hear the ugly details, to feel something of what Rose had felt at that moment. To let Rose know she was willing to share her pain.

Rose fixed her gaze on the window as a sudden wind gust drove powdery snow against the pane. "Mother and I had just come back after one of her wanderings, you know how she'd just take off." Her voice was flat, getting out the details but skipping over the feelings so she could keep going. "As we came in the door, I heard this low mumble from Dad's bedroom."

Rose's breathing came fast and shallow, she was seeing it all again. "I crept over and opened the door a crack. They were in bed. Dad was on top of Iris, naked except for a sweat-stained undershirt. Iris' dress was up around her waist, her eyes closed tight as he moved above her." She turned to Daisy. "That image has never left me, Dais, it's burned in my brain. His white backside, Iris' white legs splayed out on the dark blue quilt. The one Gran Parsons made."

"Dear God," whispered Daisy.

Rose grabbed a tissue from the box on the table. She wiped her eyes and took a deep breath. "I rushed Mother upstairs to her room and covered her up in bed, clothes and all. She kept murmuring something over and over, 'Bad, bad.' So I figured she'd seen them before."

Daisy tried to picture the scene, tried to imagine what Rose had felt as she'd looked through the door that day. It had been the end of innocence for her sister, a young girl already dealing with a harsh life. "Rose, I know I said to tell me but stop if you want to."

"No, I'll tell it like you asked." Rose took another tissue, blew her nose and started again. "I cowered in Mother's bedroom in a state that's hard to describe, but most of all I was numb. Then I began to feel weak, like I might faint, so I stretched out on the bed beside Mother.

"Suddenly, I heard the slap of bare feet outside the door. I peeped out, saw Iris barrelling down the hall, her underwear in one hand, yankin' her dress down over her hips with the other. 'Close the damn door,' she snarled, as she sailed by. So then I knew she'd seen me."

Daisy had reached overload. Her head felt too heavy, like a cannonball sitting on her shoulders. "My God, Rose, what you went through. And Iris, all this time we just thought she was cruel."

"She *was* cruel," Rose snapped.

"Well, I just... Never mind, go on." Daisy saw that Rose had no sympathy for Iris.

"I was afraid to go down for supper," Rose continued, "so I stayed in Mother's room all night. The next morning, Iris threw some toast on the table and the three of us ate breakfast. I kept waiting for something to happen but nothing did. Either Iris hadn't told him, or else he didn't give a damn. And things carried on like it was just another day."

Rose smiled a weak smile. "Funny what you think about when you're young. I used to think the alders overheard everything that happened in that house, that they kept our secrets in the leaves. I'd imagine going out to the Alder Bed and shaking these damn alders 'til the leaves went flying, and all the bad memories went flying away with them. Flying away to hell, where they belong." She shook her head. "The things we do to keep going!"

"You had to handle it all on your own."

"Like I told you, Dais, t'was Dad sent you over to live with Gran and now you know why. He wanted you out of the way. Wasn't long before he took Mother to the hospital, then he sent me to Whitbourne. He gradually got rid of us so he and Iris could carry on what they were doing."

"Everyone suffered in silence, you, Mom, even Iris, though she didn't act like it." Daisy's voice was ragged, her throat half strangled with tears. "Poor Mom, her mind couldn't take it all in. By the time she got to the hospital, it was too late." The tears were running freely now. "The letters say she didn't ask about home. Sh-she forgot all about us!"

"I know, Dais. But home for Mother only meant suffering. Maybe that's why she disappeared into her own world, that way she couldn't feel the hurt." Rose swiped a tissue across her eyes. "Breaks my heart to think about that last morning. She was so thin, her hair falling out in places. But so excited about going in the car."

She thumped a fist on the table. "And there's that bastard all spruced up, couldn't wait to get going. Jumping in the car, waving to us as they drove away!"

"The letters said she'd cry out at night sometimes," said Daisy, quietly, "bother the other patients. Her mind must have been in turmoil."

"By God," muttered Rose, her anger building. "I'm gonna have it out with 'em, starting with Iris. Been working myself up to it for a while now. She may be the doctor's widow, with her nice clothes and all, but she was hard as nails. Hard to Mother and hard to us, too."

"Maybe she had to stay angry to stay sane."

"No excuses, Dais! Since Lex showed me that stuff, I haven't been able to sleep. I just lie awake thinking how frightened I was all the time, knowing they wanted me out of the way." She dabbed at her eyes. "I remember him giving Iris little gifts and I was jealous 'cause he treated her special. God forgive me, I was."

She shot Daisy a determined look. "Yes, by God, it's time we told her what we think. I'm gonna bring it all up, everything. You needn't be there if you don't want to but I'm tired of being tormented like this. Lex started it and I'll finish it!"

Thirty-One

The snow storm had roared all night. Steve had been out shovelling all morning, his own yard and the yards and lanes of the older people who lived nearby. Daisy was glad he had something to do besides lying on the daybed, looking out the harbour with that hang-dog look on his face. Steve wasn't one for forced confinement.

He came in for lunch, his face red from the cold, his sandy hair wet with sweat. "Got the yard done," he said, watching her dish up the pea soup. "I was wondering if I should go over and shovel in front of Iris'. The snow's drifted up to her front windows."

"Yeah, maybe you should. It's not likely she'd ask."

"Saw Rose go in there earlier." He breathed in the steam wafting from his bowl. "Smells good, Daisy. Fresh buns too! Y'know, you'd be a good cook if you stayed home." Daisy let Steve's familiar, old joke pass without the usual comeback. She anticipated a visit from Rose soon.

She was at the kitchen table, leafing through a True Story magazine, when she spied Rose steaming across the Long Bridge all out. She was wearing Calvin's big, blue parka that reached almost to her ankles, and she had a long, red scarf tied around her face and knotted behind the fur-lined hood. Daisy had to smile. "Certainly not a fashion model today," she muttered.

After stamping her feet in the porch, Rose poked her head around the kitchen door. "Sorry, I brought in a ton of snow." Red-faced and out of breath, she untied her scarf and extricated herself from the parka. "God, the wind! Cold as a witch's tit out there," grumbling as she leaned over the stove to get warm.

Rose glanced around the kitchen. "Where's Steve? Gone in the Legion for a beer, I suppose. Calvin is over there feelin' housebound. I told him to go next door, listen to old Bob Morris tell him some lies."

Daisy hung Rose's coat behind the stove to warm up. "Steve went off with his snow shovel. Thought he'd go out around, see if any of the older folks need to be dug out. 'Course he could be in the Legion by now, usually finds his way there eventually." She was anxious to hear Rose's account of the visit. "Steve said you were over at Iris' this morning," she prompted. "Did you have it out with her?"

"Yes, I was over there," Rose replied, warming her hands at the stove. "Had to do it now, easier for me to do something while I'm still mad." She settled at the table while Daisy poured tea. "Iris was making bread. Seemed in a good mood so we chatted about the weather, things like that, for a few minutes. Then I said, 'Iris, when we were growing up, you and Dad were pretty thick. More than thick,' I said.

"Iris stopped what she was doing, gave me that look that used to scare the shit outa me. But I kept going. I said, 'Daisy and I remember how hard you and Dad were on poor Mother.' But then I ran out of steam. Mumbled something like, did she see it different from us, that kinda thing. I don't know, I was so nervous I can't remember what I said."

"It's a wonder she didn't throw you out."

"Well, the old Iris would've hauled off and nailed me. But she sits back, looks at me for a few seconds and says, 'Y'know what we should do, you, me and Daisy? We should have a talk. Check with Daisy and let me know when it's a good time.' Rose frowned. "What do you think of that? I don't know what to make of it, myself."

Daisy's eyebrows shot up. "My God, suppose she wouldn't kill us would she? Still, that's what we want, to find out everything about those not-so-good old days. What should we do?"

"Well, I don't think she'd kill us. Curse and roar, maybe, call us ugly names. But we won't know anything unless we go." Rose's mind seemed made up. "Best time for me is after supper, Peter and his

243

father will be settled in for the night. I'll say I'm goin' over to your place and you say you're coming to mine. Don't matter, the men never listen anyway. How 'bout Monday, that okay? I'll let Iris know."

**

The cold night sky was awash with stars as Daisy left the house and headed for the Green, where she and Rose had agreed to meet. Her stomach felt hollow with nerves as she took up her post in the shelter of a huge boulder. Five minutes later, Rose came hurrying along. "Hope we're doing the right thing," Daisy whispered.

"Tis now or never, Dais, don't get fainthearted."

They waded through the snow, back to the house by the Alder Bed, the house that harboured all their secrets. Rose stood for a moment on the top step. "When I'm here, I can almost see Mother with her basket, the day she left for the hospital."

"I do, too," said Daisy, shivering more from nervousness than cold as she waited down below. She looked back across the bridge to her house, Lena's house. She'd only been a kid when she went over there to live. And so full of hate for being hauled out of school to become a servant, as she'd thought of it at the time. Turned out she was spared a lot of the agony poor Rose had to live through. Gran Parsons had saved her from that.

Iris was taking her time coming to the door. Rose tapped again. "We'll beard the lion in her den," she whispered, trying for a joke to calm her nerves.

The houses on the Point were all lit up, everyone in for the night, sheltering from the cold. Like I should be, thought Daisy, as the lighthouse on Jean's Head flicked on and off, on and off. Doing its duty, watching over the bay as it had done all these years.

The door finally opened. "Come on in." They followed Iris in through the porch. Lambs to the slaughter, thought Daisy.

**

PART FOUR (Daisy)

It was hot in the kitchen, the new oil stove going full blast. Daisy breathed in the delicious smell of fresh bread. Iris seemed to bake a lot of bread, maybe it helped pass the time. On the table she saw a forty-ouncer of Captain Morgan, three quarters full, and three glasses.

"I must say, Iris, you got it pretty comfortable," said Rose, as she looked around. "Don't you think so, Dais? And new plumbing. Not much like when we were growing up. Never had many bathrooms, did we?" Rose was already sounding hostile.

"A proper bathroom is great," commented Daisy, mostly to stop Rose from going on. "Steve put ours in when Lex was in Grade five. 'Course he cursed like a sailor the whole time but he finally got it done with some help from Calvin. Got no patience, Steve."

Iris smiled briefly and went into the pantry, came back with a yellow, plastic bowl full of potato chips that she placed on the table. She pulled a pack of Rothman's cigarettes out of her pocket, threw it beside a blue ashtray with *Blue Star Beer* printed in white on the lip. "There, we're all set." She started to pour the rum. "Oops, forgot the mix." She went over to her new fridge and brought out two bottles of Coke.

Iris looked good in her pale green, sweater set, slim grey skirt and flat loafers. Nothing cheap about her, thought Daisy. The doctor must have left her well-off, or at least comfortable. Funny she didn't have a car. "You got a perm," said Daisy, noticing the tiny, white-blonde curls framing Iris' flushed face.

"Yeah," lighting a cigarette, blowing smoke over her shoulder. "Got young Edie Cook, Violet's girl, to give me a Toni." She laughed. "I'm prayin' to God it grows out soon."

"Hear from Dad lately?" Rose's glass was already empty.

"He called last night." Iris took a sip of her drink. "Complaining about the cold weather, the cost of heating the house there in St. John's. You'd think he was brought up in Florida."

"Yeah, the house Mamie left him," Rose snapped, reaching to pour another drink. "*And* a car. Got lucky there, didn't he?"

"Damn right! He used to laugh about that when he came to see me in Bay-de-Verde. Mamie is dead and he thinks it's funny that he gets all that stuff in her will. I figured he didn't need this place any longer so I asked him if he'd sell it. But he won't give me any kind of answer."

"Know what, Iris?" Rose was making short work of her second drink. "That's how the bastard'll hold on to you. He'll keep you guessing, then one day he'll move in and you'll be stuck looking after him in his old age."

Rose glanced at Daisy as if debating whether to go on. The rum won the debate. "Don't worry, old Dan is never without a scheme. He figures it'll be like the old days, he's the cock-o'-the-walk and you're his housekeeper. His slave." She gave a vigorous nod of her head. "There, I said it. Tha's what we're here for, say wha's on our minds."

Rose reached for the bottle, poured her third drink. The alcohol had turned her face blood-red, she had a mean, determined look about her. Daisy felt her shoulders tense. Rose was dancing around the main issue but she was in a mood to let it all out. There was no going back now.

Iris leaned back in her chair, looked at Rose and nodded. "I was thinking the same thing, Rose. He'll soon be seventy. Still fairly well, bit of a heart problem but not too serious, at least that's what he said. If his liver hangs on he could live another ten years, and you know what? I can hardly stomach it when he comes for two or three days."

She lowered her eyes. "I know you don't understand why I want the house. It's something that's stuck in my mind, I'll explain it to you sometime. But when I own the house, I'll tell him what I think of him and tell him to stay away from me."

Daisy was trying to think of the right thing to say to this when Rose piped up. "Christ, Iris, never thought I'd hear you say anything 'gainst the ol' man," slurring her words now. "All I see when I think back is you and him t'gether. Might as well say it, more like man and wife than father and daughter."

Rose took a swig of her drink, wiped her mouth with the back of her hand. "I kept the secret all those years, festering inside my brain like a worm. Only told Daisy last week." She took another swig, her anger intensifying. "I'm dyin' to hear your side o'things, Iris, dyin' to hear it."

"You're right, Rose," said Iris. "The way we got on was nothing like father and daughter. It started when he came back from Boston. He began to treat me special and I really liked it. I was almost thirteen. Developed early, thought I was real grown up.

"All the time he was gone, Mom was sick a lot, or pregnant. To me, she always seemed to be carrying a baby or having one. Eventually, she more or less gave up so I was the housekeeper, doing the work of a grown woman. And feeling sorry for myself, I suppose. Anyway, when he started giving me all that attention, I ate it up."

By now, Daisy was so tense she thought she'd explode. It was clear that Rose hadn't finished yet. Hopefully, she wouldn't push Iris too far and cause a racket.

Too late! Rose jumped to her feet. "You treated Mother like shit, Iris!" her voice rising. "And I could do nothing about it. My own mother, sufferin' under you and that bastard and I was too young to help!"

Overcome by grief, with nothing left to give to the fight, Rose collapsed back in her chair. "All the times I thought of killin' him," she murmured. "And the bastard, acting like it's nothin' what he's doin'. Christ, I felt like killin' the both of ya."

Sniffing back tears, Rose reached for the bottle again. Daisy moved her hand toward the glass but Rose pulled it away. "No, Dais," she snapped. "Don't worry 'bout me drinkin' too much. I need it, or s'help me God I'll go down the wharf and drown myself!" She sloshed the rum into her glass and gulped it down.

Iris sat with her head lowered against Rose's rage. "The first time was the day he heard about the bank crash," she said, quietly. "I was fourteen, didn't have a clue about bank crashes. He was acting all shocked. He was worried, he said, there was going to be a Depression. He didn't feel well, had to lie down. Would I keep him company?" She glanced at Rose before going on.

"I followed him into the bedroom. Stretched out on the bed beside him, arms stiff at my side. It didn't feel right but he seemed upset and I felt sorry for him. He started telling me about his Connor grandmother, how she said he had the Irish melancholy. He was sad most of the time, he said, and I was the only one in his life who kept him going. I was special." Her smile was grim. "Real good talker when he wanted to be.

"It went from there, was part of my life from then on. I didn't know how to stop, or even if I wanted to. After a while I knew he'd never let me because as kind as he was at times, he could be just as mean." She glanced at Rose again. "And I found I could be mean, too."

"Damn right you were mean," Rose snapped. "And the way you treated Mother, you had no pity at all!"

Iris kept her eyes on the table. "I know, I was terrible to Mom. If there's a God I'll never be forgiven. But you and Mom were in the way of me and what I wanted most. That's not easy to say, Rose, but I'm being honest."

Her voice broke. "God, the beatings I took when he thought I was going out with boys, which I was! But still I craved his attention. It's hard to explain, even to myself. One day he'd be kind, the next he'd ignore me. And I lived for the times he was kind."

As Iris reached for the Kleenex box on the window sill, Daisy saw the pain etched on her face. She was beginning to see something of the hell her sister had lived through. "I'm so sorry, Iris."

Iris nodded briefly. "And poor little Baby Marie. I think of her every day."

At the mention of the baby, Rose perked up. "I do, too. I used to think the old man was the father but I don't anymore. Marie was too good and pure to come from him." She sank back again and closed her eyes.

Iris took a slug of her drink. "By the time I was a woman, I was so screwed up I didn't know if he was my father or my husband. I knew I was talked about all over town, but nothing mattered except how he was gonna treat me that day."

Thump! Rose's head hit the table. Iris jumped up and pulled her over to the daybed. "Lie down there, Rose. You can still hear what we're saying." She came back to the table.

"I'll tell you how it all came about, Daisy, how I came to realize things and why I'm telling you. I daresay Daddy told you I married

Ben Simms, the doctor I went into service for. He was older than me so I wasn't interested at first. Besides, I was missing Daddy, he was working on the base in St. John's at the time." She shook her head. "Can you imagine, a twenty-four-year-old woman thinking about her father like a boyfriend or something? It's disgusting!"

Daisy sat glued to her chair, a sharp pain throbbing in her temples as she tried to take in what Iris was telling her. Tried to imagine how Iris had coped all these years.

"Anyway, after the war, I half thought he'd come and get me," Iris continued, "but he was used to the city by then. Guess we all knew he was never cut out for fishing. He liked cities, taverns, and yes, women. Especially widow women like Mamie Doolen who had money. It was Boston all over again for him, except now he didn't have to work.

"So, yes, he abandoned me down there in Bay-de-Verde without a thought." She paused, her eyes intense on Daisy "S'pose if he could do it to Mom he could do it to me, right?"

Daisy caught her meaning right away. "Right," she snapped, remembering the long-ago anger. "You were all for it when he left Mom in St. John's that time."

Iris nodded. "I know. Anyway, not long afterwards, Ben asked me to marry him. I figured why not. He was a decent man. Well-respected, which is more than I can say for the other ones I was seeing. Besides, I'd be the doctor's wife instead of his servant and I'd be respected, too."

"Did you care for him at all?"

"To be honest, I saw him as a way out of being a servant for the rest of my life." She gave Daisy a wry grin. "I was thirty-one by then, an old maid as they say. Daddy and Mamie drove down that summer, one of their royal tours in Mamie's big Buick. I told him I was married to Ben and his face lit up. He liked the idea! And you know what? I felt hurt. Jesus!"

"Yes, I can see that." Strangely enough, Daisy really did understand how Iris would feel hurt after all she'd been through with the old devil.

"The marriage was good, better than I had a right to expect. Sure, it caused some talk at first, the doctor marrying the servant girl. But Ben loved his work and the people down there loved him, so it passed. He was sixty when he died, way too young. But I was lucky to have him, he was very wise. And patient. After we were married, he gave me time to get used to him, to a normal way of living. And he made me see things in a different way."

"Wait a minute," said Daisy. "I'll put the kettle on, make some coffee for the drunk. Can't take her home plastered."

"Anyway," Iris continued, "one day about a year before he died, Ben came home from his rounds. He flopped down on the couch and asked for a drink, something he never did. When I asked what was wrong, he mumbled something like 'that bastard Hank Sturgess, doin' dirt with his ten-year-old daughter,' something like that.

"When I heard it I got a shock, like I might faint. I ran into the kitchen, the words going around in my head. *Doin' dirt with his daughter.* Ben followed me, thinking I was sick I suppose. And right then it came out. That happened to me, I said."

Daisy knew her face must be mirroring her thoughts. "I know what you're thinking," said Iris. "Can't have been too big a shock, it was going on for years. And I really can't say why it hit me like that, at that moment. Maybe because of Ben, the way he pitied that girl. Maybe because I knew he'd be kind, I don't know. But I ended up telling him everything."

"Oh, God! How did he take it? Must have been a shock." Like it was to me, Daisy thought.

"Ben was wonderful. He took the time to explain how Daddy trained me, as he put it, right from the start, so eventually he could go ahead and do what he wanted. I fought against the idea. Told him no, it wasn't like that, Daddy never manipulated me like that.

"Ben watched me go back and forth, screaming at him sometimes, even threatening to leave him. It took a while before I started to accept what he was telling me. But even now, I have days when I think it can't be, Daddy couldn't have been so evil. But he was.

"I didn't hold anything back from Ben, Daisy. I told him how I treated Mom and you two, how I resented having to be in charge of the house." Iris looked away. "How glad I was when Daddy made you leave school and go over with Gran Parsons. I'd have him all to myself then. There'd still be Rose, but she was young."

Daisy felt the sudden welling up into her eyes.

"I know, you'll always regret having to leave school. It was your favourite thing in the world." Iris leaned over, lightly touched Daisy's arm. "I don't expect to be forgiven for the things I did, not by you, not by anyone. But now you know I'm not hiding anything.

"Ben said maybe I could come back someday, when I was ready, and tell everything, then I might start to forgive myself." She sat back, her eyes searching Daisy's face. "And now I'm ready. Ready to forgive myself and ready to confront him. But first, the house. Because it all goes together, doesn't it?"

"Yes it does, and I'm glad you're moving forward. But it's not you who needs forgiveness, Iris, it's him! I'm sorry for what you suffered. It took a lot of courage to come back and face us, we should thank you for that."

Daisy felt drained. Suddenly, everything she used to believe seemed upside down. She longed to be home by herself, to sit in the dark and think. "I'll pour the coffee, you get Rose on her feet. I'll tell her everything tomorrow, after she feels better."

Iris smiled down at Rose. "Certainly can't hold her liquor."

"I hope he sells you the house, Iris." The words had come rushing out, a dam bursting under sudden pressure. "He owes you that and a lot more." Iris looked up quickly, and just as quickly turned her head away. But not before Daisy had seen the blue eyes brimming full.

"Okay," said Daisy, flustered now at the emotions swirling between them. "Let's get some coffee into Rose so I can take her home. I hope Calvin is in a good mood."

**

Walking back across the Green after piloting Rose home, and calming the waters with Calvin, Daisy's thoughts turned to Iris and the events of the evening. She'd never imagined things would turn out this way. She'd been bitter all those years, never stopped to consider things from Iris' point of view. Iris had been so vulnerable back then, no wonder she'd craved the old man's attention. And no wonder she'd seemed angry all the time.

Tomorrow, Daisy thought, I'll explain it all to Rose. She'd lived through the turmoil, she'd seen the sexual abuse Iris had suffered. If anyone should understand what Iris had gone through, it was Rose.

But Rose might see things in a different way. She might see the bond between Iris and the old man, even the abuse part, as contributing to the hardship their mother had suffered. Or maybe as the *reason* for the hardship their mother had suffered.

It would take a while for Rose to let go of the anger she'd harboured for so long. But Daisy would help her figure it out over time.

And wasn't it strange, the way Iris still called the old man "Daddy." Would she ever break the bond she'd had with him for so long?

PART FIVE (Iris)

Betrayal causes a wound, the more to be vicious by.

(David Adams Richards) *River of the Brokenhearted*

Thirty-Two

Monday, October fifteenth, 1962. Iris smiled a wry smile as she glanced around. Here I am, she thought, Iris Connor, Mrs. Ben Simms, a widow formerly of Bay-de-Verde. She was back in the old house by the Alder Bed. Back where she'd grown up, and grown up pretty fast at that!

She was all nerves this morning, and tired from a sleepless night. She'd spent an hour staring at the toast, trying to decide if she could keep it down, but her stomach wasn't up to it. She pushed herself up from the table and cleared the dishes. Dumped the two slices of cold toast into the garbage and dropped the plate into the dishpan. Then she wandered out to the back steps and looked out over the grove of alders to the Brook beyond, a scene she'd looked at a million times before except now the alders were thicker.

Iris had been twenty years in the wilderness. Not *banished* to the wilderness, exactly, as some people might have wished, but not entirely off to Bay-de-Verde of her own accord, either. She'd had no choice but to go into service, she had to have a way to live.

She remembered the heartsick emptiness she'd felt on arriving at the doctor's house in Bay-de-Verde. The war had just started, Daddy had signed on to work on the new American Base in St. John's. Fort Pepperrell Air Force Base. It broke her heart to see his excitement, his willingness to leave her behind without a thought.

"This war is gonna be good for Newfoundland," he'd crowed. "We went bankrupt trying to help the Brits in WWI, they never even thought to pay us back. This time, there's cash money coming in from everywhere and I'm gonna get some."

For three years, from 1937 when Rose left to go into service in Old Perlican, to around 1941 when he took the construction job, Iris had had him all to herself. They'd lived secretly as man and wife, as Rose had so correctly put it the night her sisters came to the house to have it out with her. But poor as church mice, hardly enough to eat half the time.

There was nothing for a man to do back then but fishing so that's what Daddy did, nothing. Except a little bootlegging. Marcus had that operation back in the woods near Big Pond. At the time, Iris had thought these years were the happiest of her life. What an idiot!

Thanks to her marriage to Ben Simms, her time in Bay-de-Verde had turned out fine in the end. But that stage of her life was over. After Ben died in '59, she'd had time to reflect. Thanks to Ben, she understood how the old man had handled her. And the old house, where she'd been abused and misused, had become a symbol for her. A symbol of loss.

Iris had pictured herself owning the house. Changing everything around, knocking down walls, making it her own. Taking back the place where he'd had the power. Taking back *her* power. Daisy and Rose would probably never fully understand why she'd want to come back here. But maybe, when they were all more comfortable with each other, she'd try to explain.

Last fall, she'd asked Daddy to rent her the house and he'd agreed. She hadn't seen him over the winter but since the spring he'd been coming out for visits. The hard part was pretending to be nice until he agreed to sell. Then she'd confront him! That was something she hadn't been able to do before.

He used to come to Bay-de-Verde in the summer, acting as if nothing had happened. Iris had been an independent woman for years then, but she still couldn't look into these dark eyes without mixed feelings. Love and fear and shame combined, like always. She hadn't been ready to stand up to him then, but she was ready now. Once the house was hers, she'd tell him exactly what he was, and what should be done to him. She'd tell him to fuck off. Move into a seniors' home in St. John's like other old people his age, and never show his face here again.

The next few days would be crucial, he was coming for his last visit until next spring. He wouldn't usually drive out from St. John's after October. He was afraid of bad weather, and shaky as hell from all the years of drinking. Realistically, he could pop off any time, so this might be her last chance. Everything must be finalized while he was here, before he went back for the winter.

Iris waited through the afternoon for his car to pull up at the front steps. Her nerves were raw, she was consumed with the sense that time was running out. All those visits over the summer, letting him think she was the old Iris, had taken a toll. Sometimes, after he'd left to go home, she had to run to the toilet and vomit.

She thought of Baby Marie, the child she'd had when she was nineteen or so. In her mind, it was never "the baby," it was always "Baby Marie." If Baby Marie had lived, she'd be twenty-eight now. Iris couldn't imagine it. Her daughter would be older than Lex, Daisy's girl.

But it was unlikely the child would have grown up sound, not the way the poor little soul had come about. Iris didn't know for sure who the father was, she'd been doing things with boys for years before she got pregnant. But the baby had never seemed healthy, that's why she thought it might have been his. "Poor Baby Marie," she whispered aloud, as she paced the kitchen. "You were cursed from the start."

Iris lived with the knowledge of that every day, the knowledge of that and many other things. The way she'd neglected the baby to please Daddy and left little Rose, only twelve at the time, to look after her. Rose had loved the child like it was her own. Later on, she'd even named her own daughter "Marie." Iris hadn't been at all surprised to hear that. The child had died of polio, another Marie lost to an early death.

The way Baby Marie had died never sat right in Iris' mind. She remembered the day before, Dan sending Rose to Parker's Store for Friar's Balsam. "It's for Gran," he'd said, "she burned her arm." Iris had wanted to ask Gran about it but she was afraid of the answer she'd get. She'd never mentioned the suspicion to a soul, not even Ben. It was just too evil.

Iris poured a drink to calm her nerves and tried to concentrate on making supper. He'd soon come rolling in like the tide, dragging along all sorts of dirt and debris with him, all the bad memories clinging to him like kelp on the rocks. She'd keep him happy while he was here, jolly him along so he'd be in a good mood when she brought up the subject of the house.

**

"Jesus, Iris, I'm bushed after that drive. Open me a beer, would ya'?" Dan took the bottle of Black Horse and drained it before he'd even sat down. "Stopped at the liquor store in Harbour Grace on the way along," he added. "Got four cases of beer and three bottles of Captain Morgan dark. I know my girl likes a rum toddy now and then."

"Oh, good," said Iris. She remembered back then, after her mother had gone to the hospital, how they used to drink together in the old house. He'd pour moonshine into two glasses and pull out her chair, acting all proper. "Care to join me?"

Iris would be overcome with feelings; excitement, love, pride, shame, confusion. They'd sit at the table in the lamplight, laughing and chatting about nothing in particular, and she'd feel like the most special girl in the world. The man was a born actor.

"No more moonshine," Dan was saying, as if he'd read her mind. "Thanks to Confederation and the Old Age Pension, I can afford the good stuff." He gave her a sly wink. "Not to mention dear old Mamie's contribution." Iris bit her tongue. Anything he had was nothing to do with his own efforts. He was a leech, he lived on the blood of others.

Dan poured them each a drink and they sat down to the supper of fish and chips she'd put together. Watching from the corner of her eye, she waited to see if he'd mention the house. She'd told him over the phone that she wanted to talk about it.

By the time she poured tea, she could stand it no longer. "So, have you thought any more about the house?" blurting out the words, frustration driving her on.

She could tell by his face that he'd been waiting to see if she had the nerve to mention it. He could hardly keep from smiling as he carefully laid his fork and knife across his plate. "Well, come to think of it, I haven't." He sat back and looked at her. Then he shrugged. "But now you bring it up, maybe it's time. I'll mull it over some more."

"No hurry," she replied, sounding casual but her insides were churning. "It's not like the house won't be here if you sell it to me, you can come here any time. We've got some good memories of the place, we'll always have that."

After supper, they went into the front room. "Watching TV with my favourite people," he said, "Captain Morgan and my Iris." His tongue was getting thicker by the hour.

Iris stayed with him 'til ten, then she got up to go to bed. "I'll lock the door before I go up."

He yawned. "Okay. I'll have another drink and watch this "Gunsmoke" rerun. I watch TV a lot now. Some of the shows are pretty good, help pass the time anyway."

"Goodnight."

"Oh, Iris, never mind the door. I might go down the Alder Bed for a stroll later. It's a clear night, the air is nice and fresh. Not like that oily, salty shit that passes for air in St. John's."

**

Iris lay in bed and listened to him rummaging around downstairs. At eleven o'clock, he turned off the TV and staggered out into the porch. Came back in for a few minutes, probably getting his windbreaker, then he left again.

Iris was on edge as another sleepless night loomed. She thought how cagey he'd been since he arrived, not mentioning the house, forcing her to do it herself. That's how he worked, he'd push her to do it for the sake of humiliating her. Then he'd say something vague, not quite yes, not quite no, something that would knock her back but keep her hopes alive for another day. She was used to his humiliations.

She tossed and turned. Replayed his words in her mind, looking for possible tricks. The house was certainly worth more now than before she'd moved in. She'd worked hard to bring it up to a halfway decent shape. And she had lots more plans for when it was hers.

It struck her that he might want to keep it for a few more years. By then, she'd have done some more improvements, he could sell at a nice profit. To hell with that, she wanted the house now. If he had any sense of fair play, he'd just give it to her. She figured she deserved it for what she'd given him. Her young womanhood

Thirty-Three

Tuesday. Iris waited impatiently for the old man to get up, she'd made bacon and eggs. When he finally appeared, he looked like the wrath of God. Can't handle the booze like he used to, she thought. Of course, he'd never admit to any lessening of his capacity and he'd argue the point 'til Doomsday.

He slumped over his plate, too miserable to sit up straight. "Good stroll last night," he muttered. "The water is pretty with the moon shining on it. God, the times we had swimmin' down there when I was a boy. The hot sun on your shoulders, the boys shouting and cursing, trying to drown each other. That bastard Rich Gordon almost *did* drown me once. Some kin of Steve Gordon, come to think of it. Poor bugger never came back from Beaumont Hamel."

Iris saw that he was in a reminiscing mood this morning. "Glad you enjoyed it. I didn't hear you come in." But she *had* heard him, stumbling through the porch and up the stairs, making enough racket to wake the dead.

He pushed back his plate. "You made me too much, Iris. Don't eat like I used to."

"I thought of something last night," she said, starting to clear the table. Her face felt stiff with tension, she wondered if it showed. "The radio calls for a few nice days. Why not stay 'til the weekend? We'll get the papers signed, you'll have the money before you go back," trying to keep her voice steady, as if she didn't care one way or the other.

"Well, I dunno." The sly look again. "The crowd at the tavern'll be expecting me." He took out his pipe, dismissing the subject. "Smokin' a pipe now, like Max used to, remember?" He smirked. "Probably thought it made him look like a businessman. Still, it's a nice change from the fags." He turned on the radio. "Time for the news."

"The war is worsening," the radio announcer said. "The situation has ..."

"Jesus, that Vietnam thing," Dan grumbled, "that's all they talk about."

"How about their new president, John Kennedy? Handsome fella, isn't he?"

"He's okay, I guess. Long as someone don't shoot him before he can do some good. Gun crazy, the Yanks are." He shrugged. "But at least they put in a new man now and then. We can't get rid of Smallwood no matter what crazy schemes he cooks up. Ray Guy, there at the Telegram, is havin' a field day mocking him."

Dan puffed his pipe thoughtfully. "Not the man he used to be, Joey. Obsessed with that Churchill Falls thing now. He'd better be careful, it's Quebec he's dealing with. If the Feds don't keep everything fair and square, we'll lose out." Iris was used to his rants. She'd let him ramble 'til he ran out of energy, then she'd try again about the house.

"Joey was something back in the '40s," Dan droned on. "Dragged the province into Confederation by sheer will. I remember Frank Fisher, Joe's son, was dead against it. Almost had a stroke when it was signed, passed right out on the floor. Drunk too, o'course. But Frank was right about one thing. It's a deal that'll be debated forever."

He finally seemed to have run down. "About the house," Iris said, carefully. "Wouldn't you like to have the money before you go back?"

There was the smile again, he'd been waiting for her to mention it. "You got a point, I suppose." He turned to the window, peered out at the cold water of the harbour. "Tell the truth, I'm getting sick of the dirty, bloody city. And the old house on Spencer Street needs work. I can't afford to fix it up, too old for mortgages, now." He turned back, shrugged. "Maybe we should do it. All in the family after all, it's not like I can't come back to visit."

Iris stood frozen in place. "Right," keeping her voice calm, "that won't change." She walked over to the table, sat down across from him. "I never did ask. How much did you have in mind for the place? I can go to the bank today if you like."

"Well, *if* I sell, I was thinking ten thousand. But there's no need to be in a tear, Iris, it's only Tuesday," calmly puffing on his pipe. "Let me think about it."

Iris felt her face drop for a split second before she caught herself. "Okay, let me know when you're ready." Naturally, he was going to keep her on a string. But ten thousand!

**

Dan spent the rest of the day out around the community while Iris stayed home and fretted. But sharp at five, there he was at the door, ready for supper. "Dropped in on the girls," he said, cheerfully. "Thought I should see them before I go back for the winter."

Iris almost laughed out loud. As if Daisy and Rose cared!

"Daisy was more hostile than ever, thought she was gonna slam the door in my face. How does Steve put up with that one?" He looked puzzled. "Told her I might sell you the house. She acted like she already knew."

"That's funny," Iris lied. "I never mentioned it to her."

"Nothing going on at Rose's 'cept the usual chaos. The kid coming home from school, Rose bawling at him for this and that. Calvin on the daybed waiting for his supper. Jesus, what a circus! Calvin should take some control there." Iris shook her head. Dan Connor was giving advice on family life! Her mother would roll in her grave.

When Iris thought about her mother, it was with shame at the way she'd treated her, the resentment she'd felt toward her all those years ago. For being unwell, for leaving her with the housework, expecting her to look after her sisters. Then, after Daddy had come home from Boston, her resentment became even more intense. She'd looked down on her mother for being weak, for not standing up for herself.

But Iris could see now, she hadn't stood up to the old man any more than her mother had. And worse, she'd *craved* her abuse because she thought it was love. False love, she knew now.

Since Iris had been back, sometimes on a late afternoon around duckish, she walked in the Canvastown Road to the cemetery. Up the hill to her mother's grave, her heart pounding, thinking the woman might come flying out of the ground and float in the air, pointing an accusing finger at her. But all she ever saw was a mound of weedy grass and a rock marker. Lexie (Fisher) Connor. 1898 – 1936.

Iris figured Daisy and Rose had to know about these visits. Probably thought she had no right, but so far they hadn't said so out loud. Her sisters had been far more understanding than she deserved. If not understanding, at least accepting.

Iris would never tell them exactly how much she'd resented their presence in her life back then. Her jealousy and fear that Daddy would reject her and turn to one of them, her relief when Daisy was sent over to Gran's. Sisters should never hear something like that from another sister.

After supper, she and the old man had some drinks and watched TV for a while. Iris had no trouble holding her own in the drinks department. She'd been drinking with him since she'd been twelve or so, he'd sneak it to her when no one could see. After Marcus Crane had arrived on the scene, she drank openly with them. Feeling all grown-up, trying to please her father by acting a certain way. Acted like a whore is what she did! And yes, he *was* pleased.

Later, after she went to bed, Iris heard the back door slam. He'd gone for his nightly walk.

Thirty-Four

Wednesday. Iris was a wreck. She hadn't slept a wink for the past two nights, had a pounding headache that wouldn't go away. She glanced across the table at the sorry-looking sight slumped in the chair, poking at his cereal. Would he follow through on what he'd said? Or would he change his mind again, just to keep her guessing?

After breakfast, he headed to the front room with a magazine. Looked like a day of hanging around the house smoking his pipe, keeping her on a string. She'd almost given up hope when, late in the afternoon, he spoke the words she'd been longing to hear. "Maybe we should go up to the bank now, Iris."

Iris was pleased, but miffed at the same time. It was two forty-five, the bank closed at three. They probably wouldn't make it. Another of his little barbs, she thought bitterly, as she went to get her coat.

Dan started the car and they headed for Heart's Content, pulled in at the bank with five minutes to spare. "Right under the wire," he said. "You go in. I'll wait in the car, have a fag."

Twenty minutes later, Iris came out with the cheque. He'd said ten thousand, a ridiculous price for the old place, but Iris had cried poor 'til he accepted that she couldn't afford it. "There you go," still nervous that he might change his mind, "six thousand dollars."

"That's it then, Iris." He passed her the bill of sale and stuffed the cheque into his pocket. "Now my Darlin', let's celebrate!" He turned the car toward the Barrens and Carbonear. "I feel like Chinese food."

They had supper and some rums at Fong's, but afterwards he was feeling too good to go home. "Let's check out that lounge in Harbour Grace I heard about. The Pirate's Cave, is it?"

"Are you sure you're up to it?" Iris was horrified. She'd heard of the place from Lex, it was where the young people went. But she had to keep him happy. If she went against him now, he might work himself into a drunken rampage.

Oblivious to the grins on the faces of the twenty-year-olds, Dan swaggered past the tables, shoulders back like he owned the place. "An evening of drinks and dancing," he drawled, settling at a table as Iris cringed inwardly. "Just what the doctor ordered."

He bought drinks and they danced a bit. More like stumbled, really, Iris keeping him upright while the young people whispered and pointed. By ten thirty he was well on. "Maybe we should go," he mumbled, eyes half closed. "You look sleepy."

Iris almost lost it. *She* looked sleepy? He was almost comatose! But thank God they were leaving. She was exhausted, yes, but mainly she was dying of embarrassment.

A young man at the next table helped her get Dan to his feet and she steered him toward the door. He looked like hell, shirttail hanging out of his pants, sweat rolling down his face. And the grey hair plastered back with enough Brylcreem to choke a horse!

"You all right, sir?" asked the young man at the bar as they went by.

"What, you don't think I can drive home?" Dan bawled. "Nothin' wrong with me, Sonny. Not my first time in the trenches!"

The barman rolled his eyes at Iris and she nodded back. Another sad, old man, they confirmed to each other, obsessed with rolling back time, trying to be the man he used to be. But Iris knew exactly the kind of man he used to be.

**

The drive across the Barrens was wild, rocks flying as the car careened from one side of the gravel road to the other, slowing down, speeding up, Dan insisting no, he didn't need to pull over. Once back home, Iris knew he'd want to relive the event, he always did when he felt he'd done himself proud. She made a pot of coffee and pretended to smile while he smoked cigarettes and rambled on about the evening.

"Just like the old days, Iris, you and me havin' a good time. Ya' still got it, kiddo!" His eyes narrowed slyly. "Maybe, later on, I'll move in here with you. We get along good, don't we?"

Iris didn't reply. In her mind, she was thinking there was no bloody way he was moving in on her, but it was late and she was exhausted. She'd put off the confrontation 'til tomorrow. "It's eleven-thirty, I'm off to bed."

He squinted up at the clock and yawned. "Eleven thirty already? Well, there's a nice, bright moon out tonight. Think I'll go down to the Brook, clear my head." He got unsteadily to his feet. "Jesus, Brook! Couldn't these old people come up with a better name for that river? Who calls a river a brook? Stupid bastards!" Iris rolled her eyes at another familiar refrain.

Dan got up and staggered toward the porch. As he passed her chair, he reached over and squeezed her breast. "Mm-m, nice," he murmured.

And with that, a surge of rage rushed upward through Iris' body and settled in her chest with a sharp pain. Through a lightheaded haze, she spotted the Blue Star ashtray on the table. Had to fight the vision of bringing it down on his head with all the force of her disgust and anger.

She sat frozen to the chair, trying to calm herself, get her breathing under control. Trying to get *herself* under control before she made that vision a reality. It's still not over, she thought, as with a sudden flash of realization she saw the future. He was going to drag her back into the black pit.

"Might be pretty hung over tomorrow," he mumbled, oblivious to her discomfort as he threw on his jacket. "Probably spend the day getting straight, go back Friday morning."

"Yes," she said, her voice flat as the word stuck in her throat.

**

Iris lay in bed wide awake, her body stiff with anger as she relived the events of the day; the torturous trip to the bank, wondering if he'd change his mind before she had the deed in her hands, the embarrassment of being with him at the lounge in Harbour Grace.

And the way he'd grabbed her as he went by. Like she was his toy, something to play with whenever he pleased. Well, she'd completed the first task, she'd stuck it out 'til the house was hers.

But now Iris knew that she still hadn't come full circle. As much as she'd envisioned the house sale as being the end of her journey, something else would be required of her before she could rest.

Thirty-Five

Thursday. Iris had been up since daylight. She'd sat in her chair by the window, watching the clouds gathering over the bay and thinking. In the end, she thought, it's come down to survival.

She got out her bankbooks and went over her finances. The house had taken almost all of what Ben had left her. From now on, she'd have no one but herself to depend on.

Iris had learned early on that doctors are loved but not always paid with money. She never knew what was coming through the door as payment, a chicken, sometimes, or a bag of potatoes.

Once, an old lady had come with a note from her son saying he'd give Dr. Simms fifty pounds of fish next fall, when he got back from the Grand Banks. Ben had saved the man's wife from dying at the birth of their last child. Women were always dying from having babies.

Of course, Ben had left her the big house in Bay-de-Verde, too. She'd sold it for fifteen thousand. Her Old Age Pension was years away, she'd have to count pennies from now on. Or, as Lex had jokingly suggested in one of her freewheeling monologues, try to find a Sugar Daddy.

Lex had dropped by last weekend, she'd been home for Thanksgiving. She was in her third year at MUN now, another year and she'd get her teacher's degree. Iris was proud of Lex, although it was Daisy who deserved the credit for raising her, for nurturing her lively disposition. And she enjoyed Lex's outspoken manner, she was a lot like Rose that way. You could see Daisy in her, though, she could be intense at times, and stubborn.

Iris had felt close to Lex since the summer she'd given her a place to stay in Bay-de-Verde. Sometimes she wondered whether she'd made Lex a substitute for Marie, whether she was trying to feel what it would be like to be a mother to the daughter she'd lost. But she figured there was no harm in it, as long as she didn't step on Daisy's toes.

**

Iris glanced at Dan as he finally shambled into the kitchen around nine. He looked even worse than usual this morning, his skin almost yellow as his liver drowned in alcohol.

"Think I'll lay off the booze today," he said, trying to force a piece of toast down his gullet, "at least 'til after supper. Get in shape to drive back tomorrow." Iris rolled her eyes. Quite the sacrifice he was making there!

He spent the morning dozing in the Lazy-Boy while Iris hovered. He had to recover, she was counting on it. Thank God, by mid-afternoon he was showing signs of life. "I need a booster," he mumbled, heading for the bottle in the pantry.

He poured a drink, carried it back to his throne and watched Iris going about the house. "You're a looker, Iris," grinning that dirty grin. "Next to you, poor old Lexie was like a faded rose. Or a weed!" chuckling at his own joke.

Iris said nothing. She was used to his snide remarks about her mother, his cruel jokes. She was ashamed to say she wasn't innocent in that regard, either.

He got up to pour another drink. Then he heaved back in the chair, sighing like a contented man. By the time the second drink was gone, he'd drifted off again.

Iris woke him up in time for supper. "Damn Lazy-Boy, worse than a sleeping pill," he grumped, yawning and stretching as he came to the table. "You made me too much again, Iris. My stomach is nish, I'm still recuperating from yesterday."

After supper, he headed back to the front room with his cigarette and his glass of rum. "Why don't you watch the TV news now," said Iris, "while I go upstairs to tidy up. I won't be long."

She gave it an hour. When she went back down he was stuck into the TV, a new drink of rum at his elbow. "Look at that," he murmured, pointing at the screen as Iris watched soldiers crawling out of muddy trenches and running toward gunfire, jumping over bodies as they went. "World War I." His voice was quiet. "Hell on earth, more like! The shock to your system, you never get over it."

Iris was taken aback at the sorrow in his voice, the regret. It was the first time he'd ever said anything to her about the war. But she didn't reply. There were too many emotions rushing around inside her.

"Shoulda stayed in England af'wards," he went on. "I was still a young man, only twenty-one. Good lookin' fella, too. Could have got a job over there, made a new life away from this God-forsaken place." He shrugged. "Too late now," brushing away silent tears. "Pour yourself a drink, Iris, get us some o'them chips you bought yes'day." His words were thick, like he had marbles in his mouth.

Iris turned quickly and went into the kitchen. That's Dan Connor all over, she thought. He'd stay in England, no matter that he had a wife and child here. Well, maybe he *should* have stayed. She'd have been raised by the Fishers, got a good education, married well. She'd have had a chance at a decent life.

They watched Perry Mason and a quiz show, Iris trying her best to concentrate. At eleven she got up from her chair. "I'm feeling a bit pickish, think I'll make a lunch."

"Nothing for me, Iris, not on top of the rum. Spoil a good buzz." He checked the time. "Think I'll go down the Alder Bed now, get some air. Need a clear head for driving back tomorrow. Goddamned Mounties everywhere, makin' their ticket quota."

"It's a bit nippy out there," Iris called from the kitchen. "You might need a sweater under your windbreaker," continuing to play her part in the charade. She heard him knocking into the furniture as he struggled with his jacket. "Come here, I'll help you with it."

She held the jacket while he shoved his arms into the sleeves. "I'll be in bed when you get back," sitting back down to her tea and toast. "Have a good walk."

He stood for a moment, gazing down at her. "Still Daddy's girl, aren't ya?" He stumbled forward, kissed the top of her head. "Yes shir, Daddy's girl."

Iris managed a tight smile. "I'll have breakfast ready in the morning."

He staggered out into the porch singing the old Irish tune he liked, the one they always played at his tavern. "*If I were a blackbird, I'd whistle and sing...*"

Iris watched from the porch window as he weaved through the back yard, stumbling into the woodpile on his way, cursing as he went. He was really under the weather tonight. The half a sleeping pill she'd dropped into his drink earlier was doing its job.

**

The idea had come from Lex, although the girl didn't know that. Lex had dropped by one evening last summer looking down in the dumps, Iris thinking nothing of it at the time, just a young woman thing.

But Lex had started going on about her grandfather; the "old boozer," how much she despised him, all the lives he'd ruined. "Y'know, Aunt Iris, I know all about the way you guys grew up, you and Mom and Aunt Rose."

And just like that, Lex had told her what she'd done. Iris couldn't believe what she was hearing. Lex had conned her way into the Riverview Hospital and read her grandmother's file! "I showed it to Mom and Aunt Rose," she said, in her matter-of-fact manner. "Since then, they've been straightforward about everything."

The thing was, Lex didn't seem to bear any ill will toward Iris for the things she'd discovered. "He was the adult, Aunt Iris. He worked on you, made you feel cared for. We studied these perverts in psychology, how they groom their victims. There's more of them around than you might think. "

Iris had been so touched, and grateful, at Lex' generosity, her maturity, that she'd almost cried. Had to pour a drink to settle herself down. Poured one for Lex, too, she didn't think Daisy would object, the girl was nineteen after all. "Thank you, Lex," she'd said. "I really appreciate those words."

But Lex had been on a roll. "Sometimes," she'd continued, her mood lifting as she sipped her rum and coke, "when I can't get to sleep at night, I play a game in my head. I think about all the different ways I could do away with the old boozer if I was so inclined."

Iris was used to Lex and her off-the-wall comments, but she'd been appalled at this. "Lex, that's terrible!"

"It's just thoughts, Aunt Iris, no one ever got hurt from thoughts. Or we'd all be dead!" As Lex rambled on, Iris had found herself listening more carefully.

Eventually, Lex had tired of the topic. "Getting late," she said, yawning loudly. "Must get back across the bridge before Daisy sounds the alarm." Adding on her way out the door, "You should be a shrink, Aunt Iris. I feel better now."

That night, as Iris went up to bed, she'd had to shake her head at the things the young ones talked about those days. It wasn't so long ago you'd hardly dare speak to a grandfather, let alone talk about killing him.

**

Iris watched from the porch window as the dark figure melted into the blackness of the alders. The timing was perfect. In the summer, the swimming hole would be swarming with kids. But now, late in the fall, the Alder Bed was deserted.

She remembered the dream she'd had last night, one she'd had a few times over the past year. Something about a rag doll with red hair and a polka dot dress. The doll is in a cradle, crying. Daddy picks it up and starts to pat its back, but suddenly, without warning, he grabs it by the bright red hair and rips off its head. It wasn't hard to figure out the meaning.

Iris knew it was evil, what she was about to do, but there'd be no moving forward until she was free of him. She'd realized that last night when he grabbed her breast, that and the sly remarks about moving in. He was never, *ever*, going to leave her alone. Owning the house wasn't enough, she had to take it further.

"God forgive me," she murmured, as, heart pounding, she charged upstairs to change her clothes. "I'll live with the knowledge of this, too."

She stripped off her skirt and blouse and pulled on the black slacks and dark sweater she'd laid out on the bed earlier. Then she raced downstairs, out to the porch where she threw on the old, black jacket she'd brought from Bay-de Verde, the one Ben used to wear on his walks. It still smelled of his aftershave. A black stocking cap to cover her hair and she was ready.

She crept through the alders, trying to ignore the coil of tension expanding inside her, a snake eating away her insides. Just as she crouched in the trees at the end of the path, mentally measuring the six feet of stones between herself and the old devil, the moon broke out of the clouds. Oh no! Everything was lit up like Christmas morning, the river, the trees, the houses on the hills above.

She watched him stumbling about with a lit cigarette in his fingers, the smell of Brylcreem heavy in the night air. "I baptize you, Pleasant River," making the sign of the cross with the cigarette before throwing it away. Iris felt irritated at his foolishness. It was doubtful the cross would make a difference to *that* sinner.

As he pushed his hands deep into his trouser pockets and started toward the water, a huge blanket of black clouds drifted across the moon. A sign from a higher power, thought Iris, as a comforting semi-darkness enveloped her. She tensed her body so she'd be ready to spring when the time was right.

It had to be the right time or he might overpower her. Daisy sometimes commented that the old man had nine lives and it was easy to see why. He'd lived through two wars, chronic alcoholism, all kinds of health problems and the odd car accident. Who could say but he mightn't live through this, too?

Iris hesitated as she contemplated the terrible sin she was about to commit. She'd loved this man throughout her childhood, through the lonely years she was away. She thought of herself at fourteen, sensing his dark eyes on her as she cooked supper, feeling his hand brushing her cheek as he passed.

But then there were the beatings. And the way he'd kept her guessing, kept her walking on eggs for fear of losing his affection. The way he'd casually tossed her aside. The tears fell silently down her cheeks and landed on the dark stones below.

Breathing a quick prayer to an unfamiliar God for strength and forgiveness, she took a deep breath, sprinted across the stones and landed the blow. He pitched face down in the shallow water, kicking his legs and rolling side to side, trying to free his hands from his pockets.

Now she had to move him out into deeper water or he might lift his head and start shouting, or free his hands and grab her. She was about to take hold of the back of his jacket when he somehow rolled over. The outline of a pale face rose out of the dark water. "Iris?" the voice barely a whisper.

Driven by pure terror now, Iris pushed with all her strength and rolled him back onto his stomach. Then she grabbed the collar of his jacket with one hand, his belt with the other and pulled him further out from shore.

"This is for all of us," she murmured, holding him down with both hands, "Mom, Daisy, Rose and especially Baby Marie. It's my gift to them. But it's for me, too. Me, Iris."

She felt a welling up of emotion from her chest, into her throat, her eyes, but couldn't hold it back. "Thanks to Ben," she sobbed, quietly, "I know how you c-controlled me. Well, I'm taking back the control. And I'm taking back the house where you used to rule the roost."

He made a last weak attempt to raise his head but it was no use. She felt it, the moment he gave up fighting. Then she lifted her hands.

His body floated gently away with the flow of the river, as it continued its journey to the Long Bridge and the freedom of the harbour.

**

Iris crept out of the water, staying low, careful not to make splashing sounds. She darted into the shelter of the alders, looked all around, watching and listening. Everything was quiet except for her sobs. Deep bursts of grief that she muffled with the collar of her jacket.

She was wet through and shivering uncontrollably, nervous effects of what she'd just done. Iris knew there'd be lots of after-effects as time passed, bad dreams, moments of regret and guilt. But she'd take whatever came. Because she knew that if she and Daddy had ended up living here together again, he'd drive her mad, too. Just like Mom.

Exhausted and stiff, she limped slowly back through the Alder Bed, back to the house. Her house. Anxious to get out of her wet clothes, she dragged her weary body upstairs to her bedroom, the bedroom her mother had slept in after she'd been banished from the one downstairs.

She reached into the closet for her warm, flannel pyjamas and her eyes fell on the old, brown sweater. It had been among the few bits of clothing belonging to her mother when she'd moved here. Iris had thrown the rest of it into a garbage bag but when it came to the sweater, she couldn't seem to discard it. She'd tried, twice pushing it into the bag and pulling it back out, before quickly rolling it into a ball and throwing it up on the shelf in the closet. As to the reason why she felt compelled to keep it, she'd put that aside for a later time.

She pulled the sweater down from the shelf. It was unravelling at the elbows from where her mother would sit in the rocking chair by the hour, resting her arms at the side. "I'll always see her ghost in that chair," Iris murmured as, clutching the sweater to her face, she fell onto the bed, her body wracked with tears of shame and loss.

She woke sometime later, still in her wet clothes and shivering with cold. The clock said three A.M. She got up, put on her warm pyjamas and her quilted robe, and stripped the sodden sheets from the bed. Then she grabbed a blanket and, stumbling with exhaustion, she went downstairs.

She lay down on the daybed to wait for the morning and whatever would come of her actions as she sounded the alarm for her missing father. She was wide awake now, her mind full of random images from last night. Disturbing images, ones that she knew would visit often in the years ahead.

Daddy was gone. Whatever demons he'd lived with, the demons that had made him cross the sacred line between father and child, had been put to rest. And Iris would live with her decision.

THE END

Printed in Canada